HAV

JAN MORRIS was born in 1926, is Anglo-Welsh, and lives in Wales. She has written some forty books, including the Pax Britannica trilogy about the British Empire; studies of Wales, Spain, Venice, Oxford, Manhattan, Sydney, Hong Kong, and Trieste; six volumes of collected travel essays; two memoirs; two capricious biographies; and a couple of novels—but she defines her entire oeuvre as "disguised autobiography." She is an honorary D.Litt. of the University of Wales and a Commander of the British Empire. Her memoir *Conundrum* is available as a New York Review Book Classic.

URSULA K. LE GUIN has published twenty-one novels as well as volumes of short stories, poems, essays, and works for children. Among her novels are *The Left Hand of Darkness* and *The Dispossessed*, both winners of the Nebula and Hugo awards.

HAV

Comprising

LAST LETTERS FROM HAV
HAV OF THE MYRMIDONS

JAN MORRIS

Introduction by
URSULA K. LE GUIN

NEW YORK REVIEW BOOKS

New York

THIS IS A NEW YORK REVIEW BOOK
PUBLISHED BY THE NEW YORK REVIEW OF BOOKS
435 Hudson Street, New York, NY 10014
www.nyrb.com

Last Letters from Hav first published in 1985

A catalog record for this book is available from the Library of Congress

ISBN 978-1-59017-449-4

Printed in the United States of America on acid-free paper.
10 9 8 7 6 5 4 3 2 1

CONTENTS

Introduction

When *Last Letters from Hav* was published (and short-listed for the Booker Prize) in 1985, Jan Morris's well-deserved fame as a travel writer, and the unfamiliarity of many modern readers with the nature of fiction, caused unexpected dismay among travel agents. Their clients demanded to know why they couldn't book a cheap flight to Hav. The problem, of course, was not the destination but the place of origin. You couldn't get there, in fact, from London or Moscow; but from Ruritania, or Orsinia, or the Invisible Cities, it was simply a matter of finding the right train.

Now, after twenty years, Morris has returned to Hav, and enhanced, deepened, and marvelously perplexed her guidebook by the addition of a final section called "Hav of the Myrmidons." To say that the result isn't what the common reader expects of a novel is not to question its fictionality, which is absolute, or the author's imagination, which is vivid and exact.

The story is episodic, entirely lacking in "action" or "plot" of the usual sort; but these supposed narrative necessities are fully replaced by the powerful and gathering direction or intention of the book as a whole. It lacks another supposed necessity of the novel: characters who, while they may represent an abstraction, also take on a memorable existence of their own. Like any good travel writer, Morris talks to interesting people and reports the conversations. And people we met in the first part of the book turn up in the second part to take us about and exhibit in person what has happened to their country;

but I confess I barely remembered their names when I met them again. Morris's gift is not portraiture, and her people are memorable not as individuals but as exemplary Havians.

This lack of plot and characters is common in the conventional Utopia, and I expect academics and other pigeonholers may stick *Hav* in with Thomas More and company. That is a respectable slot, but not where the book belongs. Probably Morris, certainly her publisher, will not thank me for saying that Hav is in fact science fiction, of a perfectly recognizable type and superb quality. The "sciences" or areas of expertise involved are social—ethnology, sociology, political science, and above all, history. Hav exists as a mirror held up to several millennia of pan-Mediterranean history, customs, and politics. It is a focusing mirror; its intensified reflection sharply concentrates both observation and speculation. Where have we been, where are we going? Those are the questions the book asks. It poses them through the invention of a place not recognized in the atlas or the histories, but which, introduced plausibly and without violence into the existing world, gives us a distanced, ironic, and revelatory view of everything around it. The mode is not satiric fantasy, as in the islands Gulliver visited; it is exuberantly realistic, firmly observant, and genuinely knowledgeable about how things have been, and are now, in Saudi Arabia, or Turkey, or Downing Street. Serious science fiction is a mode of realism, not of fantasy; and *Hav* is a splendid example of the uses of an alternate geography. If, swayed by the silly snobbery of pundits as contemptuous of science fiction as they are ignorant of it, you should turn away from *Hav*, that would be a shame and a loss.

It is not an easy book to describe. Hav itself is not easy to describe, as the author frequently laments. As she takes us about with her in her travels of discovery, we grow familiar with the delightful if somewhat incoherent Hav of 1985. We climb up to its charming castle, from which the Armenian trumpeter plays at dawn the great lament of Katourian for the knights of the First Crusade, the "Chant de doleure pour li proz chevalers qui suent morz." We visit the Venetian Fondaco, the Casino, the Caliph, the mysterious British Agency, the Kretevs who inhabit caves up on the great Escarpment through which the train, Hav's only land link to the rest of Europe, plunges daily down a zigzag tunnel. We see the Iron Dog, we watch the thrilling Roof-Race. But the more we learn, the greater our need to learn more. A sense of things not understood, matters hidden under the surface, begins to loom; even, somehow, to menace. We have entered a maze, a labyrinth constructed through millennia, leading us back and back to the age of Achilles and the Spartans who built the canal and set up the Iron Dog at the harbor mouth, and before that to the measureless antiquity of the Kretevs, who are friends of the bear. And the maze stretches out and out, too, half around the world, for it seems that Havian poetry was deeply influenced by the Welsh; and just up the coast is the westernmost of all ancient Chinese settlements, which Marco Polo found uninteresting. "There is nothing to be said about Yuan Wen Kuo," he wrote. "Let us now move on to other places."

Achilles and Marco Polo aren't the half of it. Ibn Batuta came to Hav, of course, all the great travelers did, and left their comments, diligently quoted by the Havians and Morris. T. E. Lawrence may have discovered a secret mission there; Ernest Hemingway came to fish and to carry off six-toed cats. Hav's glory days of tourism were before the First World War and again after it, when the train zigzagged through its tunnel laden with the cream of European society, millionaires, and right-wing politicians; but whether or not Hitler was actually there for one night is still a matter of dispute. The politics of Hav itself in 1985 were extremely disputable. Its religions were various, since so many great powers of the East and West had governed it over the centuries; mosques and churches coexisted amicably; and indeed the spiritual scene was so innocuous as to appear feeble—a small group of hermits, reputed to spend their days in holy meditation, proved to be cheerfully selfish hedonists who simply enjoyed asceticism. And yet, and yet, there were the Cathars. Late in her first visit, Morris was taken in darkness and great secrecy to witness a sitting of the Cathars of Hav—a strange ritual conclave of veiled women and cowled men. In some of them Morris thought she recognized friends, guides, the trumpeter, the tunnel pilot...but she could not be sure. She could not be sure of anything.

On her return twenty years later, some things appear to be all too certain. The old Hav is gone, destroyed in an obscure event called the Intervention. The train is gone, a huge airport is under construction. Ships come in to a destination resort called Lazaretto! (the punctuation is part of the name) of the most luxuriously banal kind, where, as a middle-aged lady tourist remarks, one feels so safe. The strange old House of the Chinese Master is a burnt ruin; the new landmark is a huge skyscraper called the Myrmidon Tower, "a virtuoso display of unashamed, unrestricted, technically unexampled vulgarity". The British Legate is at least as sinister and much slimier than his predecessor, the British Agent. Most of the city has been rebuilt in concrete. The troglodytic Kretev are housed in hygienic villas, and the bears are extinct. The age of postmodernism has arrived, with its characteristically brutal yet insidious architecture and propaganda, its reductionist culture of advertisement and imitation, its market capitalism, its factionalism and religiosity forever threatening terror. Yet we find pretty soon that Hav is still Hav: the maze, the labyrinth, is still there. Even the elevator of the Myrmidon Tower is indirect. Who in fact is running the country? The Cathars? But who are the Cathars? What does the M on the Myrmidon Tower really stand for?

Morris says in the epilogue that if Hav is an allegory, she's not sure what it is about. I don't take it as an allegory at all. I read it as a brilliant description of the crossroads of the West and East in two recent eras, viewed by a woman who has truly seen the world, and who lives in it with twice the intensity of most of us. Its enigmas are part of its accuracy. It is a very good guidebook, I think, to the early twenty-first century.

—URSULA K. LE GUIN

But what if light and shade should be reversed?
If you press the switch then, will you turn the darkness on?
Avzar Melchik, *Bağlılık* ('Dependence')

Preface

There can be few people nowadays who do not know the whereabouts of Hav, but when I first went there in the 1980s it seemed an almost chimerical city. Many visitors, of course, had described it in earlier days, marvelling at its curious monuments, pontificating about its history, catching something of its atmosphere in memoirs, novels and poetry –

> . . . the green-grey shape that seamen swear is Hav,
> Beyond the racing tumble of its foam.

Nobody, however, had written a proper book about the place, at least in modern times. It was almost as though a conspiracy had protected the peninsula from too frank or thorough a description.

But the cataclysm of 1985, known in Hav nowadays as the Intervention, made the name of the place familiar wherever newspapers are read. As it happened, I had arrived there some months before to write a series of literary letters for the magazine *New Gotham*, leaving just as catastrophe struck. When the essays were published in book form I called them *Last Letters from Hav*, because I assumed that the character of the city I had got to know, if not the city itself, must have been obliterated. Hav had seemed to me a little compendium of the world's experience, historically, aesthetically, even perhaps spiritually, and could surely never be the same place again.

Two decades later, when I had resolved to write no more books, I received an unexpected invitation from the Hav League of Intellectuals to revisit the city. I was surprised, because I had heard that *Last Letters* had been banned there, but thinking that it might result in an addendum to my original study, I accepted the offer and went back to Hav in the spring of 2005. I found it astonishingly resuscitated, different in character, certainly, from the city I had known, but hardly less allegorical of feel.

Denied entry to the United Nations in the years after the Intervention, Hav enjoyed diplomatic relations with only a handful of foreign states, stayed aloof to all regional groupings, and as a theocracy severly discouraged contacts with most of the rest of the world. However, in this ambiance of religious fundamentalism and state inhibition, political movements and activists of many kinds had found their way to Hav, and had made it in many ways a paradigm of our twenty-first century zeitgeist.

So in this volume we see the place stereoscopically, so to speak: in the first part through the misty lens of my letters of twenty years ago, in the second part rather more clearly, but still opaquely – for although carefully selected journalists have been able to visit Hav since the Intervention, and many travel magazines have advertised its dazzling tourist resort of Lazaretto, whether by intent or inherence it is still a destination like no other. As a contemporary Havian *anjlak*-poet has written,

> Intricate of intricacies,
> Twine-twisted,
> As a warren above wasteland
> I cherish the town – chasing its own tale.

ONE

LAST LETTERS
FROM HAV

Six Months in 1985

Frontier Station

The Escarpment

Megalith

PALAST

Arable and Grazing Land

Casino Cave

Salt Flats

Yuan Wen Kuo

CHINA BAY

THE BALAD

CANAL

1 Grand Mosque
2 Great Bazaar
3 Palace
4 Katourian's Place
5 Boulevard Cetinje
6 Pendeh Square
7 House of the Chinese Master

Castle

Central Station

The Hermitage

SERAI

Malaya Yalta

MEDINA

NEW HAV

The Port
Lazaretto

S.Pietro

S.Spiridon

Pyramid Rock

Ferry Station

Conveyor Bridge
Iron Dog

0   15
Miles   5   10

HAV
1985

MARCH

Locomotive No. 5 KOLCHOK

I

At the frontier – the tunnel pilot – L'Auberge Impériale – morning calls

I did what Tolstoy did, and jumped out of the train when it stopped in the evening at the old frontier. Far up at the front the engine desultorily gasped, and wan faces watched me through crusted carriage windows as I walked all alone down the platform to the gate. There was no pony trap awaiting me of course (Tolstoy's reminded him sadly of picnics at Yasnaya Polyana), but a smart enough green Fiat stood in the station yard, a young man in sunglasses and a blue blazer beckoned me from the wheel, and in no time we were off along the rutted track towards the ridge.

Very unusual, said the driver, to find a customer at the station these days, but he made the journey twice a week anyway, there and back, under contract to the railway. This was the tunnel pilot's car, he explained, and he was Yasar Yeğen the tunnel pilot's nephew, the pilotage being a hereditary affair. In his great-grandfather's time they had done the trip with a pony cart, and in those days, when the tunnel was considered one of the wonders of the world, all manner of great swells used to leave the train up there for the experience of the spectacle. Why did they need a pilot for the tunnel? The Porte had insisted on it, for southbound trains only, as a token of the Sultan's sovereignty after the Pendeh settlement; and ever since then, for more than a century, while Porte, Sultan and Czars too had all passed into history, a member of the Yeğen family had boarded the Mediterranean Express at the frontier stop, and formally ushered it through the escarpment.

Dust billowed behind us as we bounced over the snow-streaked plateau; ahead of us there stood a solitary tall stone, a megalith upon a mound; and then suddenly we were on the rim of the great declivity, and over it, and plunging down the ancient and spectacular mule-track, the celebrated 'Staircase', which appears in all the old engravings crowded with pack-trains, wandering dervishes, beggars squatting on rocks, platoons of soldiers with pikes and muskets, great ladies veiled in palanquins, vastly turbanned dragomans and gentlemanly horsemen in fly-netted pith helmets – 'a very inconvenient approximation', as Kinglake called it, 'of Jacob's Ladder'. The coming of the railway ended all that, and now the track was altogether empty – hardly anybody used it, Yasar Yeğen told me, except Adventure Tours in four-wheel-drive buses, and the cave-dwellers who inhabited the western face of the escarpment. So we proceeded gloriously unimpeded, skidding helter-skelter around those once-famous zigzags, and occasionally evading them with boisterous short cuts between the outcrops.

Halfway down I looked back, and there I saw, issuing from a squat chimney near the crown of the cliff, a pillar of black smoke which showed that the Express was on its way, chuffing subterraneously down its own spiralling descent within the limestone. 'Don't worry,' said Yasar, 'I am never late,' and sure enough, when we slithered to a showy stop on the gravelly clearing at the tunnel mouth, it was only a few minutes before we heard the train's resonant wailing cry from the bowels of the mountain. A gust of sooty smoke out of the big black hole – a cyclopean eye groping through the murk – a powerful emanation of steam, grease and coal dust – and there it was, tremendously emerging from its labyrinth, a huge locomotive of dirty red with a cowcatcher and a brass bell, its crew leaning from each side of their cab, as they reached the daylight, wearing goggles and greasy cloth caps, but bearing themselves as grandly as ships' officers on their flying bridges. The train eased itself to a stop with a mighty hissing of brakes, steam and smoke, and beneath the numerals on its cab I could just make out, not quite obliterated even now, the old Cyrillic characters of the Imperial Russian Railways.

A tall elderly man swung himself from the footplate, wearing a sober dark suit, remarkably unblemished, and a black felt hat in the Ataturk mode. He turned to salute the engine-driver when he reached the ground, and then walked in a distinctly authoritative way towards the Fiat. Hastily Yasar, smoothing his hair and blazer, jumped out of the car to open the back door, and almost involuntarily I got out too, so imposing was that approaching figure. The tunnel pilot looked as though the world and all its movement depended on him. The train seethed and simmered respectfully behind his back. He had a bristly grey moustache, possibly waxed, and on his chest he wore a brass emblem, larger than a mere medal, more like the insignia of some chivalric order, which incorporated, I saw as he neared me, the silhouetted form of a very old-fashioned steam engine. He strode directly over to me, bowed low and kissed my hand, grunting 'Dear lady' in a blurred and throaty sort of way, 'Dirleddy', as though he had often heard it said but had never analysed it. Then he stepped into his car, the door was closed gently behind him, and I hardly had time to thrust my money into Yasar's hand before they were away, hurling dust and rubble in their wake, breakneck up the precipitous bends of the escarpment. I sprinted for the train, dispassionately observed by those same pale faces in the carriage windows, and was just in time to scramble aboard before, with a more perfunctory hoot and a clang of couplings, it moved heavily off into the flatlands.

It was dusk by now as we crawled very, very slowly towards the city. Everything looked monotonous out there, and cold, and shadowy, and silent, and grey. We were crossing the marshy salt-flats which have always acted as a cordon sanitaire, and a field of fire too, between the coast settlements and the escarpment. They looked horribly forbidding, brackish wastelands bounded to the east by low brown hills – which one of them, I wondered, had Schliemann first claimed to be Troy? There was a line of tall iron windmills, and a few lights flickered palely in the marshes; and when, clattering over a bridge, we entered the first purlieus of the city, they too seemed sufficiently unwelcoming, with their shambolic buildings of mudbrick and clapboard, some painted a gloomy blue, with scrabbly yards, and clumps of corrugated-iron shanties, and gravel football pitches here and there, and an occasional tall chimney, and dim unlit streets. Sometimes an open fire blazed, and a few figures crouched around it. More often everything in sight looked lifeless, perhaps, abandoned.

The train moved so laboriously through these unlovely suburbs, frequently stopping altogether and ringing its bell mournfully all the way, that by the time we were in the city proper it was pitch-dark. The lights outside were all very faint, and I could see nothing much but burly dark shapes in silhouette, a power station, a dome, a square tower, what looked like a minaret, and a general monumental mass: and so, well after midnight, we lurched at last exhaustedly, as though the rolling stock were all but worn out too, into the vestigially brighter lights of the Central Station, which seemed to be immense, but turned out to have, in the event, only the one platform. '*Hav!*' a great voice boomed. '*Hav Centrum!*'

In a matter of moments, it seemed to me, my few fellow-passengers had all scuttled away into the dark, and I was left alone upon the platform, wondering where to spend the rest of the night. But enormously facing me I saw an advertisement made, as in mosaic, of brightly coloured china tiles. On the right it offered a stylized depiction of Russia, onion domes, troikas, fir forests. On the left, bathed in golden sunshine against a cobalt sea, was the city of Hav, with elaborately hatted ladies and marvellously patrician beaux sauntering, a little disjointedly where the tiles met, along a palm-shaded corniche.

Florid in the middle, in Russian Cyrillic, in Turkish Arabic and in French, a sign announced the presence of L'Auberge Impériale du Chemin de Fer Hav, and immediately below it a cavernous entrance invited me, along red-carpeted corridors lined with empty showcases, to a kiosk of glass and gilded iron-work in which there sat a stout woman, smiling, in black.

'You encountered the tunnel pilot, I hear,' she remarked unexpectedly when I presented my passport for registration. 'He is my cousin Rudolph. He was named, you may be interested to know, after a Crown Prince of Austria who came here long ago, and took the pony cart with my great-grandfather to see the train come from the tunnel.'

'Your family meets everyone.'

'*Used* to meet everyone, should we say? Whom did we not meet? All the crowned heads, all the great people, Bismarck, Nijinsky, Count Kolchok of course many, many times. You should see the pictures in the pilot's office at the frontier – everyone is there! Even Hitler came once, they say, though we did not know it at the time. Our last great lady was Princess Grace – I met her myself, such a lovely person – they had a special car waiting for her, over from Izmir, they said it was the biggest car that ever went down the Staircase, even bigger than the Kaiser's . . .'

Chatting in this good-natured way, Miss Fatima Yeğen signed me in and showed me to my room, which was very large, like a salon, and had thick curtains of faded crimson. So, I thought as she stumped away down the corridor, late in a life of travel I am in Hav at last! A big blue-and-white samovar stood in the corner of the room, and there was a picture of a rural winter scene signed T. Ramotsky, 1879 – the very year, I guessed, when they had fitted out the Imperial Railway Hotel for its original guests. A palpable smell of eggs haunted the apartment, mingled with a suggestion of pomade, and when I drew the curtains there was nothing to be seen outside but the well of the hotel, lugubriously illuminated and echoing with the clatter of washing-up from a kitchen far below. At the foot of my bed was a television set, but when I turned it on it was showing a black-and-white Cary Grant film dubbed into Turkish; so I went to sleep instead – confusedly, as in a state of weightlessness, having no idea really what lay outside the walls of L'Auberge Impériale du Chemin de Fer Hav, and fancying only, in my half-waking dreams, the bubble of the samovar, the drab grey salt-flats, the windmills, and the procession of kings, dukes and chancellors winding their way with plumes of swirling soil, like defiances, down the mule-track from the frontier.

But I was awoken in the morning by two marvellous sounds as the first light showed through my shutters: the frail quavering line of a call to prayer; from some far minaret across the city, and the note of a trumpet close at hand, greeting the day not with a bold reveille, but more in wistful threnody.

2

*Legend of the trumpet – to the market – scholarly shopper –
Katourian's Place – all Hav – Missakian breakfasts*

Hardly had the last note of the trumpet died away than I was
dressed and on my way down the silent hotel corridors
towards the daylight.

The legend of the trumpet is this. When at the end of the
eleventh century the knights of the First Crusade seized Hav
from the Seljuks, they were joined by hundreds of Armenians
flocking down from their beleaguered homelands in the north-
west. Among them was the musician Katourian, and he
became the cherished minstrel of the Court, celebrating its
feats and tragedies in beloved ballads, growing old and grey in
its service.

In 1191 Saladin, after a siege of three months, forced the
surrender of the Crusaders, and on the morning of the Feast of
St Benedict the Christians left the Castle with full courtesies of
war and marched to the galleys waiting in the harbour. Their
Armenian followers were left to face the fury of the Muslims,
and as the last of the long line of Franks passed through the
Castle gate between the rows of Arab soldiery, the musician
Katourian, feeble and bent by now, appeared on the breast-
work high above and sang, with more power and emotion
even than in the heyday of his art, the most famous of all his
great laments, 'Chant de doleure pour li proz chevalers qui
suet morz'. It rang across the city as a magnificent farewell, so
the fable says, and with its last declining cadence Katourian

plunged a dagger into his breast and died upon the rampart, known from that day to this as Katourian's Place.

Moved by the tragic splendour of this gesture, Saladin ordered that in honour of the minstrel, and of the Christian knights themselves, the lament should be sung each morning, from the same place, immediately after the call to prayer. The Arabs never did master the words of the song, which concerned the immolation of a group of otherwise forgotten Gascon men-at-arms, but the melody they subtly adapted until it sounded almost Muslim itself, and at dawn each day, throughout the long centuries of Islamic rule, it was sung from Katourian's Place. The British, during their half-century in Hav after the Napoleonic wars, substituted a trumpeter for the muezzin's voice; the Russians who followed honoured the old tradition, and the governors of the Tripartite Mandate, after them. And so it was that on my first morning I was hastening towards my opening revelation of the city to the echo of a dirge from the European Middle Ages.

I passed through the deserted station (the train still standing there lifeless) and stepped into the yellowish mist of the great square outside. I could hardly see across it – just a suggestion of great buildings opposite, and to my right the mass of the Castle looming in a dim succession of stairs, terraces, curtain walls and gateways, only the very top of the immense central keep, Beynac's Keep, being touched with the golden sunshine of the morning. Though I could hear not far away a deep muffled rumble, as of an army moving secretly through the dawn, the square itself was utterly empty; but even as I stood there, striding down the last steps from the Castle came the trumpeter himself, down from the heights, his instrument under his arm, huddled in a long brown greatcoat against the misty damp.

'*Merhaba*, trumpeter!' I accosted him. 'I am Jan Morris from Wales, on my very first morning in Hav!'

He answered in kind. 'And I am Missakian the trumpeter,' he laughed. '*Merhaba*, good morning to you!'

'Missakian! You're Armenian?'

'But naturally. The trumpeters of Hav always are. You know the legend of Katourian? Well, then you will understand' – and after an exchange of pleasantries, expressing the hope that we might meet again, 'not quite so early in the morning, perhaps', trumpet under his arm, he resumed his progress across the square.

Which reminded me, as the mist began to lift, of somewhere like Cracow or Kiev, so grey and cobbled did it seem to be, and so immense. It was hardly worth exploring then, so instead I followed that rumble, which seemed to have its focus somewhere away to my left, and found myself in a mesh of side-streets I knew not where, joining the extraordinary procession of traffic that makes its way each morning to Hav's ancient market on the waterfront. Pendeh Square, the great central plaza of the city, is closed to all traffic until seven in the morning, but the thoroughfares around it, I discovered, were already clogged with all manner of vehicles. There were pick-up trucks with brightly painted sides. There were motorbikes toppling with the weight of their loaded sidecars. There were private cars with milk-churns on their roofs. Men in wide straw hats and striped cotton *gallabiyehs* and women in headscarves and long black skirts lolloped along on pony carts, and a string of mules passed by, weighed down with firewood. They moved, for all the noise of their engines and the rattle of their wheels on the cobblestones, in a kind of hush, very deliberately; and I found myself caught up in the steady press of it, stared at curiously but without comment, until we all debouched into the wide market-place at the water's edge, where fishing-boats were moored bow to stern along the quay, and where as the sun broke through the morning fog all was already bustle and flow.

In every city the morning market, the very first thing to happen every day, offers a register of the public character. Few offer so violent a first impression as the waterside market of

Hav. Apparently unregulated, evidently immemorial, it seemed to me that morning partly like a Marseilles fish-wharf, and partly like the old Covent Garden, and partly like a flea-market, for there seemed to be almost nothing, at six in the morning, that was not there on sale. Everything was inextricably confused. One stall might be hung all over with umbrellas and plastic galoshes, the next piled high with celery and boxes of edible grass. There were mounds of apples, artistically arranged, there were stacks of boots and racks of sunglasses and rows of old radios. There were spare parts for cars, suitcases with images of the pyramids embossed upon them, rolls of silk, nylon underwear in yellows and sickly pinks, brass trays, Chinese medicines, hubble-bubbles, coffee beans in vast tin containers, souvenirs of Mecca or Istanbul, second-hand-book stalls with grubby old volumes in many languages – I looked inside a copy of *Moby Dick*, and stamped within its covers were the words 'Property of the American University, Beirut'.

In a red-roofed shed near the water, shirtsleeved butchers were at work, chopping bloody limbs and carcasses, skinning sheep and goats before my eyes; and there were living sheep too, of a brownish tight-curled wool, and chickens in crude wicker baskets, and pigeons in coops. Women shawled and bundled against the cold sold cups of steaming soup. On the quay Greek fishermen offered direct from their boats fish still flapping in their boxes, mucous eels, writhing lobsters, prawns, urchins, sponges and buckets of what looked like phosphorescent plankton.

Almost any language, I discovered, would get you by in Hav – not just Turkish, but Italian, French, Arabic, English at a pinch, even Chinese. This was Pero Tafur's 'Lesser Babel'! Some people were dressed Turkish-style in sombre dark suits with cloth caps, many wore those wide hats and cotton robes, rather like North Africans, some were dark and gypsy-looking, a few were Indian, some were high-cheeked like Mongols, and some, long-haired and medieval of face, wearing drab mixtures of jeans, raincoats and old bits of khaki uniform, I took to be the Kretevs, the cave-dwellers of the escarpment. Tousled small dogs ran about the place; the Greeks on their boats laughed and shouted badinage to each other. Moving importantly among the stalls, treated with serious respect by the most bawdy of the fishermen, the most brutal of the butchers, I saw a solitary European, in a grey suit and a panama hat, who seemed to go about his business, choosing mutton here, fruit there, in a style that was almost scholarly.

He was followed by a pair of Chinese, who saw to it when their boss had made his decisions that his choice was picked from its tank, cut from its hook or removed unbruised from its counter, and placed in the porter's trolley behind; and I followed the little cortège through the meat market, along the line of the fishing-boats, to the jetty beyond the market. A spanking new motor-launch was moored there, blue and cream, like an admiral's barge, with a smart Chinese sailor in a blue jersey waiting at the wheel, and another at the prow with his boat-hook across his arms. Gently into the well, amidships, went the crates of victuals; the European adeptly stepped aboard; and with a snarl of engines the boat backed from the quay, turned in a wide foamy curve, and sped away down the harbour towards the sea.

'Good gracious,' I said to one of the Greeks, 'who was that?'

'That was Signor Biancheri, the chef of the Casino. Every morning he comes here. You've never heard of him? You surprise me.'

'You should go up to Katourian's Place,' the trumpeter had told me 'but wait for an hour or two, until the sun comes up.' So now that the sun was rising above the silhouette of the Castle, and its warm light was creeping along the quays and striking into the cobbled streets behind, I walked back across the still empty square and clambered up the steep stone steps to see for myself the city this remarkable populace had, over so many centuries, evolved for itself

I passed through barbicans and curtain walls, I clambered

up shattered casements, I entered the immense gateway upon which Saladin had caused to be carved his triumphant and celebrated proclamation: 'In the name of God, the Merciful, the Almighty, Salah ed Din the warrior, the defender of Islam, may God glorify his victories, here defeated, humiliated and spared the armies of the Infidel.' And immediately inside, on the half-ruined rampart beside the gate, I found a second inscription, in English, upon a stone slab. 'In memory', it said, 'of Katourian the musician. Erected by subscription of the Officers of Her Majesty's Royal Regiment of Artillery in the Protectorate of Hav and the Escarpment, AD 1837. *Semper Fidelis*.'

On the platform beside the plaque, the very spot where Katourian is supposed to have killed himself, I spread out my map and looked down for the first time upon all Hav. The last morning vapours were dispersing, and the greyness of the night before was becoming, as the sun rode higher in the sky, almost unnaturally clear – the blue rim of the sea around, the low hillocks to west and east, the line of the escarpment, still in shadow, like a high wall in the distance. Salt gleamed white in the wide marshlands. There were patches of green crops and pasture to the north-east, and curving across the peninsula I could see the line of the canal cut by the Spartans during their long investment of Athenian Hav. Here and there around the coast, fishing-boats worked in twos and threes; rounding the southern point went the scud and spray of Signor Biancheri's provision launch, hastening home to breakfast.

Now I could get the hang of the place, for the Castle stands on the bald hill which is the true centre of Hav, and which was for centuries the seat of its power too. To the north of it, away to the salt-flats, extended the hangdog suburb where Hav's multi-ethnic proletariat, Turkish, Arab, Greek, African, Armenian, lives in a long frayed grid of shacks and cabins. It was marked on my map as the Balad, and it looked altogether anonymous, blank like a labour camp but for the spike of a minaret here and there, one or two church towers and brick-work chimneys, a stagnant-looking lake in the middle of it and a power station spouting smoke at its southern end. The railway track cut a wide swathe through the Balad, and parallel to it ran a tram-line, about which in places swamped dense clusters of figures, some in brown or black, some in white robes – ah, and there came the first tram of the morning, pulling a trailer, already scrambled all over by a mass of passengers clinging to its sides and platforms. I watched its lurching progress south – through those shabby shanty-streets – past the power station – out of sight for a moment in the lee of the castle hill . . .

. . . and turning myself to follow it, I saw spread out before me downtown Hav around the wide inlet of its haven. To the west, at the other end of the castle ridge, stood the vestigial remains of the Athenian acropolis, its surviving columns shored up by ugly brick buttresses. Away to the south I fancied I could just make out the Iron Dog at the entrance to the harbour, and beside it the platform of the Conveyor Bridge was already swinging slowly across the water. A couple of ships lay at their moorings in the port; on the waterfront the market was still thronged and bustling. And at my feet lay the mass of the central city, the Palace, the brightly domed offices of government, the circular slab of New Hav, the narrow crannied streets and tall white blocks of the Medina.

A red light was flashing from the prison island in the harbour, but even as I watched, it was switched off for the day, and instantly a hooter somewhere sounded a long steady blast. Seven o'clock, Hav time! Immediately, as if gates had been unlocked or barriers removed, the first traffic of the day spilled into Pendeh Square below me, and soon the din of the market had spread across the whole city, and there reached me from all around the reassuring noises of urban life, the hoots and the revs, the shouts, the clanging bells, the blaring radio music. The fishing-boats of the market sailed away in raggety flotilla down the harbour. Sunshine flashed from the upperworks of the ships, and wherever I looked the streets were filling up, cars were on the move and shopkeepers were unlocking their doors for the day's business. A small figure appeared upon the roof of the Palace, beneath its gilded onion dome, and raised upon its flagstaff the black-and-white chequered flag of Hav (which looks bathetically like the winner's flag at a motor-race, but was chosen in 1924, I have been told, so as to be utterly unidentifiable with the flag of any one of the Mandatory Powers).

Down the hill I went. The cicadas were chortling in the grass now, and halfway down a woman with a satchel over her shoulder was scrabbling in the turf for herbs. The great square was full of life by the time I got down there – cars everywhere, a tram rattling past the station entrance, flower-sellers setting up their trays beside the equestrian statue of Czar Alexander II in the middle. Outside the Palace gates, between the palm trees, two sentries in red jackets and crinkly astrakhan hats stood guard with fixed bayonets on antique rifles. The flag flew ridiculously up above. When I reached the station entrance, and made my way towards the hotel, I looked through the glass door of the Café de la Gare, to my right, and there with his instrument upright on the table the trumpeter Missakian, head down, was deep into a pile of beans.

3

Settling in – the routine – at the Athenaeum – in a vacuum – who cares?

Here as anywhere one must settle in. One must adjust one's first impressions, which may indeed be perfectly accurate, but are sure to be partial. Already, I must say, that castle does not look quite so towering on its hill. Missakian's morning trumpet is not quite so heart-rendingly flawless as it sounded that first morning, and the TV, if still fond of old Hollywood in Turkish, turns out to transmit programmes too in French, Italian and Chinese, not to mention brand-new American soap operas in Arabic.

Seen and heard at least from residence in the railway hotel, Hav is a city of very settled habit, living to programmes that seem inflexible. Usages of routine – 'two o'clock sharp', 'as always', 'according to custom' – are much favoured by Havians. Crack of dawn comes the call to prayer and the trumpet, and soon afterwards I hear the cry of the first hawker; he sells hot oatcakes in the yard behind the station, baking them in a portable oven, and always seems to have plenty of customers – many people, Miss Yeğen tells me, make a breakfast of them before they go to work. Seven o'clock, the siren sounds, and almost at once I hear the ding-ding-ding of the first tram, clattering into Pendeh Square. At eight the angelus rings from the French cathedral, and then the steel shutters of the shops clang up, one after the other through the streets. Eleven o'clock sharp on Tuesdays and Thursdays – well, *generally* sharp – and a long blast of the steam-whistle proclaims the departure of the Mediterranean Express for Kars (or as it used to be, and still can be with minor interruptions, for Tiflis, Rostov and Moscow . . .).

At eleven-thirty *really* sharp, every day of the week, one can hear the muffled report of a gun from the prison island, San Pietro. Hav time being half an hour before St Petersburg time, ever since the days of Russian rule, eleven thirty rather than noon has been the official centre of the Hav day, the moment when all official departments close for the midday break. The shop shutters rattle down again, the trams pause in their schedules, and for most of the people of Hav a rather heavy lunch is followed by three or four hours of idle siesta, even in the winter months – until as the evening begins to draw in everything starts up all over again.

The prison gun goes off once more at half past eight in the evening, and the working day is over. Nowadays, those who do not go home to supper with TV linger on till ten or eleven in the cafés and restaurants of New Hav, or go out to dinner in Yuan Wen Kuo, where things stay open later, or find disreputable indulgences, so Miss Yeğen says, in the back-streets of the Medina and Balad slums. But I am told that in the old days the climax or focal point of the evening, at least in the summer season, was the midnight arrival of the Express, to disgorge its complement of grandees and celebrities before a wondering crowd at the platform barricade. Now the train seldom arrives before two or three in the morning: and by then, as we know, nobody is awake in Hav but Miss Yeğen in her cubicle at the hotel.

One must also settle in, here as everywhere, in the official or administrative sense. This has proved a surprisingly pleasant experience. 'You must go to the Serai,' said Miss Yeğen, 'and register at the Aliens Registration Office, or else *zam*, you will be on my cousin's train without a first-class ticket, on your way to Kars.' So I went along to the Aliens Office, round the back of the government buildings, and there, presenting my passport, and

Evidence of Solvency (namely my American Express credit card, which so far as I know is accepted by nobody here), I met Mr Mahmoud Azzam, Deputy Controller of Aliens.

'Dirleddy,' said Mr Mahmoud Azzam – for this form of address, I now realize, is generic to courtly gentlemen of Hav, whatever their language – 'I see you are a writer. So am I, when I am not being Deputy Controller of Aliens, and you really must allow me, since it is now almost eleven thirty, to introduce you to some of our confrères. Do please take lunch with me in what you might call our headquarters, the Athenaeum Club – just around the corner.' Mr Azzam was in his late twenties, I would judge, and rather progressive of appearance, having long sideburns and a droopy moustache, besides wearing in his lapel a badge saying in Turkish *Balinaları Öldürmeyin*, 'Save the Whale'. He did not look Athenaeum material, so to speak, especially when, having packed away his files and put his three or four pens in his breast pocket, he took me round the corner and I saw the club-house before me. It was built by the Russians, and looked all you would expect of an Athenaeum, dorically pillared on a single floor, grandly porticoed, green-shuttered, Minerva-crowned of course – in short, if a little down-at-heel, distinctly of the literary or scholarly élite. Was this really Mr Azzam, I wondered? No less pertinently, I mused, eyeing my own dusty sandals and less than immaculate slacks, was it entirely me?

But I need not have worried. Hardly had we climbed the front steps, entered the tall portico (bees' nests clustered under its eaves), and pushed open the big front door, when a comforting hubbub reached us – loud talk, much laughter, even snatches of singing. 'We are all intellectuals here,' said Mr Azzam, as though that explained everything, and thus encouraged, holding my copy of Braudel's *The Mediterranean in the Age of Philip II*, Volume II, as if in credential, I accompanied him into the maelstrom.

The whole of the ground floor of the Hav Athenaeum, which I surmise was once hall, dining-room, bar and silent library, is now a gigantic kind of common room, as in some extremely avant-garde university. Cafeteria, bar, sitting-room, office, library, seemed to be strewn at random around this immense chamber. All was in a state of exuberant vigour. Everyone was talking very loudly, as at a cocktail party, except for those bent over books and magazines in the library wing, and there were knots of people arguing and gesticulating over drinks, and people shouting to one another from one end of the cafeteria queue to the other. Even the elderly women behind the counter replied to orders in screeching fortissimi. It was not at all how I imagined an Athenaeum.

And another un-Athenaeum-like thing: hardly anybody there, except the counter-women and me, seemed much more than thirty years old. Men and women, they looked like so many students – not even associate professors, I thought, at the most research graduates. They greeted me very breezily as we elbowed our way through. 'Hello old thing,' said a man in big horn-rimmed glasses, provoking a storm of 'Hush', 'Anton, so rude', and 'Take no notice, dirleddy', and from a young woman behind us in the queue came the cry 'Braudel! That monster!'

I asked her afterwards, when we came to share a table, why she cherished this exotic antipathy – it is not common, after all, to feel so fiercely about illustrious scholars.

'Why, because in God knows how many pages of God knows how many volumes, he never even recognizes the *existence* of Hav.'

This raised ardent waves of assent from our companions – 'shame, shame', 'quite true', 'notorious', etc. 'Fair play, Magda,' said Mahmoud Azzam, 'surely he mentions us in footnotes?'

She ignored him. 'And do you know why?' she asked me urgently, looking me very close and hard in the face. 'Because the French wish to refuse our being. They do not wish us to have existed. They failed to keep us after their infamous occupation in 1917, and so they want us not to be. They are a very jealous people. They know Hav has been for centuries, for aeons, a centre of art and civilization – long before France was thought of! – so if they cannot have us, and pretend us to be French, like Guadeloupans, or what-have-yous in the Pacific Sea, then they do not want us to be.'

A frenzied discussion followed this outburst, some supporting Magda, some telling me to take no notice of her, some declaring the Italians to be much worse than the French, some blaming the Americans, some fondly remembering visits to Paris, some going on to talk about wine, or Sartre, or Yves Saint Laurent ('You have met Yves? he is my hero') . . . 'We are intellectuals you see,' Mahmoud bawled in my ear. 'There is no subject that we cannot discuss, and all subjects make us angry:'

So now I am a member of the Athenaeum – it will make me feel at home, Mahmoud says. More than that, I am a colleague of Mahmoud and Magda and the man with the horn-rimmed glasses, whose name is Dr Borge, and so, despite my age, a temporary member of the intellectual establishment. Why *were* they all so young? I ventured to ask the other day, and there was a short silence before Mahmoud replied, 'Ah, well, you see in 1978 there were certain scandals here, and the leaders of the affair – the Prefects? is that the word in English? – they were all members of the Athenaeum. Many, many members, most of the older ones, resigned then.'

'Huh,' said Magda, 'or were *made* to resign . . .'

I asked no more. I knew my place. Still, I wonder what did happen in 1978? I wonder who the Prefects were?

Hav days pass swiftly, but somehow hazily. I know of nowhere in the world where the purpose of life seems so ill-defined. It is perfectly true that in the past Hav has played an exceedingly important role in history – has sometimes seemed indeed, as Magda would claim, the very centre of affairs, a crux, a junction of great traffic, not just the run-down terminal of the preposterously anachronistic Mediterranean Express. Especially down at the harbour, I can often imagine the days when the dhows and galleys lay alongside in a clamour of commerce, and the camel caravans from remotest Central Asia, all bales, and straw, and buckets, and ropes, and arguing Turcomans in long robes, assembled sprawled and grunting on the quays beside the warehouses!

But those purposes have long gone, and more than any other city I know Hav seems to live in a hazy vacuum. They used to say of Beirut that, just as aerodynamically a bumble-bee has no right to fly, so Beirut had no logical claim to survival. Even more is it true of contemporary Hav, which has no visible resources but the salt and the fish, which makes virtually nothing, which offers no flag of convenience, but yet manages to stagger on if not richly, at least without destitution.

History has left Hav behind, and our own times too, like Professor Braudel, have wilfully ignored the place. Its modern reputation is murky. Its political situation, vague enough even when you are in the city, is a blur indeed to the world at large. There is no airport, no proper highway into the peninsula, no harbour deep enough for big ships, and only a trickle of tourists ever bothers to make the long and extremely inconvenient journey on the train. Not one foreign news agency or newspaper maintains a correspondent in Hav. Only the British have a consul here, though the Turks possess their own Delegation Office in the Serai, and Hav has no missions abroad.

Were it not for the vessels in the harbour, the train twice a week, and the vapour trails of the airliners flying high overhead to Damascus, Teheran and the further east, it would often feel as though the place occupied its own entirely separate plane of existence, insulated against everywhere else.

All this makes the ponderous routine of Hav seem strangely introspective. Who cares? one soon comes to feel. Who cares if Missakian sounds his trumpet on the rampart? Who cares if the train is late, or what the Prefects did? Who cares if the gun goes off? Only the city itself, whose memories are so long, whose character is so elaborately creased or layered, and into whose idiosyncratic attitudes I find myself all too easily adapting.

4

*My apartment – the Serai – bureaucrats – legations – the King
of Montenegro – guards and a victim*

Less than a month in Hav, and I feel myself a citizen already. I
write now at my table upon the balcony of my own small
apartment – bedroom, dining-room with fringed velveteen
table cover, kitchen, bathroom whose magnificent shower,
entitled 'Il Majestico', is tiled with majolica flowers and fruits.
Above me lives my landlady, Signora Emilia Vattani, below me
are the consulting rooms of an elderly Lebanese psychiatrist,
and below that again is the Ristorante Milano, formerly I am
told one of the best restaurants in the city, now just a genial
Egyptian coffee shop.

If I go up to the roof of the house, where Signora V. maintains a genteel garden, with a pergola and two urns, I can see
protruding above the rooftops to the west the spirally gilded
onion domes of the Serai, the very centre of all life in Hav. The
Russians built it, of course, as a deliberate expression of their
own expansionism, but the great complex long ago became an
exclamation of Hav's own proud if ambivalent personality,
and stands towards the city today as the Eiffel Tower does to
Paris, or the Opera House to Sydney.

You know how curiously separate the Vatican feels, within
the enveloping tumult of Rome? Well, the Serai is rather like
that. It also reminds me of the Forbidden City in Beijing, old
Peking, that fantastic retreat of the Emperors which the Communists have turned into the most extraordinary of public

parks; for though in Russian times the Serai was closed to all but grandees and officials, and the public was kept at bay by formidable Cossacks, nowadays anybody can walk through its gardens, which provide indeed an agreeable short cut from Pendeh Square to the Medina. Often I take a picnic lunch there, and eat my salami and oatcake on a bench immediately outside the Governor's Palace, in what was His Excellency's private pleasance. It is still dingily delightful, with fountains sporadically spouting, arbours, gravel walks, and in one corner a little *cottage orné*, now used as a potting-shed, which was built by one of the early Russian governors as a present for his wife.

One hears tales of stately receptions here, with the wide French windows of the downstairs rooms open to the evening air, a military band playing on the terrace and half the nobility of Russia gossiping and flirting in those arbours. Tolstoy was a guest at such a function in 1885, and got into a furious argument with a cocksure captain of artillery, though in his second autobiography he simply says that he found the society of Hav 'unappealing'. Rimsky-Korsakov, on the other hand, who arrived here as an officer on a Russian warship two years later, was enchanted with everything he saw, played one of his own compositions on a grand piano in that very garden, and years later adapted the melody of the Hav trumpet call for the recurrent theme in *Scheherazade*.

No ravishing tunes sound through the garden now, but still the atmosphere of the place is genial. The governors of Hav are elected for five-year terms of office, generally towards the end of their careers as state councillors, and to judge by photographs are usually portly gents of aldermanic style. I have not yet met the present incumbent, but once when Fatima Yeğen and I were sitting beside the fountains during her lunch break from the hotel we saw him emerge upon the balcony on the *piano nobile*, looking comfortably replete and holding a champagne glass in his hand. He caught sight of us and raised his glass. We waved. 'Such a charming man,' said Fatima. 'When he was younger he was the handsomest man in Hav, bar nobody.'

The Palace and its gardens are flanked, right and left, by the offices of the administration, each with four onion domes to balance the grand central dome of the residence. The whole ensemble looks like a cross between the Brighton Pavilion and St Basil's Cathedral in Red Square, and forms an anomalously exuberant centrepiece to the city. Though the candy colours of the domes are a little muted now, by dusty age and neglect, still seen down the streets of New Hav, or through the tumbled alleys of the Medina, when the sun is right they seem to shimmer there like huge billowing screens of silk. This fanciful and light-hearted ambience is strikingly at odds with what goes on beneath them, for I doubt if there are any government offices more morosely addled with bureaucracy than the administrative offices of Hav.

Ostensibly they are divided into ministerial sections. Actually, since it was the enlightened idea of the Imperial Russian Government to house all its officials on huge open-plan floors, two to each block, everything seems to have spilled over long ago into everything else, and it is almost impossible to know, if you have business to transact there, in what department you are at any one moment. Come with me now, for instance, into the ground-floor offices of the North Block, nominally the precincts of the Hav Census, the Salt Administration, the Arable and Pasture Board, the Office of Languages and the Muslim Department of Wakfs. Entering this room is rather as I imagine entering the hospital at Scutari might have been, before Miss Nightingale got there. Even in the middle of the morning it is dark inside, and scattered bare electric light bulbs burn, giving everything a cavernous or cellar-like appearance. Hundreds of electric fans are massed in clusters on long rods from the ceiling, and the windows are covered with loose matting to keep the sun out. The entire room is filled with a mass of identical wooden desks, several hundred of them surely.

Some are protected by makeshift partitions of plyboard, cardboard or even loose canvas, while others are walled about with piles of books and ledgers. Many have been enmeshed in electric wires, plugged into light sockets above, which hang down like life-support systems to provide power for kettles, radios or winter heaters, while over them all runs a complicated pattern of pneumatic message tubes.

At every single desk a man sits, hunched, sprawling or occasionally straight-backed at his work, and each seems to be engulfed in a hill of paper. Wherever you look, everywhere across that nightmare floor, there are heaps, wodges, stacks of paper – paper tied in huge bundles, paper stuffed into sockets, paper spread out on desktops, or cluttered in trays, or strewn across the floor, and through it all the bureaucracy seems to be impotently floundering. The room is in a condition of sluggish diligence. Typewriters clack somewhere, occasionally a telephone rings, girls move unhurriedly up and down those tattered ranks, collecting dockets or returning files, waiters in stained white jackets dispense Turkish coffee and glasses of water from silver-plated trays, and ever through the tubes above one can hear the message cylinders, rattling across the intersections towards some unimaginable clearing centre out of sight.

'May I help you?' asks a peripatetic supervisor, carrying a large and battered clipboard.

'We are looking for the Department of Temporary Contributions.'

'Ah, that will be our Monsieur Tarbat, let me see now, Section A10 I believe' – he consults his board – 'ah no, he has passed to Section K . . . it must be – let me see – I think perhaps it's a branch of Domestic Registrations . . . I wonder now – patience, *mesdames*, forgive me –'

But at that moment we catch fight of our friend Boris, a keen member of the New Hav Film Society, accepting a coffee from a passing waiter. 'Temporary Contributions?' he laughs. 'Forget it, nobody has bothered about them since the end of the concessions. Put it out of your minds – enjoy yourselves!'

'Excellent advice,' says the supervisor, moving on.

Behind the Serai, in a ceremonious half-circle, stand the former legations. These were built on the edge of the old parade ground when the Russians first opened Hav to diplomatic representation, and are now given over to less lofty purposes, the British consul (who is called the Agent, actually) living at the former British Residency above the harbour. The legations are like a little museum of lost consequence, so many of their proud sponsors having vanished with the great convulsion of the First World War, but they are also a display of *fin de siècle* architectural styles. Thus the French built theirs, now the Hav Academy of Music and Dancing, in a sprightly Art Nouveau style, rich in coloured glass and ornamental lamp brackets, while the Americans next door erected one of the earliest steel-construction buildings in Europe – a building which, though now turned into the somewhat disconsolate Hav Museum, still looks by Hav standards remarkably up-to-date. My own favourite, though, is the wonderfully eccentric mansion at the northern end of the crescent, which is built partly of wood and partly of massive rusticated stone, and is splendidly embellished with balconies, external staircases, decorative busts, half-timbering and twisted chimney-pots in a style I can only describe as thoroughly Balkanesque. This was the legation of the Montenegrins, during the short-lived monarchy of the Black Mountain.

Nicholas I, the one and only king of Montenegro, had close links with Russian Hav. Two of his daughters married Russian Grand Dukes, he was an honorary Field-Marshal of the Imperial army, and his Ruritanian capital of Cetinje was modelled upon the arrangements of the Czars. Every year, when the Russian aristocracy descended upon the peninsula by train from the north, Nicholas was disembarked upon its shores from the south, having sailed there in state on board the royal yacht *Petar Njegoš*. In the years before Sarajevo he was one of

Hav's most familiar celebrities, contributing to all charities, attending all summer balls, gracing every garden party, sitting through every ballet and even having a street named in his honour – the Boulevard de Cetinje, an entirely unnecessary but properly dignified thoroughfare which the Russians cut through the Medina in 1904 in order to reach their bathing station beyond the western hills.

It was not surprising that when the Russians invited specified powers to open legations in Hav the Montenegrins were among the first to accept. No conceivable diplomatic interest required the representation of the Black Mountain in this inessential station, but the King welcomed the chance to build himself a villa in such a prime position, within the Forbidden City so to speak. The legation is generally claimed to be a replica of his own palace at Cetinje, but it is really no more than an idealized approximation, being, as it happens, rather bigger and much more comfortable.

At eleven every morning the guard changes outside the Serai. This is an engaging spectacle. Since the departure of the Russians the gubernatorial guards have always been Circassians, recruited in Turkey. They are a stalwart crew, and provide solaces of many kinds, so the common rumour says, for both the wives of high officials, and the high officials themselves. Their pageantry is fine. They move less like soldiers than stage performers, in a flourishing, curly style, marching to a modified goose-step, swinging their arms exaggeratedly, and wearing upon their faces stylized smiles of ingratiation, or perhaps self-satisfaction. Their orders I take to be shouted in Circassian, since nobody I have met understands a syllable of them, and they are armed with rifles inherited from the Russians for which there is, I am assured, no longer any ammunition.

No matter: the ceremonial life of the Serai is essentially easy-going anyway. The old protocol of the Russians has been whittled away, rule by rule, precedent by precedent down the years, and the nearest the Governor comes to any kind of grand-ducal progress nowadays is an occasional outing in his official barouche to pay a call upon the leader of one community or another. Then the guard lines up to see him off, smiling indefatigably, and the barouche is followed out of the Palace yard, across the avenue of palms, by a pair of jolly postilions wearing their astrakhan hats at a jaunty angle and equipped with gleaming swords.

But here, even in Hav, all is not picturesque flummery around the seat of power. Even the lovable Serai, it seems, has its anxieties. As it happened, when I was walking across the square one morning last week the Governor did come clopping out in his carriage, hauled by four high-stepping but rather shaggy greys, and followed by those stagy postilions. The guard saluted them as they passed, and they turned to the right, down the narrow street beside the South Block in the direction of the Medina. Hardly had they gone, however, than I heard a commotion of shouting and counter-shouting. I ran to the corner at once, and was in time to see one of the postilions, dismounted, thwacking a young man over the shoulders brutally with the flat of his sword. The youth slid to his haunches against the wall, his hands over his head. The postilion agilely remounted and cantered after the disappearing cortège.

I ran to the spot as fast as I could, and the young man looked up at me with a gaunt and melancholy face. 'What's happening?' I cried. 'Are you all right?' But he answered me – how disconcerting! – with a spit.

Hav Rig

5

New Hav – a survivor – national characteristics – Germans of another kind – 'that old ogre'

Immediately outside my window is the circular Place des Nations, supervised by a large statue of Count Alexander Kolchok, the last and most famous of the Russian governors. It was erected, so the plinth says, 'IN HOMAGE', by the administrators of the Tripartite Mandate, and shows him in court dress, loaded with medals and holding a scroll. Very proper, because if it were not for Kolchok there would have been no mandate, and no Place des Nations either.

Lenin never came to Hav, so far as is known (though a film made by Soviet dissidents is supposed to show him shamelessly dissipated among the flesh-pots). When in 1917 the news of the Revolution reached Russian Hav, which had been a demilitarized zone throughout the First World War, Kolchok the Governor immediately declared the place a White Russian republic, and called for help from the Western Allies. A French brigade was sent from Salonika, and Hav remained in a kind of limbo until in 1924 the League of Nations declared its mandate over the peninsula, and appointed Kolchok, the last Governor under the old dispensation, the first Governor under the new. He it was who, until his death in 1931 (he is buried here), presided over the unique experiment in international reconciliation which was Hav between the wars.

The delegates at Geneva invited three powers to take control of the peninsula, and to establish commercial concessions there: France because, so Magda would say, there was no choice – the French army was already on the spot, and unlikely to budge; Italy, because the Italians demanded parity with the French as a Mediterranean power; and in a stroke of unexampled idealism, the Weimar Republic of Germany, which was not then even a member of the League. Hav kept its old Russian forms of government, but with an elected instead of a nominated assembly; and across the harbour from the Medina there arose the international concessionary quarter of New Hav. It is in the very heart of this circular settlement that I have my apartment, looking down on the Place des Nations and the triumphant Count.

Actually he does not look *altogether* triumphant, because the open space around him, once so elegant, is now sadly run-down, while he himself is patchy with verdigris and bird droppings. The formal gardens are overgrown and weedy, the railings sag, and as I look down now I see a couple of figures swathed in brown stretched out asleep upon the benches. Still, the statue remains the focal point of New Hav. A wide tree-lined ring road surrounds the Place des Nations, and from it run the three boulevards which divide the international quarter, Avenue de France, Viale Roma, and Unter den Südlinden – which is shaded in fact not by limes but by lovely Hav catalpas.

The grand plan of Hav was imposed by the League, but within each national segment, served by smaller streets, the concessionary powers could do as they liked. From the start, all three parts developed strong national characteristics, and even now I know almost without thinking, as I wander through New Hav, which quarter I am in. The smart restaurants, the fashion houses and the clubs have gone, to be replaced by Greek and Syrian stores, import–export agents, homelier eating houses and the offices of dubious investment banks; but it is the easiest thing in the world, early in the evening especially, when the cafés are filling up and the young people are strolling arm-in-arm beneath the shade of the trees towards the Lux Palace or the Cinema Malibran, to summon up New Hav in its brief but glittering heyday.

Here, for example, in some fusty draper's shop I sense even now the charm of the boutique it used to be, and here a frieze of senators, helmeted soldiers and grateful Africans transports me instantly to Mussolini's Anno XIV. How earnest the peeling Gymnasium, with its busts of Goethe, Schubert and Beethoven! How sadly plush the Hotel Adler-Hav, with its velvet upholsteries, its gilt sofas and the tarnished mirrors of its Golden Bar, 'the longest bar on the Mediterranean'! The names of the streets, often the names of the shops too, still speak of other countries far away; and even today, though the faces you see around you are overwhelmingly Levantine often you will hear blurred deviations of French, German or Italian along these nostalgic pavements.

And of course there are a few living survivors of the international regime, which lingered on increasingly inchoate until the abolition of the concessions in 1945. Of these the best known is Armand Sauvignon the novelist, who came to Hav as a young attaché with the French administration in 1928, and wrote all his books here (his fictional Polova is really Hav). He is in his eighties now, a widower for twenty years, and lives amidst his large library in an apartment overlooking the French cathedral. He embodies in himself, as it were, the whole history of New Hav, start to finish, and talking to him is like reliving the whole brave but somehow unreal initiative, street by street, character by character. He has a long beaky nose, a creased brow, and an odd mannerism of pursing his mouth between sentences, and all these features combine to give his company a more or less continual irony.

His first job was to be French observer at the concessionary courts, which dealt with all cases involving nationals of the mandatory powers, but whose judges were appointed directly by the League. 'Such a collection, you can have no idea! It was like a music-hall. We had judges, I swear to you, who never saw a court of law before. The convenor would hiss at them 'Twelve years', 'Deport him', or 'Insufficient evidence', and His Honour would gather his robes around him, put on his gravest face, and do what he was told. It was killing! We had a judge from Texas, I remember (you must realize Americans were not so worldly then), who used to bring his accordion with him to court, to entertain us between cases. In the evening it was the thing for us young attachés, the Italians, the Germans, ourselves – we were all good friends – to go out to the Palace of Delights in Yuan Wen Kuo; once after a particularly gruelling fraud case, I remember, hour after hour in the hot courts, we all went out there to relax, and who should we discover playing his accordion in the Hall of Fair Beauties but old Judge Bales, surrounded by girls and half-incoherent with opium!'

'You seem to have lived merry old lives.'

'In the early years, very merry. Things changed later, as the world changed. But when New Hav was really new we were intoxicated by it all. You must remember the Great War had not long ended, we were lucky to be alive at all, and here we were working together in this place almost as though our peoples had never been enemies.

'Besides, in the twenties and thirties Hav was extremely smart. My Polova was no exaggeration. The Russian aristocrats were still in their villas here, living on the last of their jewels and ikons, and when the Casino was opened, about 1927 I think it was, anybody who had a steam-yacht in the Mediterranean came to Hav sooner or later. People used to take the train from Paris to Moscow especially to catch the Mediterranean Express down here – you should talk to the tunnel pilots, they have amazing things to recall.

'You see that poor old hotel there, the Bristol? It doesn't look much now, does it? but believe me it was as smart as any hotel in Europe for a few years. Noël Coward wrote most of *Pastiche* there, did you know? I met him at the Agency one evening, a tiresome person I thought him. Hemingway used to go there too – they will still mix you a very nasty cocktail called Papa's Sting, I believe . . .

'All the great performers came. Goodman, Chevalier, the Hot Club de France. We met them all. My first chief here was a very great swell, the Marquis de Chablon, and he virtually set up a court at our Residency. The Germans and the Italians had nobody so *soigné*, the governors after Kolchok were nonentities, so really the social whirl of Hav revolved around us. For a young man, and especially a young artist, it was a dream. Out of season we had to find our own pleasures – shooting on the escarpment, pony-racing, the Palace of Delights of course. But in the summer, my God! we lived like millionaires!'

We were strolling as we walked, in the warm of the evening, among the straggly press of the boulevards, and their mingled smells of food, dirt, jasmine and imperfectly refined gasoline. We had walked all through the Italian quarter, and down past the Schiller Fountain (in whose water ugly fat carp swam in the half-light – 'like submarines', said Sauvignon. 'Don't you think so? – yellow submarines') and we were in his own territory now, on the pavement opposite the Bristol. He took my arm. 'You have half an hour?' he said. 'Join me in an aperitif – and a glimpse of the past.'

We passed through the huge dark foyer, where an old porter rose to his feet as Sauvignon passed by, and a clerk behind the reception desk, in open-necked pale-blue shirt and gold necklace, murmured a greeting; we passed the almost empty dining-room, decorated with large now-brownish murals of Parisian life; and pushing open a brass-handled double door inlaid with figures of seahorses and mermaids, we entered the Bar 1924. It was absolutely packed. Every table was full, but an obliging waiter, recognizing my companion, squeezed a party of young Lebanese together and found room for us. The air was full of Turkish tobacco smoke; the waiter thrust before us a stained typewritten list of archaic cocktails – Sledgehammers, Riproarers, Topper's Special, and yes, Papa's Sting! Blaring above it all, deafeningly vigorous and brassy, there was jazz.

It was an elderly combo which, spotting Sauvignon through the haze, dipped its instruments in welcome: a grizzled black trumpeter, a trombonist with rimless spectacles, a gentlemanly Chinese pianist, a grey-beard playing bass and a middle-aged elf in a red shirt frenzied at the drums. They performed with a somewhat desperate enthusiasm, I thought, a repertoire of long ago. Sometimes somebody shouted a request – '"Honey-suckle Rose"!' '"A-Train"!' '"Sentimental Journey"!' The pianist had a small cup of coffee on his piano. The trumpeter occasionally groaned 'Yeah man . . .' but more in duty than in ecstasy. '"Yellow Submarine"!' called Sauvignon during a pause in the music, and as the trombonist broke into an approximate lyric – '*Weallivinayellersummerine*' – he raised his Manhattan towards me in a toast. 'To yesterday's youth,' he said.

Above the door of No. 24 Residenzstrasse – in the old German quarter, hardly a stone's throw across the Viale Roma from my apartment, there is a modern plaque in German. It commemorates the fact that between 1941 and 1945 members of the German anti-Nazi resistance movement, *der Widerstand*, were given refuge there under the clandestine protection of the German concessionary administration.

The development of New Hav, and its last apotheosis during the Second World War, was as extraordinary as its beginning. Isolated there on that distant foreshore, with poor communications and the loosest of supervision from Geneva, the three regimes developed almost autonomously. The Italians, who saw themselves from the start as colonists, threw themselves enthusiastically into Mussolini's imperial designs, putting up *fasces* all over the place, erecting ostentatious murals depicting Mare Nostrum or Africa Revicta, proudly welcoming Marshal de Bono when he paid a visit after his conquest of Ethiopia, and eventually refusing even to receive the timid representatives of collective security who now and then arrived on the train from Switzerland. They had high hopes, Signora Vattani has confided in me (her husband, she claims, was an 'important official' in the administration) – they had high hopes of taking over the whole of Hav, if ever war gave them a chance, and when war did come they openly disregarded the laws of neutrality by re-provisioning Italian submarines in the harbour.

The French treated Hav above all as a place of pleasure and prestige. They wished their quarter of New Hav to be a show-case of French panache. They sent stylish magnificos to be their Residents, the smartest young men of family to be their administrators. They sponsored visits by eminent musicians and French drama companies. The French gracefully gave way to their partners when it came to matters of political priority or protocol, but they saw to it that their quarter was much the most inviting, and made sure that, as Armand Sauvignon says, the social life of Hav revolved around their handsomely Moorish-style Residency on its artificial hillock. When France fell to the Germans in 1940 the Resident of the day, the ineffably fashionable Guyot de Delvert, unhesitatingly declared for Vichy, had banners portraying Marshal Pétain flying all down the Rue de France, and no longer sent social invitations to the British Agency.

The Germans' was the oddest role. 'Those Boches,' Sauvignon told me once, 'really, to a well-brought-up young man direct from the Sorbonne, they were like people from another planet.' Subjects as they were of liberal Weimar, they set out to make their quarter of New Hav its properly representative outpost. 'You would never have believed it! You could do anything over here, you could assume any personality you pleased. I never saw such cabarets – even the Egyptians were shocked sometimes. The place was full of drug-addicts, poets, homo-sexuals, pacifists, God knows what – everyone you met was writing a novel. I used to go over there to the Café München whenever I felt the pressures of social life too great for me, and I was sure to find myself in a group of writers or artists, some actually from Germany, but Turks too, and Syrians, and really people from everywhere. I met Thomas Mann there once. He asked me what was the right way to pronounce *mésalliance*, I remember . . .'

I constantly hear astonishing stories about the behaviour of the German diplomats during the Second World War. Signera Vattani thought it traitorous – 'They should all have been shot, if you ask me.' Others thought it truly heroic. There were only two German Residents during the entire history of New Hav, and they both stood firmly in the German liberal tradition. The second of them, Heinrich von Tranter, was appointed to office in 1932, the year before Hitler came to power. By guile and social influence, and some say by the connivance of von Papen, the impenetrable German Ambassador in Ankara, he managed to hang on to his post throughout the Second World War, and made Hav a secret refuge and headquarters for Germans opposed to the Nazi regime.

'We knew nothing,' Signora V. fervently assures me. 'We had no idea what was going on. Do you think we would have allowed it, endangering our own men and ships? Why those ruffians were in daily touch with the British Agent, giving him all sorts of information all the time!'

But had not Fatima Yeğen told me that Hitler himself was supposed to have visited Hav during the war?

'He did, he did, he came down incognito in a special car on the train with that von Papen. We knew nothing of it, we had no idea, and then on the Tuesday morning I was crossing Unter den Südlinden to get some sausages at the German delicatessen – they had excellent sausages throughout the war – and I looked up and there was von Tranter's big black car coming slowly down the boulevard, and a motor-cycle escort all around it, and who should be sitting in it but Hitler himself, with von Tranter beside him and von Papen sitting in the front with the driver. I was never so astonished. Look, I was saying to everyone on the pavement, look, it's Herr Hitler! but half of them didn't believe it even when they saw him for themselves. The very next morning he was gone again, they say. We were told a U-boat picked him up at Malaya Yalta and took him to Italy.'

Yet even Hitler, if he really did come (and if you believe that, in my opinion, you will believe anything), even Hitler apparently did not suspect what was going on under the aegis of his own swastika at 24 Residenzstrasse. Throughout the later years of the war a steady stream of German dissidents and resistance workers were smuggled through Turkey or by sea to Hav, where they coordinated escapes and clandestine missions secret even now. It was perfectly true, as Signora Vattani so scornfully alleges, that von Tranter was in touch with the British in Hav: this was a main point of contact between the German underground and the Western Allies. If the Fascists of the Italian quarter did not know what was going on across the Viale Roma, the British Secret Service certainly did, and time and again its agents and interrogators came into Hav by submarine from Cyprus and Egypt.

To many people these wartime conspiracies were the ultimate justification for the whole experiment of New Hav, but the German quarter was to acquire an ironic new reputation later. Von Tranter survived the war but died in mysterious circumstances at his home near Augsburg in 1947, and when the concessions came to an end Germans of a very different kind moved into Hav, well-fed, muscular men of undisclosed resources, with their stalwart wives and sometimes lissom mistresses. They kept themselves as closely to themselves as had von Tranter's hidden wards, living communally in the vacated villas of Russian noblemen, guarded by burly bodyguards behind wire fences. They were, it is said, members of Odessa, the clandestine organization of former SS officers, and through Hav they are supposed to have channelled immense illegal funds, arranged the disappearances of criminal colleagues, and organized fraternal networks throughout the world.

I am assured they have nearly all gone now – most of them are dead – but when Armand and I were walking one evening along the harbourside promenade of New Hav we were passed by a bent and slender elderly man of thoughtful appearance in a well-cut tweed suit and a felt hat. He bowed slightly to Sauvignon, and the Frenchman raised his hat in return. 'You see that old man?' said my companion when we were out of earshot. 'There are people in Israel who would give a million francs to discover his whereabouts.'

'You're never tempted?' I asked.

'No, my dear. If there is one thing I have learnt from Hav, it is the uselessness of revenge. To be alive is punishment enough for that old ogre.'

6

Spring – flora and fauna – the Kretevs – the day of the snow raspberry – my yellow hat

Away beyond the Serai domes one can see the outlines of the western hills, where the Greeks built their pleasure-houses (so archaeologists assure us) and the Russians after them. When I came to this apartment they looked brown and melancholy, like so much else in Hav. Then, almost as I watched, they became perceptibly greener and happier. And yesterday, when I went out on to my balcony with my morning coffee, lo! they were a magical blush of pinks, blues and yellows.

'The spring of Hav!' announced Signora V. emotionally. 'It is not', she added, as she invariably adds, 'as it used to be' ('in the Duce's day', I almost interjected), 'but still it is a kind of miracle. How wonderful nature is even in these distant places.'

I have acquired a car now. It is a 1971 Renault, and according to Fatima, who arranged the deal for me, it was once the tunnel pilot's transport. So in the afternoon I drove out to the hills to see the spring flowers for myself – swiftly through the wrinkled alleys of the Medina, along the fine big road the Russians built to take them to their pleasures, across the remains of the Spartan canal until the low hills rose on either side of me, speckled with neglected olive trees, decrepit villas and overgrown gardens. And the Signora was right: a miracle it was. Every patch of broken ground, every gulley, every broken-down Grand Duke's or Sturmbannführer's terrace was lyrically overlaid with flowers, half of them strange to me – flowers something like buttercups, but not quite, flowers very nearly bluebells, flowers not unrelated to asphodels or recognizably akin to primroses – and there were clambering plants with pink petals wandering everywhere, and up the gnarled trunks of the olive trees a sort of blossoming moss flourished. The combined scent of all these flowers, and many another herb, scrub and lichen no doubt, resolved itself into something peculiarly pungent, not unlike a sweet vinaigrette dressing, and overcome by this I lay out there flat on my back encouched in foliage. There was not a soul about. All those once blithe houses, with their tattered awnings and their sagging pergolas, seemed to be utterly deserted. Far away over the canal the towers and gilded domes of Hav, the great grey-gold mass of the castle, looked from that bowered belvedere like a city of pure fiction.

It was absolutely silent there. I heard not a bird nor a cricket, was stung by no ant, bitten by no wandering gnat. Though Heaven knows Hav is no showplace of hygiene, I sometimes feel it to be almost antiseptically sterile. There seems to be a shortage of everyday bug, bird or rodent life. The other day I had lunch at the Athenaeum with Dr Borge, who likes to describe himself as Botanist, Anthropologist and Philosopher, and I put this point to him. 'You are right,' he said, as philosophers will, 'and you are wrong. You must realize that here in Hav our conditions of life are unusual. We are at once maritime and continental, Triassic and Jurassic, marsh and salt, lime and mud. Our fauna is not lavish, but as your Bard would say, it is true to ourselves!'

Such animal life as there is, sustained by this rare combination of soils, climates and geological origins, really is sufficiently peculiar. Once or twice in the greenery immediately below my balcony I have seen a strange little snouted creature snooping in the dusk, black, soft and low on the ground. This is the Hav mongoose, *Herpestes* hav, a mutation of the Indian mongoose brought in by the British to deal with the snakes; there is a stuffed specimen in the museum's little zoological collection, and it looks to me less like a mongoose than a kind of furry anteater.

Then the Hav hedgehog, *Erinaceus hav*, is odd too, since it is tailed, like a prickly armadillo, and the Hav terrier is like a little grey ball of wire wool, and I believe the troglodytes breed a pony of Mongolian origins on the foot-slopes of the escarpment. Some people say the so-called Abyssinian cat, now so fashionable in Europe and America, really came from Hav, in the kit-bags of British soldiers; as it happened, the British garrison here was closed in the same year as the 1868 expedition to Magdala in Ethiopia, and it is suggested that some sharp characters among the returning soldiery conceived the idea of putting a new 'rare African cat' on the market. The modern Hav cat does not look much like the slinky patricians of Western fancy, but he is often distinguished by having extra claws on his front paws – the extra-toed cats which still swarm about Ernest Hemingway's house in Key West are claimed to have Hav ancestry.

Out on the marshes there are sheep, guarded by hangdog Arab shepherds (and hangdog they might well be, there in those dismal wastes). They are dull stringy creatures, but around them there often romp and scamper, as though in a state of permanent hilarious mockery, lithe and fleecy goats – so tirelessly jerky, springy and enterprising that from a distance, when you see one of those listless flocks like a stain on the flat-lands, the goats prancing around it look like so many little devils.

I don't know what the British Resident's original cattle were like, when they arrived from England on the frigate *Octavia* in 1821, but the Hav cattle of today, who are all their descendants, would win no rosettes at county shows. Disconsolately munching the scrubby turf in their pastures at the foot of the escarpment, they seem to have gone badly to seed, having long pinched faces, heavy haunches and protruding midriffs. They have never been crossed with any other cattle, Dr Borge tells me, but I suspect the poor wizened cows among them would welcome the arrival, on some later *Octavia* perhaps, of a few lusty newcomers.

There are foxes, they say, on the escarpment. There are certainly rabbits. There used to be wolves; the last of them, allegedly shot by Count Kolchok himself on 4 June 1907, is mounted in the entrance hall of the Serai's North Block, looking a bit the worse for death. And only the other day, I read in *La Gazette*, a member of the Hav Zoological Society claimed to have spotted, while snake-hunting on the escarpment (where the mongoose never did thrive) a female Hav bear.

This rarest of European bears (*Ursus arctus hav*), which looks from pictures rather like a miniature grizzly, has repeatedly been declared extinct. Hunting the survivors was one of the fashionable pastimes of the *fin de siècle*: the King of Montenegro shot three or four, and you may see the skin of one still hanging in his wooden palace at home, in Cetinje. As late as the 1930s, though the Tripartite Government had declared the animals protected, hunting parties used to go out from the Casino equipped with all the paraphernalia of safari, and sometimes claimed to have shot one: it was during one of these expeditions that Hemingway, so legend says, deliberately jogged the elbow of Count Ciano, thus saving the life of a bear offering a perfect shot upon the skyline ('You fool,' said the Count. 'You fascist,' said the writer).

Anyway, the bear apparently survives, nobody is quite sure how. The terrain of the escarpment is difficult and infertile, yet *Ursus arctus hav* has never, it seems, wandered over the crest into the easier flatlands of Anatolia, and has rarely been sighted in the Hav lowlands either. There were reports in the 1950s that a covey had somehow made themselves a lair within the escarpment tunnel – maintenance men reported seeing animal eyes glowing in alcoves as they went by on their trollies, and for a time amateur zoologists went backwards and forwards on the train, to and from the frontier station, unavailingly hoping to catch a glimpse of them. More persistently, rumour has the Kretevs sheltering the bear in their warren of caves at the western end of the escarpment, either because they believe it to be holy, or just because they are fond of it. 'The troglodytes',

Dr Borge told me learnedly, 'possess a special relationship with the animal world, not unlike I believe that of the ancient Minoans. You are aware of the Minoans? They venerated a monster, you will remember, within a labyrinth. Perhaps our Kretevs cherish other creatures within their caves?' It seemed improbable, I suggested, that only thirty-odd miles from the cafeteria of the Athenaeum such mysteries could persist. 'Ah,' said the young doctor, 'but you have not met the troglodytes. You do not know their obstinacy.'

Actually I have met some of them – I cultivate their acquaintance at the morning market, and have even struck up a sort of friendship with one of their more articulate stall-holders, who learnt some English as a merchant seaman, and whose name sounds to me like Brack. I concede, though, that of all the manifestations of nature in Hav, the Kretevs seem the most elusive. Talking the arcane unwritten language which, it is said, no foreign adult has ever mastered, crouched over their stalls with long tangled hair often half-bleached by the sun, their nondescript clothes set off by many bracelets and ear-rings, down at the market they seem to me like a race of gypsy Rastafarians, visiting the town from some other country altogether. Even Brack claims never to have set foot within the circuit of New Hav.

Yet they form a still living bridge between the city and its remotest origins. In the second or first centuries before Christ, the theory is, Celts from the Anatolian interior found their way to the edge of the great escarpment and saw before them, probably for the first time in their lives, the sea. So blue it seemed, we are told, so warm was the Mediterranean prospect, that they called the place simply 'Summer' – still *hav* or *haf* in the surviving Celtic languages of the West, just as 'Kretev' is thought to be etymologically related to the Welsh *crwydwyr*, wanderers. They were a continental people, though, a people of the land mass, and they never did settle upon the peninsula proper, forming instead troglodytic colonies in the raddled limestone caverns where their descendants still live. Their fellow-Celts of the interior presently evolved into the Galatians; and it was the poor Kretevs that St Paul had in mind when he wrote in his Epistle to the Galatians of 'your ignorant brethren living like conies in the rocks of the south'.

They are like strange familiars of the peninsula, and on one day in the year they perform a truly magical or mythological service to the city of Hav, whose foundation their presence here so long preceded, and from whose affairs they remain so generally remote. At dawn one morning, usually near the beginning of February, their gaily decorated pick-ups come storming into the morning market with far more than their usual gusto, blowing their horns fit to wake the Governor and out-blast Missakian's trumpet. They are not unexpected, since it happens every year, and the market throws itself immediately *en fête*. Every truck horn blows, every ship's siren hoots, and all the market people line the street to greet them. They are bringing, or rather one of the trucks is bringing, the first of the snow raspberries.

Almost the last too, for this supreme delicacy is to be found only on three or four days of the year, when the early spring suns melt the last of the escarpment's winter snows. Like the dragon-fly, the snow raspberry is born only to die. It sprouts mushroom-like overnight, without warning, and by noonday it is gone. It grows only in shaded crannies of the limestone, and only the cave people know where to look for it, or are there to pick it anyway. Brack says he was first taken out to gather the snow raspberries when he was five years old.

The arrival of this fruit in Hav is like the arrival of the first Beaujolais Nouveau in Paris, or the first grouse of the season in London, but much more exciting than either. Nobody knows just when the snow raspberry will appear, and for a week or two around the end of January the morning market, they tell me, is in a high state of expectancy. Even Signor Biancheri has no prior claim to supplies – even he must await the day when, honking their celebratory way past the sleeping city, the troglodytes arrive in wild array with their small but priceless commodity. The cost of snow raspberries is phenomenal. Few people in Hav have ever tasted the fruit, and nobody outside Hav has ever tasted it at all, for if it is frozen it loses its savour altogether. I suppose the Kretevs themselves may eat a few, but otherwise almost every berry goes to the government (official receptions of the most important kind are often timed to coincide with the snow raspberry season), to Biancheri's kitchen at the Casino, or to the Chinese millionaires of Yuan Wen Kuo.

Signora Vattani claims to have tasted one in her youth, but I don't believe her for a moment. Fatima Yeğen says that the Kaiser, who was lucky enough to arrive in Hav at just the right moment, was given a basket of them to eat on his ride down the Staircase. Dr Borge claims to believe them imaginary – 'folk-loric, nothing more' – and says the Kaiser was probably palmed off with Syrian loganberries. But Armand ate one once, on 8 February 1929, when an international delegation from the League of Nations was fêted at the Palace.

'Oh it was so funny, how you would have laughed! In came this single footman, as pompous as a monsignor, carrying a silver dish piled high with these snow raspberries. The biggest ones were on the top. I was just a young attaché, at the foot of the table almost. All down the room I heard the oohs and aahs, 'wonderful', '*quelle expérience*', you know the kind of thing. But by the time the dish reached us young people at the end of the room, only a few shrivelled little red fruits remained for us. They tasted like very old dry cherries.

'My dear, you must not be shocked. We were very young and disrespectful. My dear friend Ulrich Helpmann, from. the German Residency, who was the most disrespectful of us all, placed his precious raspberry on the palm of his hand and flicked it with his right forefinger – so! – across the table at me. It missed me altogether and hit the boiled shirt of the footman standing behind my chair. I mean to say, my dear, before you could blink your eye that man had scooped it off and eaten it.

His one and only snow raspberry! He's probably boasting of it still.'

Anyway, as I was saying, spring is here. The stuttered colour-less Hav that greeted me has disappeared. The flowers are blooming in the western hills, and everything else is tentatively blooming too. Even the functionaries of the Serai, when I went to have my permit stamped this morning, were emancipated into shirtsleeves. The sentries at the Palace are in white uni-forms now, with smashing gold epaulettes, and the station café has set up its pavement tables on the edge of Pendeh Square, under the palms, beneath well-patched blue, white and green sunshades. I wore my yellow towelling hat from Australia to go to the Serai. '*Başında kavak yelleri esiyor*,' a passer-by said without pausing, which translated from the Hav Turkish means 'There is the springtime in your hat!'

7

*The Arabs – a Muslim city – the 125th Caliph – 'you seem
surprised' – Olga Naratlova – not so peaceful – Hav 001 – salt*

I can hear the call to prayer only faintly in the mornings.
Though it is electrically amplified, from the minaret of the
mosque of Malik, the Grand Mosque in the Medina, it is not
harshly distorted, as it is so often in Arab countries, but
remains fragile and other-worldly; what is more it is not
recorded, but really is sung every morning by the muezzin who
climbs the precipitous eleventh-century staircase of the
minaret. For me it is much the most beautiful sound in Hav:
just as for my taste the Arab presence in this city remains the
most haunting – more profound than the Russian flamboy-
ances, more lasting than the hopes of New Hav, less aloof than
the Chinese ambience, more subtle than the Turkish . . .

Besides, though the massive structures of the Serai may seem
dominant when you first arrive in Pendeh Square, gradually you
come to realize that it was the Arabs who really created this city.
They gave it its great days, its glory days. Although for more
than a century they were supplanted by the Crusaders, in effect
they dominated Hav for four hundred years, and they made it
rich. Through Hav half the spices, skins, carpets, works of art
and learning of the Muslim East found their way into Europe –
and not only the Muslim East, for this sophisticated and well-
equipped mart between the sea and the land, between Asia and
Europe, became the chief staging-post of the Silk Route from the
further Orient. Ibn Batuta, in the fourteenth century, called it

one of the six greatest ports of the world, the others being Alexandria in Egypt, Quilon and Calicut in India, Sudaq in the Crimea and Zaitun in China. Here the Venetians established their Fondaco di Cina, their China Warehouse, and here later the very first Chinese colony of the West settled itself in the peninsula known to the Arabs as Yuan Wen Kuo, Land of the Distant Warmth. Great was the fame of Arab Hav, attested by many an old traveller, and its last splendours were extinguished only when in 1460 the Ottoman Turks, deposing the last of the Hav Amirs and expelling the Venetians, incorporated the peninsula into their own domains and so plunged it, for nearly four centuries, into the dispirited gloom of their despotism.

When the troops of the Seljuks first arrived in Hav in 1079 they must have thought it a sorry sort of conquest. It had never come to much before – had never remotely rivalled the powerful city-states of the Asia Minor shore, Seleucia, Smyrna, Trebizond. Alexander had passed it by, both the Romans and the Persians had ignored it. By the time the Arabs got there the remaining Greek inhabitants were living in miserable squalor beside the harbour, their acropolis long since a ruin above them. The salt-flats were undrained then. Malaria was endemic. There was no road up the escarpment and the Kretevs were unapproachable. Yet here the Arabs built the northernmost of their great trading cities, and most of it is still to be seen.

To the north of the castle hill they established quarters for their slaves – obdurate infidels and prisoners-of-war – and these were to develop into the wan suburbs of the Balad. To the west they built their own walled headquarters, and this is now the Old City, or Medina. The huge public place they laid out was the progenitor of today's Pendeh Square, and the second of their great mosques, erected by Saladin after his liberation of Hav from the Crusaders, now does service as the Greek Orthodox cathedral, behind the railway station. The Staircase up the escarpment was first cut by Arab engineers, and it was they who drained the salt-marshes.

It is all there still, and above all the Medina remains, even now, overwhelmingly an Arab medieval city. It is crudely intersected by the Boulevard de Cetinje, but is still a glorious jumble of alleys and sudden squares, alive with the sights and sounds of Araby – you know, the dark and the sunshine of it, the shuffle and the beat, the sour hoof-smell from the smithy, the towering simplicity of the mosque in the heart of it all – you know, you know!

For some Muslims, if only a lingering few, that mosque is one of the holiest on earth, because a small and dwindling sect claims it to be the shrine of the Caliphate. You will remember that the Ottoman sultans, whose temporal, powers were abolished in 1924, claimed also to be the legitimate caliphs of Islam, the spiritual leaders of the faith. They were recognized as such by many Muslims of the Sunni persuasion, and even after the extinction of their sultanate, proclaimed themselves caliphs still. The deposed Mehmet V tried to establish himself in the Holy Land of the Hejaz itself, his cousin Abdulmecid maintained the claim from Paris until his death there in 1944, and a contemporary aspirant to the Caliphate, Namik Abdulhamid, who says he is 125th in the true line of descent from Abu Bakr, the Prophet's father-in-law, lives in Hav, the nearest he can get to the Turkey from which the Sultan's dynasty and all its pretenders have been permanently exiled. Yesterday I had an audience with him.

This had taken time to achieve. The 125th Caliph lives cautiously. I had a letter of introduction to him, from a man in Cairo whose name I should not mention, in case somebody assassinates him; and finding it difficult to discover just where the Caliph resided, this I presented to the Imam at the Grand Mosque. For a week or two there was no response. Then one evening an excited Signora Vattani told me there had been a call, good gracious Signora Morris, a call from the Caliphate! I was to be ready to be picked up at the apartment the following evening, five o'clock sharp. But five o'clock came and went without a sign, and next day I was told, without apologies, to be ready that night instead. Twice more I waited, twice more no caliphian car arrived; it was only on the fourth evening that, exactly at five as the man on the telephone had said, the doorbell rang and a big black American car, of the fin-and-chrome era, awaited me outside.

There was a chauffeur in Arab dress, but the car's back door opened from the inside, and there sat a dapper middle-aged man in a black suit, sunglasses and that almost forgotten badge of Ottoman respectability, a tarboosh. 'A tarboosh!' I could not stop myself exclaiming '– can you still buy them?'

'The Caliph has his own supplier, in Alexandria – Tadros Nakhla and Sons, you may perhaps know the name? Very old-established.'

He introduced himself as the Caliph's Wazir, and as we drove across the square he apologized for the inconveniences of the past three days. I would understand, he was sure. The Caliph was vulnerable. One had to be careful. It seemed an inadequate excuse to me, but I let it pass, and the Wazir went on to explain that because of certain, well, entanglements of a historical nature the 125th Caliph found it necessary to live in the strictest security – all through history, he reminded me, the Caliphate had been an office of the greatest delicacy – I would recall what happened to Omar in the mosque at Kufa!

Down the Boulevard de Cetinje we sped, and out of the Old City, and before we reached the canal we turned up a gravel track, shaded by tall eucalyptus trees. 'People say', remarked the Wazir, 'that this house was built for Count Kolchok's mistress, the lovely dancer Olga Naratlova. True? False?' He shrugged his neat shoulders. 'It makes a nice little story. The Caliph likes the fancy.' It looked an imposing love-nest, as we passed through lavishly ornamental gates, crossed a wide yard, and were debouched upon a portico whose doors were instantly opened by two swarthy men in khaki drill, one each side ('Assyrians,' the Wazir said breezily as we entered, as though they were deaf mutes). Through a bare but still luxurious hall

. . . down a marbled corridor . . . two more Assyrians at a double door . . . and there rising courteously to greet me from a silken sofa was Nadik Abdulhamid.

He wore a red tarboosh too, and a suit of exquisite pale linen, and shoes that looked like lizardskin, and he held in his left hand a string of ivory prayer-beads, and in his right a cigarette in a long holder. He was clean-shaven, with heavy blue eyes and a becoming tan. All in all the pretender to the Caliphate was very suave, and not I thought very caliph-like, and he gestured me suavely to the sofa, and suavely offered me a cigarette from a silver box engraved in Arabic, and most suavely, as we talked, flicked his own ash into what looked like a solid-gold ashtray.

'You seem surprised. I am not what you expected? Tell me frankly, what did you expect?'

Someone blackly bearded, I said, and sage, and dressed in the robes of holiness.

'Then you would have been perfectly satisfied with my father. He was all that! Nobody was much sager than my father! But I decided long ago that I would be myself. As you would say, the world must take me or leave me.'

And did not this worldly persona make him enemies?

'Oh yes, I should say so. Imagine what they think of me in Iran, or even in Saudi Arabia! They hate me very much. Do you know that I have never been allowed to make the holy pilgrimage to Mecca? If I went there they would tear me limb from limb.'

Coffee arrived, flavoured with camomile, together with biscuits on little scallop-edged plates, and the Caliph asked if I would like to see something of the house. 'You know its history, I dare say? Count Kolchok built it for his mistress, the dancer Olga Naratlova, who came to Hav with Diaghilev. Everything was taken from the house when Kolchok died, but I have had her portrait painted *in memoriam*' – and he showed me on the wall above our sofa a large and sickly representation, doubtless taken from a photograph, of a dark turn-of-the-century beauty, full-length, leaning in a dress of satiny red against a truncated column.

'What became of her?'

'Ah, you must ask the Bolsheviks. She went home to Russia in 1918, and was never heard of again.'

Poor Olga. She sounds a lonely figure, hidden away here in such secluded luxury, and she is lonely still, for hers is the only portrait in the whole of the Caliph's house – 'And just think what the *Ikhwan* would say, if they knew I had *her*!' Otherwise the house, or as much as I saw of it, was severely undecorated. Spindly gilded armchairs and sofas were the nearest it got to creature comfort, unless you count the elaborate television, video and hi-fi equipment which the Caliph kept in his private sitting-room ('You may not be aware of it, but the Caliphate is a principal shareholder in Hav TV, so it is necessary for me to keep in touch . . . ').

On we went, among the grand, beautifully kept but still desolate rooms, through the office where two male secretaries sat surrounded by files and typewriters with a telex in the corner; we were bowed to here and there by silent Assyrians, interrupted once by the Wazir for a brief reminder about that evening's later arrangements ('A most excellent fellow,' said the Caliph. 'Did you like him? He would make a fine husband for you') until on the terrace at the back of the house we stood before the small octagonal mosque, a marble miniature of the Dome of the Rock, which the Caliph had built, he told me, for his private use.

Two more Assyrians guarded it. 'I dare say you are also surprised', said the Caliph, 'to find all these Assyrians. They are new to the Caliphate. I recruit them in Iraq, where as you may know for some generations they served the British military authorities, guarding camps, airfields and so forth. They are Christians, you see, with no particular allegiance to any state or power, and so very suitable to our needs. You must realize, Miss Morris, that my situation is precarious. Many people hate me, many people wish to use me.'

While the Western powers took no notice of him, he said, the Communists courted him. He had been to Moscow several times. He had many followers in Bokhara, Tashkent, and more recently in Kabul. 'You may perhaps have seen my picture at the May Day parade in Red Square in 1983? The late Mr Andropov was always especially good to me.' As for the Muslims of the Middle East, some of them loathed him, some would die for him, he claimed. 'The Iranians have twice tried to have me killed, once with a bomb in an aeroplane when I was travelling in Egypt, once here in this very house, with a gunman in the garden – you see, there are the bullet-holes still! Not everything in Hav, you know, is as peaceful as it seems. When you have been here a little longer you will come to realize that.'

And the Turks? The Caliph smiled a knowing and even more suave smile. 'The Turks will not allow me over that escarpment' – and he pointed through the trees to the distant dim line of the northern hills. 'I am a non-person to the Turks. And yet you know, Miss Morris, between ourselves – off the record, as they say – traditionally caliphs have been adept at travelling incognito, and so it is with me. I have been over that escarpment many times. I have many, many friends in my forebears' country. That is why they are afraid of me in Ankara, in Washington even – a flick of my finger, they think, and I could start revolution – as if I would want to! Even my sage father had no such plans.

'But still it is pleasant to go here now and then. How do I travel? Ah, that I cannot tell you. Suffice it to say that there are certain people not unconnected with the railway administration who have been for many generations faithful adherents of the Caliphate . . .'

Laughing heartily, conspiratorially and sophisticatedly, all at the same time, the Caliph called for an Assyrian to show me to the waiting car. 'You must remember, if you ever need anything, any help that the house of a caliph can afford, or if you wish to marry the Wazir after all, you are to telephone me at once. And now', he concluded unexpectedly, 'you must allow me to excuse myself, for it is time for my evening prayers.' With a gentle bow, and a smile full of self-amusement, he disappeared inside his little sanctuary.

His telephone number is Hav 001. I doubt if I shall ever ring it, but still my visit to Nadik Abdulhamid left me with a paradoxical sense of stability or at least of continuity. I have no idea how authentic is his claim to the Caliphate, and by his own account he leads a tricky kind of life, but there was something about his presence that made Hav feel still in the mainstream of Arab affairs, still in touch, however surreptitiously, with the debates, the feuds and the aspirations of Islam.

It is not all romantic illusion, either. Even today, they tell me, a remarkable proportion of Hav's Arabs have made the pilgrimage to Mecca, unlike the poor Caliph, and there is a regular flow of students to the University of Al Azhar in Cairo. Much the best-selling tapes at the Fantastique Video and Hi-Fi Shop in New Hav, so its manager tells me, are second-hand cassettes from Egypt, supplied by seamen from the salt ships.

The salt ships! I forgot to tell you! Today the strongest link of all between the Arabs of Hav and the Arabs of Arabia is the trade in Hav salt, whose wide sad pans I saw that first evening on the train. It is said to have been the Greeks who first discovered that salt extracted from the Hav marshes had aphrodisiac qualities: shiploads of it, they say, were sent to Attica, and according to Schliemann it was the salt that led Achilles to set up his base on Hav's western shore. By the Middle Ages the power of Hav's salt was so well attested that some scholars think it was the first reason for the Arab seizure of the peninsula.

It was largely to work the salt-flats that the Arabs established that huge slave quarter, and when the Venetians struck up their commercial alliance with the Amirs salt became the staple of their triangular trade with the Egyptians. The great merchant convoys, assembling with their escorts off Crete, would sail first to Hav to ship salt, often having to fight terrible battles with the Turks along the way, then to Alexandria to exchange it for spices and ivories, before returning rich and glorious home.

After the expulsion of the Venetians the Arabs of Hav exported the salt themselves. By then it had long been prized, as it still is, all over the Muslim world. Ibn Batuta had tried it in Tunis as early as 1325, and was much impressed:

> It is of a texture not remarkable in itself, being in colour and composition much like other salts, but hidden, within its grains is a power of youth and vigour beyond the accomplishment of the most learned apothecaries. I have tasted this salt for myself (though the merchants of the place, who are extremely greedy, demand disgraceful prices for it) and I can vouch before God that its powers are real.

Six centuries later, when I crossed the Omani desert with the Sultan of Muscat and Oman in 1956, one of his slave-cooks confided in me that the Sultan would eat no salt but salt from Hav.

Thus it is that an exotic trade still binds this city to the Arab countries across the sea. The salt merchants of the Medina stand in line of the Seljuk camel-men, with their myrrh, their gold, their silks, cloves and gingers; and true successors to the dhows and feluccas of medieval Hav are the white salt-ships for ever passing in and out beneath the changeless scrutiny of the Dog.

8

On the waterfront – the Fondaco – Chimoun and the
Venetians – more Arabesques – tramps and colliers –
a dawn visitor – the Electric Ferry

Very often now, as the days warm up, I rise with the trumpet,
and taking my notebook, and sometimes my sketching pad, I
walk down to the waterfront. I like to watch the market people,
and exchange a few words with Brack; and later I often take
my breakfast at one of the waterfront cafés, sitting outside and
drawing pictures as I eat.

You must imagine the harbour of Hav rather like a small
fiord, twisted by its central Hook so that from the quaysides of
the city you cannot see the open sea, only bare sloping hillocks
on each side. On the east bank, beyond New Hav, stands the
isolated white villa that is the British Agency, and was once the
British Residency, surrounded still by its green compound,
with a tangle of radio-masts on its outbuildings and a landing-
stage below. On the west bank, beyond the market and the
Medina, there is nothing much but a scatter of small houses,
the tower of a navigation light and a semaphore, like an old-
fashioned railway signal, with black balls on a mast above. Set
against the mottled jumble of the Old City and its markets, the
grandiose domes of the Serai, and New Hav seedy but symmetrical on its eastern shore, the harbour of Hav looks all green,
wide, cool and spacious. It reminds me sometimes of a little
Sydney Harbour, and sometimes of Bergen.

*

The historical tone of it, even now, is set by the Venetians who dominated its commerce for so long. There are two small islands in the harbour, and from my usual vantage point on the quay they look exactly like islands of the Venetian lagoon – those 'humped islands' that Shelley celebrated, running away from a far grander waterfront towards a colder sea. This is not surprising, for the buildings on them are mostly Venetian: the nearer island, still called the Lazaretto, was the Venetian quarantine station, now a jolly pleasure-garden. The further and larger one, still called Isola San Pietro, still crowned with a campanile, was leased to the Venetians as a place of confinement for prisoners-of-war and their own miscreants, and the gloomy barracks they built upon it are today Hav's only penitentiary – '*a windowless, deformed and dreary pile, / Such a one as age to age might add, for uses vile . . .* '

Then to my left, heavily arched and graced with sundry escutcheons, most of them so worn away as to be unrecognizable, stands the Fondaco di Cina, the biggest Venetian commercial building outside Venice, through which in its heyday an astonishing proportion of all the eastern trade, from Russia, from Central Asia, from the Levant, from Persia and of course from China itself was trans-shipped. In medieval times there were repeated rumours that the Venetians were about to annex Hav, as the last in their chain of islands and peninsular strongholds guarding the eastern trade routes, and looking at this building it is easy to understand why. Though it was built in Arab territory, it is an unmistakably imperial structure – just as commanding as anything the Serenissirna erected in Crete, Cyprus or Corfu. It was partly a warehouse indeed, and partly a hostelry for the Venetian merchants resident in Hav, but it was also a base for the Venetian galleys based here, with slips and sheds alongside for their careening and repair. The sheds are still there, like aircraft hangars: on top of the stone pillar outside there used to stand the Lion of St Mark, bravely demonstrating his gospel upon this waterfront of Islam.

The Fondaco now is everything under the sun, as ancient

waterfront buildings ought to be – in the West it would long ago have been prettied up with souvenir hops and net-hung restaurants. There are chandlers and junk shops, and alcoves stacked with crates, sacks and broken baskets, and hole-in-corner currency dealers, and financial concerns in upstairs offices whose small name-plates are hard to make out in the shadows of their passages – Cosmopolitan Forwarding SA is one, and another is Ahmed Khalid, Hav, Dubai and Jeddah. Mr S. Assuyian announces himself as Lloyd's Agent and Representative of Lloyd Triestino. World-wide Preferential Shipping Tariffs are offered, in several languages, by a firm surprisingly named Butterworth and Sons. The great central courtyard of the Fondaco, where once the silks and spices were stored, is now an apparently insoluble shambles of trucks, wagons, cars and motorbikes, squeezing themselves in and out through the narrow street entrance at the back. And above the grand front gate on the quayside, in the apartment I suppose of the old Venetian factory governor, sits Mr Chimoun, the Captain of the Port, a masterly Lebanese.

Masterly in a kind more suggestive, even romantic, than exactly functional. Mr Chimoun seems to me to have either a less than absolute grasp of the affairs of his port, or else a most delicately selective technique – 'two blind eyes', somebody has suggested to me. But he shows a fine aesthetic appreciation of his office and its meaning. 'When I sit here at this table,' he told me the other day – (not by the way some grand furnishing of the *seicento*, only an old deal desk piled with out-of-date reference books and letters of lading), 'when I sit here and look out at that splendid view – look, do you see? there is the campanile of San Pietro – when I watch our great ships sailing in' (which they all too seldom do) 'and hear the bustle of the merchants below' (he meant the hooting of trucks unable to get out of their parking place) 'and when I hear the gun go off as it has for a thousand years' (the Russians instituted the midday gun, in 1875) 'then do you know I feel myself truly to be some great signor myself – who knows? a Dandolo, a Grimaldi? You cannot think what a tremendous feeling it is, to be sitting at this table.'

At that moment the gun *did* go off, and Mr Chimoun suggested I might care to lunch with him at the café inside the courtyard, where they serve the great speciality of the Hav waterfront, urchin soup. The place was packed, every close-jammed table slurping with urchin-lovers of all ranks, from Magda the Braudelophobe, who was in a corner with two important-looking gentlemen, probably expellees from the Athenaeum, to dock-workers in their blue denims smoking between mouthfuls at long trestle tables. The soup was delectable: just as in some rare Corsican wines, perhaps one in a case of twelve, you can taste the heavenly scrub-fragrance of the *maquis*, so through the sea-urchins of this dish, the one native gastronomic miracle of Hav, every now and then there drifts a sweetish tangy sensation, more a bouquet than a taste, which is claimed to come from the gently waving sea-herbs of the northern coves.

'I much regret', said Mr Chimoun when the waiter brought the bill, 'that the rules of my office do not permit me to entertain you to this meal, since you are not on official business. But I trust you have enjoyed it.' Not very Dandolo-like, I could not help thinking: my share was 25 dinars – 40 new pence.

But anyway the working harbour now is much more Arab than Venetian. The language one hears is chiefly Arabic, and they are mostly distinctly Arab-looking financiers, with short clipped beards and digital gold watches, who emerge from the premises of Cosmopolitan Forwarding SA. Though the fishermen are all Greeks from the off-shore island of San Spiridon, the rig of their boats, the Hav rig, is recognizably Arab of origin, and very beautiful it is – a double lateen rig, with a jib, giving the whole vessel a most gracefully slanted appearance; the boats all have engines nowadays, but they often use their sails, and when one comes into the harbour on a southern wind, canvas bulging, flag streaming, keeling gloriously with a slap-slap of waves on its prow and its bare brown-torsoed Greeks exuberantly laughing and shouting to each other, it is as though young navigators have found their way to Hav out of the bright heroic past.

The only foreign ships trading regularly into Hav are Arab – the salt-ships, especially built for the trade, shallow enough to tie up at the Salt Wharf east of the Fondaco. They fly Panamanian flags actually, and were built in Norway, but they are Arab-owned, their crews are mostly Arab, and their only voyages take them back and forth, back and forth, between Hav and the Arabian Gulf. Monotonous duties, monotonous names too – *Queen of the Salt*, *King of the Salt*, *Emperor of the Salt* – but they do not look unlovely; they are low in the water, rakish, and when one of them lies alongside the wharf with its air-conditioners humming, its decks spotless and its paintwork all agleam, you might almost take it for some Arab prince's pleasure-craft (though Brack, who sailed in them for some years, seems to think the crew quarters down below rather less than sheikhly).

Out of the East too comes most of the casual sea-traffic which noses its way into the inner harbour. This is a great place still for the vagabond trade. Browning's Waring – '*What's become of Waring, / Since he gave us all the slip?*' – may have been last seen laughing in the stern-sheets of a bum-boat at Trieste, but he had his Hav period too: his real name was Alfred Domett (he eventually became Prime Minister of New Zealand) and it was here that Kinglake met him in 1834, finding him 'much as we knew him of old, only turned a chestnutty hue'. It was by sea that Hemingway first came here; arriving macho-style on a Syrian schooner but soon gravitating to the cocktails, roulette tables and steam-yachts of Casino Cove. And it was on board an Italian tramp from Alexandria that the poet C. P. Cafavy, in a rare break from the routine of his Egyptian office, sailed into Hav in 1910 to write one of the most sensual of his lyrics:

> He did not expect me. I had wandered far
> since we had met in the tavern at Aleppo . . .

Tramp steamers of a kind still come, and perhaps bring poets sometimes. They appear to bring little else anyway and seem to sail away with not much more – a few boxes of this or that, sometimes inexplicably a couple of old cars. They are mostly Syrian or Greek – sometimes Greek Cypriot, which is why we get Cypriot wines in our restaurants (the labels ripped off; just in case, and often the single word VIN substituted). Sometimes they seem to have come to Hav to die, and lie there at their moorings apparently abandoned, their decks flaking with rust, only the dimmest of lights shining, when night-time comes, from somewhere deep beneath their hatches. But they always revive unexpectedly, and when I turn up on the quay in the morning there goes the old *Malik*, or *Achelaos*; or *Thyella*, bravely puffing away, belching clouds of black smoke, down past San Pietro to the Hook and the open sea.

Coastal colliers come too, with fuel for the power station; they are unloaded at their own jetty, well down the harbour, by hundreds of labourers with sacks and baskets, and long after they sail away again a cloud of black dust is left in the air behind them. Small tankers tie up beside the oil-tanks near by, miscellaneous motorized dhows appear from nowhere in particular, and occasionally one sees those twos and threes of futuristic Japanese trawlers that seem to find their way into every corner of the Mediterranean.

Other traffic is harder to categorize. Once when I was down on the waterfront very early indeed, before the trumpet had blown or the market had properly opened, I heard a rumble of engines up the haven, and there came stealing out of the half-light an extremely un-shipshape motor-torpedo boat, *sans* guns or torpedo tubes. It flew a faded Stars and Stripes, and when it tied up, three young men in jeans and T-shirts emerged from wheel-house and engine-room to stretch themselves upon the quay.

'Hi,' they said, as though we were at Sausalito or Martha's Vineyard.

'Hi,' said I.

'You from Chimoun?' said one.

'Certainly not. I'm just waiting for the market to warm up.'

'Oh *I'm* sorry,' he said, 'I thought maybe you were from Chimoun.'

'Is he expecting you?' I asked. They all laughed at that. 'Expecting us?' they said. 'He'd better be.'

As you see, it is an irregular kind of port. They say it is inadequately dredged or even charted, which is why I have never once seen a plutocrat's yacht from the Casino enter the inlet – only Signor Biancheri's supply-launch foams confidently in and out. Mr Assuyian the Lloyd's Agent is alleged to have died years ago. It is a port of louche and easy anarchy, and its only signs of authority are Mr Chimoun behind his desk, the chequered flag above his building, and the venerable guard-ship, provided by the Italians in 1940 (it used to be their Yangtse gunboat *Arnaldo Carlotto*), which is the nearest thing to a Hav navy, but which seldom moves from its mooring at the Lazaretto.

One charming institution, nevertheless, does bring a gentle suggestion of order to this haphazard haven. It is the Electric Ferry. Looking rather like a floating London taxi, being black, all-enclosed and the same at each end, this little vehicle sets slowly and silently off promptly at seven each morning from the Fondaco on its journey across the harbour – to the market, the two islands, the New Hav promenade and then back the same way to the Fondaco, its last trip ending precisely at midnight. Its passengers are few, but its manner is inexorable. Young Chinese run it, keeping it very clean, collecting their fares in leather pouches and issuing tickets stamped in red ELECTRIC FERI HAV: and one of the most characteristic sounds of this city is the bang, bang, bang which precedes its arrival at the quay – the noise of its slatted seats being punctiliously slammed back on their hinges, to face the other way for the next voyage.

House of the Chinese Master
(after Bourdin, 1927)

9

The Roof-Race

It is 5 May, the day of the Roof-Race. As the horse-race is to Siena, as the bull-running is to Pamplona, as Derby Day is to the English or even perhaps Bastille Day to the French, so the day of the Roof-Race is to the people of Hav.

It is not known for sure how this fascinating institution began, though there are plenty of plausible theories. The race was certainly being run in the sixteenth century, when Nicander Nucius described it in passing as 'a curious custom of these people'; and in 1810 Lady Hester Stanhope, the future 'Queen of Palmyra', was among the spectators: she vociferously demanded the right to take part herself, and was only dissuaded by her private physician, who said it would almost certainly be the end of her.

In later years the Russian aristocracy made a regular fête of it, people coming all the way from St Petersburg simply for the day, and lavish house-parties were organized in the villas of the western hills. Enormous stakes were wagered on the outcome; the winner, still covered with dust and sweat; was immediately taken to the Palace in the Governor's own carriage for a champagne breakfast and the presentation of the traditional golden goblet (paid for, by the way, out of an annual bequest administered by the Department of Wakfs).

Today gambling is theoretically illegal in Hav, but the goblet is still presented, more prosaically nowadays at the finishing line, and the winner remains one of the heroes of Hav for the rest of his life – several old men have been admiringly pointed out to me in the streets as Roof-Race winners of long ago. The race is so demanding that nobody over the age of twenty-five has ever run it – no woman at all yet – and only once in recorded history has it been won by the same runner twice; so that actually there is quite a community of winners still alive in Hav – the most senior extant, who owns the pleasure-garden on the Lazaretto, won the race in 1921.

The most familiar account of the race's origins is this. During a rising against the Ottoman Turks, soon after their occupation of Hav, a messenger was sent clandestinely from Cyprus to make contact with the patriotic leader Gamal Abdul Hussein, who was operating from a secret headquarters in the Medina. The messenger landed safely on the waterfront at midnight, but found every entrance to the Old City blocked, and every street patrolled by Turkish soldiers. Even as he stood there wondering how to get to Gamal, at his house behind the Grand Mosque, he was spotted by Turkish sentries and a hue and cry was raised; but far from retreating to his boat, whose crew anxiously awaited him in the darkness, without a second thought he leapt up to the ramparts of the Medina, and began running helter-skelter over the rooftops towards the mosque. Up clambered the soldiers after him, scores of them, and there began a wild chase among the chimney-pots and wind-towers; but desperately leaping over alleyways, slithering down gutters, swarming over eaves and balustrades, the messenger found his way through an upper window of Gamal's house, presented his message, and died there and then, as Hav legendary heroes must, of a cracked but indomitable heart.

Such is the popular version, the one that used to get into the guide-books – Baedeker, for instance, offered it in his *Mediterranean*, 1911, while adding that 'experienced travellers may prefer to view the tale with the usual reservations'. Magda has another version altogether, concerning the exploits of an Albanian prince, while Dr Borge regards the whole thing as pagan allegory, symbolic of summer's arrival, or possibly

Christian, prefiguring the miracle of Pentecost. Most Havians, though, seem to accept the story of the messenger; and in my view, if it wasn't true in the first place, so many centuries of belief have made it true now.

The course is immensely demanding. It begins, as did the messenger's mission, with the scaling of the city wall, beside the Market Gate, and it entails a double circuit of the entire Medina, by a different route each time, involving jumps over more than thirty alleyways, culminating in a prodigious leap over the open space in the centre of the Great Bazaar, and ending desperately in a slither down the walls of the Castle Gate to the finish. The record time for the course is just under an hour, and officials are posted all over the rooftops, beneath red umbrellas like Turkish pashas themselves, to make sure there is no cheating.

Virtually all Hav turns out for this stupendous athletic event. All shops and government offices are closed for the day, and almost the only person who cannot come to watch is Missakian the trumpeter, because it is his call from the castle rampart which is the signal for the start. In former times the race was run at midnight, as the messenger supposedly ran, but so many competitors died or were terribly injured, tripping over unseen projections, misjudging the width of lanes, that in 1882 the Russians decreed it should be run instead as dawn broke over the city – to the chagrin of those young bloods whose chief pleasure, if we are to believe Tolstoy, lay in seeing the splayed bodies falling through the street-lights to their deaths. But if it was well ordered in Russian times, when Grand Duchesses came to watch, it is less so now: the race itself may be properly umpired and refereed, but the spectators, conveniently removed as they are from the actual course above their heads, are left absolutely uncontrolled. 'You are strong,' said Mahmoud, inviting me to join him at the great event, 'we will do the triple.'

This meant so positioning ourselves that we could see the

three climactic moments of the race, one after the other – the start, the Bazaar Leap and the finish. For *aficionados* this is the *only* way to watch, and over the years dozens of ways of doing it have been devised. Some use bicycles to race around the outer circle of the walls. Some are alleged to know of passages through the city's cellars and sewers. Our system however would be simple: we would just barge our way, with several thousand others, down the clogged and excited streets from one site to the other.

Forty-two young men took part in the race this morning, and when we hastened in the half-light to join the great crowd at the Market Gate, we found them flexing their muscles, stretching themselves and touching their toes in a long line below the city wall. Two were Chinese. One was black. One I recognized – he works at the Big Star garage, where I bought my car. One was Mahmoud's cousin Gabril, who works for the tramways company. Several wore red trunks to show that they had run the race before, in itself a mark of great distinction, and they were all heavily greased – a protection, Mahmoud said, against abrasions.

The eastern sky began to pale; the shape of the high wall revealed itself before us; from the mosque, as we stood there in silence, came the call to prayer; and then from the distant castle heights sounded Missakian's trumpet. The very instant its last notes died those forty-two young men were scrabbling furiously up the stonework, finding a foothold here, a handhold there, pulling themselves up bump by bump, crack by crack, by routes which, like climbers' pitches, all have their long-familiar names and well-known characteristics. A few seconds – it cannot have been more – and they were all over the top and out of sight.

'Right,' said Mahmoud, 'quick, follow me,' and ruthlessly pushing and elbowing our way we struggled through the gate into the street that leads to the Great Bazaar in the very middle of the Medina. In sudden gusts and mighty sighs, as we progressed, we could hear spectators across the city greeting some spectacular jump, mourning some unfortunate slither – first to our right, then in front of us, then to our left, and presently behind our backs, as the runners finished their first lap. 'Quick, quick,' said Mahmoud to nobody in particular, and everyone else was saying it too – 'quick, only a few minutes now, we mustn't miss it, come along, dirleddy' – and at last we were beneath the vaulted arcade of the bazaar, lit only by shafts of sunlight through its roof-holes, shoving along its eastern axis until we found ourselves jammed with a few hundred others in the circular open space that is its apex.

We were just in time. Just as we got there we heard a wild padding of feet along the roofs above, and looking up we saw, *wham*! one flying brown body, then another, then a third, spreadeagled violently across the gap, rather like flying squirrels. One after the other they came, momentarily showed themselves in their frenzied leaps and vanished, and the crowd began to count them as they appeared – *dört*, *bes*, *alti*, *yedi* . . . Twenty-five came over in quick succession, then two more after a long pause, and then no more. 'Eight fallen,' said Mahmoud. 'I hope my cousin was not one' – but by then we had all begun to move off again, up the bazaar's north axis this time, to the Castle Gate. Now the crush was not so hectic. Everyone knew that the second half of the race was run much slower than the first – though the light was better by now; the terrible exertions had taken their toll. So we had time to conjecture, as we moved towards the finish line. Was that Majourian in the lead at the bazaar, or was it the formidable Cheng Lo? Who was the first Red Trunk? Had Ahmed Aziz fallen, one wondered – he was getting on a bit, after all . . . In a great sort of communal murmur we emerged from the bazaar, hurried down the Street of the Four Nomads, and passed through the Castle Gate into the square outside.

There the Governor was waiting, with the gold goblet on the table before him, attended by sundry worthies: the gendarmerie commander in his white drills and silver helmet, the chairman of the Assembly, the Catholic, Orthodox and

Maronite bishops in their varied vestments, the Imam of the Grand Mosque, and many another less identifiable. There seemed to be a demonstration of some kind happening over by the Serai – a clutch of people holding banners and intermittently shouting: but the gendarmes were keeping them well away, and the dignitaries were not distracted. They did not have long to wait, anyway. Those spurts of wonder and commiseration grew closer and closer. The Governor joked benignly, as governors will, to ever-appreciative aides. The churchmen chatted ecumenically. The gendarmerie commander resolutely turned his back on the scuffles by the Serai. Splosh! like a loose sack of potatoes the first of the roof-runners, without more ado, suddenly fell, rather than jumped or even scrambled, down the sheer face of the gateway, to lie heaving, greased, bruised and bloody at the Governor's feet. Every few seconds then the others arrived, those that were still in the race. They simply let themselves drop from the gate-tower, plomp, like stunt-men playing corpses in western movies, to lie there at the bottom in crumpled heaps, or flat on their backs in absolute exhaustion.

It looked like a battlefield. The crowd cheered each new deposit, the dignitaries affably clapped. And when the winner had sufficiently recovered to receive his prize, the Governor, taking good care, I noticed, that none of the grease, blood or dust got on his suit, kissed him on both cheeks to rapturous cries of 'Bravo! Bravo the Victor!' rather as though we were all at the opera.

'Who won?' demanded Missakian, looking up from his beans and newspaper as we entered the station café for our breakfast.

'Izmic,' said Mahmoud.

'Izmic!' cried Missakian disgustedly, and picking up his trumpet he blew through it a rude unmusical noise.

10

To Little Yalta – 'fresh start' – Russian Hav – Diaghilev and Nijinsky – the graveyard

Boulevard de Cetinje, which slices its way so arrogantly through the Medina, turns into something nicer when it crosses the canal and winds into the western hills. Though it is little more than a rutted track now, you can see that it was once an agreeable country avenue. Many of its trees are dead and gone, but the survivors are fine old Hav catalpas, sometimes so rich, if decrepit, that they lean right across the road and touch each other. Halfway to the sea, at a crest of the road, there is a little wooden pavilion, showing traces of blue paint upon it; at weekends a girl sells fruit, biscuits and lemonade there, to lugubrious Havian music from her transistor, and outside there are pretty little rustic tables and benches, and the remains of a flower-garden.

This is the road the Russians built, purely for their own convenience, in the days of Imperial Hav. Many a memoir mentions the little blue pleasure-pavilion on the road to the sea. And when, like the princes and Grand Duchesses; the generals and the courtesans of long ago, you emerge from the hills a few miles further on, there before you, on a wide sandy bay beside the glistening sea, stand the houses of the small bathing resort they used to call Malaya Yalta, Little Yalta. They are hardly houses really, only glorified bathing huts, to which the servants would hurry beforehand with food and wine, to get the samovars going and put out the parasols, but from a distance they look entertainingly imposing. Each with its own wooded stockade, they are merrily embellished with domes, turrets, spires, ornate barge-boarded verandahs and ornamental chimney-pots. It looks like a goblin Trouville down there, full of colour and vivacity: it is only when the road peters out at the remains of the boardwalk that you find it all to be a spectral colony, its fences collapsed, its verandahs sagging, its paint-work flaked away, its comical little towers precariously listing, and only three or four of its once-festive houses at the northern end remaining, occupied by sad families of Indian squatters.

Even the ghosts of those who were happy here have left the seashore now.

There are a very few old Russians, still alive in Hav, who can just remember the bright pleasures of Little Yalta. The most prominent of them is Anna Novochka, who lives alone with a housekeeper in the very last of the old patrician villas of the western hills still to be inhabited. She is a dauntless old lady. Though she is now in her nineties, and almost penniless, she dresses always in bright flowing colours, blouses of swathed silk, brocade skirts which I suspect to have been made out of curtain fabric. 'We Russians', she likes to say, 'are people of colour. We *need* colour, as other people need liberty.'

I often go to see her, to take tea in her sparse and airy drawing-room (where pale squares upon the walls show where pictures used to hang), followed often enough, as we talk into the evening, by glasses of vodka with squeezed lime juice. She was not always called Novochka. Like many of the Russians who stayed in Hav after the Revolution, she adopted a new name of her own invention: she says it means 'Fresh Start'. Her housekeeper is Russian too, but of more recent vintage; she came to Hav via Israel five or six years ago, and is, so Anna tells me, totally disenchanted with everything. She does look rather sour. Anna herself on the other hand is the very incarnation of high spirits, and in her I feel I am meeting the miraculously preserved mood of Imperial Hav itself.

For Russian Hav was nothing if not high-spirited. It was, of course, very artificial and snobbish, like all such colonies – 'Why must you always be talking of Hav?' says Chekov's Vasilyev to his friend Gregory (in *An Affair*). 'Isn't our town good enough for you then? In Hav you never hear a word of Russian, I'm told, nothing but French and German is good enough down there.' But it seems to have possessed a certain underlying innocence. The Russians eagerly accepted Hav, under the Pendeh Agreement of 1875 as their only outlet to the Mediterranean (having lost the Ionian Islands to the British half a century before), and as a stepping-stone perhaps towards those Holy Places of Jerusalem which meant so much to them in those days. They knew well enough, though, that strategically it was useless to them – its harbour hopelessly shallow, its position fearfully vulnerable. To these disadvantages they cheerfully reconciled themselves, and instead set out to make the place as thoroughly agreeable as they could.

Politically, of course, it was an absolute despotism – Hav had never been anything else – but the Russian yoke was light enough, minorities were not suppressed, opinions were given reasonable latitude. At the end of the nineteenth century indeed Hav became a favourite destination for young Russian revolutionaries on the run, until in 1908 somebody blew up the Governor's private railway coach, and Count Kolchok was obliged to accept a detachment of the secret police.

Even the grandiose buildings around Pendeh Square – more grandiose still before the Cathedral of the Annunciation and the Little Pushkin Theatre were burnt down in the 1920s – even those somewhat monstrous buildings are generally agreed to be fun. They may have been intended to blazon Russia's Mediterranean presence to the world, but at least they did so exuberantly, Anna says that in her girlhood, before the First World War, they used to be positively dazzling in their golds and blues, their gardens exquisitely maintained and the gravel of the avenue in front of the Palace raked and smoothed so constantly that it looked like 'coral sand, when the tide has just gone out'. And the villas in the hills, where most of the richer Russians preferred to live, seem, if Anna's memories are true, to have been the happiest places imaginable.

'You must realize there are so few of us. We were all friends – enemies too of course, but friends at the same time. Many of us were related. I had three cousins living in Hav at one time. Kolchok himself was a relative on my mother's side. And when *le haut monde* came down for the season from Moscow and St Petersburg, why, we knew all of them too – or if we didn't, we very soon did. It was like the very nicest of clubs. And everyone felt freer here, far from the Court, without estates to worry about, or serfs I suppose in the old days. We were Russia emancipated!'

In the high summer season Hav was terrifically festive. To and fro between the villas went the barouches and the horsemen, laughing in the evening. Trundling hilariously down the road to the sea went the bathing parties, stopping at the blue pavilion to clamour for lemonades. Ever and again the waltzes rang out from the garden of the Palace, and the coaches and cars jammed the great square outside, and the lights shone, and long after midnight one heard the footmen calling for carriages – 'Number 23, His Imperial Highness the Grand Duke Felix . . . Number 87, the Countess Kondakov!' Little sailing-boats with canopies used to take the ladies and children for decorous trips around the harbour, to the Lazaretto pleasure-gardens, down to the Iron Dog, while the young men sometimes rented dhows to sail around the southern point and meet their families at Malaya Yalta.

'Were you never bored, with so much unremitting pleasure?'

'Never. But then I was only a little girl, remember. I see it all through the eyes of childhood. Never have I been so excited, never in all my life, as I used to be when we were taken to the station to see the first train of the season arrive. It was a fixed day, you know, announced beforehand in the *Court Gazette* and so on, and the first train was one of the great events of the year. We were allowed to stay up especially! We would all wear our best clothes, and all the barouches and luggage-traps would be waiting out there in the square – oh, I remember it so clearly! – and it used to seem like *hours* till the train arrived. We could hear it hooting, hooting, all the way through the Balad.

'And then, when it came at last, the excitement! All the grand ladies in the latest fashions, fashions we'd never seen before, and the gentlemen in their tall hats, with carnation buttonholes, and Kolchok would be there to greet whatever princess or Grand Duke was on board, and then he'd go around welcoming old friends and kissing cousins and so forth, and everybody else would be embracing their friends and laughing, and we children would be hopping up and down with the fun of it. And then all the servants jumping off from the coaches behind, and the bustle and fuss of getting the luggage together, and out we'd clop from Pendeh Square like a kind of army. It was so colourful, you have no idea. When we got home, before we children were packed off to bed, we were allowed to have a cup of cocoa with the grown-ups.

'My father said to me once, "Whatever you forget in life, don't forget the pleasure of this evening with our friends." I never have, as you see. I can hear him saying it now! And now all those friends are gone, only one old woman living on and remembering them.'

Between 1910 and 1914 the supreme event of the Hav social calendar was the annual visit of the Diaghilev Ballet to the Little Pushkin Theatre. Diaghilev first came to Hav in 1908, was fascinated by the place, and was easily persuaded to bring his company from Paris for a week at the height of the season each year. Diaghilev in Hav became, for those few brief summers, one of the great festivities of Czarist Russia, and hundreds of people used to come by special train for the performances.

A huge marquee was erected in Pendeh Square for the week, and there after each night's performance dancers and audience alike dined, drank champagne, danced again and ate urchins into the small hours, in a magical aura of fairy lights and music, beneath the velvet skies of Hav. In 1910 the French novelist Pierre Loti, then a naval officer, was in Hav for one night during the first Diaghilev season, his ship having anchored off-shore. 'It was like a dream to me', he wrote afterwards, 'to come from my ship into this midnight celebration. The music of the orchestra floated about the square and rebounded, I thought, from the golden domes of the Palace. The ladies floated in and out of the great tent like fairies of the night – white arms, billowing silk skirts, shining diamonds. The men were magnificent in black, with their bright sashes and glittering orders, Diaghilev himself occupying the centre of the stage. And in and amongst this elegant throng there flitted and pranced the dancers of the ballet, still in their costumes – fantastic figures of gold and crimson, moving through the crowd in movements that seemed to me hardly human. When I walked across the square to the picket-boat awaiting me at the quay I saw a solitary figure like a feathered satyr dancing all alone with wild movements up the long avenue of palms outside the Palace. It was Nijinsky.'

It was said of Nijinsky that he was never happier than he was in Hav, and he is remembered still with proud affection. 'I saw Nijinsky clear' is a leitmotif of elderly reminiscence in Hav, among Arabs and Turks as often as among the Europeans of the concessions. He used to love to wander the city by himself, an image so unforgettable that old people describe him as though they can actually see him still. Sometimes he would be on the harbour-front, watching the ships. Sometimes the trumpeter, arriving at Katourian's bastion, would find the great dancer already there. He liked to go to the station to see the train leave in the morning. And Anna one day, hunting among her souvenirs in a black leather box full of papers, pictures, twists of hair, postage stamps, imperial securities – 'Securities! Some securities!' – produced for me a photograph of Nijinsky taken on an outing, it said in spindly French on the back, in 1912.

There were only two figures in the picture, against a background of sky and bare heathland. One was the Iron Dog, full face. Beside it, ramrod stiff, wearing a kind of peasant jerkin and baggy trousers, Nijinsky stared expressionless into the lens, his hair ruffled by the wind.

The Ballet Russe, they say, was deeply influenced by its association with Hav. Bakst the great designer was seduced by the peculiar colour combinations he found here – the Russian dazzle of golds, crimsons and bright blues set against skies, seas and heathy hills that expressed a different sensibility. Benois was so taken with the Hav costume – straw hat and *gallabiyeh* – that he introduced it into the fair scenes of *Petrushka*. Diaghilev himself seems to have been calmed and comforted by the city's blend of the heady and the sombre, the exhilarated and the brooding; he is buried in Venice, but Anna says she herself heard him say that he would like to lie in the little Russian graveyard overlooking the sea in the western hills of Hav.

The graveyard is forlornly neglected now, though its windbreak of dark cypresses makes it visible from far away, like a war cemetery. It lies on a slope of the hill, looking out over the western bay and Pyramid Rock; from its lower graves you can just see the faded baubles of Little Yalta. Dominating the plot is the tall obelisk that marks Count Kolchok's grave, with a portrait in bas-relief and a long Russian epitaph. There are a few lesser obelisks, and a couple of broken columns, and some mourning angels. Mostly, though, they are simple crosses, some of wood, that mark the last resting places of Hav's Russians. Often their inscriptions have long been obliterated, by the heat, and the winds off the sea; everywhere the coarse grass grows, and here and there the scrub off the heath has broken through the surrounding wall. Soon it will have obliterated all but those obelisks, and an elevated angel or two.

I I

A quality of fantasy – around the great square – House of the Chinese Master – New Hav – a bit of a lark – the Conveyor Bridge

When Marco Polo came to Hav in the thirteenth century, he was struck not so much by the wealth or power of the city, but by something unusual to its nature. 'This is a place of strange buildings and rites, not like other places.' Modern Hav is not perhaps exactly beautiful – it is too knocked about for that, has been infiltrated by too many shabby purlieus, frayed by too many reverses of fortune. But it does still possess some quality of fantasy, something almost frivolous despite its ancient purposes, and this is caused I think by its particular criss-cross mixture of architectural styles, which makes many of its buildings feel like exhibition structures, or aesthetic experiments. Add to this piquancy of melange a certain flimsiness of construction – Hav bricks are small and slight, Hav roofs look lightly laid upon their joists – and the impression is given of a monumental but neglected folly, built by a sequence of playful potentates for their own amusement down the centuries.

The one Hav prospect that occasionally gets into picture-books, having been painted by numberless artists of the T. Ramotsky school, is the view looking northward from the waterfront towards the castle. Deposited here without warning out of the blue, you really might be at a loss to know where on this earth you were. To the right stands the hulk of the Fondaco, built of red brick brought from Venice, with its four squat corner towers, its machicolations, and its arcading half-filled now with hoardings and concrete walls. In the background, splendidly blocking the scene, the hill of the acropolis is crowned with the ruin of the castle, Beynac's keep mouldering at the summit, Saladin's gateway good as new below. To the left rise the walls of the Medina, protruded over by wind-towers, minarets and the upper floors of the huge merchant houses beside the bazaars.

And in the centre, seen across the busy traffic of the quay, is the official complex created by the Russians to celebrate their presence on this southern shore. The square itself, with its equestrian emperor in the centre, is said to be bigger than the Grand Square at Isfahan upon whose proportions the Arabs originally based it, and is bounded left and right by double lines of palm trees; between the eastern avenue the tramline runs, between the western is the gravel footpath along which Loti saw Nijinsky dance, originally preserved for Russian officials and their ladies, now a favourite public dalliance. The waterfront end of the square is marked by a line of bollards, placed there by the Venetians and made from captured Genoese guns; at the other end, where the winding path to the castle starts, there is a handsome double terrace, with urns and lions couchant on it, and in the middle a big circular fountain which, for all its dolphins, nymphs and bearded sea-gods, alas no longer founts.

Then to the east and west, more like pavilions than substantial buildings, rise the showy display pieces of Russian Hav, Serai on one side, station on the other. Their symbolism is extravagant, and entertaining. They represent Mediterranean Russia – the achievement at last of a dream as much aesthetic, or imaginative, as political. High above them tower the gilded onion domes, capped with gay devices, which instantly summon in the mind bitter steppes and snowy cities of the north – something of the sleigh and the fur hat, the samovar and perhaps the OGPU too – Mother Russia, at once smilingly and authoritatively embodied, here at the end of the railway line.

But below these bright globules, which somehow manage to be a little grim, as well as flashy, the architects Schröter and Huhn (who also designed the gigantic garrison cathedral at Tiflis, up the line) built in a very different allegory: for the tall arches and arcades below the domes, the gardens surrounding them, the inner courtyards and the long interior corridors are built in what architects Schröter and Huhn conceived as Southern Eclectic. Ogive arches in multi-coloured brick sustain that Slavic roofline, and there are high balconies with hoods, as in great houses of Syria, and even *mashrabiya* windows here and there. The courtyards are Alhambran, with prim patterns of orange trees; the tall shuttered windows of the wings might be in Amalfi or the old part of Nice.

Seen in the general rather than the particular, against the high silhouette of the castle hill, this ensemble really is rather spectacular, a little muted though its colours are now, a little skew-whiff some of its shutters and rickety the less frequented of its balconies: and especially seen from the Electric Ferry, sliding quietly across the harbour, all those strange and disparate shapes, the towered severity of the Fondaco the bright domes, the stark castle walls above, seem as they shift one against the other oddly temporary, as though one of these days the Grand Hav Exhibition must come to an end, and all its pavilions be dismantled.

The most celebrated architectural hybrid of Hav is the House of the Chinese Master in the Medina, directly outside the west entrance of the Great Bazaar. In the Middle Ages, when the Venetians were paramount upon the waterfront of Hav, the Chinese established a financial ascendancy in the city, and in 1432 the Amir was obliged to allow them a merchant headquarters actually within the Medina walls – hitherto they had been confined to their own settlement of Yuan Wen Kuo. They built it essentially in the glorious Ming style of the age, to plans said to have been sent from Beijing by the architect of the Qian Qing Gong, the Palace of Heavenly Parity in the Forbidden

City; but they were subtle enough to make of it something specific to Hav. It is the westernmost of all the major buildings of Chinese architecture, and some say the finest Chinese construction west of the Gobi: discovering it for the first time out of the darkness of the Great Bazaar is perhaps the most astonishing aesthetic experience Hav can offer.

Imagine yourself jostling a way through those souks, shadowy, dusty, clamorous, argumentative, and approaching gradually, past charm-hawker and water-seller, blaring record shop and clatter of iron-smiths, the small yellow rectangle of sunshine that marks the end of the arcade. So great is the contrast of light that at first there is nothing to be distinguished but the dazzle itself; but as you get closer, and your eyes accustom themselves to the shine, you see resolving itself out there what seems to be a gigantic piece of black fretwork – multitudinous squares, triangles, circles and intersections, with daylight showing intricately through them. Is it some kind of huge screen? Is it something to do with the mosque, or an antique defence work? No: when you reach the end of the corridor at last, and step outside into the afternoon, you realize with delight that you have reached Qai Chen Bo, the House of the Chinese Master.

It *is* a house, and a very large one, but its inner chambers and offices, long since converted into a warren of tenements, are surrounded by a nine-sided mesh of elaborately worked black marble, forming in fact an endlessly spiralling sequence of balconies, but looking from the outside wonderfully lacy and insubstantial. The building is eleven storeys high, deliberately built a storey higher, so legend says, than any of the Arab structures of the city, and it is capped by a conical roof of green glazed tiles, heavily eaved and surrounded by pendant bobbles. It is reached by five wooden bridges over a nine-sided moat, once filled with fish and water-lilies, now only with rubbish: at each angle of the moat a separate small circular pool festers. The building is hemmed in nowadays by nondescript brick and concrete blocks, but still stands there sublimely individual and entertaining – after five hundred years and more, much the liveliest building in Hav.

In 1927 Professor Jean-Claude Bourdin of the Académie française wrote a pamphlet about this building. All sorts of allusions, it seems, can be read into a construction that looks to the innocent eye no more than a splendid *jeu d'esprit*. The fundamental shape of the building is, of course, that of the pagoda, the most unmistakably Chinese of forms, with its wide eaves and its gently tapering flanks – the Arabs were to be left in no doubt, not for a moment, as to the nationality of the Master. In the five bridges there is apparently a direct reference to the five bridges over the Golden Water River in the Forbidden City, an allusion that would imply to the Chinese themselves, if hardly to anyone else, the presence here of the imperial authority. Then the moat itself, with its nine unblinking eye-pools, is claimed by Professor Bourdin to be a figure of the Lake of Sleepless Diligence, while the high corridor which bisects the ground floor of the building, west to east, is said to be exactly aligned upon Tian Tan, the Temple of the Heavens in Beijing. Finally, so Bourdin thinks, the whole edifice, so complex and deceptive, is a sophisticated architectural metaphor of the maze.

Well I'm sure he was right – he was a corresponding member of the Chinese Academy, too – but for me the House of the Chinese Master, whatever its subliminal purposes, is above all the most cheerful of follies. It is a building that makes nearly everyone, seeing it for the first time, laugh with pleasure, so droll is its posture there, so enchantingly delicate its construction, and so altogether unexpected its presence among the severities of medieval Islam. Here is what other visitors have written of it:

> *Pero Tafur, 1439*: 'I have seen no building like this masterpiece, not in Rome, Venice or in Constantinople, and indeed I think it is the most remarkable and delightful of all buildings.'

Nicandur Nucius, 1546: 'The House of the Chinese Master at Hav is the merry wonder of all who see it.'

Anthony Jenkinson, 1558: 'In that part of the city where the Amir lives is a tall tower built by the Chinamen, exceeding ingenious and merry, so that had it not been for the severe scrutiny of the Mussulmans close by we would fain have burst out laughing at the spectacle.'

Alexander Kinglake, 1834: 'Do you remember when we were boys together we would make houses in the trees for our childish entertainments? Well, you must imagine all the tree-houses that ever were constructed pushed all on top of one another, and crowned with the wide straw hat that our good Mrs W used to wear to church on Sundays.'

Mark Twain, 1872: 'If I hadn't seen it with my own eyes I would have said it was more probably the House of the Chinese Teller of Tales – but there it was before me, and I could not have told a taller tale myself.'

D. H. Lawrence, 1922: 'A hideous thing. Restless, unsatisfied, And yet one could not help smiling at the vivid, brisk and out-flinging insolence of it.'

Robert Byron, 1927: 'Surrounded by the sombre piles of Islam, the House of the Chinese Master burst into our view in a flowering of spectacular eccentricity. It was impossible to leave the city after so brief a glimpse of this prodigy; sighing, we resolved to come back in the morning. "You don't want to see inside now?" nagged the wretched guide. "Alas, it is not allowed," said David at once. "We are Rosi-crucians."'

But I will leave the last comment to Sigmund Freud, who lived for a time in modest lodgings on the eighth floor of the house:

It is difficult for me to express how profound an effect this experience has had upon me. It is as though I have lived within the inmost cavity of a man's mind – and that the mind of a Chinese architect dead for five hundred years. No number of hours spent in analysis with my patients has brought me nearer to the sources of personality than the weeks I spent, all unthinking, in the House of the Chinese Master.

I suppose you could say the very notion of New Hav is cross-bred – critics certainly thought so when it was founded, and historians sometimes say so now. It was certainly a quixotic gesture, to choose this remote and inessential seaport for so advanced an experiment in internationalism. As to the construction of a brand-new city to house the concessionary areas, that was variously considered at the time as either an act of preposterous extravagance, or else a project nobly worthy of the age that was dawning after the war to end all wars.

An international committee of architects was invited to design New Hav, and the plan they drew up was patently consensus architecture, a little dull. What it lacks in genius, however, it makes up for in an unexpected and sometimes comic caprice of detail. The idea was to balance the roughly circular walled city of the Arabs, on the western side of the harbour, with a second walled city on the eastern side, leaving the Serai and the castle in between. The harbour gate of New Hav opening on to a promenade upon the western quay, looks directly across the harbour to the Market Gate of the Medina. At the same time, the northern axis of the new city was to be aligned upon the castle hill, so that you could see the rock of the acropolis from the very middle of New Hav; but since this did not in the event prove possible in the city's geometrically tripartite form, the northern boulevard had to be twisted out of true, causing agonizing disputes between the French and the Italians, whose concessions it separated (in the end the Italians were compensated by being given possession of the promenade upon the harbour).

Everything else about New Hav is excessively symmetrical,

and there is almost nothing that is not balanced by something else, and almost no vista that is not suitably closed. From the central Place des Nations, below my balcony, radiate the three dividing boulevards, Avenue de France northwards towards the Serai and the castle hill, Viale Roma westwards to the harbour, Unter den Südlinden eastwards towards nowhere in particular. The city was supposed to be a physical representation of the League's visionary initiative – a place of reconciliation and cooperation, of unity in variety. Its circular shape was meant to symbolize eternal peace, and each boulevard was planted with a different species of tree (planes, catalpas and ilexes) to express the joy of amicable difference.

The façades of Place and boulevards are all uniform – grandly neoclassical, in a Beaux-Arts style, arcaded at street level, mansard-roofed above – and they are marked with elegant tiled street-signs, in four languages, contributed to this old haven of the Armenians by the Armenian Pottery in Jerusalem. But the liberty allowed to the powers to do what they liked in their own quarters saves the place from sterile monumentality. Resolutely internationalist though they were, none of the three could resist the claims of patriotism when they were let loose on the side-streets, and there are few facets of French, Italian or German architecture that are not represented somewhere within the pattern of New Hav. There are mock-Bavarian inns. There is a music-hall (the Lux Palace) straight from Montmartre. There is a classic Fascist railway station, modelled on Milan's, which since no railway enters New Hav, was used as the Italian Post Office instead. If the French decided to build a cathedral, what else but a little Rheims would do? If the Germans wanted a Residenz, what but a small *Schloss*? Though everything is cracked and peeling now, it is all there to this day, Beaux-Arts to Bauhaus, neo-Imperial to late Nihilist (the Casa Frioli in the Italian quarter, a marvel of swirled concrete decorated with mosaics of glaring purple, is the least avoidable building in New Hav).

Two world-famous architects are represented. The glass-and-concrete Maison de la Culture in the French quarter, with its stilts and green cladding, is one of Le Corbusier's less inspired works: in it, between the wars, everyone from Colette to Malraux gave lectures on The Meaning of Frenchness or Allegory in Provençal Folk-Dance. More importantly, you may notice scattered fitfully through the German quarter a certain distinction of design in matters electrical: lamp-standards, light-switches, even a few antique electric fires and toasters all seem to obey some central directive of taste. This is because the German administration entrusted the power system of its quarter to the Berlin company AEG, and it was their great consultant architect Peter Behrens who, during a visit to Hav in 1925, drew up designs for the whole electrical network. Unfortunately he had no say in the power station, which had been built by the Russians and supplied the whole peninsula, but within the German quarter everything electrical was his – the bold transformer station, like a whale-back beside the Ostgatte, the powerful street-light pylons, the solid square switches of brown Bakelite. Of course much of it is lost, but even now, so ubiquitous was Behrens' influence, there is a kind of subliminal strength to the style of the German quarter which is distributed, I like to think, directly through the frequently fused and multitudinously patched circuits of AEG-Hav.

For the rest, there is nothing of supreme quality. It is all a bit of a lark. All was done, one feels, even the Italian Post Office, in a spirit of genial optimism, elevated sometimes into parody. Architectural purists of the 1920s sneered mercilessly at New Hav, and Lutyens, invited to attend its formal opening in 1928, said privately that it reminded him of the ghost train on Brighton pier, so dizzy did it make him, and so often did damp objects slap him in the face.

But at least it possesses, as few such artificial towns do, an air of hopeful guilelessness. Just this once, it seems to say, just for this moment, even our separate patriotisms are merely amusing. And most guilelessly amusing of all, to my mind, are

the three arches by which each radial boulevard, as it debauch-
es into the central Place, is ornamentally bridged. I can see all
three from my terrace, if I lean out far enough. Close to the left
a replica of the Bridge of Sighs ambiguously links our quarter
with the French. Further round the Place, the Avenue de
France is spanned by a squashed and potted representation of
the towered bridge at Cahors. And opposite me stands an elevated Brandenburg Gate, splendid indeed when a No. 2 tram
comes storming underneath with its rocking red trailer.

Armand thinks them all very silly, but he should not scorn
Hav's follies, for the most gloriously ludicrous of them all was
contributed by his own country. In those days it was an official
French custom to distribute among Francophone communities
across the world small iron replicas of the Eiffel Tower, still to
be seen in places like Mauritius or Madagascar. It was thought
improper, I suppose, to make such an offering to Tripartite
Hav, so instead the French government presented the Conveyor
Bridge which spans the harbour mouth beside the Iron Dog,
perhaps ten miles south of the city centre, as a gesture of
France's profound respect for the people and civilization of the
peninsula. Only the French could build conveyor bridges –
archetype was Lanvedin's magnificent Pont Transbordent at
Marseilles – so its unmistakable outline on the finest site in Hav
would be a perpetual reminder of French skill and generosity.

No matter that almost nobody wanted to cross the harbour
down there, or that the elaborate solution of a conveyer bridge
was perfectly unnecessary anyway. The French mind was
majestically made up, and to this day the bridge operates with
the help of generous subsidies from Paris – besides being,
thanks to its regular maintenance by French engineers, the
most efficient piece of mechanism in Hav. Twelve times a day
its platform, slung on steel wires from the girders high above,
sets off in a gentle swaying motion across the harbour mouth,
guided by a captain wearing a derivation of French naval uniform in his small wooden cabin in the middle. The pace is

measured. The machinery is silent. A long chequered pennant streams from the cabin roof. To the north you can see the castle, rising on its rock above the city, to the south the Mediterranean sea lies blue, green and flecked with foam. Below you, perhaps, a white salt-ship slips elegantly out of the haven for Port Said and the Red Sea. In all Hav there is nothing much more foolish than the Conveyor Bridge – but nothing much grander, either!

12

*The Iron Dog – graffiti – on Greeks – on Greekness –
something haunting*

Last week, for the first time, I stood like Nijinsky beside the
Iron Dog.

You can reach it direct from the Medina, but I preferred to
approach the beast from the east, snout-on so to speak; so I
drove through the German gate of New Hav after breakfast,
took the rough track around the back of the British Agency,
and arrived at the Conveyor Bridge in time for the nine o'clock
crossing (which for myself I think of as a flight, so airy is the
motion of that platform beneath its spindly wires, with its
wind-indicator swirling and its pennant streaming bravely).
The other passengers were all Greeks – a man in a truck, three
black-shawled women with an empty pony cart. As we
approached the western shore, I noticed, the eyes of us all, even
the captain's, were drawn to the enigmatic creature on its high
headland; and when we drew level with it, almost at the same
height as our platform, all the women crossed themselves.

For the bridge disgorges its passengers a little way inland
from the Dog, and you must walk back along the windswept
moor to get to it. No good taking the car, for there is no track,
and the ground is thick with scented scrub – so scented that it
fills the air with its fragrance, and is said to give an intoxicat-
ing bouquet to the water from the spring which, sprouting
halfway up the sea-cliff, is thought to be the reason why the
Greeks landed here in the first place. The wind blew about me,

then, the captain waved from his high gazebo, and through the perfumed sunshine I walked towards the most celebrated of all Hav's monuments.

It was not, when I reached it, how I had foreseen. From a distance it looks all stark arrogance, its head held so high, its tail outstretched, its legs, slightly splayed, planted fiercely in the ground. It has been called the Iron Dog at least since the eleventh century, when the Crusaders wrote the earliest descriptions we possess; but so relentless does it appear, especially in photographs, that some modern scholars have declared it to be not a dog at all, but rather the fox that young Spartans were supposed to take into the hills, to gnaw at their bellies and make men of them. 'I can never see a picture of that animal', wrote T. E. Lawrence, who subscribed to the theory himself, 'without feeling a pain in my tum.'

But when you get close to the figure, such notions seem implausible. Whatever else he may be, the Iron Dog is certainly not a fox. His face is genial. His legs are implanted not ferociously at all, but playfully. His elongated tail streams eagerly, as though he is only waiting the word to spring after grouse or gazelle. He is made of bronze, with the remains of gilt showing on it, but so subtly is he structured, and so infinite are the little cracks of time and weather that layer his skin, that the material looks more like wood, and makes the figure seem remarkably light – especially as its big metal plinth has long since disappeared into the soil, turf and scrub.

The Iron Dog is about six feet high, paw to ear, and there are many graffiti on his hide. There is the famous rune, companion to that on one of the Arsenal lions in Venice, which proclaims that men of the Byzantine emperor's Norse bodyguard once landed on this peninsula. There are indecipherable scratches in Greek. A very hazy M.P., on the animal's rear flank, is popularly supposed to be Marco Polo's. There are some marvellously flowery little ciphers which have been identified as the marks of Venetian silk merchants, and scores of stranger devices, apparently of all ages, which seem to have some cabalistic meaning. Henry Stanley the explorer, who came here after the opening of the Suez Canal in 1869, has signed himself shamelessly beneath the animal's chin. More disgracefully still a large crowned eagle, deeply and professionally chiselled, commemorates the visit here of Kaiser Wilhelm, on his way to Jerusalem.

Disgraceful, and yet . . . There is something intensely moving about those mementoes, cut, all down the centuries, in the skin of so ancient a beast. I found a stone and added my own emblem (I will not tell you what), establishing my line of succession, too, to the first of all the peoples who have put ashore in Hav. Here as everywhere, one likes to lay claim to the heritage of the Greeks.

The modern Greeks of Hav certainly enjoy it. If I have been told once, I have been told a thousand times about the lost glories of the Hav acropolis, about Schliemann and Achilles, about the great Spartan assault, in the fourth century BC, whose siege-work was the still recognizable canal, and whose triumphant trophy is supposedly the Iron Dog. 'Hav is essentially a Greek city,' said the Orthodox bishop boldly when I went to see him in his palace beside the cathedral. 'It is the last of the Greek colonies along the shore of Asia Minor.' But then he is profoundly prejudiced against everything Turkish, including Turkish geography. He frequently calls the Turkish people barbarians, and once publicly declared them to be the enemies of God. I asked him if this was not playing with fire, Hav being where and what it was. He merely shrugged his brawny shoulders. 'I think what I think, I say what I say.'

Others of the Greek community are more cautious. The Greek shops and loan offices which have always proliferated in the Balad rarely announce themselves in Greek script nowadays, and many of their owners, I am told, have adopted Turkish or Arabic names. Several people important in the administration are supposed to have concealed Greek origins.

'Do you really suppose your friend Mahmoud is an Arab? Some Arab! He's no more Arab than Missakian's Armenian!'

'Missakian's not Armenian?'

'Of course not. He's pure Greek, anyone can see that, like half the people in this place who call themselves Armenian, or Jewish, or Syrian . . .'

'Dear God,' I said to Magda one day, trying to assimilate all these confusions, 'I don't think I shall ever master the meaning of Hav.'

'The meaning of Hav is easy,' she said coldly, 'it's the meaning of Greeks that's hard.'

Certainly theirs is a somewhat shadowy presence in the city. There seem to be no Greeks at the Athenaeum. I have noticed none in the bar of the Adler-Hav, or listening to the jazz at the Bristol, and there were certainly no Greek names on the roster of the roof-runners. Signora Vattani scoffs when I remark upon these facts. 'Of course there are no Greeks in *society*. Greeks are shopkeepers. You never saw a Greek in New Hav, in the old days, unless he was delivering the groceries. If you want to meet Greeks, you must go to the Balad.' But the bishop gave me different advice. 'To see the Hav Greek as he really is – to see the true Havian, in fact – you should visit San Spiridon. You have seen the Iron Dog. Now go and see the people who created it.' He himself was born on the island, and he gave me, there and then, a letter of introduction to his sister Kallonia – 'It means beautiful in our dialect,' he said, 'but I'm sorry to say she isn't.'

A ferry goes there once a day, out in the morning, back in the afternoon, so yesterday I drove to the ferry station, which is near the south-eastern extremity of peninsular Hav, and joined the islanders for the crossing. The little steam-boat was packed to its gunwales – women in black sitting on piles of their own parcels, powerful men with moustaches smoking bitter pipes, young bloods with motorbikes singing to the music of their transistors, children scampering every-where, mules, horses, brawny dogs with spiked collars, the inescapable priest in his tall black hat and a few cheerful girls in cotton frocks.

The crossing takes half an hour – the ferry-boat is elderly, the currents there, sweeping in and out of China Bay, are very strong – and by the time we had tied up at the island dock, I swear, nobody on that ship was unaware of my purposes. I could almost hear the intelligence running around those decks. 'She's a writer – Iron Dog – Greeks – Kallonia Laskaris – saw the Bishop – Kallonia – writer – Iron Dog . . .' And when we disembarked, amid a little harbour settlement of tin shacks that looked more like western Canada than eastern Mediterranean, three or four of the women, and an indeterminate number of dogs and children, guided me up the hill through the celery fields to the Laskaris house, which seemed to occupy the very centre and apex of the island.

Well, it was true, Kallonia was not very beautiful, but she was extremely kind, and in no time at all she had fixed up a lunch for me – 'just to meet a few of our people, you must get the *truth* about us in your writing'. But first she detailed her daughter Arianna, eleven years old, to show me round the island. This was not difficult. It is only about a mile round, and is speckled all over, as by pimples, with small stone houses like Kallonia's own, each with its pergola and its garden. The only village is the little ferry-port, and the church (St Spiridon's, naturally) stands all alone on an islet at the southern tip, approached by a stone causeway. There is not much else – a couple of taverns, a shop or two, a disused cinema (every house has its TV aerial). The fishing-boats were nearly all at sea just then, but when they came back, so Arianna said, each would be moored directly outside the owner's home, some at little wooden landing-stages, some in docks cut alongside the houses.

By the time we got back to the house the luncheon party was already assembled and the food was on the table beneath the pergola – smoked mullet, shrimps, tomato with fetta cheese, lots of celery, ouzo. The company, six or seven men, rather more women, greeted me courteously; the priest I had seen on the boat, the chairman of the fishing cooperative, some miscellaneous elders and their wives. Once we were settled, they tucked into their victuals in vigorous silence. They seemed to have huge appetites. 'Now you see', said the priest, 'what the Hav Greeks are really like.' In the city, he said, they had been oppressed for so long that they had lost their national characteristics, and had become subdued and inhibited. Evasive too, somebody said between mouthfuls. One would not know, seeing them in their poky shops and offices, that they were of a great seagoing race, a martial race – it was here after all that Achilles built his fortress, here that the Spartans created the Iron Dog! They had lost their gaiety, too, and their sense of comradeship – yes, and even their ancient culture, which flourished now only on San Spiridon, whereas once, all the old historians said, Hav had been a very cradle of Hellenism. Now the city Greeks had been forced into subterfuge and secrecy. 'What you see now', said the priest, waving his arms around the assembled company, who had fallen into rapt and solemn attention, 'is the Greekness of Hav as it always was – here alone, on our beloved island.'

After the meal they sang songs to me. Somebody fetched a mandolin, and some younger people began to dance on the terrace beneath the pergola, weaving an intricate, fairy-footed step. But happy and grateful though I was, well fed, well ouzo'd too, the more I watched and listened to them, somehow the less Greek those Greeks really seemed to be. There was something odd about them. Were they really Greeks at all? All the externals were there, of course, clerical beard to fetta cheese, but something else, something more profound, seemed to be wrong. Their faces did not look quite like Greek faces, ancient or modern: there was a hint of something oriental to them, just the faintest suggestion of eye and cheekbone, as in the faces pictured by the old Hav portraitists. Then their bodily shape was not quite Greek either, being stringier, or tauter, or more sinewy. Their earnest ethnic loyalties seemed to me more Arab in style than Hellenic. Their ravenous appetites surprised me. Their music sounded less like melodies of Crete or Athens than of places well to the east of us, while the performance of the dancers on the terrace began to remind me uncomfortably, in its silent, deft and expressionless zeal, of tranced dervishes!

Perhaps it was the ouzo. But when they took me down to the port to catch the ferry home I happened to mention the graffiti on the hide of the Iron Dog. Out of the corner of my eye I saw Kallonia, the bishop's sister, crossing herself like the women on the ferry.

Today I mentioned these peculiar sensations to Dr Borge, as we lunched together at the Al-Asima, in the Great Bazaar. He looked at me in a penetrating way. 'You are walking on quicksands,' he said. 'I will say no more. We cannot rewrite history. Nevertheless, when you have a moment take a look at a picture of the dragons on the Ishtar Gate at Babylon – not the lions, the dragons. See what you make of them.'

I went to the Athenaeum the moment we parted, and found a photograph of the dragons, proud but not vicious beasts, made of glazed brick, with jaunty serpents' tails and heads held high. I was none the wiser, though. I could see the resemblance, of course, to the Iron Dog, but so what? What could he mean? Magda says she has not the faintest idea. 'He's an old fraud anyway.' But the mystery of it, the strangeness of those Greeks, the presence of the Dog there, graffiti-scarred upon his headland, haunt me rather.

JUNE

British Agency

13

At the Victor's Party

I have been into the Palace, and met the Governor. A month after the Roof-Race the winner, by then assumed to have recovered from the ordeal, is honoured at a gubernatorial garden party, the Victor's Party, which is one of the great public occasions of the Hav year. It takes no great social clout to be invited, though Signora Vattani did look rather miffed when the big official envelope, stamped rather than embossed with the Governor's emblem (a Hav bear, rampant, holding a maze-mallet) plopped through our letter-box for me. Before the war, she said, she always used to go with her husband, but of course (with a sniff) everything was so different now . . .

Long before I reached the Palace gates I could hear the thump of military music over the traffic of Pendeh Square, and the party was evidently in full swing by the time I presented my invitation to the smiling sentries, and had been stentoriously announced by the footman at the door of the central salon. The Governor was there to receive his guests. 'Dirleddy, I have heard so much of your presence here. You are welcome to Hav! Allow me to introduce our guest of honour and our hero, Irfan Izmic.' Izmic looked very unlike that heap of blotched, greased and bloody flesh which had dropped from the Castle Gate four weeks before. He was in a smart tropical suit now, his hair slicked, his moustache urbanely trimmed, in his lapel the red ribbon which winners of the great contest wear until the end of their days. 'Delighted, dirleddy,' said he. 'Honoured to meet you,' said I, and so I was left, as one is left at garden parties the world over, hopefully to circulate.

I was happy enough to do so. It was a grand festivity to watch. Partly in the garden, partly in the salon beneath the chandeliers, the confused society of the peninsula milled, ambled or was clotted, offering for my contemplation a splendid cross-section of *Homo hav*. The noise was considerable. Not just the military band played, resplendent in white and scarlet in the little garden bandstand, but two other musical ensembles worked away indoors. In the blue drawing-room a piano quartet, three ladies and the urbane Chinese pianist I had last seen thumping jazz in Bar 1924, played café music with much careful turnings of pages and rhythmic noddings of heads. In the pink drawing-room a folk group of six girls and six men, dressed alike in straw hats and *gallabiyehs*, performed in penetrating quarter-tones upon flutes, lutes and tambourines.

Through these varying melodies the Havians shouted to each other in their several languages, so that as I wandered through the crowd I moved from Turkish to Arabic, from Italian to Chinese to surprisingly frequent enclaves of English – for as I have discovered from the Athenaeum, Hav intellectuals in particular love to talk English among themselves. Mahmoud was there and introduced me to his hitherto unrevealed wife, who looked like a very pretty deer, but seemed to speak no known language at all. Dr Borge was there and told me to ignore the folk-artists banging and fluting away in the other room, as they were pure phonies – 'One of these evenings I'll take you to a place I know and let you hear the real thing.' Magda, in yellow, was accompanied by a handsome-bearded black man, and who should be with Fatima (brown silk, helping herself to urchin mayonnaise from the buffet) but the stately figure of the tunnel pilot himself. 'I hear you have bought one of our old cars,' he said. 'A wise purchase. We keep them scrupulously.'

Presently the Governor adjourned with his guest of honour

to a wide divan, covered with carpets in the Turkish way, which stood just within the French windows of the salon, looking out on to the garden. There they were joined by the Governor's wife and daughter, ample ladies both, in long white dresses and small tilted hats, who draped themselves side by side at the end of the divan, slightly separate from Izmic and His Excellency, and looked to me suggestively like odalisques. In twos and threes the citizenry took their turn to wait upon this court, and were greeted I noticed with varying degrees of condescension.

When for example athletic young men, with shy young wives, went over to grasp Izmic by the shoulder or pretend to rumple his hair, the Governor was all jollity, his ladies sweet with smiles. When elderly Turkish-looking gentlemen went, without their wives, sometimes the Governor actually rose to his feet to greet them, while his ladies adjusted their skirts and all but tidied their black hair. Others seemed less graciously received. I could not hear what was said, from my peregrinating distances, but I got the impression that sometimes the exchange of courtesies was curt. The Caliph's Wazir, though greeted by formal smiles, did not last long at the divan. A group of Greeks was all but waved away, and went off laughing rather rudely among themselves. And when Chimoun the Port Captain approached the presence with his svelte and predatory wife, I thought for a moment the Governor seemed a little nervous.

Magda and her black man, each holding a plate of langoustines, pressed me to a garden bench, in the shade of a fine old chestnut, from where I could view this intriguing pageant *in toto*. From there it all looked very colourful, very charming – the splash of crimson from the band in the corner, the bright dresses and gaudy hats, the wonderfully varied wandering wardrobe of kaftans, *gallabiyehs*, white uniforms, tight-buttoned suits and ecclesiastical headgear – and in the middle, intermittently revealed to us between the comings and goings of the guests, the Governor there on his divan, with his ladies and his champion, looking now so unmistakably Levantine that I almost expected him to pull his feet up under him and sit cross-legged on his rugs.

'I suppose you are thinking,' Magda remarked, 'what a pretty scene!' and her friend laughed cynically.

'Well it *is* a pretty scene,' I replied.

'You are so innocent,' Magda said, 'for a person of your age. You cannot have travelled much, I think. You sit here smiling around you as though it is a little show. You think it is all lobsters and urchins and nice music. Believe me it is much more than that.'

'You can say that again,' said her companion idiomatically.

'This is almost the only time in the whole year', she went on, 'when all these people meet at the same time. Do you suppose they are here just to talk about the Roof-Race, or congratulate the Governor's daughter on her smart dress from Beirut? No, my friend, they're talking about very different things.'

'They're talking about money,' said the black man.

'Certainly,' said Magda, 'they're talking about money. And they're talking about power, and many other things too. They're not just here for fun. Look at them! Do they look as though they are having fun?'

They did actually, since half of them were stuffing urchins into their mouths, and many were laughing, and some were looking at the garden flowers, and others were deep in what seemed to be very absorbing gossip. But I saw what Magda meant. It was not exactly a *blithe* party. Currents I could not place, allusions I could not identify, seemed to loiter on the air. Separate little groups of people had assembled now, and appeared to have turned their backs on all the others. The longer I looked at the Governor the less he seemed like the benevolent figurehead of an idiosyncratic Mediterranean backwater, and the more like one of those spidery despots one reads about in old books of oriental travel, crouching there at the heart of his web.

'Well what d'you suppose they all *want*?' I asked.

'Ah,' said Magda sententiously, 'if we knew that, we would know the answer to life's riddles, wouldn't we?'

'That's for sure,' her friend added.

As I passed through the salon on my way out, having said my goodbyes to the divan ('Charmed, charmed,' murmured the two ladies, and the Governor bowed distractedly from the waist, being deep in talk with the Maronite archbishop), a man in well-cut sharkskin intercepted me. He was Mario Biancheri of the Casino. He had heard I was about, he said, and as we had friends in common in Venice, wondered if I would care to visit the Casino, which was difficult to enter without an introduction. 'You can drive out, of course, but it's a terrible road – you really need four-wheel drive. But if you're prepared to get up early you could come with me in the launch one morning when we return from the market. We would see that you got home again. You would be amused? Very well, signora, it's fixed.

'By the way, did you enjoy the food? We did the catering. If you are planning to do any entertaining yourself we shall be delighted to help – we need not be as expensive as we look!' And so in the end I was seen off at the door of the Palace, past the Circassian sentries, beneath the onion domes, away from the mysteries of that somewhat dream-like function, with a brisk quotation of sample prices – 'You prefer a sit-down meal? Certainly, certainly.' As I walked across the square the bands played on: thump of Souza from the garden, 'Chanson d'amour' from the blue room, and a reedy wheeze and jangle of folk melody.

14

Mystery of Mr Thorne – Hav Britannica – in spite of all temptations – luncheon at the Agency – Lawrence Sahib and the Turkish gentleman – 'very pale'

The British Agent's name is – well, I will call him Thorne. His wife's name is – well, let us say Rosa. They are the only English residents in Hav, and he is the only foreign diplomatic representative. He keeps very much to himself. He is officially invited every year, he tells me, to the Roof-Race and the Victor's Party, but has never been to either, confining himself to private contact with the Governor or the Foreign Department when the need arises, which seems to be infrequently. He is a tall thin man, very clever I think, with a high brow and the sort of nose which, without being retroussé, slopes downwards below the nostrils to the upper lip. She was at Cambridge, where she read foreign languages, and is clever too, while affecting Kurdish jewelry and sandals with heavy gold thongs. It is touted about, naturally, that Thorne is a spy-master, and that much British and American intelligence passes through his hands. Magda says he is the original of one of John Le Carré's characters, but she can't remember which.

He is a mystery, but a mystery the people of Hav seem perfectly content to ignore. From almost anywhere on the water-front you can see his fine white house above the harbour, radio aerials sprouting from the outbuildings behind, yet hardly anybody goes near the place, and it stands there apparently aloof to the life of the peninsula. It is a tantalizing relic of the brief and not very glorious Hav Britannica.

If in 1794 Nelson had obeyed his original instructions, and attacked the peninsula of Hav instead of sailing west to invest Corsica, he might never have had his eye shot out at Calvi. As it was, the British never did have to take Hav by force, for it fell into their hands peacefully under the treaty arrangements of 1815. They wanted it for strategic reasons. They were coming to see India as the true source and focus of their power, and were more and more concerned with the safety of the routes that led there. With Gibraltar already theirs, with Malta to control the central Mediterranean, the Ionians to command the Adriatic, and with Hav flying the flag away to the east, their lines of communication through the inner sea seemed to be secure.

In those days warships were small enough to make use of Hav's poor harbour, and the British promptly established a garrison, built a Residency, an Admiralty House, an Anglican church and an ice-house, and made the Protectorate of Hav and the Escarpment a proper little tight-meshed outpost of their fast coalescing empire. Many well-known imperial figures had Hav connections at one time or another. Bold General C. J. Napier, conqueror of Baluchistan, spent some months in the city reorganizing the garrison, and wrote to his wife that it was 'a dreadful hole – worse than Sind! I am sorry for the poor soldiers, but it is the price we pay for power'. The half-mad Lord Guilford, who established an Ionic university in Corfu, paid a brief spectacular visit to Hav, swathed in his usual flowing toga, to suggest a sister establishment here: it was to be called the Trojan Academy, but protests from the Sublime Porte direct to the Crown, so Guilford always claimed, put paid to the project. General Gordon was a more frequent visitor, sometimes in the course of his duties as a military engineer (he had a scheme for resuscitating the Spartan canal as a defence work), sometimes in the pursuit of Truth: just as he believed the Seychelles to be the true site of the Garden of Eden, so he was sure that Noah's Ark had really grounded on the Escarpment, and he wrote many learned papers to prove it.

Then Kinglake came of course, the then British Resident Harry Stormont having been at Eton with him; and Edward Lear painted some agreeable pictures of the castle and the Medina; and from time to time parliamentary commissions descended upon the Protectorate, as they did upon all such petty possessions, were well fed at the Residency, watched a smart parade of the 53rd Foot, and went home expressing the view that Her Majesty's interests on Hav were being diligently safeguarded. Frigates of the fleet put in sometimes. Garden parties were held on the Queen's birthday. An undistinguished succession of Residents came and went; the best known was perhaps Sir Joshua Remington, who having just escaped bankruptcy by the fortunate chance of his appointment by Lord Palmerston to the office, was lampooned by *Punch*:

> As he picked up the carver to carve,
> Said Sir, Joshua, 'We'll never starve.
> For thanks to LORD P.,
> And the powers that be,
> Whatever we haven't, we've HAV.

So for half a century the Protectorate lived the familiar life of a British overseas possession. It was not the happiest on the roster, for nearly everyone loathed it (the mosquitoes were terrible then, the drinking-water was often brackish and the food was described by Napier as being 'fit only for monkeys – if for them'). Old pictures, nevertheless, make life for the imperialists look quite bearable. We see the officers in their shakos, the ladies beneath their parasols, parading the quayside outside the Fondaco, admiring the view through telescopes from Katourian's Place, or enjoying *fêtes-champêtres* in the then empty western hills. Here in stilted sepia photographs Chinese women in wide coolie hats sell them silks and souvenirs ('Buying keepsakes in the Protectorate'), and here a visiting cricket team, very stiff at the wicket, extremely alert in the field, plays the officers of the garrison on the green outside St George's Church.

Cricket continued to be played in Hav long after the end of the Protectorate; some of the Russians took it up, and as late as 1912 we read of a match between Prince Bronsky's XI and a team from Corfu. A few other British legacies died hard, too. The honorific 'Dirleddy' has been inherited, I take it, from the etiquette of the Victorian empire-builders. The version of '*Chant de doleure pour li proz chevalers qui sunt morz*' played by Missakian nowadays was arranged by a garrison bandmaster. Not only the cows and mongooses, but all the Indians one sees in Hav are migrants of the Pax Britannica – they came originally as servants and camp-followers. A few places have kept their British names – China Bay, The Hook, Pyramid Rock, the triangular rock which rises out of the sea off little Yalta – and a few reactionaries still like to call the Balad 'Blacktown'.

Most of the meagre monuments of British Hav may still be identified. Westminster never put much money into the place, so that the buildings were mostly ferry-built and second-rate, but still in one form or another they have survived, their origins generally long forgotten. The Residency thrives still as the Agency – the name was adopted by agreement with the Russians in 1875, and British consuls in Hav have called themselves Agents ever since. The Anglican church however, its steeple knocked off, is now used for the storage of oil drums by the Greek fishermen, while the open space in front of it, where they used to play cricket, is now one of the market truck parks (and I have found no trace of the tombstone, mentioned in several imperial memoirs, of the officer who, 'having recently achieved his Captaincy in the Royal Engineers, Left this Station to Report to the Commander of a yet greater Corps . . .').

If you look closely at the barrack block between the Palace and the old legations you will see that its southern wing was verandahed in the Anglo-Indian manner, until the Russians stripped it of its iron-work, and the former Admiralty House, at the southern end of the Lazaretto, is now the agreeable if decrepit restaurant of the pleasure-park. As for the ice-house which stood on the eastern quay, Count Kolchok turned it into a private retreat, in whose cool chambers, if we are to believe the gossip, he often enjoyed himself with the dancer Naratlova; but it was demolished when they built the promenade of New Hav.

And one British commercial concern, out of several which made their modest fortunes from the Hav connection, is active to this day. One morning I walked into the offices of Butterworth and Sons, World-Wide Preferential Shipping Tariffs, and asked if there was actually a Mr Butterworth. Certainly there was, they said, Mr Mitko Butterworth – would I care to meet him? And there he was, the last living representative, one might say, of the Protectorate of Hav and the Escarpment – a swarthy man in his thirties, shirtsleeved below his swirling electric fan, with large gold cuff-links and round wire spectacles. Yes, he said, he was the great-great-grandson, he thought, of the Oswald Butterworth who had, in 1823, followed the flag to Hav and set up his shipping agency in that very office within the Fondaco.

Oswald had hoped, he told me, to make Hav once more the great entrepôt for the whole of the Levant trade, perhaps even the Russian trade, as British contemporaries were even then making Hong Kong the chief outlet for the wealth of China. That had never happened, but still the Butterworths had moderately prospered, outlived their several competitors, and become so much a part of Hav life that they had successfully ridden out all subsequent ebbs and flows of political circumstance.

And did he feel himself, I wondered, to be British still? He shrugged and laughed. 'When it suits me to feel British, I feel British, but it is very seldom. And rather hard. Work it out yourself. Oswald Butterworth married a Bulgarian, and there has been no new British blood in the Butterworth family since then. What am I – one thirty-secondth British?' And to my astonishment, for it seemed altogether out of character, he burst into loud song:

'In spite of all temptations,
To belong to other nations,
I remain one thirty-secondth of an E-e-e-e-nglishman!'

When Mr Thorne invited me to lunch, which he called tiffin, at the former Residency, I mentioned Mr Butterworth and his improbable command of Gilbert and Sullivan. 'Yes, I've heard about him,' the Agent said without a smile, 'but he's not a British subject. There are no British subjects here. There may be some Maltese, but they are no longer our responsibility. I have never met this Butterworth.'

'Perhaps we should invite him out, darling?' said Rosa. 'He sounds amusing.'

'I think not,' replied the Agent.

We were sitting in considerable, but somehow dullened splendour. The house was recognizably an Anglo-Indian villa, translated here from the banks of the Hooghly, but had long lost its imperial panache. The big mahogany table was handsome, but scuffed here and there. The silver was handsome too, but might have been better polished. The Indian manservant who waited on us wore a white jacket not exactly dirty, but sort of grey-looking. We ate fish with Hav cabbage, and drank white wine which I suspect to have been Cypriot. I was the only guest. 'How nice', said Rosa, 'to see a new face. Isn't it nice, Ronald?'

'Very nice,' said Mr Thorne.

Around us on the walls were portraits of the men who had presided over the Hav Protectorate from that house – florid, well-fed Britons every one, lavishly splayed with insignia of various orders, and sometimes in military uniform. The Agent identified them all for me – 'General Ricks who made something of a fool of himself in the Crimea, Sir Joshua Remington who became Lord Remington of Hav – you may know the limerick, 'Whatever we haven't we've Hav?' – Harry Stormont who was something of an artist, we have one of his paintings in the library in fact, and Sir Roland Triston, and Sir Henry Walton-Vere, the only Anglo-Indian of the lot, surprisingly enough, and Lord Hevington, and General Stockingham, and . . .'

I had hardly heard of any of them, and my mind wandered rather during this recital, concentrating instead on the fish, which was good but bony. What *were* we doing there, the Agent, his Rosa and I, eating mullet at the rubbed mahogany table from Calcutta, recalling the ineptitudes of General Ricks at Sebastopol, drinking wine we should not be drinking, in that queer little alien enclave above teeming and tumultuous Hav?

After lunch we sat on the verandah, among pots of flowering ferns, looking down to the harbour below us, where one of the salt-ships was just rounding the Hook, and the Electric Ferry was slowly crossing the gap between the Lazaretto and San Pietro. I said it reminded me of Sydney. Rosa said it reminded her of the Helston River. Mr Thorne said of course the British never did quite know where they were in Hav. Sometimes they thought of it as an extension of India, sometimes as an outpost of Constantinople – 'We still call our waiters "bearers" but our watchmen "dragomans", and they always call me Sahib. "Rivers of history", one might say. You remember the quotation? No matter.'

I had heard something interesting of the house. I had heard that in 1913, when T. E. Lawrence, Lawrence of Arabia, was engaged on an archaeological excavation in Mesopotamia, he had met here the young Turkish officer Mustafa Kemal, later to be known as Attaturk. And it is said that this secret meeting between the Oxford don, who was a British agent, and the most formidable of the Young Turks was to have an incalculable influence upon the course of the First World War and the post-war settlement; for Attaturk is supposed to have promised that he would use his influence within the Turkish army to allow the Arab revolt, already germinating in British minds as well as Arab ones, so to succeed that in future years British influence would be paramount in the Middle East. As it turned out, Attaturk was the very Turkish commander who allowed the forces of the Arabs, under British patronage, to capture Damascus, thus ensuring British suzerainty in those parts for another forty years: if the story is true, then the white Agency above the harbour of Hav played a clandestine role of enormous significance in the history of the British Empire, of Israel, and of the world between the wars.

'I dare say', Mr Thorne was saying, 'that you may think the survival of this Agency an anachronism. Some of my colleagues do. But our duties here have always been specialized. We are an independent window, as it were, upon the eastern Levant. Here in Hav we can make contacts denied to diplomatic missions in places closer to the mainstream. I would not like you to go away with the impression that we are merely idle lotus-eaters – that's what Kinglake called Stormont, you know, the Resident, in his time – "a plump and idle lotus-eater".'

'No, plump we may be,' interjected Rosa, who is, 'but idle certainly not. Lucky old Stormont hadn't got a radio link, had he?'

The conversation moved on, by way of Wales and the British monarchy, to the subject of 24 Residenzstrasse. 'I hope you don't believe all the bizarre things they say about it,' said Mr Thorne quite crossly. 'Von Tranter was as thorough a Nazi as anyone else, I can assure you, and worked hand-in-glove with von Papen throughout the war. Putting up that plaque was a disgrace. As for the poppycock about Hitler coming to Hav, believe me, if he had ever been within a hundred miles of this Agency, he would never have got home alive.'

It seemed a good moment, as we appeared to have entered cloak-and-dagger territory, to raise the story of Lawrence and Attaturk. This was evidently unwelcome. 'Lawrence did come to this house,' said the Agent, in a formal tone of voice, 'but the visit was purely private. He came as the guest of the then Agent, a somewhat eccentric man called Winchester, the first man in Hav, as a matter of fact, to ride a motorcycle. His interest was in the barrow-graves of the salt-marsh, at that time supposed to be Minoan, now known to be troglodytic. He stayed some ten days, and then proceeded overland to his dig in Iraq. Anything else you may have heard', said Mr Thorne conclusively, 'is totally unfounded.' Thus on a detectably minatory note the Agent's hospitality came to an end, and with 'So lovely to see a new face' from Rosa, and 'You must come again some time' from Mr Thorne – 'how long did you say you were staying?' – I was shown to my car and waved fairly perfunctorily down the drive.

Hardly was I around the corner and in the shrubbery, out of sight of the house, when an elderly man in green *gallabiyeh* and turban urgently signalled me to stop. 'Excuse me, memsahib,' he said, 'I am head dragoman here. Bearer says you ask about Lawrence Pasha – I tell you truth now. My father was dragoman here then, and he remembered visit of Lawrence Pasha very well. Now I tell you, *at same time Turkish gentleman stayed in this house*. Mr Thorne not tell you that I think. British prefer to forget that. But my father remember very well, and he knew who that Turkish gentleman was, *he knew* . . . He remembered very clearly, and many times he described to us Lawrence Pasha riding Winchester Sahib's motorcycle up and down this drive. He never rode motorcycle before, but very fast he rode, very very fast, very dangerous and once, my father said, that Turkish gentleman went for ride on back seat of motorbike, and when they came back to this house he was very pale.'

I have asked several people at the Athenaeum what they know of the Lawrence story, but they do not seem very interested, just as they see nothing to be wondered at in the fact that the fishermen's oil store used to be an English church, and seem indifferent to the presence of the white house with its radio masts above the harbour. 'All I want from Britain is the Beatles,' Magda said to me one day: for their tastes in Western music are years behind the times.

15

*To Casino Cove – dreaming? – a call from Dodo – hard and
steely – Solveig and the champagne – a remarkable menu*

It was the loveliest of pearly mornings, all warm and still, the
sea as calm as urchin soup, the castle shimmering in the warm
sun behind us, when Mario Biancheri, his Chinese henchmen
and I scudded away from the market quay on the day of my
initiation into Casino Cove.

Nothing else was moving on the water, but all around us, as
we swept in a wide showy curve from the waterfront, the city
was awakening. The first traffic was just entering Pendeh
Square, on the New Hav promenade somebody was doing cal-
listhenics, and the gardener was already up and about in the
flower-beds of the British Agency. At the coal wharf a coaster
was unloading in a haze of sooty dust. I sat in the stern of the
boat, and thought that Hav had never looked so lovely – gone
all its seediness, all its decay, from this perspective, on such a
morning! Round the Hook we swept, and the hills rose green
and fresh on either side, and under the Conveyor Bridge,
whose platform was swinging, entirely untenanted except for
the captain, from one tower to the other – and there was the
Iron Dog glaring down at us from the headland, and before us
the open sea, veiled in a thin morning haze, stretched away to
Cyprus and distant Africa.

It looked an entirely open sea – as so often, Hav felt utterly
alone in the world. But when we had rounded the southern
point, passed through the San Spiridon channel, and entered

the wide declivity called China Bay, busy life began to show – and life altogether separate from that of the city we had left behind us. It was like entering a different ocean. There were scores of Chinese fishing-craft about, their crews grimly working at nets or riggings. There were marker buoys everywhere, and schools of those apparently abandoned boats, silently bobbing, which give a particular mystery to every Chinese shore. Sometimes Biancheri waved at the fishermen, but they responded only in an abstracted Chinese way: once our helmsman shouted something, but nobody answered.

Straggling over its hillocks now I could see Yuan Wen Kuo, brown and huddled, and then we were around the next point, and before us on a tight little cove, hemmed about by steep cliffs, thickly greened by woods, half-obscured by the masts and upperworks of a dozen large yachts, stood the buildings of the Casino. They did not look like Hav at all. They were low, and pink-washed, and had pale tiled roofs, and seemed to breathe, even at that distance, the very *numen* of immense wealth. Biancheri caught my eye and made a face, wry, amused, half apologetic, implying 'Well, there we are, for what it's worth . . .' I shouted a response above the din of the engines. 'Breakfast should be good,' I said.

Breakfast was. The hotel was still asleep, so Biancheri and I ate alone upon the wide restaurant verandah, with its yellow-cushioned furniture, its bright flowering plants, its apparently numberless and weightless Chinese servants, the yachts gleaming across the lawn and the lovely cove beyond. Biancheri laughed to see me, as the steaming coffee arrived with corn-flakes and Oxford marmalade. 'You think you are dreaming? But there's no *Times*! What a shame! We must complain to the management!'

Presently the management joined us, in the elegantly suited and delicately after-shaved person of Monsieur Tomas Cheval-laz, a Swiss, he told me, who had worked in his time at the Mandarin Hong Kong, the Connaught in London and 'a pub of my own at home'. The Hav Casino, he told me, was quite different from them all. It was unique. Since its beginnings in the late 1920s it had never had to advertise – all was by word of mouth, or by inheritance. Now it was a private club, and as old Pierpont Morgan remarked about the owning of steam-yachts, if you had to ask how much it cost, you couldn't afford it. 'In the twelve years I have managed this place, I can remember only about a dozen of our guests who did *not* arrive on their own yachts.'

He identified some of the boats lying there below us – this one a Spanish industrialist's, that one a shipowner's, another the matrimonially disputed property of an American actor – and by now a few of the guests were trickling on to the terrace for their breakfasts. Most of them slept very late, Chevallaz said, having been up most of the night at the gaming tables; and some of them, as everyone knew, preferred to sleep the sleep narcotic, which is why he would be grateful if I did not mention present guests by name – 'In Hav nobody minds, it is when they get home to their boardrooms . . .'

Those who did appear looked anything but drugged. They were the lean, lithe kind, smooth-tanned, and had probably already played a game of tennis, or been swimming, or at least gone for a jog through the trees. They all seemed to know each other intimately, and exchanged greetings across the tables in variously accented English – 'You're looking rather terrific' – 'My dear, I had a call from Dodo,' or, 'Kurt says he's never going to eat urchins again.' They seemed to me nationless and quite timeless. They might have been from any decade of our century, or earlier. They were the stuff of Carlsbad, Newport, Monte Carlo in the thirties, even Hav itself in the days of the Russians. 'Have you heard from Scott?' they asked each other. '*What* a pity Otto isn't here!'

'You see,' said Chevallaz as we walked over the sprinkled lawns to his office, 'our clients are different from others. They cannot fly to Hav. They can hardly drive. They would be mad to come by train. They can really only come in their own ships, or their friends' ships, and that's what makes them feel like rich people from other times. You are quite right. And when they are here, here they stay. As you know, they're not encouraged to take their yachts into the city harbour, where they'd probably sink, and it's a frightful track over the cliffs here. Why move? I doubt if one of our guests in a thousand ever goes into the city, and we much prefer it that way.'

All around his office were portraits of the Casino's famous guests. There were kings, statesmen, authors, bankers, actresses, great ladies of the social circuit. There was Noël Coward – 'To dear André – happy days!' – and there was Hemingway in a bush shirt – 'To Hav . . . ?' Coco Chanel was fuzzed and misty, in the photographic style of the day. Maurice Chevalier was wearing his boater. Winston Churchill painted on the beach. Thomas Mann looked haggard. And no, could it be – ? 'Yes, I'm afraid so, though I'm not sure he ought to be there. He is supposed to have come to Hav, you know, secretly during the war, and legend says he was picked up by a U-boat at the cove here. We don't know the truth, but my predecessor hung the picture there anyway. I'm often told I should remove it, but I don't know . . . he's not the only villain on the wall.'

His mother loved him anyway, I suggested. 'In that case he did *not* come here,' Biancheri said. 'Nobody who comes to the Hav Casino ever had a mother.' It is clearly not a place rich in the milk of human kindness, and as we wandered around that morning, from pool to solarium, from kitchens to gambling rooms, something very hard and steely seemed to impregnate the air. Almost everyone who works at the Cove is Chinese, and the responses we got from the staff were taciturn, just as the buildings themselves, fitted out in every last degree of luxury, seemed nevertheless devoid of comfort. Above the roulette tables Chevallaz showed me the hidden mirrors and monitors which ensure that the billionaires below do not cheat (not that any of them try – they are much too clever for that). In the restaurant he showed me the one-way mirrors behind which less exhibitionist celebrities prefer to dine – seeing but unseen.

Wherever we went young Chinese in olive-green fatigues seemed to be prowling around holding night-sticks. 'Please don't ask me', said Chevallaz, 'if they have guns too.' Security, he said, was one of his chief headaches, especially as so many of his guests brought their own bodyguards too – 'See that guy over there?' – and leaning against the wall of one of the bungalows was a tall heavy man in white tennis gear, holding a walkie-talkie and looking distinctly bulged around the hips. There had been sufficient mayhem at the Cove in its time, Chevallaz said – did I know about the Tiananmen affair? No? Ah well, it was a subject he preferred to stay clear of anyway. 'I'm only an employee, and I like my job.'

And who were his employers? Oh, the same Chinese syndicate, *mutatis mutandis*, that had founded the Casino back in the 1920s. All the money was Chinese – well, almost all – he had heard some European money had slid in, one way or another, after the war. And the Hav government – it had no share? Better not know, he implied.

'*Jan*, my dear,' came a loud deep voice from a patio. It was Solveig, a Swedish actress of my acquaintance, so Chevallaz left us together – 'I'll send coffee over,' he said.

'Jan, how amazing, of all people! You're alone? God, I wish I were, but you know how Eric is, he's so terribly friendly with everyone, and here we are stuck in this absurd place.'

'You don't like it?'

'Darling, how could one? It's absurd, obscene. Nothing but millionaires and Chinese people everywhere, and gambling – you know I hate gambling. I suppose you're living in some delicious garret somewhere. You *are* lucky. Sit down at once, sit here, tell me everything!'

I told her about Signora Vattani and my apartment in New Hav, and about the harbour, and the onion-domed Serai, and the snow raspberries, and Missakian's trumpet, and the Athenaeum, and Brack and Kretev. How absolutely perfect, she cried, she could hardly wait to see it all for herself. How could she get into Hav? Well, I said, I supposed she could get hold of a jeep or something to get her up the cliff track, and down the edge of the salt-marsh, and through the Balad; or alternatively she might persuade Signor Biancheri to take her on the market launch, though that meant getting up at about three in the morning.

At that moment the coffee arrived, together with a bunch of fresh roses, a bottle of champagne and a bowl of fruit. 'When you have enjoyed your coffee,' said a note in Chevallaz's fastidious hand, 'I hope you will drink my health in something a little stronger.' Tacitly we abandoned Solveig's visit to Hav.

'What a marvellous man Chevallaz is,' she said.

'Marvellous,' I agreed, 'and he knows his business, too.'

'There is somebody else here you may know,' said Biancheri, showing me into the bar, and sure enough, the moment I saw the face of the head barman, I remembered him from Venice. Seeing his bitter-sweet smile there, reaching across the bar to shake his hand, gave me a most curious sense of *déjà vu*. And when I looked around the cramped but indefinably expensive little saloon, too, all seemed creepily familiar to an old habituée of Harry's Bar: the same sorts of faces, the same loud talk, the same confident laughter, the same weather-eye on the door to see if anyone who matters is coming in. 'But not,' said Biancheri, joining me with a gin-fizz in a corner of the room – 'not *altogether* the same food that you are accustomed to get from Ciprianis. I think you will agree that our restaurant menu is something a little different.' He was right. Could there be such a menu, I wondered, anywhere else on earth? Not only were there the old stalwarts of classical French and Italian cooking – not only the inescapable pigeons' breasts and raw mushrooms of the cuisine nouvelle – not only roast beef for traditionalists, jellied duck for Sinophiles, bortsch for nostalgia, couscous, pumpkin pie – there was also a fascinating selection of Hav specialities.

You could eat sea-urchins grilled, meunière, baked, stewed, in batter, with ginger garnish, as a pâté, in an omelette, in a soup or raw. You could eat roast kid in the escarpment style, which meant cold with a herb-flavoured mayonnaise, or barbecued over catalpa charcoal from the western hills. You could eat the legs of frogs from the salt-marshes, which are claimed to have a flavour like no others, or Hav eels, which are pickled in rosemary brine, or the pink-coloured mullet which is said to be unique to these waters, and which the Casino likes to serve smoked with dill sauce, or the tall sweet celery which grows on the island of the Greeks, or a salad made entirely, in the inexplicable absence of lettuce anywhere on the peninsula, of wild grasses and young leaves gathered every morning in the hills above Yuan Wen Kuo. You could even eat a dish, otherwise undefined, listed as *ours hav faux*.

This was only a joke, said Biancheri, though in the 1920s Hav bear really was eaten sometimes at the Casino. Now the false bear was no more than a bear-shaped duck terrine. 'But then,' he added, 'it is all a joke. For myself I prefer scrambled eggs.'

I did not stay for lunch, anyway. As the hungrier plutocrats began to drift out of the bar towards the restaurant, Biancheri walked down with me to the waiting launch, where the boatswain started up his engines as he saw us approaching, and the deckhand untied the hawser to push off. 'You will find something to sustain you on the way home', said Biancheri, 'in the after cabin': and so as we splashed and sprayed our way back to Hav I sat in the stern like Waring, laughing, and eating bread, cheese, apples and Greek celery, washed down with ice-cold retsina. The Chinese bowed soundlessly when I stepped ashore beneath the Fondaco.

16

Hav and the maze – artistic cross-breeding – on poetry – on pictures – on music – Avzar Melchik – honouring an emblem

You may wonder what a maze-mallet is, such as appears in the paws of the bear on the Governor's emblem, and why a maze should be configured on the fretwork of the House of the Chinese Master. Forgive me. The maze is so universal a token of Hav, appears so often in legends and artistic references of all kinds, that one comes to take it for granted.

The idea of the maze has always been associated with Hav. The first reference to a Hav maze-maker comes in Pliny, who says the greatest master of the craft 'lived in the peninsula called by the people of those parts Hav, which some say means the place of summer, but others the place of confusions'. An ancient tradition says that the great labyrinth of Minoan Crete, in whose bowels the Minotaur lived, was made not by Daedalus, as the Greeks had it, but by the first and greatest of the Hav maze-makers, Avzar, who was kidnapped from the peninsula and blinded when his work was done: it is perhaps this remote fable that encouraged archaeologists, for many years, to suppose a Minoan connection in Hav, and to claim traces of Cretan design in the fragmentary remains of its acropolis.

Later it used to be said that the whole of the salt-flats, with their mesh of channels, conduits and drying-basins, were originally nothing more than a gigantic maze, fulfilling some obscure ritual purpose, and of course it has been repeatedly suggested that the caves of the Kretevs, which have never been scientifically explored, are not really caves at all, but only the visible entrances of an artificial labyrinth riddling the whole escarpment. How proper it seemed to Russian romantics, that the Hav tunnel should spiral upon itself so mazily within the limestone mass!

There is an innocuous little maze of hedges and love-seats in the Governor's garden, and one or two are rumoured to be hidden within the courtyard walls of houses in the Medina. Otherwise there are no Hav mazes extant, and for that matter none historically confirmable from the past. Yet the spirit of the maze has always fascinated the people of Hav, and the tokens of the maze-maker, as they have been fancifully transmitted down the ages, are inescapable in the iconography of the city: the mallet, with which Avzar at the beginning of time beat his iron labyrinth into shape, the honeycomb which is seen as a natural type of the maze, the bull-horns which are doubtless a vestige of the supposed Minoan link.

Some scholars go further, and say that the conception of the maze has profoundly affected the very psyche of Hav. It certainly seems true that if there is one constant factor binding the artistic and creative centuries together, it is an idiom of the impenetrable. The writers, artists and musicians of this place, though they have included few native geniuses, have seldom been obvious or conventional. They have loved the opaque more than the specific, the intuitive more than the rational. Pliny said they wrote in riddles, and declared their sculptures to be like nothing so much as lumps of coral. Manet on the other hand, visiting Hav as a young man in 1858, wrote to his mother: 'I feel so much at home in this city, among these people, whose vision is so much less harsh than that of people in France, and whose art looks as though it has been gently smudged by rain, or blurred by wood-smoke.'

For myself I suspect this lack of edge has nothing to do with mazes, but is a result of Hav's ceaseless cross-fertilization down the centuries. Hardly has one manner of thought, school of art, been absorbed than it is overlaid by another, and the result, as Manet saw, is a general sense of intellectual and artistic pointillism – nothing exact, nothing absolute, for better or for worse. You can see it at the museum in the folk-art of the peninsula, which is a heady muddle of motifs Eastern and Western, realist and symbolical, practical and mystically unexplained; and you can see it all around you in the architecture.

The Arab buildings of Hav, for instance, were less purely Arab than any others of their age. It was not just a matter of incorporating classical masonries into their buildings, as often happened elsewhere: the Corinthian columns of Hav's Grand Mosque were made by the Arabs themselves, and on many of the tall merchant houses of the Medina you may see classical pilasters and even architraves, besides innumerable eaves and marble embellishments, derived from the House of the Chinese Master. The one great Chinese building in the peninsula is a mish-mash of architectural allusions. The British built their Residency as if they were in India. And we have seen already with what adaptive flair architects Schröter and Huhn, when the time came, mixed their metaphors of Hav. It is the way of the place – "rivers of history"! You remember the quotation?

Very early in Hav's history the arts began to show symptoms of cultural confusion. 'The language of these people,' Marco Polo wrote, 'which is generally that of the Turks, contains also words and phrases of unknown origin, peculiar to hear.' They were, linguists have only recently come to realize, words of the troglodytic language, a fragile offshoot of the Celtic.

The earliest known poet of Hav was the Arab Rahman ibn Muhammed, 'The Song-Bird', who lived in the thirteenth century: in his work occur words, inflexions, ideas and even techniques (including the alliterative device called *cynghanedd*) which seem to show that in those days a Celtic poetic tradition was still very much alive in this peninsula. It has even been lately suggested that Rahman may have been in touch with his

contemporary on the far side of Europe, the Welsh lyric bard
Dafydd ap Gwilym. Here in Professor Morris David's translation are some lines from the Song-Bird's poem 'The Grotto':

> Ah, what need have we of mosque
> Or learned imam,
> When into the garden of our delights
> Flies the sweet dove of Allah's mercy
> With her call to prayer?

And here in my own translation is part of Dafydd ap Gwilym's
poem 'Offeren y Llwyn', 'The Woodland Mass':

> There was nothing there, by great God
> Anything but gold for the chancel roof . . .
> And the eloquent slim nightingale,
> From the corner of the grove nearby,
> Wandering poetess of the valley, rang to the multitude
> The Sanctus bell, clear its trill,
> And raised the Host
> As far as the sky . . .

Coincidence? Or perhaps, more probably than actual communication between the two poets, some empathy of tempera-
ment and tradition. Celtic words had disappeared from the
Hav poetic vocabulary by the seventeenth century, but still the
poet Gamal Misri was writing of the natural world in a way
quite unknown among other Muslim poets of the day, and
dealing with religious matters in idioms astonishingly close to
those of his contemporaries far away on the western Celtic
fringe – idioms that would have cost him dear in Egypt, Persia
or Iraq. This is his startling evocation of the Attributes of
Allah, again in David's version:

> He can see as doth the Telescope, to the furthest Stars.
> He knows of the ways of man as the Compass knoweth
>   the Pole.
> He doth create Gold from Dross as doth the Alchemist,

> And as the great Advocate doth argue for us before the
> Courts of Eternity . . .

Visual artists, too, even in the great days of Islamic Hav, did
not hesitate to risk the disapproval of the faithful by painting
living portraits – not simply stylized representations, such as
you find in Persian miniatures, but formal portraits of real people, sitting to be painted as they would in the West. The so-called
Hav-Venetian school of painting, which flourished throughout
the sixteenth century, was unique, producing the only such
genre in the Islamic world, and there are no examples of its
work outside Hav. Even in the city they are very rare. A few
are thought to be in private hands, but the only specimens on
public display are five hanging in the former chapel of the
Palace, which is open to the public at weekends. They are very
strange. Large formal oil-paintings of merchants and their
wives, dressed in the Venetian style but looking unmistakably
Havian with their rather Mongol cheeks and hard staring eyes,
their painters are unknown, and they are signed simply with
illegible ciphers and the Islamic date. They are hardly, I think,
great works of art. They look as though they have been painted by not terribly gifted oriental pupils at the atelier of
Veronese, say, being very rich in colour and detail (pet terriers,
mirrors, the House of the Chinese Master in one background,
the harbour islands in another) but queerly lifeless in effect. I
suspect myself that the artists were Chinese; for they remind
me of paintings done for European clients in Canton in the
eighteenth century, though their technique is far more sophisticated and their subjects are altogether more sumptuous. The
Havians are immensely proud of them, and forbid their copy-
ing or reproduction – but that may be only a relic of the days
when their very existence was kept a secret, lest Islamic zealots
harm them.

I really do not think Havians excel at the musical art. They are
adept enough at Western forms, and addicted to Arabic pop,

but the indigenous kinds seem to me less than thrilling. Dr Borge was as good as his word, and took me last week to the 'place he knew', which turned out to be a dark café in one of those morose unpaved streets of the Balad, between the railway line and the salt-flats. Here, he said, the very best of Hav folk-music was to be heard. The night we went the performers were a particular kind of ensemble called *hamshak*, 'sable', because they specialized in elegiac music, and this made for a melancholy evening. They were all men, dressed in hooded monk-like cloaks supposed to be derived from the habits of Capuchin confessors who came here with the Crusaders. Their instruments were rather like those of the folk-music group at the Victor's Party, only more so: reedier, wheezier, janglier still, and given extra density by two drummers beating drums made of furry animal skins ('Hav bear skins,' said Dr Borge, '– no, I am only joking'). We drank beer, we ate grilled fish with our fingers, and through the sombre light of the place the music beat at us. Sometimes, apparently without pattern, one or another of the musicians broke into a sad falsetto refrain ('Reminiscent isn't it', said the young doctor, 'of *cante hondo*?'). Sometimes, in the Arab way, the music suddenly stopped altogether and there was a moment of utter silence before the whole band erupted once more in climactic unison.

It was more interesting than enjoyable. It *was* rather like *cante hondo*, having sprung I suppose from the same musical roots. But the clatter of the tambourines and the clash of the cymbals reminded me irresistibly of Chinese music, such as one endures during the long awful hours of the Beijing Opera, while the plaintive notes of the flutes seem to come from some other culture entirely. Could it be, I wondered, that in Hav music, as in Hav medieval poetry, some dim Celtic memory is at work? Anything was possible, the Philosopher said; and when after the performance I put the same question to the band leader, a suitably cadaverous man with an Abraham Lincoln beard, his eyes lit up in a visionary way. 'Often I feel it', he said, 'like something very cold out of the long ages' – a sufficiently convincing phrase, I thought, to catch his inspiration's meaning.

Out of the long ages certainly comes the genius of Avzar Melchik, the best-known Hav writer of the twentieth century, whose personality I can most properly use to cap this brief digression into criticism. If there is nothing overtly Celtic in his work, there is much that is undeniably mazy – even the given name he adopted, you may notice, is that of the great maze-man of legend.

Melchik, who died in 1955 (the year in which he was tipped as a likely rival to Haldór Laxness for the Nobel Literature Prize), wrote in Turkish and in French and sometimes in both at the same time, alternating passages and even sentences between the languages. He was never in the least Europeanized, though – Armand dismisses him as a mere provincial – and his novels, if you can call them novels, are all set in Hav. They are powerful evocations of the place, through which there wander insubstantial characters, figures of gossamer, drifting for ever through the Old City's alleys or along the waterfront. Melchik so detested the invention of New Hav that he refused to recognize its existence in his art, and though his stories are set in the 1940s and 1950s, the Hav that they inhabit is essentially Count Kolchok's Hav, giving them all a haunting sense of overlap.

There is no doubt that Melchik was obsessed by the idea of the maze. Every one of his books is really its diagram. But in his most famous work, and the only one widely known in the West, he turns the conception inside out. *Bağlılık* ('Dependence') is the tale of a woman whose life, very gently and allusively described, is a perpetual search not for clarity but for complexity. She feels herself to be vapidly self-evident, her circumstances banal, and so she deliberately sets out to entangle herself. But when at last she feels she is released from her simplicities – has reached the centre of the maze in fact – she finds to her despair that her last state is more prosaic than her first.

Soon after finishing *Bağlılık* Melchik died. He was unmarried, and lived a life of supreme simplicity himself in a small wooden house, hardly more than a hut, on the edge of the Balad. It is now kept up as a little shrine, with the writer's pens still on his desk, his coat still hanging behind the door, and beside the china wash-basin, for all the world as though he has just been called into another room, the copy of Pascal's *Pensées* which he is said to have been reading on the last day of his life. An elderly woman acts as caretaker, paid by the Athenaeum, and told me when I visited the house that she felt the shade of Melchik ever-present there. 'When I make myself a cup of coffee in the kitchen, I often feel I should make one for him too.'

'And do you like this ghost?'

She thought for a moment before she replied. 'Have you been to his grave?' she asked. 'Perhaps that will answer the question for you.'

So I went there. Melchik was a Maronite Christian, and he is buried in the Maronite cemetery behind the power station. His grave is not hard to find – it stands all by itself at the northern corner within a hedge of prickly pears. You can see nothing of it, though, so formidable is this surrounding barrier, until you are within a few feet: and then you find it to be, not a slab, or a cross, or an obelisk, but a twisted mass of iron, like a half-unravelled ball of metallic wool, mounted on a stone slab with the single word 'MELCHIK' just visible within the tangle. He designed it himself.

I saw what the caretaker meant. Could one exactly *like* such a spirit? Nothing, I thought, so cut-and-dried: but even there, all the same, where Melchik was represented only by those crude bold letters within the meshed and worried metal, I felt his presence burning.

Few places, I must say, honour their emblems more loyally than Hav honours its generic and imaginary maze. This city may not look especially labyrinthine, but behind its façades, I am coming to realize, beneath its surfaces bold, bland or comical, there lie a myriad passages unrevealed. Perhaps even the subterranean short cuts of the Roof-Race enthusiasts are only allegorical really!

Of course all cities have their hidden themes and influences – New York has its Mob, Rome its Christian Democrats, London its Old Boy Network, Singapore its Triads, Dublin its Republican Army, all working away there, out of sight and generally out of thought, to determine the character of the place. The unseen forms of Hav, though, seem to me harder to define than any, so vague are they, so insidious, and I find it difficult to enunciate the feeling this is beginning to leave in my mind. It is a tantalizing and disquieting sensation. It is rather like the taste you get in the butter, if it has been close to other foods in the refrigerator; or like the dark calculating look that cats sometimes give you; or the sudden silence that falls when you walk into a room where they are talking about you; or like one of those threadbare exhausting dreams that have you groping through an impenetrable tangle of time, space and meaning, looking for your car keys.

JULY

Castle Gate, Medina

17

Summer – exiles – Freud – Anastasia – going native – varied refugees – meeting a Nazi – 'and me!'

High summer is on us, and I see why the British loathed the Protectorate so. 'Oh what a foretaste of hell this is,' poor Napier wrote home to his wife, and he was accustomed to the miseries of Karachi. It is not merely that Hav is hot – it is no hotter than anywhere else in the eastern Mediterranean – nor even that it is particularly humid. The trouble is an oppressive sensation of enclosure, a dead-end air, which can make one feel horribly claustrophobic.

They say the suicide rate is high, and I am not surprised. When I look out from my terrace now the citizenry below looks all but defeated – prostrate on park benches, or shuffling dejectedly along the pavements beneath floppy straw hats and parasols. Out in the Balad, where there are no trees, and not much greenery either, it is far worse; the dust lies thickly in those pot-holed streets, the shacks with their iron roofs are like ovens, and the people sprawl about like so many corpses, beneath shelters rigged up of poles and old canvas.

There is no air-conditioning in Hav, except at the Casino (and perhaps a few very rich houses of Medina and Yuan Wen Kuo). We depend still upon revolving fans, upon wind towers, upon the shades and awnings which now cover every window, and in the Palace at least, upon electrically operated punkahs – huge sheets of tasselled canvas waving ponderously about to stir a little fitful breeze through the stifling salons. Those massed fans are twirling desperately now beneath the high ceilings of the Serai, but even so, Hav being Hav, many of the more senior clerks take all their files into the gardens, and are to be seen scattered over the brown dry grass with their documents spread around them and thermos flasks close to hand. Signora V. spends most of the day sitting on the roof reading old magazines, and the urchin soup at the Fondaco café is served chilled, like a very exotic vichyssoise.

The English hated it; and yet there is to the flavour of this stagnant city, limp and hangdog in the heat, something peculiarly seductive, rather like that smell of rotting foliage you sometimes discover in the depths of woodlands – a fungus smell, sweet and dangerous. It is a curious fact that of the exiles who have come in modern times to spend a few weeks, a few months in Hav, nearly all have come in the summer time, when the city is at its cruellest.

Armand is of course the expert on Hav's exiles, and in the heat of noon the other day, as we drank lime juice at the little refreshment stall which has sprung up on the promenade, I asked him how he accounted for this odd preference.

'It is simple.' (Everything is simple to Armand Sauvignon.) 'Hav is like some exile itself, and never more so than in these terrible days of July and August. *Ergo*, like goes to like, and your wandering poet, your dreaming philosopher, your Freud or your Wagner feels most at home here when everything is at its worst.'

'Drinking iced lime juice,' said I, 'beneath a sunshade on the promenade.'

'Ha! *Touché*! But they did not always live like us!'

Nor did they. By and large the Hav exiles have lived anonymously, or at least obscurely, during their time in the city. I went one day to the apartment in which Freud had his lodgings, when he came to Hav in 1876 to search for the testes of the eel. Seconded by the Department of Comparative Anatomy at Vienna University, he had already failed in this task at Trieste, but the Hav eel has the reputation of extreme virility, frequenting as it does the irrigation canals and brackish pools of those aphrodisiac salt-marshes, so he transferred his researches here. The newly installed Russian administration allowed him to use as a laboratory the old ice-house, not yet converted to Count Kolchok's purposes, and he found himself lodgings in the House of the Chinese Master.

To my surprise I discovered that he is remembered there still. Clambering up the spiral staircase, now strewn with litter and scratched with incomprehensible slogans, I found the eighth floor, in Freud's time one big apartment, divided into four tenements; but when I knocked at the first door, and asked if this was where the scientist had stayed, 'Yes,' said at once the tousle-haired young woman who opened the door, 'come in and see.' It was an ungainly room she showed me – wedge-shaped, with only a narrow wall at the inner end, and a single window at the other looking through the marble mesh outside to the roofs of the Great Bazaar – and it was in a state of homely chaos, which the woman casually did her best to reduce, picking up clothes and papers from the floor as we entered, and clearing a pile of sewing from the sofa to give us sitting space.

'It was my great-grandmother's place then – she was Austrian, she came here as governess to a Russian family, but married a local man. Of course Freud was unknown in those days, and nobody took much notice of him. It was only in my father's time that people began to be interested.'

'Lots of people come to see the place?'

'Lots? Not lots. Perhaps seven or eight a year. Sometimes they are interested in Freud, sometimes in eels! My husband does not welcome them, but then it was my family that Sigmund lived with, not his.'

'Sigmund!' I laughed. 'You know him well!'

'Yes, yes, I feel I do. He is very kindly remembered in our family – such a nice young man, we were always told, with his funny stories and his jokes. Besides, we have little things of his here that bring him close to me' – and opening a drawer she brought out a black leather box, embossed 'S.F.', and showed me its quaint contents. There was a comb – 'Freud's comb?' 'Sigmund's comb, certainly' – and a silver-gilt pen, and a letter from the Trieste laboratory of the comparative anatomy department wishing him luck – '*After 400 Trieste eels, my dear old boy, you deserve to find your quarry among the salts of Hav*' – and a silhouette in an oval frame which portrayed, she said, Freud's mother. 'And here', she said, 'is a funny rhyme that Sigmund left for my great-grandmother when he went away.' It was four lines of German, in a clear script, which I will try to translate into verse:

To my dear Frau Makal:

> If you find, upon eating an eel,
> A part [*körperteil*] you would rather avoid,
> Please pack up that bit of your evening meal
> And send it to young Dr Freud.

For poor Freud, having dissected those 400 eels in Trieste, examined another 200 during his six weeks in Hav, and never did find a testes – a curious failure, remarks his biographer Ernest Jones, for the inventor of the castration complex!

It was historical chance, of course, that brought Anastasia to Hav in the height of summer – if indeed she came at all. Of all this city's exiles, voluntary or compulsory, real or legendary, she is the one Hav most enjoys talking about, partly because people here are still enthralled by the Russian period of heir history, but chiefly because romance says her vast collection of jewelry is still hidden somewhere in the peninsula.

As to whether she really came, opinions vary. Count Kolchok swore to the end of his days that she did not, and Anna Novochka also denies it: pure tosh, she says – 'If she was ever here, would I not have known of it?' On the other hand there is a strong tradition in the Yeğen family that in August 1918 a girl arrived on the train in a sealed coach, all curtains drawn, together with three servants and a mountain of baggage – to be met at the frontier by a car from the Serai, while the baggage was picked up by mule-cart at the central station and taken to the western hills.

Others say Anastasia arrived on board a British warship, which anchored beyond the Iron Dog and sent her in by jolly-boat, while wilder stories suggest she struggled by foot over the escarpment, helped by Kretevs – even living for a time, so it was imagined in a recent historical novel, in one of their caves. I often meet people who claim that their parents met her, though never it seems in very specific circumstances, only at some ball or other, or at the railway station. There is a legend that she was at Kolchok's funeral – and a fable, inevitably perhaps, that she succeeded Naratlova as his mistress.

But nobody offers any very definite theories as to what became of her. Perhaps she went on to America? Perhaps, when Russian rule ended in Hav, she simply faded into the White Russian community here, adopting another name as Anna did? Perhaps she was murdered by the KGB? Perhaps she is still alive? Far more substantial are speculations about her treasure, which seems to have grown over the years until it now sometimes embraces most of the Russian crown jewels. The existence of this trove is taken very seriously. The Palace with its outbuildings has been combed and combed again. Little Malta, a very popular site, has almost been taken apart. Every weekend you see people with metal-detectors setting off for the derelict villas of the western hills, and Anna has a terrible time keeping intruders out of her garden – 'and I ask you, if there was treasure in my flower-beds would I be living like this?'

I have an open mind about Anastasia, but it is intriguing to think that, if she really did escape to Hav, her exile might well have overlapped with that of Trotsky, who spent a secretive month here in the summer of 1929. This is well-documented. He was photographed arriving on the train (the picture hangs in the pilot's office), and he lived in an old Arab house just within the Castle Gate of the Medina – hardly a stone's throw from the Palace compound so recently vacated by Kolchok and his Czarist apparatus. Melchik has described the arrangements in his novel *Dönüş* ('The Return'): the gunmen always on the flat roof of the house, the heavy steel shutters which closed off the central courtyard in case of a siege. When Trotsky went out, which was very rarely it seems, he was hemmed all about by bodyguards; when he left for France, at the start of the fateful wanderings that led him in the end to Mexico, it is said he departed on board a private yacht. The house is now occupied by a Muslim craft school, and the only reminders of Trotsky's stay are the shutters still attached to the courtyard pillars – very reassuring, the headmaster told me waggishly, when pupils show signs of rebelling.

It has been suggested that Hitler's probably apocryphal visit to Hav may have been sparked by Wagner's paradoxical fondness for the place. Paradoxical because there seems to me nothing remotely Wagnerian about Hav, and its summer discomforts (the composer's three stays were all in July) do not seem at all to his taste.

He was apparently compelled, though, by the brooding wall of the escarpment, by the mysterious anachronism of the Kretevs in their high caverns, and by the idea that in Hav the Celtic gods of the old European pantheon had somehow found their last apotheosis. He lived here in conditions of heroic austerity – none of his habitual silks and velvet hangings – in a wooden house near the railway station, burnt down during the fire of 1927 which also destroyed the Cathedral of the Annunciation and the theatre. There he was constantly visited, it is said, by wild men from the escarpment, Greeks from San Spiridon, Arabs and blacks; he even took to dressing Hav-style, they say, in striped cotton and straw hat.

But then the advantage of going native in Hav is that nobody knows what native is. Now as then, you can take your choice! Chopin, for example, when he came here with George Sand in 1839 after their unhappy holiday in Majorca, chose to live in the Armenian way, rented a house in the Armenian quarter of the Old City and briefly took lessons in Armenian with the city trumpeter of the day. On the other hand James Joyce spent nearly all his time at the Café München, the famous writers' haunt on Bundstrasse, while Richard Burton the explorer, as one might expect, went entirely Arab, strode around the city in burnous and golden dagger, flagrantly snubbed the British Resident, and was rumoured to have got up to terrible things in the darker corners of the Medina – he himself put it around that he had decapitated a man in a bath-house.

Almost the only visiting celebrity not to adopt the ways of the city, in one way or another, was Edward Lear the painter. He set up his studio respectably in a house overlooking the harbour, took on many pupils both English and Havian, and described Hav as 'a very snuffyuffy, scrumdoochian kind of place'.

There have been many enforced refugees, from many countries and many situations, who have found in this confused and eclectic city a temporary haven. Even as I write, I see one of them on a park bench below. I know him slightly. He is dressed anachronistically even by Hav standards, for he presents an image direct from the American 1960s: his hair is long and pig-tailed, his moustache is droopy, he wears baseball shoes and patched jeans frayed at the bottom. His guitar is propped against the bench beside him, and he is fast asleep – head back, mouth slightly open, arms on the back of the bench showing (I happen to know) a tattooed dove of peace on one bicep the words ROLLIN' STONE on the other. He is in his late thirties, I would guess. He is known in Hav as Bob.

Scores of young Americans, evading the draft for the Vietnam War, found their way to Hav in the sixties and seventies, min-gling easily enough with the travellers on the hippie route to Afghanistan and Katmandu who used, in those days, some-times to stop off in the peninsula. As far as I know Bob is the only survivor, having scornfully disregarded the amnesty which took most of the draft evaders home to the United States. He is rumoured to be rich really, and to be supported by subsidies from his family, but I doubt it: he busks with his guitar for money, a familiar figure on the waterfront and the pavements of New Hav, and once he took me to his lodgings, a bed-sitting-room in the German quarter plastered all over with anti-war posters, pictures of Joan Baez and Dylan, and touching colour snapshots of his mother and father, gazing into the dark little apartment, with its crumpled bed and chipped mugs by the sink, out of a well-tended garden in Iowa.

Look over there now, through the gateway to the promenade, and you will see, dangling their legs over the edge of the quay, two fugitives of another sort. They are stocky men in their thirties, unshaven rather, in brown baggy trousers and open-necked shirts. Their hair is quite long now, but it was close-cropped when I first saw them, shortly after my arrival in Hav. Unlike Bob, who knows everyone, they are extremely aloof, lodging in a Turkish boarding-house near the central post office, and supporting themselves certainly not by busking, but rumour says by subventions from the British Agency (which is to say, it is knowingly added, the CIA).

They are, we are told, deserters from the Soviet army in Afghanistan, and arrived in Hav nobody knows how – some say by sea. They are supposed to have been thoroughly interrogated by Mr Thorne and his assistants, and then let loose in the city. They seem quite happy. One is a skilled mechanic, and sometimes does odd jobs for people, if he can be made to understand what is needed – very few people speak Russian in Hav now, while the two deserters speak nothing else. The other is variously rumoured to be a fighter pilot and a colonel in the KGB. When I try to speak to them, they smile pleasantly and say nothing. Magda says they would be admirable recruits for the Athenaeum.

Of course they may not be deserters from Afghanistan at all. Another theory is that they are dissident Russian artists, scientists or writers, kept here in reserve, so to speak, until the Western powers feel their propaganda value will be most useful. This has happened before. In the 1950s a distinguished young Russian physicist arrived on a boat from Syria, and immediately made his way to the British Agency. There he stayed for some months safe, sound and secret, awaiting the apposite moment.

But one day a senior British official arrived by train from Ankara supposedly for a last de-briefing of the man, or perhaps a final indoctrination, and thereafter nothing was ever heard of the refugee again. The name of the senior official is lost too: but I wonder, could it have been H. A. R. ('Kim') Philby?

Pace Armand, much the best-known refugee in Hav today is that meditative old Nazi he first pointed out to me – do you remember? – as being very much wanted by the Israelis. The Mossad do not seem to have been searching very hard, for Oberführer Boschendorf is to be found, most days of the week, buttonholing people with his story in the pleasure-gardens of the Lazaretto.

I often go there myself, for I love to watch the solemn Hav children enjoying themselves on the biplanes, steamrollers, cocks and wooden camels of the elderly roundabouts, and one afternoon Boschendorf picked on me. 'Please, please, I know you are a writer, I want you to know the truth' – so we went into the old Admiralty House café, and placing his hat carefully on the seat beside him, he told me his tale.

It was perfectly true, he said, as I had doubtless learnt, that during the late war (he always called it the late war) he had been involved in the deaths of Jews, but it was not out of racial hatred. It was because he had cherished since childhood a deep, a truly mystical empathy for the destiny of the Jewish people – 'but am I ever believed in Hav, this snake-pit, this Babylon? Never!' His obsession began when he had been taken as a boy to the Passion Play at Oberammergau. 'The sublime and awful meaning of it! A Jew, the noblest of Jews, condemned to death by his own people – but only, as I realized in revelation that day, as their own imperishable contribution to the destiny of all humanity. It was they themselves that they were sacrificing upon the Cross. Christ was but the image of all his people, the Jews but an enlargement of Christ!'

At first he had seen Hitler and the Nazi party as the embodiment of all evil, the Anti-Christ – 'how I suffered for the Jews with their horrible yellow badges and their degradations'. But then came the war, and he first heard of the Final Solution, the plan to exterminate all the Jews of Europe. 'It was a second revelation to me. The Jews, the Christ-people, were to be sublimated at last in total sacrifice, and join their archetype upon the Cross. I saw it all in ecstasy, those tragic millions, deprived of all but their heritage, in pilgrimage to their own Calvaries. I could not imagine – it would take a Wagner to imagine! – what it would mean for the future of the world, and I came to see Adolf Hitler, as I had long seen Pontius Pilate, as a divine instrument of redemption. I saw all the mighty energies of Germany, beset by enemies on every front, directed to the sacred task – inspired!'

Boschendorf got himself into the SS, and was concerned, as a junior administrative officer, with paperwork for Eichmann's death-trains; but he was never charged with war crimes, and came to Hav after the war not through the tortuous channels of Odessa, but by paying his own fare on the Mediterranean Express. This anti-climax seemed to prey upon his mind.

'They will not listen! They do not hear! Am I a criminal? Am I not rather an agent of God's passion? Was I not to the Jews as Judas was to his master, no more than the means of holy destiny? Have I not risked death to bring them death?' Suddenly unbuttoning his jacket and baring his chest, he showed me tattooed there a Star of David – 'There, as they branded the Jews entering upon their fulfilment so they branded me, at my instructions, Hauptsturmführer, SS, with the badge of the Chosen!'

'Quick, Herr Boschendorf–'

'*Dr* Boschendorf.'

'–quick, button up your shirt, everyone is staring at you.'

'WHY?' he shouted. 'Must I be ashamed of my badge?' He rose to his feet and displayed his chest right and left across the café, whose customers were in fact assiduously pretending not to notice. 'MUST I BE ASHAMED?'

One or two of our neighbours now offered me sympathetic smiles, as if to say that they had seen and heard it all before, and the waiters, to a man, conscientiously looked the other way.

'Oh I know what these people' – he threw a hand around the room – 'have been telling you. That's Hav! That's Babylon! They say I am wanted in four continents, don't they? But do I hide myself? Do I hide my badge of sacrament? The Israelis know and respect me for my love of their people, for whom I shed their blood . . .'

I thought he was going to break down. 'I saw you that day with Armand Sauvignon. Did you believe what he told you? Do you know what he did in the late war? He it was, when Jews arrived in Hav, who saw to it that they were shipped to France, and thence to Germany – but he did it not in love, but in hatred. Ask anyone! Oh, we all know Monsieur Sauvignon, novelist, gentleman of France, hypocrite.'

He calmed down presently and politely paid his bill. The head waiter bowed to him respectfully as we left the café. 'I so much enjoyed our talk,' Boschendorf said, 'and feel relieved that you are now in possession of the truth – always a rare commodity in Hav. Use it how you will.' He asked me if I would care to join him on the Electric Ferry back to the Fondaco, but I said no, I would stay on the island a little longer, and watch the children on the merry-go-round as the fairy lights came up.

Who else is sheltering, here in the haven of Hav? A few Israeli deserters, and a few Syrians, who are said to enjoy regular get-togethers at which they damn each others' governments indiscriminately. Plenty of Palestinians, they say. The Caliph's Assyrians. Perhaps one or two of Boschendorf's old comrades.

A clutch of Libyans, often to be seen, heads together, gloomily eating kebabs at the Al-Khouri restaurant in the bazaar.

And me, of course, and me. 'What are you running away from?' Magda asked me once. I said I wasn't running away from anything. 'Of course you are,' she said. 'In Hav we are all running.' Perhaps we are, too, each of us finding our own escape in this narrow sultry cul-de-sac. Like many another cage the peninsula of Hav, blazed all about by sun, trapped in dust and moulder, offers its prisoners a special kind of liberation. The harsher, the freer! When the sun goes down on these summer days I feel the city to be less than itself, and look forward impatiently to the hot blast of the morning.

18

Among the Chinese – Feng Shui in Hav – the Palace of Delights – piracy – X's story – ad infinitum

To Yuan Wen Kuo last night, for dinner with M, in the cool of the July evening. We ate early at the Lotus Blossom Garden, and afterwards wandered agreeably around the streets thinking how pleasantly unremarkable everything looked. The Chinese consider it lucky to live in uninteresting times, and it seemed to me that by and large they go to some lengths to live in uninteresting places, too.

Ten miles across the peninsula from the city of Hav proper, which is by any standards unusual, the Chinese have created a town of their own which seems quite deliberately its antithesis: a town without surprises, homogenous in its slatternly makeshift feeling, and imbued with all the standard Chineseness of all the Chinatowns that ever were – the tireless crowds and the smell of cooking, the piles of medicinal roots and powders, the shining varnished dead ducks hanging from their hooks, the burbling bewildered live ones jammed in their market pens, the men in shirtsleeves leaning over the balconies of upstairs restaurants, the severe old ladies on kitchen chairs, the children tied together with string like puppets, as they are taken for walks in parks, the rolls of silk from Shanghai, the bookshops hung with scroll paintings of the Yangtze Gorges, the nasal clanging of radio music, the clic-clac of the abacus, the men playing draughts beneath trees, the disconsolate sniffing dogs, the rich men passing in the back seats of their Mercedes, the poor men pedalling their bicycle rickshaws, the buckets full of verminous threshing fish, the labourers bent double with tea-chests on their backs, the dubious little hotels, their halls brightly lit with unshaded bulbs, the glimpses of girls at sewing-machines in second-storey windows, the fibrous black-ened harbour-craft, the old-fashioned bicycles, the shops full of Hong Kong television sets, the Yellow Rose Department Store, the Star Dry-Cleaning Company, the pictures here of Chiang Kai Shek peak-capped against a rising sun, there of Mao Tse-Tung bare-headed against the Great Wall – in short, the threshed, meshed, patternless, hodge-podge, sleepless, dili-gent and ordinary disorder of the Chinese presence.

How I enjoyed it last night! As we loitered around the streets of Yuan Wen Kuo, digesting our Sautéed Chicken with Wolf-berry (recommended to me in Beijing long ago as a specific against depression), I felt extraordinarily reassured by the pro-saic activity of it all. I felt in fact, in a calm illogical way, as though I were enjoying a brief spell of home leave from the front.

Perhaps this is what the architects and soothsayers had in mind when, so many centuries ago, they laid out on this inconceiv-ably distant shore the pattern of the first Chinese city west of the Gobi Desert. The principles of Feng Shui, the Chinese art of relating buildings to their landscapes, are easy to recognize in Yuan Wen Kuo. Two low hillocks, still bare but for an orna-mental tea-house on each of them, stand here half a mile or so from the water's edge, facing south-west. Nothing could be more suitable. Though down the generations the shape of the town has inevitably been blurred, essentially Yuan Wen Kuo still lies, as the Feng Shui men doubtless decreed, between the benevolent arms of the Azure Dragon, the White Tiger, and the Black Tortoise – the three protective ridges which protect it from the north. Halfway up the hill they laid out the main street, for Feng Shui insisted that a site should be commanding, but not exposed; though there are a few rich villas now near the summit of the slope, the ridge itself remains bare to this day, except for the semaphore mast overlooking the fishing-harbour at the eastern end.

We are told that the imperial architect Han Tu Chu himself decreed the original ground-plan, but architecturally Yuan Wen Kuo never seems to have been anything special. Perhaps, being so far away, and so vulnerable, the Chinese thought it was hardly worth spending money on expensive buildings there. Marco Polo dismissed it cursorily. 'There is nothing to be said about Yuan Wen Kuo. Let us now move on to other places.' Ibn Batuta thought it 'mean and dirty, with small nar-row houses and thieving people', and was glad to get back to the civilized comforts of the Medina, where he was told of a charitable fund established especially to help the victims of extortion in Yuan Wen Kuo. Possibly it was the unimpressive character of the place that encouraged the Chinese authorities, when the time came in the fifteenth century, to build the House of the Chinese Master with such fine extravagance.

By acumen and experience Yuan Wen Kuo survived the Ottoman period – Chinese money from Hav became highly influential in Constantinople – and the town came vigorously into its own again with the arrival of New Hav, which was mostly built by Chinese contractors, and which offered endless opportunities for Chinese speculators. The Palace of Delights (which with its more discreet annexe, the House of Secret Wonders, had existed in Ibn Batuta's time) arose anew as a great pleasure-dome in the middle of Yuan Wen Kuo, and among the Europeans of the concessions became *the* place to go for a racy evening out. As for our own times, they tell me that hardly a development in the Gulf, hardly a new hotel in Abu Dhabi or a university in Oman, fails to send home its quo-tient of profit to the Chinese financiers of Hav.

The Palace of Delights, by the way, is still there, an ugly con-crete block set in a scrubby garden, and is still in its modest way a place of pleasure: there is a restaurant in it, and a con-cert hall, and there are rival information departments set up by the local factions of Communist China and Taiwan – each with its glass-fronted cabinet full of propaganda booklets, each staffed, as I discovered when I once laboured up the bare concrete steps to their offices, by young men and women with time on their hands to explain their respective points of view until Tuesday week. In its great days, though, the Palace of Delights was something altogether different. I know several people who remember it from the days between the wars, and they make it sound terrific.

There was not just one restaurant then, but a regular covey of them, each serving a different Chinese cuisine, on a different floor, to the music of a different band. Then four or five night clubs pullulated until dawn, and there were fortune-tellers, and beauty parlours, and shops of many kinds, and performing animals, and photographers to take your picture dressed as mandarin or empress, or alternatively not dressed at all. Magicians made rabbits vanish on staircases, fire-eaters stalked the corridors, there were story-tellers, gambling-booths, sideshows offering freaks or dancing-girls or distorting mirrors. You could get married at the Palace of Delights. You could find an amanuensis to write a letter for you, or a wizard to cast you a spell. I have been told that more than a thousand people worked there, and throughout the 1920s and 1930s the profits were immense.

The clientele of the House of Secret Wonders (which has been pointed out to me as a low wooden building, now half-collapsed and covered with tangled creeper) is claimed to have been too distinguished to list – Armand says that in his last years Kolchok himself was a regular customer. The most intriguing rumour I have heard concerns a tall young Englishman with a pale gingery beard, who was said almost to have lived in the place for several months in the years before the First World War. He seemed to be well-off, he had lodgings in a Chinese apartment house along the road, and he apparently had nothing whatever to do with Europeans. After a time he vanished, and people forgot all about him; it is only in recent years that he has been tentatively identified as that queer and beguiling recluse Sir Edmund Backhouse, who lived for most of the rest of his life in Beijing, and deceived the whole world of oriental scholarship with his fake scrolls and fantasies.

I often go to Yuan Wen Kuo. I like to have lunch on the Boating restaurant in the harbour, and spend the afternoon sketching from its deck, kept cool, with lemonades and thoughtfully adjusted canopies by its obliging owners. I love to watch the fisher-people at work, especially when on festival days they dress up their boats with huge heraldic flags, pennants and trailing crimson dragons, giving them a wonderfully piratical splendour.

Actually, piracy used to be notorious among the Hav Chinese. Fast pirate craft roamed the eastern Mediterranean out of Yuan Wen Kuo, ravaging the Syrian trade routes, preying upon the traffic of the Dardanelles, raiding isolated villages on the coasts of Cyprus and Lebanon. Even the Venetians, partners in profit to the Hav Chinese, often had occasion to complain about their piracy on the high seas, and in the fifteenth century there were persistent rumours of collusion between the terrible Uskok pirates of the Adriatic and those of Yuan Wen Kuo; a Chinese seaman was among those beheaded after the capture of an Uskok ship by the Venetians in 1458, and to this day in the Yugoslav village of Senj, the old Uskok headquarters, people of faintly oriental cast are said to be descendants of Hav Chinese (though some withered scholars scorn the whole story as merely a semantic confusion between Hav and the Dalmatian island of Hvar . . .).

'I suppose you think,' said M last night, 'that there are no pirates left in Yuan Wen Kuo? You're wrong. I'll introduce you to one right now.' In the twilight we walked up the hill to one of the grand houses at the eastern end of the ridge, immediately below the semaphore, and there we were immediately invited in for coffee by X, as I had better call him, who is one of the Chinese directors of the Casino. This was a very urbane

experience, Old Money in the truest sense, since it was originally made out of the silk trade with the Venetians. X is
Harvard-educated, his wife was at the Sorbonne, and their
house is full of books, pictures Western and Chinese, advanced
hi-fi and little Hav terriers. Marvellous vases and ceramic
beasts stand about the rooms, and it would not surprise me
to learn that some paintings of the Hav-Venetian school are
hidden away upstairs. We had our coffee alfresco, looking
down over the sea, and it was true X talked in an authentical-
ly piratical way about financial coups and deeds of daring –
about his success in exploiting the insecurities of Hong Kong,
his lucky investments in Singapore during the Japanese occupation, his personal loans to the Castro administration and his
profitable stakes in Tanzania. I did not like to ask him if Hitler
really had come to Casino Cove, or how well he had known
Howard Hughes, but presently M said, 'Go on, tell Jan about
Tiananmen.' X, who was otherwise anything but taciturn, at
first seemed reluctant, but 'Go on,' said Madame X too, 'tell
her, where's the harm now? It might be useful, anyway.' And
this is what I learnt from Bluebeard's lips.

For years, said X, a group of rich men in Yuan Wen Kuo,
calling themselves the Crimson Hand, had supported an active
partisan movement against the Communist government in Beijing. They had nothing to do with the Kuomingtang in Taiwan.
They were fanatical monarchists, dedicated to the restoration
of the Manchu dynasty to the imperial throne of China. Many
of the mysterious events reported out of China could be attrib-
uted, X said, to them: for example, the supposedly accidental
plane crash which in 1971 killed Marshal Lin Biao, Mao's
appointed successor. It was rumoured that they had links with
the Gang of Four, and that if all had gone well for them the
Cultural Revolution would have been climaxed by the deposi-
tion of Mao and the restoration of the imperial dynasty to its
throne in the Forbidden City.

In 1960 their directors in Hav had conceived a spectacular
coup: they decided to abduct the old man who had been,

briefly in his childhood, the last Emperor of China, then working as a humble clerk in Beijing. They would bring him to Hav
as the rallying-point of a great monarchist movement which
would, they hoped, sweep all through the world of the overseas
Chinese. It would not be a difficult operation, they thought. The
Chinese authorities were proud of pointing out Pu Yi, so
docile, so well-adjusted to events, as he took the morning bus
from his home in the suburbs to his work at a ministry office.
Foreigners often saw him, sitting there in his blue work suit,
and sometimes spoke to him. His responses were always ideologically correct.

The Crimson Hand's plan was to have a pair of partisans
board that morning bus and ride with it until Pu Yi got out at
his usual stop at the northern end of Tiananmen Square. He
would then be seized in the confusion of the crowd, bundled
through the mêlée of the morning commuters into a waiting
taxi, and spirited away to Hong Kong and eventually to Hav.
Everything was arranged, the get-away taxi, the route to
Kwangchow and thence to Hong Kong, where the Crimson
Hand had many friends. A dozen dummy runs were tried.
Diversions were arranged in Tiananmen Square – a couple of
bicyclists were to collide, some subversive leaflets were to be
found upon the pavement.

But the very moment they laid hands on Pu Yi as he stepped
through the opening door of the bus, they themselves were
grabbed by the four harmless-looking passengers stepping out
before him, and by two equally innocuous commuters behind
their backs. The last of the emperors might be politically cooperative but never for a moment, forty years after his deposi-
tion, did the authorities let him out of sight, and the secret
policemen of his final bodyguard had not failed him in their
duty. The conspirators were quietly executed; Pu Yi continued
to take the bus to work until his retirement and peaceful end.

'I hear the Crimson Hand is lying low these days,' said M.

'So I understand,' X replied, 'and yet I have it on very, very
good authority that they are grooming their own successor to

the throne of the Manchus right here in Hav – rather like' (he said to me) 'your friend the Caliph!'

'Can you imagine?' laughed Madame X, pouring us more coffee.

'*Can you imagine?*' mimicked M, as we walked down the hill again. 'In that house you can imagine anything, can't you? You can imagine X himself as Emperor of China!'

But down in the town the Crimson Hand seemed an improbable fancy. It was almost midnight, yet all was as usual among the Hav Chinese: the tireless crowds and the smell of cooking, the piles of roots and powders, the dead ducks and the live ones, the bright bare lights in hotel lobbies, the rickshaws and the limousines, the clic-clac and the threshing fish, and so *ad infinitum* . . .

19

A horrible thing – without religion – Topolino – walking to the hermits – 'on the terrace' – the Cathars – a séance – Mahmoud disappointed

A very strange and horrible thing has happened in Hav. Somebody broke into the old Palace chapel and slashed two of the priceless portraits of the Hav-Venetian school which hang inside. The city buzzes with it. The vandals left no explanatory message, but simply daubed a large red tick beside each ruined painting, as though to say that their mission had been accomplished.

Who could have done it? Why? I suggested diffidently to Mahmoud that the motive might have been religious. He dismissed the idea. 'Hav', he said, 'is not a religious place.'

St Paul would have agreed. There are three references to Hav in his epistles, and none of them are complimentary. Besides complaining about its inhabitants' feckless ineptitude – 'for be not like the people of Hav, who cannot cut wood nor build houses' – he calls them Godless, lustful and not to be trusted. It used to be said that a Pauline epistle to the Havians themselves existed somewhere, in an Anatolian monastery perhaps, or hidden away at Athos: if so, it would make uncomfortable reading for this citizenry.

The Crusaders also found the indigenes of the promontory, by then a mixture of Arabs, Africans, Syrians, Greeks, Turks and Kretevs, spiritually uninspiring. Beycan, in a letter to

Raymond of Toulouse, described them as 'worthless and incorrigible', and a contemporary illuminated picture of the castle at Hav shows the inhabitants outside its walls looking horridly gnomish and dog-like. Even the Muslims, it seems to me, have never quite converted this city, though they have been calling it to prayer for nearly a thousand years: the mosques are full enough on Fridays, the Imam of the Grand Mosque is powerful, the presence of the Caliph is never forgotten, but one never feels here the mighty supremacy of the faith, the grand saturation of everyday life, that gives Islam elsewhere in the East its sense of absolute ubiquity. One can hardly imagine a Hav taxi-driver pausing to say his prayers at midday, just as he is unlikely to have dangling at his windscreen an icon of the Virgin Mary or his patron saint – only a plastic model of the Iron Dog, or a little pair of running shoes.

Of course nearly every faith is represented here. There are mosques Sunni and Shia (tucked away in the depths of the Balad). There is a small Buddhist temple at Hen Chaiu Lu, and one sometimes sees its yellow-robed acolytes buying saffron at the morning market. The synagogue is in the old Scuola Levantina of the Venetian Jews; two aged monks are alleged to survive from the Russian monastery of the Holy Ghost, destroyed in the great fire of 1928. The Anglican church may be full of oil-drums, but the Roman Catholics still worship at the French cathedral, the Orthodox Greeks are in Saladin's mosque, the Lutherans still have their chapel next door to the old Residenz, and sundry Maronites, Copts and Nestorians maintain their places of worship, tentative or robust, here and there across the city. The Indian squatters of Little Yalta have built themselves a rickety little Hindu temple by the sea. Once when I was wandering through the Balad in the evening I heard loud enthusiastic singing in an unknown tongue, and walking up an alley to investigate found a happy congregation of black people in full flood of Pentecostal conviction.

But I think it may be true, as Mahmoud said, that Hav as a whole, Hav *in genere* so to speak, is without religion: and as a pagan myself I enjoy this wayward scattering of spirituality, this carefree pragmatism, which makes me feel that I might easily run into those fundamentalists in the Cathedral of St Antoine one day, or find nonagenarian Russian monks helping out with the Buddhist rites.

However I have repeatedly heard of a remarkable deviation from this general rule. Signora Vattani first told me of the hermitage in the eastern moors. She told me that before the war there arrived in Hav from nowhere in particular a strange young Malian nicknamed Topolino, 'Little Mouse', after a small Fiat car popular then.

He dressed himself in a rough brown habit, like a Franciscan, and began giving extempore pavement sermons: and though he was really neither a monk nor a priest – just a layabout, Signora V. says – though his political views seemed almost communist and his religious ones inchoate, though he was disgracefully impertinent to the Italian Resident, and for that matter to the late Signor Vattani, besides using terrible language in his homilies, nevertheless he was taken up by some of the Italian families of the concession and established a kind of cult. He lived somewhere in the Balad, but was often to be encountered in his tattered brown cassock at soirées and cocktail parties, and even made an appearance sometimes at Palace festivities. For two years running, Signora Vattani says, he took part in the Roof-Race. His favourite preaching-place was the quayside immediately outside the Fondaco, which he used to denounce as a symbol of Italian imperialism.

When the war came, Topolino left the city – to avoid conscription, the Signora maintains – and with a few of his followers built himself a hermitage on the moorland south of Hen Chiau Lu. There he died in 1954, his body being unexpectedly claimed, and taken to Italy, by an eminent Christian Democrat politician ('No, I will not tell you his name – I have my loyalties') who turned out to be the Little Mouse's brother. However, I had often been told that his hermitage still existed, and last week I drove out to find it. Nobody could say exactly where it was, but all agreed that you could not take a car all the way. So I started early in the morning, with a packed lunch in a knapsack, and leaving the car at the southern end of China Bay, set off across the tufty grassland into the rolling bare moors, apparently uninhabited, that lie to the south.

It was a marvellous walk. Sometimes the Hav sky seems higher and wider than any sky anywhere, except perhaps in Texas, and on mornings like this the Hav sea, too, seems matchless – so profoundly, bottomlessly blue, so beautifully flecked with the buoys and boats of the Chinese in their wide bay, and falling so lazily, in such long slow waves, upon the silent foreshore. To the south-west silently lay San Spiridon, its church tower protruding over the ridge, and much further away, far out at sea beneath the drifting white clouds, I fancied I could see the distant smudges of other countries altogether – Cyprus? Syria? The Hesperides?

In front the moors looked empty. The magical spring flowers have left Hav now, and the only bright colours in those heathlands were occasional splodges of yellow furze and speckles of a sort of blue poppy they call in Turkish *göz kraliçe,* 'eye of the queen'. Otherwise all was brownish-green, and more brown than green. Sometimes a hawk hovered high above me. Sometimes I started a gamebird from my feet. As the sun came up every rock seemed to flicker with its lizard, and out of the earth the warmth brought a faint aroma, dry, sweet and pungent, which I took to be a memory of all the flowers that had been born, blossomed and died there. But of human life, not a glimpse looking across the moors suggested to me the battlefields of the Boer War, whose similarly treeless landscapes so often looked just as deserted, until the rifle-fire of the Afrikaners spat and blazed from hidden kopje trenches.

No Mausers, I am glad to say, opened up on me. The morning was absolutely silent. But presently, scrambling around a rocky outcrop (lizards twitching everywhere, dark lichen in declivities), I looked up and saw, on a low rise far ahead, a small patch of tangled green, like an overgrown garden, and beside it, waving, two brown-clad figures. It took me a good hour to get up there; and whenever I looked up again, there those figures always seemed to be, waving their encouragement.

They came the last half-mile or so to meet me, and when I saw them striding easily in my direction I remembered for a moment a Buddhist mystic I encountered thirty years ago in the Himalayas, who seemed hardly to walk at all over the snows, but rather to levitate. However these ascetics of Hav turned out to be anything but ethereal – light on their feet perhaps, because they were very thin, but smiling very straightforward smiles, offering me jolly greetings in Italian, and showing evidence all too clear, in their stooped old figures and arthritic-looking fingers, that they were as corporeal as anyone else. Their cassocks, tied with straw ropes in monkly style, were neatly patched. They wore rubber flip-flops, incongruously blue and yellow, upon their feet. They had straggly grey beards, and both looked to me in their seventies.

I was ashamed to find myself breathless as these old men, so agile despite their infirmities, cheerfully paced me over the moor. But they laughed my apologies aside. It was no competition, they said, since they lived such wonderfully healthy lives out there; and indeed when we reached the hermitage, and the seven other members of the community, four men, three women, crowded around to welcome me, they did look extraordinarily spry, though all were of a similar age, and gave the impression that were it not for the deep tans of so many summers on the moorland, their cheeks might have been quite rosy.

They seemed to inhabit a pergola: at least the wide shelf of the rising ground there, perhaps a hundred yards long, had been roofed with a construction of wood and wire which, covered as it was all over with wild vines, meant that the place was half indoors, and half out. It was all green and leafy, wonderfully cool, and it was bisected by a small stream which came out of a conduit above, and went splashing away through the heather towards the sea. Along this dappled belvedere were eight or nine little wooden huts, very well built of rough oak, which formed the cells of the community, together with a store-house at the end. Outside was a long trestle table with benches, and an iron stove whose chimney disappeared through the leaves of the pergola. The hermits produced water in thick white china mugs, and we all sat down at the table while they explained things.

What did they call themselves? I asked. Nothing. What were their beliefs? Nothing: they were a community of agnostics, dedicated to the certainty of uncertainty. Would they describe themselves as disciples of Topolino? No, they had simply been friends of his, who had all chosen the same course of life. How did they live? 'We have our garden, we used to do some fishing, and fortunately some of us have a little money of our own.' Four of them, they said, smiling affectionately at one another, were married couples. One of the men was a widower, whose wife had lived with him 'on the terrace', as they described their situation. The others were bachelors. 'And we are all friends,' they cried triumphantly, 'after forty-five years on the terrace!'

Forty-five years! 'Come with me,' said one of the old women, scrambling off the bench and taking me by the hand. She led me into her cabin, which was bare, and neat, and had two beds and a vase of eye-of-the-queen on the table. 'There we all are,' she said; on the wall, a little mildewed, was a photograph of a dozen laughing young men and women, wearing summer clothes but holding in front of them, each one, a cassock and a cord. 'The twelfth of April, 1940,' said my companion, 'the day we took our vows – and there's Topolino in the middle.' He looked a splendid fellow, the very opposite of a little mouse, being tall, muscular and evidently exuberant. He alone was wearing his cassock already, beneath a wide Hav hat, and he was holding a paper of some kind scrunched above his head with one hand, while with the other he waved to the camera in a gesture of delight. In the background I could see the walls of the Fondaco, and at each end of the picture two or three small boys, in short trousers, were peering mischievously around the edges of the group.

'Where are you?' I asked my companion. She showed me herself in the front row, wearing a Spanish-looking blouse with full frilled sleeves, and white trousers. 'Oh,' she said, 'I was very modern then.'

I ate my picnic lunch with them, on the trestle table, in the vine-patterned shade. They ate salads and what looked like cold noodles. I offered them some of my wine, but they said no, they hadn't touched the stuff for forty years – 'but we drank it often enough before!' They were all educated people, two of them at least speaking excellent English, and several of them French. They were Italian by birth, they told me, but now regarded themselves as being of no nationality. 'We are the people of nowhere.' Nihilists? Certainly not, for they believed that nothing and everything were the same thing. They had long outgrown any instinct for material possession, they said, but at the same time they had foresworn from the very start any striving for mystic enlightenment. They never prayed or meditated, or even read much any more. If they worshipped anything, it was life itself; if they had any doctrine, it could best be identified as a sense of humour.

Of course, said I, they had advantages over other varieties of eremite, in that they were people of intellectual resource, were evidently not destitute, and seemed to have no responsibilities towards anyone else on earth. It was true, they readily admitted. They were mostly the children of business and official families of the Italian concession, and some of them had inherited properties in Italy, which had relieved them of many worries – occasionally for instance some of their members had gone to Beirut, or even to Italy, for medical or dental treatment. Also they often bought food in Yuan Wen Kuo, all walking there and back together – 'we enjoy the exercise'. I said they must seem exotic figures, the nine of them, strolling down the main street past the Palace of Delights. 'Oh do you think so?' they said.

They seemed to me on the whole the happiest, the friend-liest, the most truly banal and the most entirely selfish people I had met in all Hav. They seemed drained of everything but satisfaction. All nine walked back with me to the start of the outcrop, and all shook my hand affectionately. I said they had been described to me as the only religious people in Hav, and this made them laugh. 'No,' said one of the old men in an uncharacteristically ironic tone of voice, 'the only religious people in Hav are the Cathars.'

And so I first heard of the Cathars of Hav. I thought it odd that nobody had mentioned them before, and when I asked about them people seemed evasive. The Cathars were somewhat like Freemasons, I heard it suggested. They no longer existed, some-body else said, or if they did, were all immensely old. Magda just laughed, when I asked her. Dr Borge looked knowing.

I learned something of their beginnings from Jean Antoine's *Hav et les Crusades*, which was published in 1893, but is still the only work on the subject. The Cathar heresy of France, it appears, probably originated among the knights of the First Crusade. They had picked up its basic ideas from the Manicheans, whose roots were in Babylonia, and whose reli-gion was based upon the existence of two equal principles in the world, the Good and the Evil, the Light and the Dark, both to be placated. The Yezidis of modern Iraq, who seem to have had Manichean origins, have come over the centuries to place far more emphasis on the Evil One than on the Good, and have been seen by foreigners as Satan-worshippers – they will not pronounce the sound *sh*, because Satan abhors it, they will not wear the colour blue, because Satan does not like it, they will not eat lettuce because Satan is associated with it, having once hidden under its leaves in time of emergency.

The Crusaders on the other hand evolved their ideas into a recognizably Christian heresy. Like Pelagianism, it postulated that Man was essentially the master of his own destiny – human will was far more important than divine decree; and it was supposed too that Satan had never fallen from heaven, but was still co-regnant with God, dividing the responsibilities of omnipotence, each pulling mankind towards opposite poles of morality. In France Catharism in a more sophisticated form so gripped the imagination of people in the south-east, particularly, that the thirteenth-century Albigensian Crusade was required to exterminate it, the last of the cultists holding out to the bitter end in the hilltop fortresses of Roussillon and Languedoc.

According to Antoine, Hav was a stronghold of Catharism among the Crusaders. Among their Armenian followers were several Paulicians, who held similar views to the Manicheans, and are said powerfully to have influenced the knights – Katourian the minstrel was one. Beynac, himself a native of Roussillon, is said to have been an early convert, and many of his lieutenants followed suit. More than that, they and the Armenians converted to their beliefs many of Hav's cosmopolitan citizens, Greek, Arab, Turkish, Syrian, so that when in 1191 Saladin put an end to Christian rule in the peninsula, and the Crusaders surrendered the castle to the sound of Katourian's lament, they left behind them under Arab rule a resolute Cathar cult of a unique kind. 'Of all the legacies that remain to us of the Crusader era in Hav', wrote Antoine in 1893, 'the most mysterious and perhaps the most resilient is the movement of Cathars, which has its connections throughout the Near East, and which long ago crossed the borders of sect or confessional, to become a fraternity still influential – 700 years later – within the body politic of the city.'

It was Fatima Yeğen who led me to the modern Cathars. Yes, she told me cautiously when I mentioned the movement, she knew of their existence, but their affairs were very secret. 'You cannot guess how secret, how private.' However she would do her best to help, and a few days later, when I was eating my picnic lunch in the Serai garden, she accosted me theatrically. 'You know the subject we were discussing – those people, you know? Come tonight to the hotel, nine o'clock, and you shall meet somebody who will tell you about them' –

and conspiratorially, looking right and left, she flitted away among the flower-beds. 'Nine o'clock sharp,' she said over her shoulder:

So that night I turned up at the hotel, where Fatima was waiting for me expectantly, nervously I thought, inside her kiosk. 'Now you must remember', she said, 'that I have sworn you to secrecy – you must not let me down.' Never, I assured her, and she stopped outside one of the downstairs bedroom doors, said, 'In there,' and left me. I entered, and two young men rose to greet me. One was Yasar Yeğen, who had driven me down the Staircase on my very first day in Hav. The other, introduced to me simply as George, was the man who had spat at me outside the Palace, when the gendarme dismounted and beat him up.

Neither mentioned our previous encounters. They shook my hand gravely, offered me Cyprus brandy from a bottle that stood, with a couple of toothmugs, on the bedside table, and said they were ready to take me to a Cathar meeting that evening.

'You must realize', said Yasar, 'that we do this only because we have heard good things of you, and we may want you to give evidence.'

'Evidence?' I did not like the sound of that.

'We want you to tell the world, if it is necessary, that you saw the Cathars of Hav this very night in *séance*.'

He was using the word, I knew, in its French sense, but all the same it gave me an eerie jolt.

'*If it is necessary*, I say. You will know. Otherwise you must swear to me that you will reveal nothing – where you have been, who you saw. You must ask me no questions – promise me.'

'I promise.'

'Very well, then we need not blindfold you. Try not to look where we are going.'

I tried hard, and it was not difficult. We rode in George's Citroën, Yasar in the back with me, and I could scarcely help observing that we sped straight across Pendeh Square, turned behind the old legation buildings, and entered the Medina by the small gateway, only just wide enough for a car, which is called Bab el Kelb, 'Dog's Gate'. After that I was lost. We went up this alley and that, more than once seemed to double back on our tracks, crossed a square or two, passed through one of the open bazaars; and finally, leaving George and the car in a yard full of iron pipes and asbestos sheeting, and half used as a football pitch, Yasar and I entered the back door of one of the towering old Arab houses which form the core of the Old City. I could see the minaret of the Grand Mosque over a rooftop to my right, but for the life of me I could not tell which side of it was facing us. Their secret was safe. I had no idea where I was.

Up some steep stairs we went, across a landing, around an open gallery above the interior courtyard of the house, up some more stairs, through what appeared to be some kind of robing-room, for there were outdoor clothes on hooks, hangers and chairs all over it, until we entered a small chamber, more a cupboard than a room, through whose wall I could hear a muffled drone of voices, sometimes a single speaker, sometimes a chorus, talking what sounded like French. Yasar closed the door. We were in utter darkness. He pulled aside a curtain then, and through a glazed and grilled little window I could see into a dimly lit room below.

'The *séance*,' whispered Yasar. 'You see the Cathars of Hav.'

Actually, now that I was there it reminded me more of a Welsh eisteddfod than a spiritualist meeting, for the forty or fifty people down there were all strangely robed. On the left sat the women, in white, veiled like nuns. On the right were the men, in black, with cowls worn far forward over their faces. And on a dais in the middle sat a dozen men whose robes were bright red, whose turbans were wound around the lower halves of their faces like Tuaregs, and whose tall wooden staves were each capped with the shining silver figure of an animal, tail extended. I could not hear what was being said. It seemed to be a sort of ritualized conference, for sometimes one of the elders spoke alone, sometimes a man or woman rose from the floor to make a contribution, and sometimes the whole company broke into the droning mechanical chant that I had heard before. 'Remember,' said Yasar, 'you know nobody here.'

I nodded, but wondered. Were not some of those veiled figures familiar to me, beneath their theatrical cloaks and hoods, behind their veils? Did not that woman in the front row, the tensely crouching one at the end – did she not look a little like – who was it? – Yes! Anna Noyochka's misanthropist housekeeper? Was it possible – surely not – but was it possible that the man speaking now, his hood deeply down over his forehead, was standing somewhat in Missakian's stance? Could they conceivably be Assyrians, those stocky men just behind him? Was it altogether fancy, or could I detect above the red veil of the most stalwart of the elders the tunnel pilot's lordly stare?

I could be sure of none of them. I was disturbed and bewildered, and began to see the most unlikely people disguised in those queer vestments among the shadows of the chamber – the Caliph, Mr Thorne, Chimoun, even crazed old Dr Boschendorf! They were probably all in my imagination, and I did not have long to search for more substantial clues, because at a word from the chief elder, and a knock on the floor from his stave, the company rose to its feet and turned towards the dais, as if they were about to recite a creed or mantra. Instantly Yasar drew the curtain and hurried me out of the room, down the stairs and into the car where George was waiting.

'You must ask us no questions,' said Yasar. 'You have the evidence, if it is needed. Remember your promise.'

'*Remember*,' said George, less kindly I thought.

'Yes, yes, I remember. But just let me ask you one thing – only one, and nothing more I swear. Who were the men on the platform, the ones in red? Were they priests?'

The young men looked at each other, and shrugged. 'I don't

know how you say it in English,' said Yasar, 'but we call them *Les Parfaits*.'

The *Perfects*!

Not Prefects – Perfects!

I told nobody about my visit to the upper room of the Cathars, but I did tell Mahmoud that I had been to see the hermits, and that they only confirmed what he had said about Hav – they were not in the least religious. He was intensely disappointed. He had thought them the great exceptions. As a matter of fact in his adolescence he had cherished the ambition of joining them one day in a life of prayer and meditation. 'They were my ideal,' he said.

'Why *didn't* you join them, then?'

'Why was I never a roof-runner? Cowardice, Jan, pure cowardice. I have lived a life of it.' Having met Topolino's followers for myself, I did not think much courage was needed to join them on the terrace: but I was not so sure about the Cathars.

20

A visit to the troglodytes

All this time (it may have crossed your mind) and I still had not clambered the escarpment to the cave-homes of the Kretevs, the most compelling of all the Havians! I wonder why? Sometimes I was afraid of disillusionment, I suppose, in this city of reappraisals. Sometimes I reasoned that I should end with the beginning, and keep those atavists for my last letter. And sometimes I felt that, what with the Cathars, and the British Agency's radio masts, and the peculiar island Greeks, I was surfeited with enigma. But I kept in touch with Brack, and at the market the other day he beckoned me over to his stall. He said that if I wanted to come to Palast (which is, so far as I can make out, more or less what the troglodytes themselves call their village) I had better come that very day – if I brought my car I could join the market convoy when it went home in the afternoon. Trouble was brewing in Hav, he said, bad trouble, and it might be my only chance. He shook his head in a sorrowful way, and his ear-rings glinted among his dreadlocks. So at three o'clock – sharp! – I drove down to the truck park, and found the Kretev pick-ups all ready to go. Brack leant from his cab and gestured me to follow him. The other drivers, starting up their engines, stared at me blankly.

Trouble? All seemed peaceful, as we drove along the edge of the Balad and into the salt-flats. The old slave settlement looked just as listless as it had when I first saw it, so dim-lit and arid, through the windows of the Mediterranean Express.

Some small boys were playing football on the waste ground beside the windmills. Away to the west I thought I could distinguish Anna's villa, in the flank of the hills, and imagined her settling down, now as always, to tea, petits fours and her current novel (she is very fond of thrillers). The usual lonely figures were labouring in the white waste of the salt-pans, and now and then one of the big salt-trucks rumbled by on its way to the docks.

But just as we left the marshes and approached the first rise of the escarpment, Brack leant out of his window again and pointed to something in the sky behind us and there were two black aircraft, flying very low and very fast out of the sea – except for the passing airliners, the first I had ever seen over Hav.

In the event I did not have to clamber to the caves, for one can drive all the way. It is a rough, steep and awkward track though, and most of the Kretevs left their trucks at a parking place at the foot of the escarpment, piling vigorously into the back of Brack's pick-up and into my Renault. Thus I found myself squeezed tight in my seat by troglodytes when I drove at last into the shaly centre of Palast – which, like so many things in Hav, was not as I expected it to be.

I had supposed it something like the well-known cave settlements of Cappadocia, whose people inhabit queer white cones of rock protruding from the volcanic surface. But Palast is much more like the gypsy colony of Sacramonte in Spain, or perhaps those eerie towns of cave-tombs that one finds in Sicily, which is to say that it is a township of rock-dwellings strung out on both sides of a cleft in the face of the escarpment. Wherever I looked I could see them, some in clusters of five or six, some all alone, some at ground level, some approached by steps in the rock, or ladders, some apparently altogether inaccessible high in the cliff face. Many had tubs of greenery outside, or flags of bright colours, and some had whitewashed surrounds to their entrances, like picture frames.

The flat floor of the ravine was evidently common ground, with a row of wells in the middle. Shambled cars, not unlike my own, were parked at random around it, stocky ponies wandered apparently at liberty, hens scooted away from my wheels. Out of some of the cave doors, which were mostly screened with red-and-yellow bead curtains, heads poked to see us come – a woman with a pan in her hand, an old man smoking a cigar, half a dozen boys and girls who, spotting my unfamiliar vehicle, came tumbling out to meet us. Soon I was sitting at a scrubbed table in Brack's own ground-floor cave, drinking hot sweet tea with his young wife, whose name sounded like Tiya, and being introduced to an apparently numberless stream of neighbours, of all ages, who came pressing into the cave.

When I say I was being introduced, it was generally in a kind of dumb show. Some of the men spoke Turkish, some a little Arab or French, but the women spoke only Kretev. We shook hands solemnly, exchanged names and inspected each others' clothes. Here I was at a disadvantage. I was wearing jeans, a tennis shirt and my yellow Australian hat, rather less spring-like now after so much bleaching by the suns of Hav. They on the other hand were distinctly not wearing the jumbled neo-European hand-downs I had expected from the appearance of their market men on the job; on the contrary, they were in vivid reds and yellows, like the door curtains, the women in fine flowing gypsy skirts, the men in blazing shirts over which their long tangled hair fell to great effect. They jammed the table all around me and I felt their keen unsmiling eyes concentrated hard, analysing my every gesture, my every response. Their faces were very brown, and they smelled of a musky scent. Sometimes their ear-rings and bangles tinkled. Whenever I was not talking they fell into a hushed but animated conversation among themselves.

'They want to know', Brack told me, 'what you think of our caves.' The caves seemed fine to me, if his own was anything to go by. It was far more than a cave really, being four or five whitewashed rooms, three with windows opening on to the common ground outside, furnished in a high-flown romantic mode, tapestry chair-covers and mahogany sideboards, and lit by electric lights beneath flowered glass lampshades definitely not designed by Peter Behrens of AEG. Everything was brilliantly clean: it all reminded me of a Welsh farmhouse, not least the miscellaneous mementoes of Brack's naval service that were neatly displayed in the glass-fronted corner cupboard. The water, I was told, had to be drawn from the wells, but the electricity came from the Kretevs' own generator.

It all seemed fine, I said. But was there any truth in the rumour that the caves really joined together, forming a secret labyrinth inside the escarpment? They did not, as I expected, laugh at this. They talked quite earnestly among themselves before Brack interpreted. 'We don't think so,' he said, 'we have never found one, but our people have always maintained that there is one great tunnel in the mountain behind us, and they say a great leader of our people long ago sleeps in there, and if we are ever in danger he will awake from sleep with his warriors and come out to help us. That is the story.' What about the treasures of the old Kretevs, the goblets, the golden horses, which I had been told from time to time were picked up on the escarpment? Then they *did* laugh. No such luck, they said, and when many years before some archaeologists had excavated the barrow-tombs down in the salt-flats, which were said to be the graves of primeval Kretevs, they found nothing inside but old bits of natural rock, placed there, it was supposed, because they bore some resemblance to human faces.

There was a thumping noise outside, and a rumble, and with a flicker the lights came on. Then we had supper. Everyone stayed for it, even the children who had been hanging about their parents' legs or staring at me from the doorway. It was goat stew in a huge tureen, with fibrous bread that Tiya had made. We helped ourselves with a wooden spoon and ate out of a variety of china bowls, some brought in from neighbouring caves because there were too few to go round. We never stopped talking. We talked about the origins of the Kretevs ('We came out of the earth, with horses'). We talked about the snow raspberries (not so plentiful as they used to be, but then that made for higher prices). We talked about Kretev art ('They do not understand your question') and Kretev religion ('We do not talk about that'). We talked about earning a living (their goat-herds, their market-gardens, their grassland where the cattle grazed). We talked about their language, but inconclusively; every now and then I heard words which seemed vaguely familiar to me, but when I asked their meaning no bells were rung, and when I invited the Kretevs to count up to ten for me, hoping to recognize some Celtic affinities, I recognized not a single numeral. What were their names again? Around the room we went, but not a name seemed anything but totally alien – Projo (I write as I heard them), Daraj, Stilts, what sounded improbably like Hammerhead. They had no surnames, they said: just the one name each, that was all. They needed no more. They were Kretevs!

Not Havians, I laughed, and that brought us to the condition of the city which lay, feeling a thousand miles away, through the string-bead curtains of that cave, and down the gulley across the salt-flats. What was happening down there? What was the vague feeling of malaise or conspiracy that seemed to be gathering like a cloud over the city? Who slashed the paintings in the palace chapel? Most ominously of all, what were those black aircraft we had seen on the way up? None of them knew. 'Bad things,' said Brack, 'that's all we know.' Were they worried? They did not seem to be. 'We are here, it is there.' Besides, they had no high opinion of life down on the peninsula. 'Do you not know', said Brack, speaking for himself now, 'what sort of people they are? Each talks behind the other. Have you not discovered? Hav is never how it says. So . . .' He splayed his hands in a gesture of indifference, and all around the table the brown faces gravely nodded, or leaned backwards with a sigh. 'We are here, it is there.'

*

And did they, I asked, ever see a Hav bear these days? Supper was over by then, and we were drinking out of a cheerful assortment of tumblers, cups and souvenir mugs from Port Said the Kretevs' own liqueur, made from the little purple bilberries which abound on the upper slopes of the escarpment, and alleged to cause hallucinations, like the magic mushroom, if you drink too much of it. There was silence for a moment. Somebody made a joke and raised a laugh. They talked among themselves in undertones. Then, 'Come on,' said Brack, taking a torch from the mantelpiece, 'come with us.' Out we trooped into the moonlit night, the whole company of us, some people scattering to their own caves to pick up torches; and so in an easy straggle, fifteen or twenty of us I suppose, torch beams wavering everywhere up the ravine, we walked up the gravel track towards the face of the escarpment. Above us the rocks rose grey and blank; all around the lights of the cave-dwellers twinkled; low in the sky, across the flatlands, a half-moon was rising. Through some of the open cave-doors I could see the flickering screens of TV sets, and discordant snatches of music reached us stereophonically from all sides. The engine of the generator rhythmically thumped.

It was a stiff climb that Brack led us in the darkness, off the sloping floor of the ravine, up a winding goat path, very steep, which took us high up the escarpment bluff, until those lights of Palast were far below us, the music had faded, and only the beat of the generator still sounded. The Kretevs, though considerably more out of breath than the hermits of the eastern hills, were not dismayed. They were full of bilberry juice, like me. The women merrily hitched up their skirts, the men flashed their torches here and there, they laughed and chatted all the way. They seemed in their element, in the dark, on the mountain face, out there in the terrain of *Ursus hav* and the snow raspberries.

Quite suddenly, almost as though it had been switched off, we could no longer hear the noise of the generator. 'When we hear the silence', said Brack, 'we know we are there' – for at the very same moment we crossed a small rock ridge and found ourselves in a dark gullet, with a big cave-mouth at the end of it. The Kretevs stopped their chatter and turned their torches off. 'We must be quiet now,' whispered Brack. In silence we walked up the gulley, and I became aware as we neared the cave of a strange smell: a thick, warm, furry, licked smell, with a touch of that muskiness that I had noticed on the Kretevs themselves – an enormously old smell, I thought, which seemed to come from the very heart of the mountain itself.

We entered the cave in a shuffling gaggle, like pilgrims, guided only by Brack's torch. It was not at all damp in there. On the contrary, it felt quite particularly dry, like a hayloft, and there was no shine of vapour on its walls, or chill in its air. The further we went, the stronger that smell became, and the quieter grew the Kretevs, until they walked so silently, on tip-toe it seemed, that all I could hear was their breathing in the darkness. Nobody spoke. Brack's torch shone steadily ahead of us. The passage became narrower and lower, so that we had to bend almost double to get through, and then opened out once more into what appeared to be a very large low chamber, its atmosphere almost opaque, it seemed to me, with that warmth and must and furriness. Brack shone his torch around the chamber: and there were the bears.

At first (though by now I knew of course what to expect) I did not realize they were bears. They looked just like piles of old rugs, heaped on top of one another, like the discarded stock of a carpet-seller. They lay in heaps around the walls of the chamber, motionless. But the Kretevs began to make a noise then, a sort of soothing caressing noise, something between singing and sighing, and all around the cave I heard a stirring and a rustling – grunts, pants, heavings. When Brack shone his torch around again, everywhere I could see big brown heads raised from those huddles, and bright green eyes staring back at us out of the shadows. The bears were not in the least hostile, or frightened. One or two rolled their heads over sleepily, like cats, burying them in their paws. One was caught by the torch light in the middle of a yawn. None bothered to get to their feet, and as the Kretevs ended their crooning and we stole away down the passage again, bumping into one another awkwardly in the silence, I could hear those animals settling down to sleep again in their soft and fusty privacy.

When we reached the open air again the moon was glistening upon the salt-flats below, and the Kretevs burst once more into laughter and conversation. They seemed refreshed and reassured by their visit to the bears, and gave me the impression that they would one and all sleep like logs that night, in their own scattered caverns of the hillside.

I did too, in my sleeping-bag in the cool back room of Tiya's cave, and got up in the morning in time to say goodbye to the market men before the dawn broke. The goatherds and gardeners were already climbing up the ravine. 'Come back again,' said Brack as he shook my hand, but I felt I never would. 'Look after yourselves,' I said in return. When I left Palast myself, a couple of hours later, all the young men had gone, and there were only women, children and old men to see me off. Their farewell was rather formal. They stood there still and silent, even the children, as I turned on the engine and started the Renault's reluctant ignition (not what it was when the tunnel pilots had it). 'Goodbye,' I said, 'goodbye.' They smiled their wistful smiles, and raised their hands uncertainly.

AUGUST

The Agent writes – symptoms – trouble – a decision in the night – saying goodbye – looking back

When I got home from my visit to the Kretevs Signora Vattani knocked on my door with a letter for me. It looked vaguely official, and important, or she would have left it on the table downstairs. She doubtless thought it was a social invitation, but it wasn't.

My dear Miss Morris [it said],

I am not certain whether in fact you consider yourself a British subject, but I think it best to let you know that according to our information the internal difficulties of Hav will shortly be coming to a head, and I consider it my duty to advise you to leave the city as soon as is convenient. You will I am sure be able to make your own arrangements.

My wife sends you her regards.

Yours sincerely,
Ronald Thorne
British Agent

I immediately went round to the Aliens Office and presented the letter to Mahmoud. What did it mean? Nothing, he said, nothing. It was just rumours, that was all. I should take no notice of it. What could the British Agent know that he didn't know? – why, he had been with the Governor himself that very morning. 'But if I were you,' Mahmoud added, 'I would not show the letter to anyone else.'

I showed it to everyone, of course, but they nearly all pooh-poohed it, or professed to. As the days passed, nevertheless, I felt the city's usual indeterminate disquiet, its habitual grumble or frisson in the air, unmistakably resolving itself into something more menacing. If I had been haunted before by the Iron Dog or the Cathars, I was pursued now by the implication of those two black aircraft.

Yes, what about those aircraft? Few people admitted to having seen them at all, but those who did said they were probably just passing over, or taking part in Turkish war games. Then it seemed to me that there were rather more of those baffling tramp steamers coming and going in the harbour, vague of destination and improbable of cargo, but Chimoun assured me that it was 'merely a seasonal fluctuation of traffic'. The gunboat moored at the Lazaretto had steam up one morning, for the first time since I have been in Hav, and that afternoon I found the Fondaco wharf screened off by canvas awnings, and was told to go round the back way by a sentry shouting down at me from the roof; I peered through a gap when he wasn't looking, but all I could see was a pile of banana boxes. The annual football match between the Salt Men and the Runners, representing in effect the Balad and the Medina, was indefinitely postponed 'owing to probable weather conditions', and it was announced in the *Gazette* that in future the Electric Ferry services would end at sunset, instead of midnight as before.

Little symptoms, symptoms in the mind perhaps. Nobody seemed to be worrying. Signora Vattani said: 'Believe me, I know what trouble is. I've seen enough of it in my time. I know when trouble's in the air.' Armand said: 'Yes, *ma chérie*, these are feelings that we all have after our first few months in Hav. It is like an island here. After a few months we pine to get off

– then we pine to get back again.' Magda said darkly: 'You're right, you're right, at last you feel it, you are becoming the true Havian at last.' Fatima Yeğen said she did not like to think about such things. I took to listening to the BBC news each night, but there was no mention of Hav.

I telephoned Ronald Thorne and asked him if he would elucidate his warning, or allow me to come to the Agency to talk about it. 'Really, Miss Morris,' he said, 'I think I have done my duty in writing to you. These are busy times for me. You must take your own counsel on these matters.' I telephoned Hav 001, too, but it was always engaged. I kept my eye on the various refugees I knew in the city, the Israelis, the Libyans, those two Russians, somehow supposing that they would be more sensitive than the rest of us to stirrings in the political atmosphere: they were still drinking in the same cafés, loitering around Pendeh Square, sitting on the waterfront, as they always did.

But by last week nobody could ignore the signs. On the Monday morning, very early, there was an explosion somewhere, and the electric power was off all day. The *Gazette* appeared with half its front page blank, and worshippers going to the Grand Mosque for morning prayers found that indecipherable graffiti in red paint had been scrawled all over its arcades. On Wednesday I was told there had been some kind of riot in the Balad, and when I walked across the square I found the Palace guards no longer in their white drill and epaulettes, with those quaint guns and those stylized smiles: they were in camouflage suits now, held automatic rifles, and seemed to be cultivating the facial expressions of martial art. 'Don't worry,' Mahmoud said, 'don't worry, that always happens at the end of July – this is their training time.' But when I drove south from the Medina later that day, intending to draw some pictures of the Iron Dog, the track was blocked with barricades, and notices said that the Conveyor Bridge was closed to traffic for essential repairs.

Now everybody was beginning to be anxious, without admitting it, without knowing why. The *Gazette* told us nothing, but nobody could fail to see the two black aircraft when they came back on Thursday morning, because they flew deafeningly backwards and forwards very low over the centre of the city, shaking the windows with the thunderous blast of their engines. There was a long, long line at the bank when I went to collect my draft. Fatima reported an unusual number of passengers leaving on the train. Somebody said they had seen all the rich yachts from Casino Cove sailing away together, as in convoy, south past San Spiridon towards Cyprus. At the café in Pendeh Square I met a disconsolate group of young Germans who had come to Hav on an overland adventure tour: they had expected to stay a week, they said, but had been ordered back up the Staircase that same night. When I asked Armand what could be happening, he said, testily: 'How can I know? I am just an old pensioner. I am no longer in touch.'

On Thursday night, soon after midnight, I heard a single protracted burst of automatic gunfire, somewhere quite close. Nothing more. I ran to my balcony and looked out across the city, but all seemed peaceful. A few people were walking along the pavement below. The last No. 2 tram was disappearing under the Brandenburg. I could see the lights of a ship moving slowly down the harbour past the dim outline of the Lazaretto. The Serai domes shone ominously above the roofs, and made me think of Diaghilev, the King of Montenegro, and Rimsky-Korsakov playing his piano in the palace garden. High above us I could sense, rather than see, the grey shape of the castle, up whose winding path, in a few hours, Missakian would be labouring with his trumpet for another day's lament – how many had the city heard, I wondered, and with what variety of feeling, since the Crusaders marched off between the silent ranks of Arabs to their waiting galleys at the quay?

I was moved by the moment, and by the thought of all the life and history, all the secrets and confusions, all the truths and fantasies, all the strains of blood and conflict that surrounded me there that night. I felt it was all mine! But though I heard no more gunfire, and though as the time passed, while I stood watching in the warm night, a profound and peaceful silence fell upon the city, yet I decided there and then to take the Agent's advice and make my arrangements to leave.

The city was frightened now. In the bazaar a myriad rumours were going about – of a coup d'état caught in the bud, of an impending Turkish takeover, a Palestinian conspiracy, a Greek plot, a kidnapping of the Caliphate or an assassination attempt at the Palace . . . Mahmoud denied them all, but was increasingly evasive. Remarkably few people, I noticed, were taking their lunches at the Athenaeum. Another note arrived for me, this time from Mario Biancheri: 'I shall not be at the market tomorrow. I have to go to Istanbul. I shall be at the Pera Palas. Ciao.'

When I went to the station to buy my ticket out, they told me that from that night the train would come no further than the old frontier. 'I can sell you a ticket, but you will have to make your own way up the Staircase – no rebates.' I decided to drive up there and abandon the car at the station, or give it to Yasar, if he was around. I spent the morning saying my goodbyes, but already it seemed Hav's brittle society was coming apart.

Fatima for instance, the first of my friends in the city, was not expected at the hotel that day, or the next either – they were not sure when she would be back, in fact. Armand was not at his apartment, nor at the Bristol, where the barman told me he had not been in for his noontime Pernod for a couple of days. I looked in at the Fondaco café, but Chimoun was not at his soup, and the two Russians were nowhere to be seen along the promenade. I had a last lunch at the Athenaeum with Dr Borge ('You see, you see!') and Magda ('Remember the Victor's Party?') but Mahmoud was nowhere to be found – 'He's probably with the Governor,' his assistant said.

I rang the Caliph again, and this time I got him. I congratulated him on not having been kidnapped. 'The Wazir will miss
you,' he said. I found Bob on the quay strumming his guitar as
usual to a little thing of his own:

> Nothin's goin' to be the same, no, no,
> Not while the years keep comin'.

He grasped my upper arm, looked me straight in the eye and
said: 'The first rule of life: you never know, you never know.'
The Signora was predictably tearful, as she accepted two
months' rent in lieu of notice, and gave me a picture of herself,
in slimmer times, to remember her by. When I threw my bags
into the front of the car old Abdu the Egyptian, from the Ristorante Milano downstairs, came running out of his door to
wish me luck – 'but you will be back – you know the saying,
"He who has drunk the water of Hav . . .!"' I gave the thumbs-
up to the Circassian sentries when I drove for the last time
around the square, and for all their camouflage gear they
responded with their old parade-ground smiles. Just as I
rounded the castle ridge, to take the road north through the
Balad, with a howl those black planes hurled themselves again
out of the eastern hills.

Above me on the Staircase a long line of cars was already
climbing. Others were following me across the flats. The winding track itself did not seem half so thrilling as it had when
Yasar raced me down it five months before, and I drove up easily enough in the lingering dust haze raised by the cars ahead.
Halfway up a Kretev stood, with his flock of goats, bemusedly
watching the traffic. When I reached the top of the ridge,
where the megalith stands, I stopped and got out of the car. It
was cool up there, and very still. Not a breath of wind blew, as
I climbed the little grass mound beside the standing stone.

Before me, over the tussocky moorland, the train stood at
the frontier station, a thin plume of smoke rising vertically
from its funnel, a clutter of cars and people all around. Once

again I was reminded of Africa, where you sometimes see the big steam-trains standing all alone, inexplicably waiting, in the immense and empty veldt. I looked behind me then, back over the peninsula: and like grey imperfections on the southern horizon, I saw the warships coming.

TWO

HAV OF THE MYRMIDONS

Six Days in 2005

Frontier ○ Station

▲ Megalith   The Escarpment

Tunnel

Arable and Grazing Land

Salt
Flats   ■ Yuan Wen Kuo

THE BALAD
and Airport

Road H1

Castle

MEDINA

Lazaretto
Island

S. Spiridon

Ferry Station

Iron Dog   Conveyor
              Bridge

0   15

Miles   5   10

HAV
2005

The Myrmidonic Tower

I

Lazaretto! – 'just arrived?'– the famous Kiruski –
old times' sake – High-tech – 'not much like the old days' –
a view from the top

The first thing you see, when you sail beneath the Conveyor
Bridge, through the Hook into the harbour of the new Hav, is
the Myrmidon Tower, the prime and very public talisman of
the Holy Myrmidonic Republic.

By the nature of things it is not often that one can enjoy first
impressions of a place twice over. But when the overnight hydrofoil brought me back to Hav, streaming in with foamy wake and
a mighty rumble of engines, it really was as though I had never
been there before. My emotions were different in kind from
those of twenty years before, but no less compelling, and I felt
just the same sensation of slightly unnerving paradox. Perhaps it
was all in the mind – the impact of the old Hav had certainly
been profound – but once again I seemed to detect some equiv-
ocation or ambivalence in the air, as we passed under the bridge
just as the sun rose, and saw that phenomenal tower before us. I
had never set eyes on it before, of course, and although it was
familiar to me from a hundred photographs, still it came as a
shock. There it stood, slim as a rake, two thousand feet of glass
and steel, and vastly illuminated above its triple helipads, dazzling even in the dawn, was its iconic device – the Myrmidonic
'M', flashing in sequential colours, red, yellow, green, blue, and
set against the Achillean helmet outlined in gold, that is the state
emblem of the Republic.

Disembarking at the Lazaretto resort is itself an unsettling experience. The minute I set foot upon the quay a porter in full Havian costume (wide straw hat, long white *gallabiyeh* striped with gold brocade) came swishing towards me. 'Dirleddy,' he said, speaking very fast, 'I think you are to be our honoured guest, you are expected, please follow me, your bags will be taken care of, welcome to Lazaretto, the name written with an exclamation mark because we believe you will find it a truly exclamatory experience.' The whole sentence was blurted out at a breath, as it were, as though by long-accustomed rote, and I remembered this as a Havian habit. The man did not wait for a response anyway, but led me at speed along tortuous shrubberied paths until we entered a hall of luxurious but queerly indeterminate design. It dazed me. It seemed like nowhere in general, but like many other places in particular, with allusions variously majestic, sinister and festive. It might be some Tolkienian grandee's palace. It was lit by flaming torches and swarmed all about by smiling servants in white and gold, bowing courteously and murmuring 'dirleddy' as they passed me.

'Welcome indeed,' said an alarmingly soignée receptionist, without much warmth. She was dressed all in gold Havian brocade, with dangling ear-rings apparently made of concrete. 'Your passport please. As a fraternal privilege you have been granted a blue pass by the Cathar League of Intellectuals. This permits you to visit Hav City and to make use of the League's facilities, but please note that it expires strictly in two weeks' time. Your passport will remain with me, your blue pass will be sufficient for identification if required. My colleague will now take you to your suite and it only remains to me to wish you a pleasant residence on behalf of Lazaretto!' – and somehow she managed to make the punctuation audible. Packing away my passport in a drawer, she summoned another minion. 'Palast One,' she said unsmilingly.

'Palast?' I queried as he led me through the shrubberies again. I seemed to remember the word. 'Yes, dirleddy,' he said, 'all the suites at Lazaretto remember places in the former Hav, before the Intervention.' Ah yes, I remembered then, Palast was the cave-quarter on the escarpment, where the troglodytes lived. And what had happened to the old Lazaretto island itself, which I remembered as the site of a rather merry pleasure-garden? Hardly a single building had been left standing on it, he told me. It had been artificially joined to its sister island of San Pietro, where Hav's gaol used to be, and given over entirely to this huge resort, Lazaretto with an exclamation mark, and to a Diplomatic Suburb, the whole dominated by the Myrmidon Tower. 'Very expensive,' said the porter, 'all very expensive, all for foreigners.' No Havian guests at all? 'No Havians, except in the Tower itself, of course, and unless our honoured foreign guests have blue passes, they are not permitted to leave the resort. But then, dirleddy,' he added, looking back at me over his shoulder, 'why would any of you want to?'

I saw his point when he left me in my quarters. From my sitting-room balcony I could see the lights of Hav City, across the bay; outside my bedroom the great skyscraper rose grandiloquently into the early sunshine; between the two vistas my rooms offered me, as an illuminated tapestry above the fireplace declared in stylized Cufic script, 'All That Your Heart Desires' – the Lazaretto equivalent, it struck me, of the notices in English boarding houses that used to forbid alcohol, loud music or Visitors After 10 p.m. But all my heart desired was sleep, so I was in bed by ten anyway.

In the morning I had breakfast at a canopied restaurant on the beach called The Salt Trade, in commemoration I suppose of Hav's ancient maritime connections, and asked for a pot of tea. 'Hav tea?' asked the waiter. 'Of course', I said. 'Quite right too', he smilingly replied, but it turned out to be horrible – bright green in colour, hard-leaved and sulphuric.

A very English middle-aged couple sat at the next table, and smiled over at me. 'Just arrived?', the woman said encouragingly.

'Crack of dawn', said I.

'Oh, you must be tired. Never mind, you're going to love it here, isn't she darling?'

'Absolutely. Nowhere better. Suites grand, climate a dream, food first class.'

'Well I don't think much of the tea', I said.

'Oh you poor thing, you probably had that awful Hav brew. They've only just started to make it, you know, and don't seem to have got it right yet. But Arthur's quite correct, in general the food's marvellous. We're the Ponsonby's, by the way, I'm Vera, he's Arthur.'

'I'll tell you, though' said Arthur, 'you don't want to experiment too much with the local stuff. Before the kerfuffle we used to stay at the old Casino here, up on the coast, and there they used to force the stuff on us rather, urchins and Hav mushrooms and all that kind if thing. Here they give you a proper choice, and if I were you I'd stick to the victuals you know.'

I thanked him for the kind advice. 'So you prefer this place to the old one?' I said.

'Oh absolutely', they both replied. 'Hundred per cent. Do you remember the mongooses, darling?'

'Do I not? Bloody animals snuffling about in the middle of the night. But fair play, they've got it all right this time around.'

'The thing is', she said to me, 'one feels so *safe* here. The security's really marvellous, it's all so clean and friendly, and, well, everything we're used to really. We've met several old friends here, and just feel *comfortable* in this environment. We shall certainly be coming again, won't we darling?'

'Oh, a hundred percent. I think it's bloody marvellous what they've achieved, when you remember what happened here.'

'Perfectly wonderful', she said. 'Well, have a lovely time, dear', she said as they picked up their bags and towels.

'Watch the sun, won't you – it's fiercer than you think.'

'And don't touch that tea again', said he. 'Stick to the old Darjeeling.'

*

Lazaretto is the one reconstruction work of Hav that has been made readily public – ostentatiously public, in fact, to the world at large. Almost as soon as the airport was completed plane-loads of foreign correspondents, travel writers and tourist promoters were flown in to see it arising from the wreckage. They called it The Ultimate Destination, Resort of Resorts, Loveretto. Architectural critics wrote learned pieces about its Myrmidon Tower, without making much sense of it, and gossip columnists welcomed news of the glitzy goings on – Princess Diana was one of the resort's earliest guests, a publicity coup which put it permanently on the paparazzi map and encouraged a stream of TV celebrities and footballers' wives from Cheshire. All the construction work was done by Chinese companies. The architects were mostly Chinese too, together with some from India and the Arab world, but I had read that they all worked under the supervision of an aged Havian philosopher named Hayyam Kiruski.

When, after breakfast, the resort's public-relations officer took me on a tour of the project, I asked her to explain this curious choice. 'You are aware I suppose', she replied, 'that the artistic heritage of Myrmidonic Hav has been essentially Minoan, in all genres. Our greatest artists down the centuries, from Melchik all the way back to Avzar himself, the supreme maze-maker, found their inspiration in the Cretan mysteries. That is why the Perfects invited our famous Kiruski to bring to this project an overriding sense of our intellectual heritage. It is an unprecedent project, you realize. There has been nothing like it in the history of civilization.'

Well, she was a public-relations person, but she may be right. The resort Lazaretto! is a vastly confusing sprawl of a dozen separate guest-houses, each with its own swimming-pool and squat Havian wind-tower, linked by a succession of bridges, hedged footpaths and pedestrian tunnels, and designed in a striking melange of moods or analogies. I am at a loss to define its style – like that reception hall, it seemed to me slightly Kremlinesque, and a bit Bedouin, with touches of the

Ottoman and underlying vibrations, so the PR lady suggested, 'of the unique evocative symbolism that is so characteristic of Hav's thought and art'.

Fine sandy beaches line the northern coast of the resort, impeccably raked, lined with cafés and patterned with chaises-longues and parasols. From there one can look across the harbour to Hav City on the northern shore. 'So near and yet so far,' the PR lady commented, 'yet there's nothing there that you can't get here.' It looked very different from the Hav I remembered. Gone was the esoteric skyline of turrets, minarets and gilded domes. Only the castle still stood on its crag high above. For the rest, all was a grey flattish blur of new buildings, low and flat, with a minaret protruding here and there, and a distant jumble of masts and riggings at the waterfront, but none of the gaudy eclecticism that made the old city so compelling.

In the southern part of the island, the former San Pietro, the foreign legations are assembled in a Diplomatic Suburb. My cicerone did not take me there. It was not part of Lazaretto, she told me, but was placed adjacent to the resort for administrative purposes. As in the old Hav, the sovereign states had been permitted to build their missions in their own national styles, 'folksy, modernist, mock-primitive, what have you,' and she was not impressed. 'The area is outside the direct remit of our famous Kiruski, and so lacks ideological certainty.' But actually, in the very middle of the whole ensemble, built on the landfill which has made the two former islands into one, the Myrmidon Tower stands, so far as I can see, utterly beyond ideology – a virtuoso display of unashamed, unrestricted, technically unexampled vulgarity.

Over lunch I told the PR person that nevertheless I would like to call that afternoon on the British Legate, in the Diplomatic Suburb. 'I can't think why,' she said, but she called the Legate for me anyway, on her mobile telephone. I asked if I could come and see him.

'What for?' he said.

'For old times' sake. I knew one of your predecessors, long ago.'

'And who might that have been?'

I thought of saying Harry Potter or Sir Homer Simpson, but restrained myself.

'I forget the name,' I said. 'It was a long time ago.'

'I see. Well come along at 3 p.m. this afternoon. You know where we are? I can give you five minutes.'

Again I considered a sharp retort, but what the hell, said I to myself, you're not going for the fun of it.

And fun it wasn't, my visit to the British Legate. I agreed with the PR lady. The Diplomatic Suburb turned out to be a drably incomplete development lot, laid out in petty avenues and crescents and a very far cry from Lazaretto! – a far cry too, from the grandiose diplomatic quarter of the old Hav. Half a dozen unprepossessing villas flew the flags of different states, and displayed half-hearted architectural features of their nationalities – here a florid touch of Alpinism, there the simulacrum of an Iowa barn – but several more were unfinished, and there were some vacant building sites, too. The British Legation had mock half-timbering and was rather like a Surbiton villa of the 1930s, even to the garden gate and the box hedges. *O tempora, O mores*, I thought to myself, remembering the colonial elegance of the old Agency.

The Legate opened the door himself when I rang the crested doorbell. He looked at his watch as we shook hands, and walked before me into a downstairs room with royal portraits above a desk and copies of *Britain Today* on a deal coffee-table. He was a plumpish man of about thirty-five, wearing an open-necked shirt beneath his suit jacket. He had a gingerish moustache and pale, protruding blue eyes, and suggested to me a middle-ranking regimental officer offered early retirement. His vowels were not impeccable.

'Now look here,' he said, 'I've found out about you since we talked, and I want to give you a few words of advice. I've had

trouble with your sort in previous postings. We had that Mary
Ann Abbott at Lagos, and that was bad enough. I'll be straight
with you. Here in Hav it just won't do. Do you understand
me? I gather they've given you a blue pass, God knows why,
but I'm not going to tolerate any hanky-panky or prying
about. You are a British subject, remember. None of that
Welsh nonsense with me. Do you get me?'

'I really only wanted to ask you–' I began, but he interrupted
me.

'Don't ask me a damn thing. If you want to ask anything,
ask at the Office of Ideology. You have a blue pass, go and ask
them. You see my situation here, I have a very small staff and
I have my work cut out for me. As for old times' sake, if I were
you I'd forget all about old times. Old times is not what Hav is
about. Old times is not what this Legation is for. Here, take
this to read on the way back to the resort. Hear, read and
inwardly digest.' And thrusting a pamphlet in my direction, he
led the way to the hall and without offering his hand closed the
door behind me.

I looked back when I got to the garden gate, and caught
sight of him watching me from a corner of his office window,
like a Parisian concierge at a lace curtain. The pamphlet was
an order from the Myrmidonic Republic, headed by the
Republican helmet-logo, and evidently circulated among all
foreign legations:

> Members of diplomatic missions accredited to the
> Myrmidonic Republic are reminded that they will be held
> accountable for the behaviour of foreign guests in the
> Republic. Reports of disrespectful conduct, circumvention
> of Republican security or privacy laws, blasphemy towards
> Cathar establishments or unauthorized intrusion into the
> affairs of the Myrmidonic Republic will invite serious
> repercussions. Foreign visitors should be advised that under
> Myrmidonic customary law private citizens are subject to
> the discipline of organs of the State, including diplomatic

missions, which are themselves permitted to operate within the Myrmidonic Republic only as licensed agents of that Republic.

No wonder, I thought as I walked back towards Palast One past the glittering entrances of the Tower – no wonder half those legations were unoccupied.

Lazaretto feels so utterly alien to all that I remember of the old Hav that when I returned to my suite I was surprised to find a letter awaiting me.

Welcome back [it said]. You are no doubt surprised to hear from me, after all that has happened in Hav since we last met, but the force of destiny can be merciful and here I am installed as general manager of Lazaretto! (spelled with an exclamation mark, please note, to show how excruciatingly fashionable we are). Remember Chevallaz, who use to be our restaurant manager? He now runs the catering here, with a staff of a thousand chefs. No, I am joking, but any complaints about the food, put them to him – not enough ginger with the sea-urchins, eels over-pickled, I know what a gourmet you are. It's all a far cry from the old Casino, but we are lucky to be here still, and there are still some friends about. Now then, mark in your engagement diary: Dinner with Mario, Casino Grill, 7.30 p.m. Monday evening! THIS VERY EVENING!! Until then, many embraces. Ciaou, Mario Biancheri.

PS. I expect you know that the book you wrote last time was banned after the Intervention, so I've never read it. I'm told it mentions me. If you happen to have a copy tucked away in your make-up bag . . .

I called home later, and this was an exhilaratingly Lazzareto experience, because it was all voice-activated. It works like this. You lightly press your door-key (a round metal representation of the Havian Maze) upon a gun-metal strip which runs around every wall of your suite, like a dado, whereupon a disembodied operator, speaking apparently out of the ether, invites you to place your call. Name the number you want, and after a few clicks and pauses the voice of your beloved replies from far away – not through a single loudspeaker, but through multi-stereos throughout the suite. You speak wherever you like – walking about, in the bath, pouring yourself a drink, and the voice from home is vibrantly all about you. The conversation ended, the last oral kisses exchanged, and a touch of the key on the tele-dado switches it off.

'Not much like the old days, eh?' said Biancheri at the dinner-table. 'Remember the black dial-phones at the old Casino? But look over there now – and there behind the bar was the very same barman whom I had known at the Casino in the old Hav, and years before that at Harry's Bar in Venice – still smiling the same Gorgonzola smile, still managing to wave a hand and polish a glass at the same time. 'You see? Not everything is gone . . .'

For I must understand, he told me, lowering his voice a little, that Hav's Myrmidonic rulers were no fools, whatever else one might say of them. 'They knew that our old team at the Casino was a good team, not only very professional, respected throughout the world, but also experienced in the sometimes circuitous ways of Hav. You understand me? They knew us, we knew them.

'At the Intervention we were scattered of course, as you will remember, but they had no difficulty in finding us. I had stayed in Turkey, old Giovanni there had gone back to Venice to retire, Chevallaz went home to his family restaurant in Zurich. It was not difficult to lure us back to help launch this some-what excessive venture. What's the phrase you have these days – over the top? OTT? Well, dear friend, if Lazaretto! is OTT, so were the opportunities they offered us.'

Chevallaz joined us then, and remarked to me that he was

glad our cat Ibsen had recovered from his wounded paw. I was
taken aback. How did he know about Ibsen? The two men
looked at each other wryly. 'My dear Signora,' said Chevallaz,
'you must realize that your telephonic system here is not exclu-
sively your own. High-tech is inter-tech in the new Hav.'

'Precisely,' said Biancheri, laughing. 'And you should
assume that if Chevallaz knows about it, by now the Security
Perfect himself is aware of your cat's misfortune. If you don't
wish to start a War of Ibsen's Paw, take my advice, Jan, don't
make use of the tele-dado in Palast One.'

I didn't know how to reply, but they soon changed the subject
anyway, and told me about their problems with the Chinese
construction workers, and their difficulties in adjusting the
demands of the hotel industry to the immemorial Havian ethos
– 'It must have been rather the same for whoever designed the
House of the Chinese Master, if he had Taoist theologians on
his back.' And what had happened to that House, I wondered,
that ancient wonder of Hav, which had amazed so many travellers down the centuries? Burnt out in the Intervention, they
told me, together with nearly all the monuments of old Hav.
The copper-domed Serai? The Montenegrin Legation? League
of Nations International Settlement, where I had lived last
time?

Gone, all gone, they said. Even the Medina was burnt to the
ground, and the slum-quarter of the Balad had been entirely
rebuilt – ideologically rebuilt, they said, *Myrmidonically*
rebuilt, and they laughed a lot. There was not much left of the
old Hav, as I would see for myself when I went over to the city
– 'You do have a blue pass, I suppose? Of course you do, or
you wouldn't be in Palast One.'

The truth seems to be that the Lazaretto island is a self-con-
tained, insulated conclave within the Myrmidonic Republic. If
visitors arrive by sea, as I did, they disembark there. If they
come by air, they are taken straight there by helicopter from
the airport. The island is in effect the Foreign Quarter of Hav,
all tourists confined there, all legations within their own

compound, rather like the districts where aliens had to live in Stalin's Russia.

But it is also the public face of the Republic. Everybody recognizes the image of the Tower. Every glossy tourist brochure portrays the luxury of the resort, with its restaurants and bars and bazaars and swimming-pools and casinos and boutiques and beaches, and the white-clad straw-hatted servants attentive at every corner. The brassily capitalist structure of Lazaretto is rigidly regulated by the Republic ('one feels so *safe*, dear'), and as everyone knows it is already one of the great international tourist destinations, attracting wealthy pleasure-seekers from half the world – 'just the same types,' said Biancheri, 'as used to come to the old Casino, only very much more so . . .'

After dinner he suggested I might like to see the view from the top of the Tower. By now the building was floodlit from top to bottom, and its lobby, sheathed in chrome, was blindingly illuminated. Soldiers or policemen were everywhere inside, wearing combat gear and toting automatic rifles, but the duty officer at the desk knew Biancheri. 'Where tonight, signor?' he said.

'No stops,' Biancheri replied. 'I would just like to show my guest the prospect from the top.'

'She has a blue pass? Show it me, please. Right. Proceed, signor. Car 7 it is'.

'Ciaou,' said Biancheri, and we stepped into an elevator. It was very large and empty, with glass sides, and when Biancheri pressed its only button it seemed to explode upwards out of its pad, like a rocket. My heart went into my mouth. I nearly fell.

'Dear God!' said I, 'you might have warned me.'

'Wait, my dear, in a moment or two you will be soothed. It is all arranged. Trust me.'

And it was true, for the elevator presently slowed, the lights were dimmed, my heart stopped pounding, and as we then sidled gently upwards I discovered that on all four sides of us there was an aquarium – an upright aquarium, as it were, extending to the top of the tower – an acquarium 200 floors deep, through whose waters, oblivious to us as we passed, a multitude of fish floated and loitered, golden, black and crimson shapes, with prickly fins or languidly trailing tails, drifting here and there in and out of the elevator's lights. Soft tuneless music played. The lights were dimmed. Up we glided through the fish and the water, weightlessly. After the detonation of our launch it was delightfully comforting.

'An old Chinese device,' Biancheri said. 'Haven't you seen the fish tanks in Chinese dentists' waiting-rooms? They were originally to calm anxious patients, but their effect is so addictive that nowadays dentists have them there for their own pleasure – like a narcotic. The Chinese who built this place carried the idea to extremes, and reversed it. First we get that almighty shock, and then in contrast we are given this lovely feeling of beauty and release. They call it Peace after Murder. It is part of The Lazaretto Experience.'

I wondered if every elevator travelled through the fish-tank in this therapeutic way, but no, it was only Summit Car 7, the number 7 being a traditional Havian symbol for contentment. It alone was non-stop, too. 'After all, the people who live here have to get off at their own floors sometimes – give them a chance!'

'And who are they,' I asked, 'when they're at home?'

But before he could reply we had reached the top, and stepped out into a second lobby, equally policed. We showed our passes. We signed a book. An electric door slid, and we stepped out on to the summit gallery. High above us blazed the great letter M, flashing its colours, and behind it Achilles' crested helmet, and above them both, invisible from the ground, were batteries of aerials and electronic dishes. There was a ceaseless hum of machinery somewhere. Below us a great glow of light emanated from the building itself, almost as though it was burning – it was like standing on top of a pillar of fire. And far down there on the ground Lazaretto was now laid out for me like a diagram, or a mathematical theorem.

Oh, the famous Kiruski had done his job well! Now I understood. It reminded me of those immense sand-drawings in the
Peruvian desert whose subjects are apparent only from the air –
spiders, crabs, monkeys that only the gods can see. Kiruski had
so arranged things that the meaning of Hav itself should be represented in this, its newest incarnation, but that only from its
utmost pinnacle, beneath the lamp of the great 'M' itself, could
it be understood. Now I saw it all, in all its allegory! There were
the lights of Lazaretto, far below us, and now I realized that all
its paths and tunnels and shrubberies and towered villas were in
the form of the circular labyrinth, the old Cathar symbol for
mystic perfection. On the other side the Diplomatic Suburb was
a metaphor of the mundane, patchily symmetrical, *sans* mystery,
sans discipline – decidedly lacking, as the lady had warned me,
ideological certainty. And high above it all, god-like in its
strength and selfishness, indestructibly the Myrmidon Tower
spread its glory, flashed its message of conviction across maze
and mediocrity, island, harbour and city itself.

'Are you all right?' asked Biancheri on the way down. 'You
look a little shaky.'

Something did seem to have happened to me up there – a
spasm of dizziness, like a transient mini-stroke. It might have
been the elevator, I told him, the rocket-jolt and the fish, Murder
and Peace, or perhaps it was the effect of all those electronics,
or just the height maybe. I thought it was more probably,
though, an overwhelming sensation of sheer *power* that had
overcome me in the tower – some kind of transcendental influence, you might say . . .

'Aha,' he said. 'Well perhaps you're right. There's a lot of
power stacked up in that building. And believe you me, they
know all about Ibsen's paw up there! Perhaps you're right!'

He walked me back to Palast One, through the garden
torches and the bazaars, and when we parted he said: 'You
take care of yourself, now. This isn't Llanystumdwy. Oh and
by the way, you can disengage the tele-dado by pressing a little
pink button behind the jacuzzi.'

TUESDAY

The Way of Genius

2

A baleful effect – expecting the answer yes – his deputies
awaited me – a magical tale – in memoriam – taking a turn

Because of the time change I woke early next morning, and
went out to my balcony to watch the dawn break. I remembered that on my very first morning in Hav, two decades
before, I had awoken to the sound of Missakian's trumpet
from the castle rampart, thrillingly echoing across the wakening
city. I stood there now in the half-light, looking towards the
distant outline of the citadel, hoping to hear that magical
reveille again.

As the sun's rim showed itself above the horizon I imagined
the trumpeter in the cold lee of the castle wall, wetting his lips
and raising his instrument as the city's minstrels had done
every morning for so many generations. But no. No silvery
trump called, to die away heart-rendingly into the mist.
Instead there suddenly sounded, tremendously amplified over
loudspeakers across the city, the lugubrious clanging chimes of
a carillon, playing music that I did not recognize but which
sounded almost fictionally antique. I was reminded, there and
then, of the prehistoric horns they keep in the National Museum at Copenhagen, found deep in a peat-bog, which are sometimes taken from their cases and played on ceremonial
occasions, and which were once described to me as sounding
'older than the bogs themselves'. And I remembered too how a
folk-band leader, in the Balad of years before, had described
Havian music as 'something very cold out of the long ago'.

So that carillon seemed – older than Hav itself, not indeed in the timbre of the instrument itself, but in the nature of its music, which seemed to employ rhythms I had never heard before, chords and intervals beyond the rungs of the harmonic ladder – rarities of nature, perhaps, like triply diminished thirds. Was it in some lost mode – Lydian, Phrygian, Havian? The effect was baleful anyway, and the loud clanging so depressed me that I went indoors and shut the window, so that the discreet rush of the air-conditioning would drown it. Poor Missakian, thought I, if he were still alive to hear it.

Just as I did so I noticed an envelope sliding beneath my door. It was stamped with the helmet logo, and was an invitation to visit the Office of Ideology at ten o'clock that morning – sharp. This sounded to me less an invitation than a summons, or at best one of those Latin interrogatives that expect the answer 'yes,' so I thought it best to accept, and made sure to be at the tunnel entrance just before ten.

Transportation is one of the many polished pleasures of Lazaretto. Wherever you are in the resort, whether you are walking down to the beach or just wandering around, within a minute or two a bright-painted resort buggy is sure to slow down beside you and ask if you need a lift – 'Welcome, dirleddy, make yourself comfortable, please; where would you like to go?'

It is especially convenient if you plan to go through the harbour tunnel to the city, because until late at night half a dozen buggies are perpetually going back and forth. All you must do is show your blue pass to the man at the gate, sign the exit book, and away you trundle into the underwater tunnel, which is gaily decorated all over with mosaics illustrating the history of Hav from Troy to the Intervention, concluding with a representation of the Myrmidon Tower, flat on the tunnel roof, whose colours gradually merge with the daylight that greets you outside. It is very stylish, very cool. 'Ideology Office, dirleddy? Hold on.'

I was sad to think that these poky little vehicles, like something off a Florida golf course, had replaced the Electric Ferry that had contributed so inescapably to the atmosphere of the old Hav, but I had to admit advantages: in a trice we had emerged from the tunnel into a city square, and the buggy-driver, removing his straw hat with a courtly air, was surreptitiously accepting my tip (for gratuities, Biancheri had told me, are forbidden not just at Lazaretto, but anywhere in the new Hav).

The square, Memorial Square, was entirely unfamiliar to me. The sea was out of sight, the waterfront was presumably behind me somewhere, and every single structure seemed to be brand-new. The buggy had dropped me before a large low building of white concrete. Its façade was plastered with a myriad Achillean helmets of marble, row upon row, rather as the Casa de las Conchas in Salamanca is studded all over with cockle-shells. I did not have to ask if this was the Office of Ideology. It had ideology written all over it. An armed sentry in white uniform and astrakhan hat, much like the military livery I remembered, gestured me inside with a charming smile, and in the severely functional lobby I was almost fulsomely greeted. It is true that I had to insert my blue pass into an identification slot, rather like putting a ticket into a railway-station machine, but the woman at the desk was wreathed in ingratiation. The Director himself, she said, was eagerly expecting me, being himself a scholar of the English language, and she congratulated me on my punctuality, a virtue much prized in Hav. It was a great pleasure to have me at the Office, declared this amiable functionary, and she herself took me up the white marble staircase to the office at the top.

'Ah, Dirleddy Morris, what a privilege to meet you,' said the trimly suited elderly man, wearing a red tarboosh, who rose from his desk to greet me. A monocle dangled from a golden cord around his neck, and what with this and the tasselled tarboosh, he looked remarkably like an Egyptian pasha of the previous century.

'Please, sit down, take comfort, and I'll join you.' Coming round to the front of his desk he sat beside me on a squashy flowered sofa and asked me if I would care for tea. 'No? Not indeed our finest Hav Broadleaf, cultivated in our new plantations on the escarpment slope? Well then, let us instead take a little chat.

'We are particularly pleased to have you as our guest, Dirleddy Morris, because here in the Office we have all perused your book, and we feel that you have an instinctive sensation, a gut-sensation as it were, for the fundamental identity, one might say the basic soul, of our beloved country.'

'I thought the book was banned,' said I.

'Banned? Oh dear me no, certainly not. For one reason and another it has been difficult to obtain in recent years, but as you see, we certainly have our hands on it here' – and reaching up to his desk he showed me a well-worn copy of *Last Letters from Hav*.

'There is one memorable passage which checked us of your empathy for the Hav meanings, and encouraged us to have the League of Intellectuals send you their invitation. It occurs on page 99.'

The page evidently had a marker in it, for he immediately opened it there. 'Would you care, dirleddy, if I reminded you of your own words? They are greatly moving to any true Havian, I think. You may remember that they demonstrate the return of fishing-boats into our harbour, and this' (he cleared his throat and put his monocle in his eye) 'is how they run:

' . . . the boats all have engines nowadays, but they often use their sails, and when one comes into the harbour on a southern wind, canvas bulging, flag streaming, keeling gloriously with a slap-slap of waves on its prow and its bare brown-torsoed Greeks exuberantly laughing and shouting to each other, it is as though young navigators have found their way to Hav out of the bright heroic past.'

*

'Those are your own words, dirleddy, and sublimital words they are. They bring the tears to my eyes to read them' – and he took out his monocle and wiped it, to demonstrate the fact – 'because they seem to see through the tumbled years into the bright heroic times of our beginnings. *As though young navigators have found their way to Hav out of the bright heroic past.* There it is, dear Miss Morris, there is the truth of us. There is the beauty of our condition, as we sail, shouting and laughing at one another, brown-torsoed into our newly reborn city. Thank you. You write as if you are yourself writing out of the soul of Hav, and that is why you are here as our honoured guest today.'

I don't suppose his was quite the sort of figure I had in mind when I wrote the piece (which I had forgotten all about), but I let that go. 'How very kind of you,' I said. 'I did wonder why the League had invited me, especially as I had heard you'd banned the book.'

'No, no, Ms Morris, I have told you. Indisputably not banned. Simply unobtainable for administrative reasons, I remonstrate you. As you will find, certain segments of it – that same glorious passage, for example – have been reprinted by this Office and intentionally circulated. We all very much hope that if you publish a sequel, bring your reflections on Hav up to the instant, we shall have the pleasure of reprinting it in full here in Hav – we would rather have it done here, because, you must know, your Western publishers are notoriously unreliable in matters of administrative cooperation. I am myself, as you may perhaps have observed, a student of English idiom, and I personally relish your use of vocabulary.

'So there we are, dirleddy. Our cards are displayed. It is an ornament to have you here, and I hope you will allow me personally to conduct you on an inspection of our new Hav. I know you have already tasted the wonder of Lazaretto. (They spell it with a symbol of astonishment, you know, just for effect – a cranky modernism, in my opinion, but you know what publicists are.) Now, you are expected for a morning conference with my deputies here at the Office, disposed for 10.30 sharp, and after an early lunch we shall spend the afternoon *en promenade*, so to speak. (We used to have a French resident here, before the Intervention – a literary cove himself, as it happens – and he always used to amuse me by his talk of going *en promenade* – so much more gentlemanly, he seemed to think, than simply taking a turn, as you or I would have exclaimed it.)'

With elaborate politesse he showed me to the door.

'My private name, by the way, is Dr Porvic, and I will now say you goodbye. See you later, alligator.'

I very nearly responded in kind, but I wasn't at all sure that he was joking.

Downstairs his deputies awaited me, five of them. They reminded me of the ideologues of apartheid who, long before, had greeted me with similar earnest solemnity at Stellenbosch in South Africa. There would be no joking with them, I knew. They sat me down on a hard chair in a small conference room, and gathered about me rather like medical students at an anatomy theatre. They were all young, all in suits and ties, all with small Achillean badges in their lapels, and they were clearly settling down to put me straight.

It was a bit like being lectured – not exactly brainwashed, just having inaccurate notions corrected. They knew, they said, of my well-known sympathy for the Havian ethos – the Director had told them about it, and they had read the Office's extracts from my book, and now wished only to make clear to me what had been achieved since the end of the Intervention.

Fundamentally, they said, the change was revelatory. When the Cathar Perfects had assumed power, after the withdrawal of the Intervening Force, they had made public the results of secret scholastic research which they had undertaken down the centuries, and which made apparent for the first time the profoundest origins of the State. As was well known, although the Cathars had been forced into anonymity in the sixteenth century, they had always been the true guardians of the Hav identity, but it had hitherto been supposed that the cult had been established here by knights of the First Crusade.

'Now then,' said they (I forget now which one of them actually said it – in my memory they seem to have spoken with one voice), 'I'm sure you are aware that the earliest known urban settlement on our peninsula was that of Troy. Schliemann himself identified its remains on the western coast, and there is no doubt that Achilles set up his camp there when the Iliadic expedition first arrived from the Aegean (there was, of course, no such thing then as Greece).

'You also surely know that Achilles brought his own bodyguard with him, Myrmidons, from the province of Thessaly in the north of what is now Greece. They sailed in their own ships – fifty of them in all. The Myrmidons long ago vanished from history, or legend for that matter, except as a synonym for fierce and dogged loyalty. By the time Achilles died they had dispersed, gone, vanished we know not where – Homer does not tell us.'

I was beginning to see the light.

'Are you beginning to see the light, Ms Morris? Dr Porvic tells us that your enlightened attitude to the meaning of Hav comes, he believes, purely by instinct. As we remember it, he tells us that you yourself come from the country of Wales – Cymru, is it? He says it is itself an often forgotten province of heroic origins, and suggests that this predisposes you, as it were, to absorb the Hav epic and its aesthetic.

'Be that as it may . . . I dare say you are aware that in the past it has sometimes been proposed that the Kretevs, the cave-dwellers of the Escarpment, were not as had previously been thought Celts from central Europe, but descendants of that lost Myrmidonic host. It is also indisputable that the Cathar cult itself drew its original inspiration from Eastern mysteries – in particular Manicheanism and related dualistic conceptions. Now DNA tests carried out by our Office ethnic scientists have indeed established that the Kretev blood-stream, or as we prefer to call it, Ethnic Authority, had no known Celtic affinities. On the other hand it showed scientifically detectable analogies to ethnicities of certain provinces of what is now called Greece.

'And here is the glory of it. During the Intervention, evidence was clandestinely discovered which proved without doubt – *we repeat, without doubt, Ms Morris* – that the ancient Cathar families of Hav, the Perfects of the ancient cult, *shared the same ethnicity.* In short, that our Cathar theocracy could claim unquestioned and legitimate descent from the Myrmidon warrior people who first came to Hav with the hero Achilles – possibly, unlikely though it sounds, through the medium of the troglodytes! It has even been suggested that Mani, the original prophet of Manicheanism, may have settled on our peninsula during his meditative wanderings. So it was established that the Cathars were, so to speak, the divinely sponsored rulers of our republic, suppressed for so many years by prejudice religious, political and ethnic.'

The five deputies sat back in their chairs, observing my reaction. It must have satisfied them. I was fascinated, and astonished. So much about the new Hav now fell into place.

'I see that the implications of this momentous certainty are apparent to you, and now you will begin more truly to understand the nature of our Republic. It is indeed revelatory. We honour, as it were, two aesthetics, one spiritual, one secular – not unlike the division of loyalties in the old Soviet republics, between theoretical Communism – Leninism, if you like – and the Stalinist State. On the one hand there is the mysterious aesthetic of the maze, which has been for many centuries the inspiration of Havian art and philosophy. It was itself perhaps introduced here from Crete – the Cretans themselves, you may remember, sent eighty ships to Troy. On the other hand. there is the more absolute aesthetic of the Myrmidonic tradition, bold, warlike, glittering. Just as the concepts of Good and Evil are accorded equal respect by Manicheans, so these two structures of thought and beauty have now been reconciled by the

Cathar theocracy, resulting in the Republic which, while grandly Myrmidonic in its outward aspects, is sustained by more ethereal principles beneath.

'Both are animated,' he continued, 'by an inner conviction, cherished by Cathars down the generations, that Hav occupies a particular transcendental position in the world at large, peculiar to itself, which is how it has maintained its separateness down the centuries. You will have noticed, perhaps, from your visit to the Tower, that when our famous Kiruski designed the Lazaretto island, he made sure that all three conditions were to be allegorically represented. The brilliance of the resort is balanced by that less lovely appendage, the Diplomatic Suburb, expressing the darker nature of creation, and high above there rises in culmination the magnificent assurance of the Tower. And the whole is embraced within our immemorial symbol of the maze.'

So there, said the directors, as one man, now I knew all.

'But you talk about aesthetics,' I protested, 'you say nothing about practices.'

'Practices?' said their leader. 'You mean political practices, economic practices, matters like that? Dirleddy, they fall outside our province. We deal in this Office with Ideology and Ethnic Authority. Day-to-day management affairs you must discover for youself – and if we are to go by Dr Porvic's assessment of your talents, we are sure you will! Ah, and here he is now!'

For the Director was waiting for me in the lobby, when I left the conference chamber with all the deputies. 'Well, how did the convening occur?' he asked to the radiant smiles of the woman at the reception desk. 'Did my deputies instruct you well?'

'Excellently, although I have to say that in some ways they left me more confused than I was before.'

Ha ha, laughed all the deputies, and Porvic did too. 'Ah, dirleddy, that is the mazian aspect of our national personality. If you would like to discuss it more deeply I will happily introduce you some of my colleagues with a profounder knowledge of it than I can myself profess, or even my learned deputies here. Best of all, I can lead you to our famous Professor Kiruski, who is the most eminent authority of them all.'

But no, I said hastily, 'I've only got two weeks,' and the Director and his deputies laughed again.

'Urchin soup?' he asked as we left the building, to the winning salute of the sentry. 'Would that satisfy your taste-buds?' I remembered the waterfront café I used to frequent, which made a speciality of sea-urchins, and attracted a wonderfully cosmopolitan, raffish and bohemian clientele. I assumed it had been buried under the concrete of his own office, but he took me round the back, and there in a cluttered alley, overshadowed by that wall of Achillean helmets, the same old café appeared to thrive.

'We forfeited so much of our heritage in the Intervention,' the Director said, 'that some of us have done our best to preserve those native institutions that survived. As it occurs, and you would not of course have known it, this café was always a gathering place of Cathars, where many adherents met to plan the continuance of the cult. It was very dangerous to be a Cathar in Hav, you know. Many of my own ancestors died for their heresy.'

We sat down at a heavy wooden table, on a heavy wooden bench, and very respectful servants, recognizing the Director, filled our soup-plates with the bubbling urchin-broth, fragrantly steaming. 'You call it a heresy? That seems ironic.'

'Well *they* called it a heresy first, when they tried to exterminate our enlightenment in the so-called Albigensian Crusade, but more recently we assumed the phrase ourselves as an emblem of our defiance. And our pride. Our heresy was, after all, the top-hole truth.'

I have never been absolutely sure what the Cathar heresy was, but having sat through one ideological lecture already that day, I changed the subject. What about the carillon and the dawn trumpet-call, I asked?

'Ah, the trumpet, Katourian's Lament, ah, what a falling-off is there. Even in Hav we make our errors. Even in Hav we have our differences of taste or historical judgement. I don't altogether know how to affirm this, but it has to be conceded that some segments of our society are, you might say, more go-ahead than others – though all working from the heart, of course, for the good of our Republic, under the guidance of our Perfects, no argumentation about that. As Avzar Melchik worded it in his greatest work – now then, how can I translate it for you – let's see . . . well, something like 'A rose without petals has lost its flavour' – you maintain my drift?

'So, the petals of my particular Office – the Office of Ideology and Ethnic Authority, to give it its full title – our petals are of traditional flavour. We are Kiruskians lock, stock and barrel. Our colleagues at the Office of Public Ritual, on the other hand are, shall we postulate, somewhat less devoted to the *status quo ante*. We have contrived to reconstruct this café in its traditional posture, because it stands within the focus of our own building, but if the Public Ritual people had the authority they would undoubtedly have replaced it with a cafeteria.'

'Dear God,' I said, spluttering politely over my soup, 'a *cafeteria*!'

'Precisely. Imagine! The trouble about the Lament arose when, after the Intervention, sympathizers of our republic in China, with whom we enjoy cordial relationships, on an old-boy basis in fact, wished to chip in a symbolical contribution to our efforts of reconstruction.'

'Decent of them,' I said, for I was beginning to get the conversational hang of things.

'Granted. But what they gave us was not hard cash but that confoundable carillon. It's mounted up there at Katourian's Place, in a little summer-house sort of place, and every damned morning it plays our national anthem – mechanically, of course, and frightfully loud.'

'Dear me. No work for Missakian, then.'

'By Jove no. Missakian Costas was the last trumpeter,

killed poor fellow on the very day of the Intervention. The shell terminated his life just as he was playing the Lament that morning, and his very trumpet is preserved in the museum – we shall see it in a moment or two.'

'But what is that anthem? I never heard it before.'

The Director assumed a mystic tone of voice, as if we were in church. 'Ah, that is a different tale,' he said. 'It is a magical tale. After the Intervention, when the Holy Cathar Government revealed itself and assumed authority, there was need for a new national hymn, more ideologically relevant. You may perhaps remember the former one? No? Well, be that as it was. Because of the ancient Cathar proscription of sacred song, it was decided that a solely melodic anthem must be sufficient to express our national gratitude. But how, dirleddy' – he asked me rhetorically – 'how, dirleddy, could a sufficient tonality be found for so exalted a function?

'The answer is: by a miracle. Unbeknownst to anyone, hidden in a wall of the Séance House was a most ancient manuscript, brought to light by the exact same shell-burst that terminated poor Missakian. Our Perfects hastened to examine it, and found it to be a hitherto unbeknownst musical score, in the medieval Catharist notation, of extreme beauty and obvious ideological reference.

'One of our brilliant young music students re-notated it for contemporary use, and that is the smashing melody, dirleddy – smashing even at the hands of that monster machine – which you doubtless heard this morning calling us all to loyalty and gratitude. Isn't that a palpable miracle? Wouldn't you say so?'

After lunch – a second bowl of soup for Dr Porvic, I noticed, on the house of course – we walked around the corner to the Museum of the Intervention, which was a building precisely the same as the Ideology Office, only smaller, and with fewer Achillean helmets on it. We were met at the door by the curator, who greeted Porvic obsequiously but hardly noticed me. The very first thing he showed us, in a solitary cabinet inside the entrance, was Missakian's badly dented trumpet, described as 'The historic instrument of Missakian Costas'. Beside it, I was touched to see, was the plaque erected on the castle rampart in 1837 by officers of the British Royal Artillery. It had commemorated the original musician, Katourian, after whom the trumpet-place was named, but Dr Melchick said it was now there to remember everyone who had blown the Lament at Katourian's Place down the generations. 'Call me sentimental,' he said, 'if you like, but I myself caused that plaque to be re-erected here' – and it seemed to me that he blushed.

Next there was a room called Animal Pride, 'in memoriam,' the curator said, 'of the Havian species exterminated in the Intervention'.

'Sad, sad losses,' murmured Porvic to me.

'Sad indeed,' the curator sanctimoniously confirmed. 'Oh the sadness of it!' The Hav bear was apparently gone at last, and a pair of them looked out at us from their specimen case in sad self-memorial. 'The Kretev troglodytes were their guardians,' said the curator, 'and when they were driven out of their caves nobody was left to champion the bears.' The Hav hedgehog had disappeared too, and there had certainly been no sighting of the Hav wolf since the Intervention.

Only the Hav mongoose, said the curator, seemed to have increased during the past twenty years, and even it had migrated out of the coastal districts into the city suburbs. 'A good thing too, perhaps,' I ventured to suggest, remembering what Arthur had said about the creatures, but the curator looked at me coldly. 'On the contrary, *herpestes hav* is one of our national emblems, a mongoose like no other, with its uniquely elongated tail. Some scholars say the Iron Dog itself was modelled upon it. It has been proposed that it might indeed be recognized as the official animal of the Holy Cathar Republic.'

Oops, sorry, I almost said, but Dr Porvic said it for me. 'Our honoured guest, though empathetic indeed to the Hav ethos, is as yet relatively innocent of its fauna, and does not realize the import of the mongoose.'

'Ideological import?' I asked.

'Quite,' said the curator, mollified, and we moved into the main rooms of the museum, the Labyrinth of Memory. There were six of them, and every inch of them, even their ceilings, wall after wall, room after room, was covered with photographs from 1985. It was like being buried alive in a ruin. Everywhere one looked there were piles of rubble, tottering walls, blackened beams, figures huddled in the shadows, burnt-out cars, skeletonic girders. I could almost smell the charred wood. I did not want to linger.

'I understand,' said Dr Porvic sympathetically. 'It is an emphatic representation. Yet it was a wonder that so few people were killed – such utter destruction, such miraculous refuge. A wonder too that the native morality of Hav, our moral inheritance, was not shattered by the bombardment. And as a final tribute to that fiery spirit, descended from our distant ancestors, those bare bronze-torsoed heros you have yourself celebrated, we have kept our museum's final room as a symbolical tribute.'

He signalled to the curator, who thereupon flung open huge double doors of oak, to reveal a single enormous oil-painting, magnificently framed, standing like an icon in the middle of the room. It was painted in the half-naif, half-oriental style known as the Hav-Venetian, and I knew at once what it showed. It showed the House of the Chinese Master, in flames.

'Our most noble public treasure, at its moment of supreme nobility.'

There stood the legendary building, ablaze on all its floors, swirled around by smoke, and all about it were charred and tumbled ruins. It alone was brilliantly illuminated, by its own lights, by the fires, by what seemed be a shaft of sunlight – or moonlight? – penetrating the black smoke to throw its ancient silhouette into relief. It was like a shrine.

'We call this the Ark of Genius. As you know, the architect of the House remains unknown, but of course the reference is allegorical anyway. It is the genius of Hav itself that this room commemorates, defiant through thick and thin, stiff upper lip despite all.'

'Who painted the picture?' I asked.

'That is the final miracle. Nobody can know. It was found torn and crumpled on the person of Missakian the trumpeter, before his burial.'

Directly behind the shrine, outside the museum doors, there was a viewing platform. From there I could see no sign of carnage. I was looking over the site of the old Serai, but I could hardly make out even its outlines, so devastating was the destruction but so complete the rebuilding. What we saw from that platform was a brand-new metropolis of mirror-glass, steel and concrete, metallic, regimented, criss-crossed with over-passes, traffic-lights blinking everywhere, teeming in an almost stylized way with traffic and pedestrians – some in Turkish-style hats and suits, some in traditional Havian *gallabiyehs*. Its buildings were flat-roofed and of uniform height throughout, except for a few shining tiled minarets, lumpish cranes and aerials. Nearly all had been built, so Porvic said, by the very same Chinese firms who had built the International Settlement sixty years before.

It was like one of those Cities of the Future one used to see at World Fairs, or in architectural journals. Touches here and there of post-modernism – here a pinnacle, there a squirl – only emphasized the intense functional feeling of everything, and I looked in vain for some familiar street pattern, the echo of a bazaar, the remnant of a park. I could hardly believe that in this very city, only twenty years before, I had lived in surroundings that were, in their peculiar way, really rather homely – the Russian domes, the German beer-gardens, the French cafés, the whole melded into a a shabby Levantine languor. Now, it seemed to me, I was looking at a cityscape machine-made, computer-calculated, absolute.

'I see you are taken aback,' said Porvic sympathetically. 'It is indeed a shock, to see new life exploding so dramatically out of desolation. But from small acorns mighty oaks do grow, and out of our destruction we have extracted a sense of symbolism, of liturgy even, that offers some public expression to the nuances of our ideology.'

I was not at all sure what he was talking about, but I obeyed him when, with a courtly bow and a screw of his monocle, he concluded: 'Pray to accompany me now, as we confirm our promised turn.'

From the front steps of the museum, in a direct straight line from the Ark of Genius, a wide pedestrian street of ceremonial, funereal or perhaps Masonic feel cut through a parade of doorless office blocks, with heavily barred windows. It was ornamented only with a single row of Achillean helmets. There was something occult about it – it reminded me of the street that runs straight as a die from the hill of Jingshan in Beijing through Tiananmen Square to the Temple of Heaven where the Emperors of China would commune with their only superiors, the gods. I recognized nothing as Dr Porvic led me solemnly down it. 'We call this the Way of Genius,' he said, and presently we reached the end of it, and suddenly saw before us, astonishing as ever among a stern circuit of new buildings, the actual House of the Chinese Master.

It was no more than a blackened ruin, of course, propped up with steel girders, its terraces sagging, the pools and bridges at its base scummy and neglected, but from the utmost point of its pagoda flew not the helmet-ensign of the Myrmidonic Republic, but the old chequered flag of Hav – the first time I had seen it since my return. And surrounding the ruin, enclosed within a gold-tipped wrought-iron fence, was a garden, almost a park, brilliant with masses of wild flowers – Hav bluebells, buttercups of the Escarpment, white saxifrage, flowering moss, poppies, and everywhere, climbing over walls and up the parapets of bridges, softening and moistening the pavements, that spectacular queen of the Havian fauna, *scrophulariaecaea haviana*, Hav toadflax, with its tall bright plumes of purple and yellow.

It was overwhelming, this sudden glimpse of the innocently

exotic. 'The Perfects themselves compassionately decreed that here, and here only, the former flag of Hav should fly, night and day, to honour that time of tragedy and revelation, and that the House should never be demolished. And the flowers of the garden? Dirleddy, when this entire city was laid waste by our enemies, leaving only a steaming and blackened wreck, when our people were living in cellars or sheltering in shattered structures, or had fled the city to the countryside – at that black moment, like a promise of recompense our own native wild flowers sprang up everywhere through the city, carpeting the ruins and the shambled thoroughfares. This little patch of our native flora has been preserved just as it was from those grim times, untouched by gardeners or improvers, playing and weaving for ever just as it did around the Master's House in its forlornity.'

It was the most beautiful thing – the *only* beautiful thing – that I had seen in the new city. The Director removed his monocle from his eye, and wiped it thoughtfully with his handkerchief, before walking me back to Memorial Square. When a buggy arrived to take me home under the water to Lazaretto he seemed quite moved.

'You do appreciate, dirleddy, do you not, that for Cathars the Intervention had a doubly allegorical intimation. It was a tragedy of course, but it was also a scouring, a purgation if you prefer. The Greek Κάθάροις, I don't have to inform you I'm sure, signifies a purgation, a catharsis in fact, and so to Cathars any kind of scouring, even the cruellest kind, carries within it a seed of perfection. Thus in an unwavering track our emblematic memory conveys us from the fire to the ruin to the flowers. And even the flowers carry a message, for the true flora of our beloved city are us, its sons and daughters.'

He paused for a long silence. 'And so farewell, dirleddy,' he then concluded, as we shook hands. 'No doubt we shall meet again.'

For a moment I considered my response. 'See you about, trout,' I said at last, and looked at him cautiously. I think the old man smiled, but I couldn't be sure.

WEDNESDAY

Warship Carlotta

3

'You never know' – league talk – on the Fondaco –
an old ship – sacred site – but I didn't go home

Next morning I again had my breakfast in the sunshine at The
Salt Trade, and there my English acquaintances greeted me
enthusiastically.

'Morning, morning, Jan!' cried Arthur. 'Come and join us,
do. Top of the morning to you!' and Vera observed that I was
looking better already – 'I did think you looked a little peaky
the other day, but I expect it was just the long journey.'

And what had I been doing with myself? they wanted to know.
They hadn't noticed me on the beach at all, in fact they hadn't
seen me since that teatime – when was it? – Monday ? – Tuesday?
'How fast time passes when you're enjoying yourselves!'

I told them the first thing I had done when I left them last
time was to call upon the British Legate.

'Very wise, very wise. Can't be too careful in these places,
even one like this.'

'Do tell us. What kind of a person is the Legate? Is he, as it
were, one of the old sort? Nowadays our Ambassadors and so
on always seem to be commercial attachés or whatever they
call themselves, so we don't generally bother to call. What's
this one like? Do tell.'

'I shouldn't pry, Vera darling, if I were you,' Arthur intervened. 'They always used to say in the old days that the Hav
Residence was a proper spy-nest, and perhaps Jan is in that
racket too!'

She laughed a tinkly, silvery laugh. 'Oh I hardly think so. Arthur spent a lot of time travelling, you know, before he retired from the company, and used to see spies all over the place, or thought he did.'

'Only joking, darling. I imagine the Legate's got quite enough to do here nowadays without bothering about espionage. Looking after himself all right, I suppose?' he said to me. 'Nice house, garden parties and all that? He doesn't have to go far for the catering, does he?'

I gave them a quick run-down of the Legate's circumstances, as they had struck me, and I was about to tell them about the pamphlet he had given me when a servant approached our table with a mobile telephone on a silver tray. 'Call for you, dirleddy,' he said to me.

'Jan?' said the caller, extremely loudly. 'Jan? Is that you? You'll never guess who this is. Remember Magda? Magda at the old Athenaeum? That's me! Yes, yes, terribly ancient but still alive and kicking, I'm happy to tell you.

'Now listen, Jan. You must come and lunch with me today. Yes, this very day. No, I won't take no for an answer. Several of your old acquaintances want to see you too. Where? Why at the League of Intellectuals of course – the Athenaeum that was, though you'll find it very different from what it used to be. I know you have a blue pass, so all you have to do is jump into one of those horrid little buggies and come straight here. They'll know where it is. No, no, Jan, I won't take no for an answer. Twelve o'clock sharp, at the League. Anton will be here? Remember Anton? And Ludo Borovic and, oh, lots of people you know, not to mention my lovely black husband.'

I didn't know any of them, but 'OK Magda,' I said, 'twelve o'clock at the League.'

The Ponsonbys were intrigued. 'So you have friends in the city?' said Vera rather querulously. 'Fancy that!'

'You see, darling, you never know,' Arthur said with a wink to me.

*

Magda was waiting for me in the hall of the League. I remembered her at once – twenty years older, her black hair turning to grey, but still dark and vibrant, as though she had something urgent to tell everybody every day, and dressed gypsy-style, as always, in a long flowered skirt and a white blouse half off her shoulders, numerous scarves and heavy brass bracelets. With her was a handsome middle-aged black man.

'You see! Here we are – just the same only a little older! You remember Henri? Of course you do – you remember, you met at the Victor's Party, the year poor Izmic won?'

Of course I did, I could say with all honesty, as from some phantasmagorical dream – the Levantine colour and queerness of that lost Hav, the Governor and the elusive Caliph and Izmic himself with his red ribbon and his smarmed-down hair, and Mazda on the arm of this proud African.

'But you may not realize that this building occupies the very remains of the old Athenaeum, where you and I first met – the one is the direct successor of the other, as it were. This is the same room!' I remembered that first meeting too, if only hazily, but as for the Athenaeum – well, nothing could be more different than the spotlessly clean and orderly club-room we now entered. It was enormous, as the old one had been, but this one was comfortable, panelled in pale Hav ash, pilastered and austerely symmetrical. It was lit by half-hidden ceiling lights, in clumps around the room were squashy sofas, armchairs and tables with spindly legs, and on the walls hung large but unexciting abstracts. If Lazaretto tended undeniably towards the nouveau riche, the League club-room struck me as modestly neo-Fascist – perhaps in the decor they used to call, in Mussolini's Italy, Rationalist.

The place was full of men and women. Some were in Hav caftans, and in one corner was a group of classically Arab-looking people, men in white kuffiyahs with silver daggers at their waists, women blackly veiled. All were talking very loudly in the manner I remembered from the Atheneaum. All were sitting – nobody standing about in conversation – but waiters in *gallabiyehs* glided industriously here and there, their trays cluttered with plates and glasses. The scene was almost disciplined. Only the noise was unrestrained.

'It feels like *déjà vu*,' I wanly remarked.

'Oh come on,' said Magda, 'don't give us that balls. It's nothing like the old place. Don't you remember the mess of everything, and queuing for our food ourselves – at that very corner over there, as a matter of fact? And what about the people – look at them! Look at that huddle of Arabs, Henri – where have they sprung from? They call it the League of Intellectuals but there isn't one in a hundred here who writes or composes or even reads! Isn't that true, Henri?'

'One in a thousand more like it.'

'Oh no, Jan Morris,' Magda said, 'don't give us any of that nonsense about old times.'

She led us to a table and chairs bang in the centre of the room, where the hubbub was worst. I wondered why.

'Because here, in all this noise, nobody can bug us.'

Pure waste of time actually, Henri said. Bugging people as Magda imagined, with hidden mikes and all that, was just a joke by now. There were much subtler means of surveillance nowadays. 'But bugger them anyway. Better safe than sorry. When we want to talk, we take a walk.'

So we settled ourselves in the middle of everything, and without anyone ordering there arrived a succession of dishes – cold goat-meat slices, chips, Hav hummus, frogs' legs, chunks of eel, urchins of course and, wonder of wonders, bowls of fruit that were defined for me as snow raspberries (canned of course, said Magda, but still . . .). From time to time people stopped by to greet us – a shifting company of Magda's and Henri's acquaintances, Antons and Ludovics and Marettas, who claimed somewhat unconvincingly to remember me, and solemnly took a single chip from our plates, or a prawn, or a lump of bass-roe, almost as a matter of ritual, before bowing and proceeding.

'We call it sharing our sustenance,' Magda said, 'which is a sort of code for sharing our convictions. We are the Sustenance folk! You have only been here half an hour, but already you have met half the true intellectuals of this so-called League. Oh, and here's another – remember Azzam, he of the Alien Office long ago? Now he's the most private of our private citizens – isn't that right, Azzam?'

Azzam delicately took a snow raspberry, and sat down with us. He was smiling gently. He had aged, but I remembered him. The earnest young bureaucrat with pens in his breast-pocket had become the stooped, scholarly-looking gentleman in a tweed shooting-jacket, carrying under his arm what looked like a sketching-pad. 'A pleasure to meet you again,' he said. 'You perhaps remember me as Mahmoud, but I am always Azzam now, don't ask me why.'

'If you want the facts,' Magda said, 'Azzam's your man. Isn't that right, Henri?'

'Azzam's the boy, definitely,' said Henri. 'Sit down, boy, give us the facts.'

'The facts are,' said Azzam, fastidiously biting into his snow raspberry, 'that there are no facts. Facts are factotum in the new Hav. Facts are faxes. Faxes are facts. Fair blows the fact on summer eve, and fierce the mountains fart.'

Magda laughed. 'Bravo, Azzam. But Ezra Pound's dead, you know. So is constructivism. So is post-constructivism. So's Braudel, Jan, isn't he? that old fraud you used to admire so much. Melchik certainly is. So just talk straight now, dear Azzam, and explain to Jan here whatever it is you're going to explain.'

Azzam smiled again. 'All right, Magda, but where to begin? How much does the dirleddy absorb?'

'Try me,' I said.

'Spill the beans,' said Henri.

'Tell her the truth,' said Magda.

'Tea?' said a passing waiter with a pot. 'Best Hav Broadleaf, freshly plucked?'

'*That's* the truth,' Azzam suddenly shouted. '*That's* the new

Hav truth! Freshly plucked broadleaf that tastes like shit, and GM snow berries out of a tin!'

Half the people in the room turned to see who was shouting but, when they saw it was Azzam, seemed to lose interest. Magda said, 'Enough already' (she loved old American movies, I remembered), and so the four of us left the League of Intellectuals, with me sheepishly in the rear.

I thought there seemed something something contrived or stagy to this episode. It was like a performance, climaxing in Azzam's blatant eccentricity. It was like a charade, in which I had played a non-speaking role.

'Man, these Brits are too quick for us,' said Henri when I voiced the thought outside the club, 'but believe us, don't disturb yourself, our Myrmidonic stiffs are too damn slow to perceive the nature of the game.'

What *was* the game, I wondered? but I was soon distracted. Out of the League, Magda led us round the back, past the Office of Ideology and down a street of blank new warehouses, until we found ourselves on the Fondaco Quay. 'There,' said Magda, 'now you *can* talk about old times!' For it was very like the waterfront I knew, only more so. It was more crowded, more bustling, more animated that ever it was in my memory. The afternoon was bright, and across the harbour I could see Lazaretto island with its topsy-turvy skyline of bobbles and wind-towers, and the immense pillar of the Myrmidon Tower flashing its signal still – from here it looked as though it was emerging from the water itself, shaking the drips off. Beyond, the hills closed in to the narrow passage of the Hook, and far away I could just make out, glistening blue-green, a stretch of open sea. It was a sparkling scene, and the activity of the waterfront matched it.

'Wow, what's happened here?' I exclaimed in delight, and they explained it to me. Since the dredging and widening of the Hook larger local craft had been able to use the city quays, and Hav's new status as a vibrant entrepôt meant that coastal shipping from a much wider area now brought their goods for unloading and re-shipping here. The really big freighters, the container ships, docked at the new deep-sea port at Casino Cove, but larger salt-ships could now tie up here, and a new traffic of dhows and traders found it profitable to sail through the Hook to Hav.

I could see it for myself. The Fondaco itself, the great Venetian caravanserai which had dominated the waterfront, had vanished, and in its place were five or six large and unlovely warehouse blocks, with a myriad aerials on their roofs and huge commercial signs all over them.. And the quays themselves were crammed with a marvellous variety of dhows, moored there side by side, sometimes three or four abreast, a jumbled mass of high poops and superstructures, fluttering flags, gangplanks from vessel to vessel, ship to shore, huge piles of crates or sacking, derricks and winches and rumbling generators. Along the quays trucks stood double- or triple-parked, nose to tail, with longshoremen stacking them with goods, foremen shouting through loudhailers, a revving of engines, a hooting of horns, and everywhere a busy mass of men and women, in dungarees or *gallabiyehs*, the wide straw hats of Hav, Arab *kuffiyas*, bright gypsy headscarves, turbans, skullcaps and occasional burkas – a tumult of humanity, always shifting, always noisy, laughing and shouting in a babel of languages. Off-shore idly lay a couple of coastal freighters, smoke drifting from their funnels, and there was a flurry of small boats. Fishing-boats with the graceful old Hav rig navigated their way among the mooring-buoys, and motor-boats scudded here and there, and out on the harbour I could see a lovely white streamlined vessel, low in the water, making its way to the salt-quay.

I was greatly encouraged by all this. 'Now you can talk of old times,' said Magda, squeezing my arm affectionately. 'Here, here on the old waterfront, the real old times survive.'

'And it is here,' said Azzam, 'that the real truth survives too – the ideological truth, that is. We can tell you now, Jan, now that we are clear of eavesdroppers, the reason for our performance at the League. Of course our conversations are bugged there, whatever Henri says, and the Office of Security knows that we and our friends – our friends of the Sustenance, as we say – talk subversively. But we present ourselves to them simply as common-or-garden silly intellectuals, econological nuts as you might say. We pretend to be crazy Greens – it was we who invented the joke that the "M" on the Tower stood not for Myrmidon but for Monsanto – rather funny, don't you think?'

'Yeah, well we are Greens too,' Henri put in, 'but not crazies.'

'Quite, but our real quarrel with our rulers is part aesthetic, part ideological, part doctrinal, part liturgical.'

'Bless my soul,' said I, 'no wonder you bring me down to the quays to talk.'

'Yes Azzam,' Magda said, 'you always make things too complicated. He's really a poet you know, Jan, a very Havian poet. His mind works like a maze. Do you know that *anjlak* about the intricacy of intricacies? That's one of his. Let me put it all more simply. What we are really against, Jan, is the Republic's philistine manipulation of history – brainwashing really – which is beginning to infect ever the most high-minded of our citizens. Let me give you an example. You've met Dr Porvic, I know, and probably found him a perfectly decent sort.'

'Absolutely, I laughed at him a bit, but I liked him.'

'Quite right too. He's a genuine lover of books and words, and I'm assured he's a good Cathar. But you must surely have realized that he is also a fool.'

'A sucker,' said Henri.

'Yes, a sucker who has been brain-washed himself and is now brain-washing everyone else. Did you get the bit about Missakian? Of course you did. How he was killed by the first shot of the Intervention just as he was sounding the Lament? Well cast your mind back, Jan dear. You were here that day. You know just as well as we do that the first shots of the Intervention were fired *in the afternoon*!'

'You don't have to be Agatha Christie', Azzam said, 'to see the flaws in that. And what about that stuff about the picture of the burning House being found on Missakian's corpse, apparently painted before the House was burnt at all? Poor old Porvic, he genuinely believes that was a miracle.'

'He believes the whole malarky, I really think he does. He honestly believes that the Cathars are descended from those ridiculous Myrmidons. And he's not alone, you know. There are lots like him. In their muddled minds they've accepted the idea that the theocracy is historically ordained – divinely ordained too, naturally.'

'What do you make of it all politically?' I asked. This seemed to floor them rather. They looked at each other questioningly.

'We are not really political animals,' Azzam said, 'we of the Sustenance. There's a lot to be said for the Republic. It's certainly better than what came before. You may question the taste, but you can't deny the speed and efficiency of the recovery. Hav is certainly richer than it was before, and much better ordered, too. Lazaretto is a great success, no question about that. What we object to is this: that it's all based upon lies. Of course that outburst of mine at lunchtime was play-acting –'

'Good stuff all the same,' said Henri.

'Thank you, Henri, but much more important is what I didn't say: that the theocracy is built upon intellectual pretence and fakery. As a result we are living lies. That's what we are fighting against: institutional lying. That's what this is all about.'

'Well, enough already,' Magda said again. 'I think Jan's heard enough. But we've got a couple of things we want to show you, Jan – don't worry, nothing ecological, just new Sights of Hav, as the tourist brochures would say, if any tourists were allowed in the city. You're very privileged, you know – all thanks to us.'

'All thanks to Dr Porvic.'

'Well, you may be right there,' said Henri. 'You're getting the picture. An invitation from us has generally come from him.'

We walked around the point from the Fondaco Quay. 'You must not suppose', Azzam said, 'that because we differ in some of our views from the Republic, we do not recognize its achievements. For example the way the Cathars assumed the defence of Hav, so soon after the first attack of the Intervention, was an inspiration to us all. We are disturbed by the arcane use they have made of the House of the Chinese Master–'

'Creepy's the word,' said Henri.

'Well, yes, creepy if you like – but we admire what they've done with the *Carlotto*.'

The Carlotto? Round the corner we walked, past the last of the warehouses, and there mounted on a high platform was a small warship. I recognized it. It was the *Arnaldo Carlotto* which used to be moored more or less permanently beside the old Lazaretto amusement park. She was built in 1918 as a Yangtze gunboat for the Italian navy, but was given to the Hav Government in 1940 to act as a guard ship for the port. Now she stood high and dry above the quay, gleaming with new paintwork. She looked brand new. Her two tall funnels were bright red, her wooden bridge was polished, her twin guns, fore and aft, were proudly elevated and over her long afterdeck a snow-white tarpaulin was stretched.

'You know her history?' Henri asked me. 'Boy, she did well. She hadn't put to sea for years when the Intervention came, but when the first warships showed themselves – you saw them yourself, right? – the old girl got steam up at once and sailed out to the Hook to wait for them. She hadn't a hope, of course, but she stood there all alone, firing away like crazy as the destroyers came through the narrows. They say it was six hours before she sank at last, blasted clean out of the water.

'After the Intervention the Cathars had her raised and rebuilt, and put her on that throne. They treat her well, don't they? They made her a Hero Ship. Folks love her, as you see.'

Certainly, queuing up the gangplank, filing around the deck, sporadic groups of sightseers toured the vessel, and I could just hear, above the hubbub of the Fondaco Quay round the point and out of sight, the insistent recorded voice of a commentary. And when after ten minutes or so the voice ceased, I heard something else too: the baffling cadences and third-tones of the Myrmidonic anthem.

'God,' said Mazda, 'there's that bloody tune again – if you can call it a tune. It comes around every ten minutes, Jan, so never stay here as long as that! I suppose old Porvic told you its story? And you believed it, of course – about the loose stone in the Séance House, and the brilliant young music student? Really. That fool Borge will do anything for them.'

Henri said: 'And have you heard what they've done with the stuff at the rock clubs? They call it the Hav Sound. Huh! Some brilliant young music student! Some fucking sound!'

Next, they said, and finally, they wanted to show me a sacred site – well, not exactly a sacred site, but the nearest thing to one that Hav possessed. 'Now of course you never knew', said Magda, 'about the Cathar *séances*, when you were here before.'

Oh yes I did, but I didn't say so.

'Not many of us did, and we certainly didn't know where they held their rites – the Lord knows what would have happened to anyone who penetrated them, which is why the whole set-up remained so mysterious. It's mysterious enough still, but not so much.'

'Come now Magda,' Azzam interrupted, 'we know no more about the Perfects now than we did then. I bet you even old Porvic doesn't know who they are, Jan, and he's one of their own bigwigs.'

'That's true enough, but at least we know where the Séance Hall used to be in those days, and that's where we're taking you now.'

It wasn't far. The streets of new Hav are as confusing in their way as the old ones were. The old ones were endlessly muddling in their intricate alleys and courtyards, the new ones blur the mind with their monotony – each one looking so like the next that it is difficult to keep track on a course through them. Except for the big motorways most of them are pedestrianized, but for me this makes it hard to judge any distance. The only building I thought I recognized as we walked was a mosque protruding above the rooftops: it looked to me like a reconstructed version of the old Grand Mosque. But it certainly wasn't far to the sacred site.

'Voilà!' said Magda, slightly ironically, when we reached a very small clearing in the middle of a cluster of housing blocks, with a narrow arcade around it. 'There's our sacred site. It was here that the Cathars used to hold their fateful *séances*, in a secret hall in an old Arab house that used to stand here. You would never have noticed it – nobody did. But inside it, or underneath it perhaps, on this very spot, all that has happened to Hav in our time was plotted and decreed.'

'That is so,' said Azzam. 'Like it or not, this is the crucible of our present.'

I wandered off by myself, thinking. Was it really here that I had, all those years before, been hurried up those steep dark steps to spy upon the Cathars below? Was it here that I had half-imagined, half-dreamed the identities of the red-cloaked Perfects, and promised never to reveal where I had been or what I had seen? I felt a pang of guilt about what I had written in the event, written in ignorance as it was, and wondered if that was why my book had been banned – evidently the Sustenance people, at least, had never read it.

In the centre of the little clearing there was a raised oblong platform of marble, with an inscribed plate of bronze on top of it. Step-ladders were placed nearby for the convenience of visitors, and while Magda, Azzam and Henri watched me from the arcade I climbed up one and bent over to read its inscription. It was in five languages, Havian, Arabic, Turkish, Chinese and English, and this is what it said:

ON THIS SITE WAS BORN
THE HOLY MYRMIDONIC REPUBLIC OF HAV
BY THE SACRIFICE OF THE CATHARS
AUGUST 17 1985
HISTORY, YOU PASSER-BY, REMEMBER!

I stood up there for a moment or two, wondering what it meant, until Magda came over and asked if I was all right. Still bemused, I clambered down the ladder, and she said: 'I know just what you're feeling. I felt it, the first time. Remember what? – that's you're thinking, aren't you? Or remember who? That's the sacredness of it, that we none of us have the faintest notion what it's all about, and probably never will. I saw your old friend Porvic standing here once in tears, and I bet you anything he didn't know what he was crying about.

'Come on, Jan, blow your nose; we'll have a last cup of tea before we trundle you off on your buggy to the delights of Lazaretto.'

'Did you ever know a lady named Fatima Yeğen?' I asked them when we went to the café for our tea. 'She was something to do with the railway.'

Magda and Henri looked blank, but Azzam said he thought he'd read something about her in *Myrmidon Mirror*, the more gossipy, he said, of the city's two newspapers. 'I think you'll find she's running the old station hotel.'

'L'Auberge Impériale,' I cried in delight. 'D'you mean to say it still exists?'

'Only in name really, only what's left of it. The station was completely destroyed, of course, and the railway itself never reopened. But I rather think the Yeğen family had some official connection with it – wasn't there somebody called the Tunnel Pilot in those days?'

Indeed there was, I told him. In my time the Pilot was Fatima Yeğen's cousin Rudolph, and if she was still alive and letting rooms I wouldn't take a Lazaretto buggy, I'd find my way to L'Auberge Impériale instead.

'Well don't expect too much,' said Azzam. 'I've only seen it from the outside, but I wouldn't fancy it myself, and alas the three of us have to be back at the League for a Sustenance discussion. Can you find your way there by yourself?'

'She's a grown woman, Azzam. It's easy, Jan. Go back to the

Fondaco Quay, and after the warehouses, before you turn the corner to the *Carlotto*, you'll see a big motorway running away from the harbour. That's August 17 Street. Walk up it for a few hundred yards and you'll find Centrum Square. That's where the station used to be and you can't miss what's left of the hotel. We'd come with you, but we just haven't got time. You must continue your investigations all alone.'

So we parted, and I walked alone in the evening through the streets of the city – streets and quays of ghosts they were to me – thinking of all I had seen there once, fancying the lights of the old British Residence across the water, imagining the little Electric Ferry bustling to and fro across the water, hearing the voices of old friends, smelling the lost scents of Hav, treading the pavements I might once have trodden until –

'Can I help you, dirleddy?' asked a smiling lady in black, sitting in a kiosk of glass and gilded ironwork.

She was much older – of course she was; her hair was white and her figure was less ample, but it was undoubtedly Miss Fatima Yeğen, the Tunnel Pilot's cousin. Out she came from her kiosk to embrace me, and of course she had a room for me, and of course we must have supper together, and there was so much to talk about wasn't there? and oh! the things that had happened to Hav since I went away, wasn't it a shame about the beautiful old tiled hotel sign? hadn't I noticed? mind the step, if I needed anything I had only to ring the bell, and how lovely it all was, and she'd be seeing me later, and she'd turned the geyser on to let me have a nice hot bath.

Azzam was, I have to admit, right. The Impériale was no great shakes, as dear Dr Porvic would have put it. It was a bum joint, as Henri might have said (in Hav all foreign slang is out of date). About half the size of the original, I suppose, it had been salvaged from the ruins of Hav Centrum, and was apparently still shored up with temporary girders and scaffolding. On one external wall, seen from the old station square outside, there still showed the fireplaces and blocked up doors of grander times.

Here and there inside, too, as I explored the yellow-painted corridors, I found reminders of the past: here a decidedly Russian-style landscape (muffled ladies in long skirts snowballing with preternaturally rosy children), here a chipped and rusted enamel advertisement (TAKE THE TRAIN! MEDITERRANEAN EXPRESS DIRECT TO MOSCOW, with a fanciful representation of onion domes and Cossacks), and standing in a dark corner cold and unpolished, a fine old samovar surmounted by a Russian imperial eagle. But they were no more than hints, really, rather than relics of what had once been there.

'Oh dear me no, Miss Morris, the Impériale is not what it was,' said Miss Yeğen, when we settled down in her cosy sitting-room for, as she put it, 'a little light something before bed'.

'But what would you do? No trains, very few visitors – only Chinese and Arab commercials, by and large – and certainly no help from the Government. They wanted to pull the place down, actually, when they pulled down the station ruins, and it was only because we all made a fuss that they let it stand.'

So making a fuss did have some effect, in the new Hav?

'Not often, but sometimes. There's not much what you might call public opinion these days. The papers don't spend much time on everyday matters – I was surprised when the *Mirror* had that article about me and the hotel, but that may have been the influence of Signor Biancheri, who's always had a soft spot for the Impériale. Still, it was certainly people making a fuss who saved the Roof-Race.'

I'd forgotten all about the Roof-Race.

'Oh feelings ran so high about the Roof-Race that those Cathars really couldn't go ahead and do away with it. They meant to, you know. When they rebuilt the Medina they were going to make no provision at all for the Roof-Race, and it was only because everybody was up in arms that they made the new course – not a patch on what it was, but something, I suppose – worth your while to take a look at, anyway.'

I said I was surprised the Cathars had given in on the matter.

'Me too,' said Fatima, 'what with them being so mad on health and safety and all that. But who knows what they really think about anything?'

And apropos of that, did she remember when, thanks to her, I had gone with Yasar and George to that secret *séance*? What had become of them?

Fatima fell silent for a moment then, while she looked about for a sugar-spoon.

'I'll tell you what,' she said. 'Why don't you borrow my car for the day tomorrow, take a turn around, see what you want to see, and then in the evening we can have a nice long chat. What do you think? You can stay another night, can't you?'

I thought so. I had my blue pass, after all. So after accepting a warm dry kiss from Miss Yeğen, off I went along the gloomy corridor to bed. There seemed to be no other guests at the Impériale that night, and all I heard as I dozed off was a gurgle of antique plumbing, and a distant barking of dogs. No steam-whistle from the station, when the Hav Express pulled in. No clanking of wagons or porters' shouts. Not another sound, until the carillon woke me like a bad dream in the morning.

THURSDAY

Myrmidon Rural
Enterprises

4

Continuing my investigations – the Chinese factor – country life – Myrmidon style – 'out of the bright heroic past'

Surely hers wasn't one of the Tunnel Pilot's cars, was it, I asked Fatima Yeğen in the morning, like the one I had bought all those years before?

She laughed a tinkly girlish laugh. 'No, no, Miss Morris, what a scream you are! They all went to the scrap heap long, long ago, like the railway itself.' And when we went out to the hotel garage after breakfast, there awaited me a stylish new Shanghai coupé, white, with a sunshine roof and CD player – 'all mod cons,' tinkled Miss Yeğen again, 'almost like Lazaretto!'

There was a map on the passenger's seat. 'I think you'll need this,' she said, and spread it out for me on the roof of the car. She was right. Except for the shape of the peninsula itself, the very topography of Hav looked different. Slap across it, from one coast to the other, there now ran a dual-carriageway motor-road (H1), following the route of the filled-in Spartan Canal and linking the city with the new port at Yuan Wen Kuo. There was no sign now of the International Settlement – 'vanished like a dream', said Miss Yeğen – and what had been the heart of the old city, where the Serai had been, and the palaces, was apparently now absorbed within a large rectangular slab labelled Medina. And the Balad, the old Arab quarter? 'Ah well,' said Miss Yeğen, 'I won't tell you that. Give yourself a surprise!'

And the rest of all I had known? The castle survived, of course, and there was evidently still a settlement on San Spiridon, the Greek island, but the old Russian pleasure-place of Malaya Yalta was not even marked, and the old motor-road up to the Escarpment was coloured in green ('Unsuitable for motor traffic').

Miss Yeğen sighed heavily as I folded up the map. 'Such changes! So much gone! But never mind, there's lots for you to see still. Enjoy yourself! "Laugh and be happy" is my motto! Tell me all about it tomorrow!'

And so, finding reverse gear with some difficulty, since the symbols on the knob were all in Chinese, I eased the car backwards into Centrum Square and continued my investigations.

I hit the H1 north of the castle hill. One way led to the Medina (20 km, said a road-sign), the other to Yuan Wen Kuo (32 km, with a picture of a steamship puffing smoke). I turned to the east, and now and then saw traces of the old canal running now one side, now the other of the highway. It was a grey morning, and the landscape was much as I remembered it: bare rolling moorland, with occasional woodland clumps, running away to the distant line of the Escarpment. Here and there patches of wild flowers, brilliant in bright blues and yellows, were revealed when sunshine momentarily broke through the clouds. No animals crosssed my path – no animals seemed to be in the moors – but streams of bulky trucks with trailers, interspersed with plush black limousines, passed in both directions along the road.

This part of the peninsula never was much populated, because of its harsh flinty soil, but it came as a shock to me when, descending a long gradual slope to the eastern shore, I found there was no sign of Yuan Wen Kuo, only a shack or two off the road and a few dingy shops.

An elderly Chinese was sitting in a bamboo chair outside one of the buildings, looking rather like a Chinaman in an old western, so I pulled off the highway and asked him what had happened. Surely the whole town, which I remembered as a perfectly ordinary Chinese settlement, had not been destroyed in the Intervention?

'No, dirleddy, much destroyed but not all. Rest all moved. Rest gone north – that way,' and he pointed to the big road behind me.

'All *moved*?' I repeated incredulously. It sounded like an Old Chinese Fable. '*Everything*? Palace of Delights? Yellow Rose Store? Big Star Floating Restaurant? They all just got up and went? Like magic?'

He thought this very funny. How he laughed, and pulled his beard, and puffed his pipe, and tilted back on his chair! No, no, no, he explained to me, very carefully. The town of Yuan Wen Kuo had been peaceably moved fifteen years before, to become the port town of the new deep-sea harbour, and the old place had been abandoned in a very short time – 'one month, two month, everyone gone. Now not much to do here except watch the cars go by.

'But Yuan Wen Kuo now very rich, dirleddy, big ships, rich people, many streets. Go and see! Back to big road, turn right. You soon be there. No, no, no, Yuan Wen Kuo no move by magic – ha, ha, ha . . .' and I heard him chuckling still, waving his pipe at me, as I turned the car around and returned to the H1.

A mile or two further on the new Yuan Wen Kuo hit me. It was recognizably Chinese still, with its garish signs and its ceaseless sense of movement, but Chinese in the twenty-first-century manner, brash, angular, blazing, like a miniature Shanghai. This Yuan Wen Kuo had been shifted from the arcane protection of its neighbouring hills, and the principle of Feng Shui, which had governed Chinese building aesthetics for so many years, had evidently been abandoned. Nothing remained of the Palace of Delights, and I saw no sign of the Kuomingtang–Communist rivalries that used to fester and flourish here. Gone, too, was the shambled homeliness I used to find so soothing, and the energy of the place was altogether more concentrated, more controlled. It was a small town still, but ostentatiously, even brutally modern, and I noticed that the ship on its civic greeting – WELCOME TO YWK, GATEWAY TO HAV – was certainly not a traditional steamer, like the ones on the highway sign, but a fiercely stylized and deeply loaded container ship. It all reminded me of one of the New Towns of Hong Kong, only rather more restrained.

I parked the car in a multi-storey park, in the middle of the town, which formed part of a sprawling civic centre, flew a large helmet-flag and was plastered everywhere with garish posters. There was a concert hall and a children's playground with trampolines. An open-ended arcade ran through the building, with a gilded canopy above the entrance, and an excessively uniformed Chinese commissionare stood at its wrought-iron gates. It looked dauntingly expensive, but Han Tu Chu Mall was not, as I expected, lined with antiquarian shops full of ivories, and scented boutiques. It was occupied entirely by the headquarters of corporations – The Hav East Corp, Peninsula Exchange, Achilles International, the Sunrise Company – all with offices too in Hong Kong, Shanghai, Taipeh or Singapore, and with showily opulent premises here. Corinthian pillars, dual marble staircases, discreet but impressive name-plates, elegant receptionists to be seen sitting at vast semi-circular desks – the whole repertoire of high capitalist display offered me a steely greeting as I walked down the arcade, and made me feel I was not in a small Chinese settlement a thousand miles from Beijing but in some powerful financial outpost of Chinese power. I remembered then that long ago Chevallaz had told me of Chinese money behind the old Casino, and when I reached the commissionaire at the other end of the mall I asked him if the Casino still existed.

'I have heard about it, dirleddy, of course,' he said, 'my father used to talk of it, but I believe it disappeared beneath the works of the port. But they still call this Casino Cove, you know. You might perhaps enquire at the Port Captain's office – straight down here, past the post office on the waterfront, not to be mistaken.'

I thanked him. He bowed. 'Ask for Mr Chimoun,' he added. 'He would be well informed about the old Hav. It was before my time!'

Mr Chimoun! I hastened down the street, past the ornately decorated Post Office with sculpted storks along the roof, past the Black Tortoise Refreshment Restaurant and the Tiger Tea-House, until I reached the waterfront. This was different from the quays down at Hav City. A squadron of fishing-boats was tied up at one side of the cove, but the big ships lay off-shore in their dozens, swarmed about with lighters and motor-launches. The quays were piled high with containers, in piles as big as houses, with mobile cranes and transporters moving ceaselessly among them.

The Port Captaincy occupied a severely functional Modernist block. The Chinese official behind the reception desk had never heard the name Chimoun. Not very enthusiastically he shuffled through the pages of a directory, and then shouted across the hall to a colleague: 'Hey, Li, ever hear of a guy called Chimoun?'

'Old guy?' asked Li.

'Old guy?' asked the man of me.

'Old by now, I suppose,' I said, 'but he used to be Port Captain.'

'Try Transient Services,' Li said, 'they use some old-timers there'; and so I found myself led along bleak corridors, past conference rooms and offices full of computers, until I reached a door marked 'Transient Enquiries (A)', and there sure enough they directed me to Mr Chimoun. 'That's Mr Chimoun over there. Chimoun! Chimoun! CHIMOUN! Someone to see you!'

For Mr Chimoun the Port Captain of twenty years before, who had born himself like an admiral and felt himself a doge, who had looked out from his stately headquarters on the old Fondaco Quay with so grand an air of possession – Mr Chimoun was now a deaf old clerk bent over a ledger-like volume, like an illustration by Boz. He stumbled over to me pushing his spectacles up his nose, and responded with a blank stare when I told him who I was. I thought he might have had a stroke, or a nervous breakdown, or had lost his memory, but no; after a baffling moment of silence he said perfectly lucidly: 'We can't talk here – we'll go to the canteen.'

As we walked there he said, rather testily I thought, 'Yes, yes, of course I know who you are. You came to see me just before the Intervention. You met Harry Gunther, didn't you? He told me about it, Richards too. Yes, yes, of course I know about you.'

In the bare and empty staff canteen bright-painted Chinese thermos flasks, lined up on the counter, were all that showed of catering or hospitality. Chimoun poured us each a cup of luke-warm tea, and we sat in a corner. 'Now then,' he said, 'what do you want to know?'

To be honest I didn't know *what* I wanted to know, although I was sure there must be something; but he forestalled me anyway.

'Because', he said, 'whatever it is, I can't discuss it. You want to know what Gunther and Richards were doing on the quay? You want to know about Biancheri? You're going to put it all into a book, aren't you, and make money out of it, and let me down? Well I'll tell you, Ms Morris, I've suffered enough already, since the Intervention, I've paid my price; you see me now a poor clerk of the Chinese, when once I had the whole port of Hav at my command, and I'm not going to say more. I am myself engaged, during my spare time, in compiling a documentary history of medieval Hav – purely as a labour of love. That perfectly occupies my mind. It's by the favour of the Perfects that I have this humble job at all, and I'm not going to risk losing it.'

'You won't even talk about the old Casino?'

'There's really nothing to say about that. You knew Biancheri, you probably met Antony Ho, what more do you want to know? It's moved on to bigger things now, anyway, as you've doubtless discovered for yourself. You're staying at the

Lazaretto, I suppose? Well then, you must have some inkling of it.'

'Yes, but–'

'No, no, Ms Morris, more I will not say. I am grateful for your visit – I see very few foreigners these days, except for crews and transients. I won't offer you another cup of this horrible tea (they grow it here now, you know, out on the Escarpment), and so must wish you goodbye, with memories of happier times. Mind how you go, Ms Morris. Mind what you write.'

'Good luck with the medieval documents,' I said, 'and go easy on the Crusaders.' But I don't think he heard, or he would have asked me what I meant by that, and I wouldn't have known.

I remembered that from the old Casino Cove there used to be a rough road westward across the peninsula towards the Balad, so I followed my nose back along the motorway until I discovered signs of it running away unmarked across the moors. I took it, hoping to see whatever there was of countryside in the new Hav. It took me across the old grazing land, in the foot-slopes of the escarpment, and I did see some signs of pastoral life. There were farm-huts sometimes along the way, and occasional herds of wizened-looking cattle, guarded by no less bloodless cow-herds. All the huts seemed to be empty. The herdsmen stood motionless beside the track, leaning on sticks or picking their noses, and watched my passing without visible interest. They all seemed to be old, and possibly half-witted, and I decided that the agricultural sector was low on the list of Myrmidonic priorities.

But presently I crossed the line of the old railway, and the now neglected Escarpment road, and skirting the salt-flats I discovered a very different rural scene. The whole of the north-west plateau, stretching away towards the coast hills and the sea, seemed to be a shimmering mass of silver plastic, billowing slightly in the breeze, interspersed with vegetable fields, greenhouses and steel windmills. Brand-new roads criss-crossed the area, and trucks crawled about wherever I looked, and there were gangs of workers among the vegetables, and the windmills whirred. I was reminded of the flower-farms of Jersey, or the windmill plateau of Lassithi in Crete, or Carolina cotton-fields. It all looked purposeful, and profitable.

A sign explained it to me – MYRMIDON RURAL ENTERPRISES – and there was a concrete office behind it, and a helmet-flag flying. 'Welcome, welcome, dirleddy,' said a gushing functionary inside. 'It's always such a pleasure to welcome visitors from across the seas – you are from across the seas, I assume? Excellent, excellent. Oh, a guest of the League of Intellectuals, I see,' said he when he examined my blue pass. 'Very good friends of ours here at Rural Enterprises – many keen brains to help and encourage us in our tasks. You are welcome *all the more*!

'And I expect you are chiefly interested – tell me if I am wrong! – in the miracle of the GM snow raspberries. Well, that happens at the Escarpment end of the Enterprise, so suppose we stroll up there now – you have the time? Excellent, excellent, dirleddy. Off we go, then.'

Of course, he went on to tell me, much of the matter they grew was grown in the orthodox way, either under glass or under plastic sheeting – 'so beautiful to see, don't you think so, especially when you drive over the ridge there – so, well, so spiritual, I always think, as though all those lovely growing things are shrouded not for death but for new life. Don't you get that feeling?'

Not precisely that feeling, I told him, but I did think it was a delightful surprise to find so much life and energy in that somewhat desiccated landscape.

'Life, yes life, life all around us,' he said as we pottered through the sheeted fields and the rich vegetable gardens, impeccably planted with rows of cabbages, beans, rhubarb, potatoes – but no lettuces, I noticed.

'No lettuces yet, then?'

'Not as yet, but we have high hopes. Some of our workers here have specialized in lettuces in their homelands, and several are employed specifically in lettuce research. For you do realize, I suppose, that most of these industrious employees you see in our fields are transients from across the seas? Oh yes, we are fortunate to find such enthusiastic sources of labour – and at such economic rates, too.'

They didn't – er – demand high wages, then?

'I can speak frankly to you? They hardly demand anything at all. They come, you see, mostly from Afghanistan and Uzbekistan, just for a season, no women or families, and having really nothing much to spend their money on here, go home relatively rich however much we pay them. They are looked after, too. Transient Services look after them very well – ship them in, put them up and ship them off again. No questions asked, anywhere. We have the best advice, from South Africa and from the United States, about the handling of transient labour. You're going on to the Balad? Well then, you'll see how well it is all organized.'

And so, to a metaphorical blast of trumpets, as it were, he displayed to me a separate, fenced enclosure where the snow raspberries were grown – some under plastic outside, some in hot-houses. 'We are still experimenting, but this is the very site where the first generically modified snow raspberry was produced, available all the year round.' With a supplementary flourish he showed me into one of the greenhouses, and there amidst a racket of machinery and a bustle of overalled workers, stood rank upon rank of wooden boxes full of the gleaming crimson fruit. 'Waiting for canning,' he said. 'Within the hour they'll be canned. Here, dirleddy, taste one while they're still fresh.'

He rummaged about for a moment or two, looking for a particularly lush one, and then fastidiously passed it to me between his finger and his thumb. It was certainly more interesting than the frozen berries at the League, but I could not help thinking that if this is what snow raspberries had always tasted like, the mystique that used to surround them was misplaced – all that fuss about the harvesting, the dinner ceremonials that Armand Sauvignon talked about, the ludicrous prices . . .

'Did you ever eat one in the old days,' I asked, 'before modification?'

'Not I,' he laughed; 'I was too poor in those days, and too young anyway. But our collaborators from across the seas assure us that, in the development of this process, none of the fruit's delicious taste has been lost. As you see, however, we are careful to grow, harvest and can them in careful segregation from other crops, in case of contamination. In this, of course, we are given valuable instruction by our associates from across the seas, and by now canned snow raspberries, under the trade name Havberry, are one of our principal products – you must surely be familiar with them, in your own homeland? No? There may be political reasons for that. In America, of course, they are very popular. Our Arab friends, too, are eager customers. Some of the container ships you must have seen at Yuan Wen Kuo are entirely dedicated to the trade.'

Before I drove away he gave me an elaborately wrapped box. 'Please take this, dirleddy, as a souvenir of your visit. It is our newest product. One day, I assure you, it will be as familiar around the world as Benedictine.'

When I was out of sight I stopped the car and unwrapped the package. Nestled inside it was a blue bottle, labelled 'Aqua Hav: 45% Proof. Genuine Snow Raspberry Liqueur'.

Beyond the Havberry plant a new hard road led southward, and a slip road took traffic on to the H1 and thence to Yuan Wen Kuo. A few miles on the road forked, and was signed to Hav City one way, Balad the other. I remembered the Balad as a very crumbled, shabby, disreputable, spiced, straggly and crowded slum quarter, through which the railway ran up to the Escarpment tunnel and a tram line ran down to the city proper.

Now everybody spoke of it rather evasively, as though not to spoil my surprise, and I soon saw why. There was no warning. I crossed a slight bump in the road and there was Balad laid out before me. The whole of it had been turned into an airport. Two huge runways ran north and south, and there was the usual airport conglomeration of sleek terminal buildings, control tower, hangars and car parks. Lights flashed, luggage carts rumbled, buses went here and there and even as I watched a black-and-white aircraft laboured into the sky. Nothing was left of the old Balad, not a hovel or mosque. Even the scummy old lake had vanished. Only rows and rows of barrack-like structures, flat-roofed and identical, seemed in attendance upon the airfield.

Billboards now lined the road: FLY HAVAIR! – SEE THE OTHER HALF! – CAIRO 450 HD! – TWO FLIGHTS A WEEK TO BEIJING! I wondered who took all these flights, since I had met nobody who seemed to travel anywhere. All the tourists, I knew, came to Lazaretto by charter flights, and the aircraft I saw standing on the tarmac at the airport, or in the aicraft park beside the terminal building, all seemed to be private jets. 'Oh, don't believe everything the ads say,' advised a uniformed Havair girl I asked in the terminal atrium. 'Those Beijing flights are really just for the Government, bringing in specialist workers and flying them out again, and hardly anyone *flies* to Cairo – it's much easier and cheaper to take the hydrofoil. Except for the foreign charters this whole airport is really just for private jets, people comng to YWK, or the GM research place, or the Medina of course, or Cathars and such going out.'

Cathars and such? But she was a busy woman, and I did not keep her from her work. Instead I went and looked out of the window at the aeroplanes. There were three Shenjen 824s in the Havair colours of black and white: almost the whole fleet, I would guess, and each named very Havianly – *Avzar Melchik, Rahman ibn Muhammed, Gunboat Carlotta*. A solitary fighter jet, heavily camouflaged, stood outside one of the hangars. And the many corporate jets which crowded the tarmac were one and all sleek and very luxurious, with curtained windows, crested doors, names in flowery Arabic, in calligraphic Chinese or discreet American advertising script. Some had bold 'M's on their flanks, simple and elegant; but remembering Azzam's joke I wondered if it stood for Myrmidon or for something else . . .

The terminal, though equipped with all the airport gimmicks, from executive lounges to shopping centres, was virtually empty, so after wandering around for a time, looking at the series of photographs illustrating the Development of Aviation in Hav, and wondering at the photograph of Ivan Rostrovich garlanded with Hav roses at the conclusion of his pioneering flight from Tabriz, and peering at the plaque, now fading a bit, which told me that the airport had been officially opened by His Excellency Anjak Creen, Myrmidonic Minister of Travel, in 2001 – after wandering for a while in this way, like anyone else in any airport anywhere, I popped into one of the airport cafés, where the young men in Hav dress at the counter were desultorily chatting, and ordered a cup of coffee.

Who should I find sitting there too but Chevallaz of Lazaretto!? He greeted me warily, it seemed to me, but warmly enough, and I told him about my visit to Casino Cove. He did not seem very interested. 'That's all over now,' he said. 'That's all behind us. We've moved on since then. Signor Biancheri's ambitions are too large for the old Casino – even Lazaretto is too small for him, I sometimes think.'

'What about you? He says you've got a thousand chefs under you.'

'Ah, he was joking, Signora Morris. Signor Biancheri is a generous man, he always speaks well of others. The truth is I am well satisfied with my position, which offers me opportunities far wider than before. I must confess to you that in the old Hav, when my responsibilities were more limited, now and then I felt the need to get away from it all – to escape, if you like, from everything. Do you know what I mean?'

Of course I did. Had not just the same thing been said to me, times beyond number, in the old Hav, and had I not felt it myself when the complexities of the place seemed to be hemming me in?

'But my position is very different now. Today, for instance, I'm off to to Riyadh for a short business stay.'

'Riyadh! Dear God! How are you going to get there? Surely Havair doesn't fly to Saudi Arabia?'

'No, no, not yet,' he laughed. 'No, business associates of Signor Biancheri are picking me up – they're flying in from Zurich in their own plane – should be landing very soon now. But you do realize, Ms Morris, don't you, that what you see here now' – and he gestured beyond the terminal windows – 'is only a foretaste of what is on the way? Havair flies almost nowhere now, almost all the traffic here is private, but why do you think they've built these two world-class runways, and this terminal to rival anything in Europe or America? It's because in a few years' time this is going to be one of the global transport hubs, and Havair will be one of the world's most important airlines. No expense spared, as they say. They've got the world's best architects to build this place – your own Lord Rogers was invited to design this terminal. They've got the best publicists working on it. They've flown in thousands of workers to do the job, and built all those barracks to house them. That big glass block over there is the Havair training depot, and there they're building a whole new airline from scratch, no expense spared, with advisers from all over.'

This spiel took me aback. I had thought of Chevallaz as a professional restaurateur, a chef by background, bred to the bourgeois world of Swiss catering. Now he sounded more like a public-relations executive.

'You don't believe me, do you, Ms Morris? You would if you knew the amount of money that's going into all this – not just on new aircraft for Havair, and all that kind of thing, but millions being spent on incentives, to make this an unrivalled staging-post for all the intercontinental airlines – and who knows, perhaps for interspace travel one day? Think of our position here. We're in the middle of everything. In the old days Hav was an almost unknown backwater – you remember that yourself – but the Intervention changed everything. Now

Hav is poised to be one of the world's prime movers. You wait! Your Heathrows and American Airlines and Emirates and Lufthansas and the whole damned aviation industry will have to watch out!'

'And where's the money coming from? Who's paying for it all?'

Chevallaz shrugged his shoulders. 'Who knows, Ms Morris?' he said. 'Who can tell? Hav still keeps its secrets – one reason all this is happening. Do you suppose it's just coincidence that this airport's code symbol is HAV? I don't suppose there is another city anywhere whose airport code is its own name! Think of the publicity advantages! It takes more than imagination to arrange a thing like that; it takes influence, and it takes persuasion. But that's the way we're going here – unique and unbeatable! Ah, there comes my plane. I'd better be moving.'

Gathering his briefcase and overcoat, and bowing slightly to me, he walked away. A black-and-silver private jet, with some sort of crest up on its fuselage, was turning off the runway to the terminal apron, and presently I saw him, escorted by uniformed officials, walking across to it. Its engines were not turned off, but its door opened, a step-ladder unfolded and I caught a glimpse of figures in black burkas ushering Signor Chevallaz aboard. In a matter of moments the plane was off down the runway and flinging itself into the sky.

'Dear me,' I said to the young men behind the counter, who had been listening to our conversation. 'Hav is certainly full of surprises. Whatever next?'

Go and take a look around New Balad, they suggested, so I did. Much of it was standard airport stuff, offices and hangars and the usual hotels (looking very empty). But there were also streets and streets of those barrack-like structures that I had seen from a distance, and of these I expected the worst. Had not the man at Rural Enterprises said they had learned a lot from the South Africans about housing immigrant workers? I remembered with a shudder the awful sheds in which the black workers of the gold mines used to be housed, with their outdoor ablutions, their treeless yards, their dormitories like concentration camps and the tin bowls they clutched as they lined up for their rations.

But they *had* learned a lot, they really had. Those featureless streets which from a distance had looked rather like Auschwitz blocks turned out to be, when I drove through them, more like something in a garden suburb. They were well built, they were brightly painted, and their accommdation, far from being loveless dormitories, was agreeable small apartments. They were generally deserted, but one block was lively with families, on the doorsteps, at the windows, on the sidewalks, gossiping in twos and threes. I recognized them at once as Kretevs, so I stopped to talk. They were mostly women with small children, and they crowded curiously about me. What a difference, I said, from their old homes in the caves of the Escarpment.

Very different they said, very sad. But then they looked at each other and laughed. Very comfortable, too, they said! No, they did not miss the caves, they preferred the central heating. Their menfolk all had construction jobs at the airport. And when the guest workers were in their quarters – they went off by bus each day to their work sites – why, then the whole place was full of life, better than those long lonely days on the Escarpment. They laughed and giggled and nudged one another. Oh yes, they said, the Cathar Government had looked after them well, after the Intervention.

At this a big old man, heavily bearded, interrupted us. 'Of course they looked after us. They needed us. Now they want to show the world how civilized they are. Why d'you think this lady is here now? Because they've sent her here to see how well they treat us. Do you think this is any way of life for a Kretev? Don't you care about the bears, you silly women? Don't you care about anything? I'll tell you, lady, what they're doing to us is ethnic engineering. We're like snow raspberries to them. They're mutating us. GM folk, that's what we are. Human snow raspberries.'

He stumped off, leaving the women giggling and the children looking goggle-eyed at me, and suddenly I remembered what the place reminded me of. It was like that huge healthy construction the Nazis built on the island of Rugen in the Baltic, to provide holiday indoctrination for the Hitler Youth.

It was still only late afternoon, so I turned in my tracks and drove south by the old rough roads, skirting the city, leaving the harbour away to my left, until I struck the old highway to the ferry station for San Spiridon, on the east coast of the peninsula. I remembered the unassuming little island community as being, in a curiously suggestive way, the heart or fulcrum of Greekness in Hav, and Fatima Yeğen had told me that it was left unscathed by the Intervention. There used to be only one steamboat a day to the island, but I guessed that things might have changed by now, and I was right.

I left the car in a car park and walked down to the little dock. No steamboat lay gently hissing there, but a gleaming streamlined hydrofoil was revving its engines. 'Just in time,' said a cheerful dockhand in sailor's gear, 'and there isn't another for an hour.' The passengers already on board had changed, too. They were certainly Greek, but they no longer looked like peasants from the Dodecanese, but more like well-dressed office-workers on a daily commute. Their string-tied suitcases and straw hampers had become briefcases and plastic shopping-bags. Their children were demure. There was not a dog or a mule or a motorbike on board the spanking little vessel, and nobody smoked a pipe. Only the inevitable tall-hatted Orthodox priest sat there with an air of authority, reading his Bible.

Except for the priest everybody looked up at me as I found myself a seat, but nobody spoke. Only when we had crossed the sound, fifteen minutes later, and were about to dock at the island, did an elderly woman sit down beside me and say: 'Haven't we met before? Didn't you come to San Spiridon long ago? Jan Morris, isn't it? I am Kallonia Laskaris.'

'Kallonia Laskaris – of course! I'd have known you any-where' – and we both laughed. 'And how is your dear little daughter, who was so kind to me that day?'

'This is "my dear little daughter" – Arianna, come over here and meet an old friend' – and there she was, an elegant young woman in her early thirties, in T-shirt and designer jeans, assuring me that she remembered very well my visit to the island all those years ago, but not very convincingly.

'I'm told you wrote about us that time,' said Kallonia. 'I won't ask if you're going to write something again, my dear – although I hope you do have a blue pass, don't you? – but you must come home with us anyway and see what's happened to our lovely San Spiridon – thanks be to God.'

I told her I only had an hour, before I must catch the hydro-foil back.

'Never mind, dear Jan. We shall do it just like we did last time. Arianna will quickly show you round the place again, and I will get in a few dear friends to meet you. You will see some changes! But our good shepherd-saint and the Holy Mother of God has protected us.'

I didn't remember Kallonia ever talking like this, and as Ari-anna led me up the hill, I mentioned it to her.

'You're right,' she said. My mother is born again. St Spiri-don is very big in her life these days – he was the shepherd-saint, you know – but then he's very big to nearly everyone on the island now. You say you noticed a difference in her conver-sation. Don't you notice any difference in the place?'

Holy Mother of God I did. Nothing had basically changed, but everything seemed rejuvenated. The fishermen's shacks were all repainted, the taverns were smart, one of the shops had become a small supermarket, the other was a cyber-café. The church, at the end of its causeway, was a brilliant white, and the celery fields were meticulously maintained.

'Not GM celery, I hope,' I said, but Arianna scoffed.

'Monsanto on San Spiridon? The saint would never allow it. And who would be fool enough to mutate Spiridon celery?'

I asked her what had happened, to recharge the island in this way, but she told me to ask the people when we got home. 'They can explain it better than I can.'

And sure enough, when we reached Kallonia's house on the top of the hill, the company assembled there beneath the pergola was only too ready to oblige. There were four or five bourgeois-looking gentlemen and their wives, and the sideburned young owner of the cyber-café, and Kallonia herself of course, and the priest I had seen on the hydro-ferry, and except for the priest they all talked at once, while Kallonia and Arianna moved among us with tumblers of Hav retsina and vine-leaf rice rolls – 'We would give you a proper meal, dear Jan, but I know you haven't got the time.'

It was the priest, of course, still wearing his hat, who prevailed over the hubbub, and emerged as spokesman for them all – spokesman for the island itself, as Kallonia whispered in my ear.

'We are grateful to our patron saint, of course, and to the Holy Mother of God' – all crossed themselves here – 'for what has happened to our beloved island and our community, but we must also be properly grateful to our Perfects and the Holy Cathar Government. For it is they who, assiduously exploring the byways of Hav's ancient history, realized that at the root of it, the core and the root, the foundation – at the bottom of it was Greekness' (murmurs of approval).

'Our forebear Achilles, it is now recognized, was the true Father of Hav. Our Myrmidonic ancestors, we now understand, were the original Cathars, and although our religious practices have diverged somewhat down the centuries, nevertheless we gratefully acknowledge that our theologies are in profoundest essences identical.' ('Identical,' confirmed one of the bourgeois gents. 'Almost identical,' murmured the owner of the cyber-café.) 'Identical,' firmly concluded the priest.)

So it was, he went on, that the Myrmidonic Republic recognized the island as – well, say the Runnymede of Hav, where Magna Carta was signed, or that field by the lake, he forgot the name, where the Swiss Confederation was established. 'It is the cradle of our Republic, and as such is generously favoured by the Perfects and the State. There was a time, we must explain to our visitor from across the seas, when to be Greek in Hav was something to be ashamed of. Our people were forced to be furtive in our Greekness. We were subdued, we lost our old Hellenic pride – our epic pride, one might say – or as one writer across the seas has written, I am told, our pride in our bright heroic past.

'But now – well, dirleddy, look around you Do we seem furtive? Are we not the Greeks of old once more?' (Cries of yes, yes, praise to the saint, praise to the Holy Mother, etc.) 'That is because we know ourselves now to be the original Havians, and the Republic knows it too!'

Happy confusion ensued, the priest beaming in triumph, the gentlemen shaking hands with each other, the ladies breaking fitfully into song, the cyber-café man telling me that of course he realized their theologies were *hypothetically* identical, the retsina flowing, Kallonia telling me she hoped I now understood a little more, until we saw from the terrace the hydrofoil returning from the mainland, and with embraces, kisses and loud good wishes in Havian Greek, I was seen off through the celery fields down to the harbour.

Stuffed full of Hellenism, then, I just had time to drive down and see the Iron Dog again. It was, after all, the most extraordinary legacy of the Greeks in Hav, placed there above the Hook, so it was claimed, by the Spartans when they were besieging the city. I knew that the nearby Conveyor Bridge had escaped the Intervention. Its destruction might have blocked the channel into the harbour, and its French subsidies had continued throughout, together with regular maintenance by engineers from Paris. Nobody had mentioned, though, the Dog.

I drove most of the way, over tussocky tracks, but had to walk the last few hundred scented yards to the high plateau above the bridge. Beyond it that animal still stood, proud and strange as ever, his tail flowing behind him, his snout extended. For the first time he struck me as some sort of heraldic beast, like a savage armorial. The wind blew, as it always does there, the container cabin lurched silently across the channel, a ship sailed by far below, and the whole scene seemed to me altogether hallucinatory, like so much of Hav itself.

I clambered down the slope to look through my binoculars at the famous graffiti on the dog's flank, but I could make none of them out. The Norse symbols, the Venetian ciphers, the Kaiser's eagle, 'H. M. Stanley' arrogantly under the creature's chin, all had been overwhelmed by enormous tangles of cyber-graffiti – those weird stylized inscriptions which are plastered bafflingly all over the western world, but which I had never before seen in Hav. They looked more than ever mysterious on the hide of the Iron Dog, high above the chasm, as if a horde of aliens had passed that way, leaving their arcane signatures behind.

I drove back to L'Auberge Impériale just at twilight, and spent the evening chatting to Miss Yeğen. We shared a bowl of celery soup ('the real stuff', said Fatima, 'like you, fresh this morning from San Spiridon'), and capped it with a glass or two of Aqua Hav. This was rather too sweet for me, but she liked it.

FRIDAY

Into the tunnel

5

To the Rialto – everything? – in the bazaar – an initiative –
the Escarpment rally – tunnel effects

'And what', asked Fatima at the breakfast table, 'are you planning for today? Do you need the car? Or are you running away
to the flesh-pots again?'

'Today', I said, 'I must go to the Rialto, and I shall go afoot.'

She thought I meant I was planning a visit to the movies, so
I explained myself less Shakespearianly. I wanted to see where
the action was, where the money was generated, where the
shakers and movers hung out.

'Ah, the *Hav* Rialto. Well you can walk there easily enough.
You can find the way, I'm sure. It's the Medina, of course, as it
always was, and around the Grand Bazaar is where it all happens – not *in* the Bazaar, but in the streets all around it. It's
nearly all new, of course – you realize that – but you'll see
some things you remember, and if you want to find out more
about the Roof-Race they've got an office down there now,
around the corner from the Grand Mosque. As it happens, I
think you know its manager. Remember my cousin Yasar, who
drove you down the Staircase when you first came? That's him.
Give him a kiss from me. He'll tell you everything.'

Everything? He'd certainly told me a lot last time, but times
have changed in Hav since then . . . I embraced Fatima,
thanked her for the bedroom and the car, gave her the rest of
the Aqua Hav and set off for the Medina. I hardly knew where

I was, so utterly changed was the city-scape, but I used as a point of reference the Castle high on its hill above the city. Nothing has changed up there, I thought to myself. Missakian is dead, but lives on in the memory of his melody. The Crusaders are still marching bravely down to their ships, and Saladin instructs his scribes just how to word the inscription on his gateway. The Venetians are up there still, watching their salt-convoys sailing for Alexandria, and I expect the officers of Her Majesty's Royal Regiment of Artillery sometimes visit their gun emplacements. The permanence of this immanent city is embodied in those old walls, thought I sententiously to myself as I followed my nose through the unfamiliar streets below.

I had expected to find the Medina, rebuilt from its own ruins, rather like Wall Street, rigid, overbearing, pompous, or at least like the new financial quarter of Frankfurt, which had similarly been reborn out of chaos. But oddly enough it turned out to be much more like the original Rialto, that tight-packed financial quarter around the famous bridge in Venice, stepped and jumbled and full of dead ends, which has survived the centuries with its scrambled character intact. Could it be that the architects of the new Hav really did have Venice in mind? Certainly the minarets of the Great Mosque, high above the offices of concrete and mirror-glass, stand there very much as the Basilica of San Marco still lords it over its red-tiled rooftops.

For they have rebuilt this financial quarter of Hav, this new Rialto, in a deliberately stylized way. Motor-traffic is banned within the spectral circuit of the medieval walls – themselves entirely demolished – and there is nothing straightforward to its plan, nothing obviously rational. It is like a pastiche. The few main thoroughfares are entangled in alleys and lanes and little squares. Perhaps the famous Kiruski had something to do with it, because in its insidious way it is a perfect allegory of the money-making world. 'Turn up on your right hand at the next turning,' says Shakespeare's Launcelot, directing a visitor towards the Venetian Rialto, 'but at the next turning of all, on your left; marry at the very next turning, turn of no hand, but turn down indirectly to the Jew's house.' So it seemed to me in the Rialto of Hav, too – the detail perfectly explicit, the whole a deliberate tangle.

At first I simply wandered – and wondered. This is a formidable place. It is a labyrinth of money. It has none of the ostentation of Yuan Wen Kuo, so brassily, flauntingly showy. Instead it is a nook-and-cranny sort of place, where you would be more likely to find one of those discreet private banks of the City of London, or the secretive institutions of Zurich, than the Bank of America, say, or the Hong Kong and Shanghai. Up every alley there seems to be another quiet institution. Modest brass plates announce the presence of the Stockholm and Copenhagen Trust Company, or Lisbon Trading, or Cosmopolitan Exchange, or Balkan & Baltic. Some of the doors are unmarked. Some of the plates need a polish – intentionally, I suspect. Even the movement of people – couriers? security men? accountants? – down the narrow side-streets and cul-de-sacs has an obscurely muffled air. The absence of traffic, too, makes it feel even more Venetian: the voices of people, the swarming footsteps of passers-by, the hum of air-conditioning and the constant ringing of telephones sound all the louder by contrast.

Hah! Here was a name-plate I recognized, among several of many nationalities in the doorway of a particularly anonymous-looking block: Butterworth and Sons, World-Wide Preferential Shipping Tariffs. I pressed a button. A man's voice said, 'Yes.'. 'Jan Morris,' said I. A long pause, then a man's voice: 'Jan Morris? Good Lord. Well I never. Come on in.' A buzz, a click, and the door was opened. The offices of Butterworth and Sons occupied the ground floor, and waiting for me in the hall was Mr Mitko Butterworth himself. 'Yes,' we cried in unison when we saw each other – '*In spite of all temptations . . .!*'

'Fancy your remembering,' we tumbled over each other in saying, and then, still laughing, he led me into his highly functional office, all chrome and electronics. 'Yes, after all these years, fancy your remembering. How did you find us? Just by chance? Certainly not through the British Legation, what? They don't like us there any more than they liked us when they were a hoity-toity Agency!'

Mr Butterworth didn't seem to have aged much, and was still in his shirtsleeves, though I noticed he had given up on cuff-links.

'Well well well, fancy that. There've been some changes made, *n'est-ce pas*? What? I suppose you hardly recognize the old place?'

'I certainly wouldn't recognize Butterworth and Sons,' I said, eyeing the suavity all around me, and remembering the musty premises of 1985.

'Yes, that's true, we haven't done badly since the Intervention. All's in order for the fifth generation of Butterworths, touch wood. Oh, how rude of me: care for a coffee? Or an Aqua Hav perhaps?'

Coffee would be lovely I said, and he winked at me as he spoke into his desk telephone. 'Very wise. Can't stand the Aqua stuff myself, but all good Havians are obliged to like it.'

The coffee arrived and we were silent for a moment until the golden-robed servant withdrew.

'You're still not Havian yourself, then?'

'No, no, no. Never. Well, not altogether. Nowadays, I must admit, I do have more than one nationality. In my business there are advantages to it.'

'What is your business, actually? I know you told me your great-great-grandfather, was it? – wanted to extend the range of the agency. Has it happened?'

Mr Butterworth stirred his coffee cup for a moment. 'Shipping agencies', he said, 'have always been complex businesses. We've always tried to move with the times, which is why we've hung on here all this time, and I think I can say we've adapted successfully to the new Hav. Those name-plates outside are all ours really, you know – subsidiary companies of ours, associate agencies, concessionaires, that kind of thing.'

'You mean the whole building is yours?'

'Well yes, in a manner of speaking. Ownership is a sort of abstraction in Hav these days. Let's say we have an enthusiastic interest in it all – how's that?'

I said I'd been at Yuan Wen Kuo the day before, and was struck by the contrast in style between it and the Medina.

'Ah well, yes, that's the Chinese way. They like a bit of flash. They're all at each others' throats anyway, and love to show off. They're much more internecine, if that's the word, than we are down here. Almost all the firms up there are Chinese, cut-throat competitors, and very big business too. They deal in *things* – things they make, things they sell, huge construction projects, all that kind of stuff. They're big on import–export – always have been. Down here we're more – well, theoretical.'

As he said this, he put his finger down the side of his nose and smirked a bit. 'Funny really,' he said. 'It used to be the Chinese who ran laundry businesses . . .'

'Are you saying . . .'

'Yes I am, more or less. Leave it at that. You see, the Chinese prefer things up front. They've been active in Hav for years and years, as you know, and they feel a bit superior to all these people around here. If you want to build an airport, fine, go and talk about it at Yuan Wen Kuo; they'll fix everything for you, money, materials, labour, technicians, the whole lot – even architects – they hoped to get that Lord Rogers for the terminal, you know. They've built the whole caboodle at the Balad.

'But if you want to ship, say, a cargo of electronics from Cuba to Abu Dhabi, or broker a deal in some debatable substance or other, or fix an exchange rate somewhere, or even arrange a tricky introduction, why, the Medina's the place, and you can't do better than consult Butterworth and Sons, Founded 1823! A long-standing British firm, as our letter-heads used to say, "To Be Trusted in All Transactions".'

'I'm sure old Oswald would be proud of you.'

'You can be damned sure of it. He'd be right at home on the new Hav. We do a lot of business with the Lazaretto, you know – wasn't Biancheri rather a pal of yours in the old days? Lazaretto's just the old man's style, I like to imagine. He was very go-ahead in his day.'

And how about the Cathars, I asked him. 'How d'you get on with them?'

'Ask no questions, my love, and you'll be told no lies – well, not many, anyway.' He laughed boisterously once again and showed me to the door. 'Where are you off to next?'

I said I was going to the Great Bazaar, to look into the matter of the Roof-Race.

'Ah yes, the Roof-Race, our Bull Run. There's money in that, too. Keep your nose clean.'

The Great Bazaar was just at the end of his street. My only remembrance of it concerned the Roof-Race, when in '84 I raced with the then Mahmoud (now Azzam) through its tumultuous arcades to catch the climactic moments of the Bazaar Leap and the finish. It was still the same shape, with its Market Gate and its Castle Gate, but that was all. It had been rebuilt after the Intervention as a shopping-mall, and was interspersed with a dozen or more coffee shops at which, as I explored the place, swarms of young people sat on sofas or stood at counters noisily talking – junior *commerçants* or financiers, I assumed, having their lunch break.

The old pattern of the Bazaar, with its myriad alleys open to the sky, had been preserved, and the shops did somehow retain a faintly Levantine air. They all had open fronts. Their produce was laid out in big trays, or hung in flouncy rows, and from their dark interiors the shopkeepers peered out, just as in the old days, like so many watchful serpents, sometimes hissing the terms of a reduction. It reminded me rather of the mock souks that have sprung up in some Arab countries, for the benefit of nervous tourists, at which even the haggling is a sort of pretence.

When I stopped for a coffee myself, and mentioned it to young people at the counter, they were inclined to agree. 'But then,' said one girl, 'the whole Great Bazaar is a con, isn't it? The Castle Gate isn't really a gate after all, and look at the Roof-Race circuit!'

I hadn't seen the Roof-Race circuit, so they took me up to a viewing site above the café. 'See what I mean?' said the girl. 'What's real about that?'

Nothing was. The old Roof-Race had been run over a ramshackle antique course full of dangerously miscellaneous obstacles, chimney-pots and wind-towers, drainpipes and balustrades, intersected everywhere by the open-roofed alleys that ran below: a medieval, maze-like course immemorially supposed to have been the route run by the legendary Messenger to reach Gamal Abdul Hussein. It was all too real, and people died running it, or jumping over the round open space that was the crux of the Great Bazaar. Now almost the whole roof of the new, concrete mall was perfectly flat, and the only obstacles were artificial bumps sometimes, rather like very high speedbumps, and concrete chimneys dotted here and there. The roof was still split this way and that, to correspond with the bazaar alleys below, but I noticed that in every case it sloped downwards to the gap, and the line of sight was clear everywhere. A white steel fence ran all around the circuit; dotted here and there were view platforms like the one we were on.

'See what I mean? All sanitized, all sham. Even the chimneys are sham – who needs chimneys now? And the jumps – you can see for yourself, they've all got safety shelves, and as for the Great Leap itself, there in the middle, they put a safety net under that.'

'Yes, but be fair, Sofy, it's still a hell of a course. I wouldn't like to run it. They've made it less dangerous, yes, but they run it so much faster nowadays that there are nearly as many accidents anyway.'

'I wasn't telling her about the danger; I was talking about the reality of it. It isn't real any more. It's all stage-managed.

Look for yourself! You can see! It's lost all meaning now. It used to be a true honour to wear the red ribbon, but who cares now?'

As we went down again they said I ought to go and talk to the people at the Race Office, outside the Castle Gate. 'Fair's fair,' they said, 'go and see what they have to say.'

So I left them ordering more coffees at the café, and walked down the main arcade and out through the great gate (itself a sort of reluctant approximation of its medieval original). Immediately outside it, on a rounded corner building, a large sign said: 'THE ROOF-RACE INITIATIVE 2012'. Display windows below were full of Roof-Race photographs, old and new, victors falling bloodied from the ramparts, art photographs of the Great Leap taken from below, groups of champions, Governors presenting the gold goblet surrounded by preposterously overdressed civic worthies, legendary winners from the past posed with laurel wreaths around their necks. In the foreground there was a photograph of some filmic celebrity holding above her blonde head a banner proclaiming: ROOF-RACE FOR THE WORLD!

I went inside. A man was sitting at a big desk, piled with pamphlets and carved in front with a gilded helmet. He was dressed in a Hav *gallabiyeh* and sported a black-and-white rosette. 'Yes?' he said.

'Could it be', I began, 'that–'

'Yes, yes, it could! Fatima told me to expect you!' He jumped up from his chair (the back of it ornamented with maze-circles) and kissed my hand enthsiastically. 'Dirleddy, what a pleasure to see you again. Do you recognize me? Do you honestly?'

I didn't, to tell you the truth. He had been a slim, racy, perhaps rather wild young man: now he was the plump epitome of middle-aged Havian respectabililty, and he talked in a committee-room timbre.

'No, I thought not. Ah well, one can't expect it – age creeps up on all of us, does it not? Prosperity too! But sit down, sit down, how can I help you?'

I told him that he could explain to me first what all this Initiative stuff was about. Why 2012? He was only too pleased to explain. It was a campaign, he said, to have the Roof-Race recognized as an Olympic sport in time for the 2012 holding of the Games.

'I must first tell you what has in recent years happened to the Race' (and as that receptionist had audibly articulated the exclamation mark in 'Lazaretto!', so Yasin made it clear to me that 'the Race' had a capital 'R'). 'You may or may not know that since the year 2000 it has been thrown open to competitors from around the world. It is now a major event on the international sporting calendar. Like the Bull Run at Pamplona – just as an example, you understand – it attracts entries from everywhere, and our Government is anxious that it should become a universally recognized feature of modern Hav. With the Myrmidon Tower, it will be something that comes to everyone's mind when Hav is mentioned.'

He sounded as though he had it by heart. 'You've said all this before, haven't you?' I said.

He laughed and shrugged. 'Oh Miss Morris, you've been in this game too long. But there we are, it's my job. I'm no longer the young man skidding down the Staircase; I am a Myrmidonic Civil Servant Grade 3. Anyway, it's like I say: they wanted it be a world-class event, and so when the Grand Bazaar was rebuilt they decreed that it must be reconceived too. Health and safety, don't you know.

'Actually they had first wanted it abolished altogether, but you know how much it meant to Havian people – there was such an outcry that the Perfects themselves intervened. But they did remodel the whole course, to make it generally acceptable to world opinion.'

'They took all the character out of it, you mean. I've just been up to see it.'

'That is not for me to say. I am only the Race spokesman.

Suffice it to say that the course has now been judged, by independent international experts, to conform to the highest safety standards. This being so, the Government has decided that it should occupy a similar status to the Cresta Run at St Moritz in Switzerland. That's also confined to a particular place, but open to all comers, and we feel confident that Hav will soon be ready to accommodate big sporting crowds – the new airport, Lazaretto and all that, all the necessary infrastructure.'

But, said I, St Moritz was a bit different because the Cresta was a winter sports event.

'Quite true, and as a matter of fact we have thought of using artificial snow machines to make the Roof-Race a winter sport too. It was thought too risky in the end, so instead we are pressing for the Race to be accepted as a sport in the summer Olympics for 2012. We've hardly started the campaign yet. We've only just opened this office. But the Government is going to use all its influence, especially of course among our economic associates, to see that we win. It will be a triumph for Hav. Lazaretto is sponsoring it, and with the new Balad airport, and of course with Havberry products becoming household names around the world, it will put us on the map at last.'

'You want to be on the map?'

'Not much. But that's my job.' He looked at me a little wistfully, I thought. 'But actually, Jan – I may call you Jan, mayn't I? – actually I hate the whole thing. I'm just paid to say all this. For me the Roof-Race was always a private affair. It was just for us, us Havians. Also it was exciting – it was, wasn't it? And of course the danger was part of it. Nobody complained in the old Hav about the danger, did they? It's only since the Intervention, and all that – making a profit out of everything, giving Hav its proper place in the world, all that balls. Health and safety, all that nonsense.

'I'll tell you what I'd really like to happen. It's too late to do anything about the Roof-Race. Trying to revive it as it was couldn't work, and the new course means it's something totally different and new, really nothing to do with the old one. But if they really must put Hav on the sporting map – give it a Cresta Run, as it were – I think they should have a car rally on the Escarpment. We'd call it the Escarpment Rally.'

Now he was warming up. 'I know the country well, as you will remember – remember whizzing down to pick up my cousin, the first time we ever met? I know the country well, and I've already worked out a route. We can use the Tunnel itself. They've taken out all the rails – the Chinese bought the lot, to ship away as scrap metal. Think of it: all those hairpin bends inside the mountain!

'I'll tell you what, Jan. Are you free this afternoon? Why don't I take you up there, and you can see for yourself? We will run our own Escarpment Rally.'

A great idea, I thought. Anything is grist to my mill, and besides, I hadn't forgotten that he was one of the two young men who had taken me to the *séance* long ago.

'Well then, suppose we meet here around two. My car's in the multi-storey. OK? I've got a group coming any minute now from the airport, but I should be through with them by then. Ideology bring them in, you know, on their way to Lazaretto. Stay and hear my recitation, if you like.'

I declined, and at that moment there arrived half a dozen rather worn-looking tourists, clearly just off a long flight, most of them American it seemed, and ushered by a tour guide in Havian rig. I hastily left, but lingered for a few moments by the door, to hear Yazin say, in his fruity official voice: 'Welcome, welcome. Before your helicopter takes you to enjoy yourselves at our great resort, I am so happy and privileged to be able to tell you something about an exciting new initiative that we are embarking upon here in Hav . . .'

I left, closed the door quietly behind me, and returned to the Bazaar for another coffee.

When I returned to the Roof-Race office Yasar was outside waiting for me. How did the recitation go, I asked him?

'It went. They loved it. I know it by heart,' and as we walked out of the Medina to the car park he added: 'They always love it. Who wouldn't? One of them said the Messenger sounded a bit like Robin Hood – oh, and one of them said they'd read about it in your book. I didn't know you'd written a book? I hope I don't come into it.'

Fortunately for me we reached the car park then – and fortunate for me too, I could not help thinking, that my book was banned . . .

His car was a trim little Honda Type R (built at their new Izmir factory, he said) and the minute he swung it out into the highway I knew I was in for a sharp ride. We whizzed – his word! – round the foot of the Castle on to the H1, and then up past the airport. Before the Havberry plant we turned off, and then we were on a rough road that went through the salt-flats towards the old Palast. This, he said, was where his rally route began.

I thought it seemed more suitable for motorbikes than for cars, but no, no, no, he said, not necessarily, and suddenly he put his foot down and we leapt over the flats leaving a vast cloud of sandy salty dust billowing behind us. There was no other traffic on the track – the big salt-wagons, he said, had their own tarmac road down the coast to the harbour – and the only signs of life were trucks moving among the flats and the big grey salt elevators steaming. This would only be the preliminary phase of the event, Yasar told me, and all too soon it was over, and we were bounding and bouncing up the first slopes of the Escarpment.

Here were the caves of the Kretevs. They were lifeless. Nobody was there. Not a tumble-down lorry stood about, no raggedy swarm of children ran after us, no bright washing hung from laundry lines. 'No bears,' I said as we bounced and joggled over the hard bumps.

'No bears, no Kretevs, no snow raspberries, no life. That's what the Intervention did to us. Only these holes in the ground.'

They did look like holes, too, like rabbit warrens perhaps, or abandoned badger setts, with the same scrabbled signs of old activity around them. I found it hard even to imagine the curious community that used to be there, so full of life and love, with their cosy troglodyte homes and their weird relationship with the bears. Could any of their tradition survive, I wondered, among the comfortable conformities of the new Balad? And then I remembered what the women had said about the guest workers, and thought that perhaps all was not lost . . .

Yasar seemed to have read my mind. 'Don't fret,' he said, grimly clutching his bucking steering-wheel and desperately changing gear around corners – his paunch made it a little difficult. 'Don't you worry, the Kretevs will find a way. They always have.'

We did not stop when we reached the top of the ridge, high above the sea to our left. Instead we raced down to the flat ground on the other side, and then, turning to the east, made an exhilarating run at top speed along the northern lee of the Escarpment – thirty miles or so along the tussocky moorland, flying over mounds and declivities, swooping around bumps, with such a roar and a rattling and a whoosh that Yasar was laughing aloud beside me. 'I call that the Frontier Run,' he said at last, breathlessly braking the car to career around a rock. 'We've been following the old frontier all the way. Now back to the station.'

We turned in our tracks to run westward along the flank of the ridge, and soon I saw where we were. All alone there stood the remains of the Frontier Station, where the Express used to stop to pick up the Tunnel Pilot, and where I had first met the young Yasar. It looked picked clean, as it were. The roof and gates and platform shelters had all gone. So had the railway lines. It might never have been a railway station at all, and it looked as though nobody had been there for years. 'Sometimes I see Kretevs here,' Yasar said. 'God knows what they're up to. They scare me rather – they look like ghosts.'

He swung the car into the cutting where the railway had run, stopped, and switched off the engine. Now the only sound was the ticking of its engine cooling, and the rush of the wind. 'Look up there,' Yasar said, pointing to the top of the Escarpment before us. I looked, I looked hard, and I could just make out, like a careless stroke of pencil lead in a drawing, a thin black line silhouetted against the sky. It was the Megalith, the high point of the old Staircase, from where I had looked back, all those years before, to see the warships of the Intervention approaching. In my mind I could see the scene as if it were yesterday. I could almost hear the blast of those black aircraft, heralding the change of all things in Hav.

'Right,' said Yasar then. 'The tunnel run.' Revving the engine hard, he slipped the clutch and we shot helter-skelter into the darkness. The Hav Tunnel, built by Roman Abramoff of the Imperial Russian Railways, used to be famous as the most daring feat of railway engineering ever undertaken, because it descended (or ascended) such a startling distance in so short a time. It avoided a precipitate surface gradient by a series of a dozen or more hairpin bends, so close together that they amount in fact to a spiral. 'Nothing like this had ever been attempted before', said Branger's *Railway Engineering* in 1878, 'and will probably never be tried again. It was Abramoff's final *tour de force.*' And when Norman Foster's celebrated Millau Viaduct was opened in France in 2005, even then the *Civil Engineering Gazette* declared it to be reminiscent, in its sheer technical virtuosity, of Abramoff's Hav Tunnel.

This was the prodigy we now threw ourselves into, in our little Honda, and no train ever descended those loops so fast. It was pitch-black in the tunnel, except for the beams of our headlights, eerily sweeping the rock walls, and the noise of our engine was deafening, echoing all around us and reverberating, I imagine, back through all the bends behind us and up to the tunnel mouth. Neither of us spoke. Like a projectile we plunged down the inside of that mountain, with never a glimpse of daylight ahead. Once a bird, startled by the noise and the headlights' beams, sprang from the wall with a frenzied flutter of its wings and disappeared into the gloom. Sometimes I felt we were twirling, like a bullet in a rifle barrel, and this sensation recalled to me the moment, only a day or two before, when we had suddenly been hurled upwards in Car 7 of the Myrmidon Tower.

The two experiences oddly merged in my mind. Both journeys, one in the light, one in the darkness, seemed somehow paradigmatic of a journey through Hav itself. The absolute nature of both, something gravelike about them, was like Hav's blanketing enigma. The solitary bird of the tunnel, the myriad bright fish of the Tower, suggested impotent reminders of life. It was a bit like being buried alive. Even my companions were a little disturbing in their charm. Something about Biancheri made me feel uncomfortable. Something about Yasar was evasive. Was it Yasar in the Tower, Biancheri in the Tunnel? The bird in the aquarium, the fish coming out of the rock? It took us only five minutes or so to rush through that tunnel, but it seemed to me that all the nagging ambiguities of Hav, all the unanswered questions, swirled around my head as the car swirled through the darkness.

Suddenly the daylight burst upon us. 'Voilà!' cried Yasar, looking at his watch. 'How was that? Five minutes flat!'

The rest of the ride, down the track of the old Staircase, seemed an anti-climax. Yasar relaxed, and slowed down. However, I hadn't freed myself of those peculiar sensations in the Tunnel. It was as though I had emerged from an anaesthetic, with snatches of a dream lingering in my head.

'Tell me something, Yasar,' I said. 'What was it you wanted me to remember, when we went to that *séance* of the Cathars?'

There was a long silence, until we came to the bottom of the track and joined the smooth road back to the city. Then he stopped the car.

'That's the end of the rally route,' he said emotionlessly, as though he had suddenly lost interest. 'And what's that you asked me?'

'I asked what it was you wanted me to remember, when you took me to the *séance* with George that time.'

'I don't know any George, and believe me, Jan, I never took you to any *séance*. You must believe that. Whatever you say about it, I will deny. No George, no *séance*. You're talking about twenty years ago, and your memory must be at fault. And I'd be much obliged if you didn't raise the matter with Fatima, either. Okay? Okay?'

'Okay of course. Just as you say. I won't ask any more – and thanks very much for the rally ride – it was marvellous.'

'Thank you, Jan. I'm sorry the matter arose. If you feel you want to know more about such things, I suggest you talk to the Caliph. I believe you know him, don't you? He's your best bet. Mention me if you like.'

So it was with slightly awkward *politesse* that we parted at the waterfront, where he dropped me at the Lazaretto buggy stand. Damn Hav, I thought to myself. Damn this two-faced, double-dealing, lying, cheating, deceptive old fox of a place.

The buggy-driver knew me, and greeted me kindly. 'Welcome home dirleddy,' he said.

'Home', I replied, 'is where the heart is.'

'Is that really true?' he earnestly enquired, as we drove sedately into the lesser tunnel.

SATURDAY

Aleykum salaam!

6

Over my Havflakes – to the Caliph's – a fact-finding mission?
– The Wazir slid in – an aerial view – 'M' for what?

'Welcome home!' the Ponsonbys cried, when I went to The Salt Trade for my breakfast in the morning. 'Long time no see!'

'Yes, Jan dear, what have you been up to? We've missed you.'

'Hush, Vera,' said Arthur. 'Remember the Official Secrets Act.'

'Oh pooh, you old fool. Come on, Jan, tell all.'

So I told them about the Escarpment rally adventure, as I ate my Havflakes, and they were much amused. 'What a scream,' thought Vera. 'Sounds a winner to me,' Arthur thought, adding that he himself had been down the Cresta Run, when he was a young man, and would do it again at the drop of a hat. 'Drop of a few hundreds pounds more like,' Vera suggested.

'Oh and by the way,' Arthur said, 'Biancheri was asking after you last night. He seemed a bit anxious. Wondered if everything was all right with you.'

'If you ask me, Jan,' Vera winked, 'that man's got a bit of a crush on you. Lucky you, at your age!'

I must have run through half a dozen address books since I was last in Hav, but to the travelling writer they are never altogether outdated. I had brought with me my 1980s version, and when I got back to my room I found the number I wanted, and spoke it into the teledado: Hav 001.

I was not surprised to hear that the number had been changed to 0082321, so I asked for that instead and heard an elderly, exquisite, faintly sacerdotal voice announce: 'His Holiness the Caliph's Residence.'

'May I speak to the Caliph, please?'

'To his Holiness? His Holiness does not normally accept unsolicited calls. May I enquire who is telephoning?'

I told him, and there was a pause. 'Then am I not correct in thinking that we have previously made your acquaintance? I am the Caliph's Wazir. Be so good as to wait for a moment or two, dirleddy, and I will consult His Holiness.'

It seemed to me that the 125th Caliph had acquired extra dignity during my absence. His Holiness indeed: I thought that was only the Pope! But when the Wazir came back on the line he sounded much more informal.

'The Caliph says yes, of course, he'll be most interested to see you again – as indeed, dear Ms Morris, so will I. Shall we send the car promptly at about four this afternoon, to pick you up at the Lazaretto buggy station?'

'That would be fine, Wazir,' said I, 'but last time you named a date the car came three days late.'

'Oh dear oh dear, did it really? – forgive us. As you know, the Caliph's situation is such that we must keep the tightest security for his protection. But now we know you, dirleddy, and believe me, the car will be there at four o'clock sharp, or I'm not the Caliph's Wazir – and I shall be in it!'

I spent the day puzzling. I wandered the wayward paths of Lazaretto, and felt myself truly inside a labyrinth. I sat in the shade at the Maze Bar, and tried to reduce my responses to the place into diagrammatic form – one factor linked with another, one experience blending (or more often not blending) with the next. I remembered the stroke-like spasm in Car 7, the confusions of the tunnel. I had lunch on the bar's terrace, looking towards the Tower and thinking about these mysteries, and in a kind of reverie over my coffee I heard a voice behind my back, and the scrape of a chair being pulled beside mine.

'I was told I would find you here', said the British Legate, rather greasily I thought. 'Mind if I join you?'

'Delighted', I lied, and waited.

'It's like this', he said. 'I feel we somehow got off on the wrong feet, so to speak, when we met the other day. I feel I was abrupt with you – I didn't quite realize the – well, the position.'

'Oh not at all', said I. 'I can well understand what a nuisance transient Britons must be to you, especially if they happen to be Welsh.'

'Yes, well, that slipped out. I shouldn't have said that. But the thing is, I wonder if I could possibly ask a favour of you?' I waited. He blew his nose.

'The thing is, I gather that this evening you're going to see the Caliph. The thing is, the Caliph is absolutely *persona non grata* with HMG. It's out of the question for me ever to meet him. I've never set eyes on the fellow. We Brits have no contact, although there's a lot we could learn from him about one thing and another.'

'So?'

'So, the thing is, I wondered, entre nous of course – I'm speaking absolutely confidentially – I was wondering, if anything that might be of interest to HM Government emerged from your meeting, would it be too much to ask if you would pass it on to me? In particular anything concerning, well, no doubt you can guess the sort of thing, the sort of person . . .'

His voice trailed away. I considered the matter. He shifted in his chair.

'I think not', said I. 'I am a private citizen, and it seems to me that if you already know of my appointment with the Caliph this evening you've been keeping some sort of surveillance over me. Whatever passed between the Caliph and me is my private business, and I will do with it whatever seems best.'

The Legate oozed no longer. 'Meaning I suppose that if it's juicy enough you'll flog it to some sleazy tabloid instead of doing your patriotic duty and reporting it to me.'

I said I was sorry. He left without a hand-shake, tucking his handkerchief into his sleeve. I walked up to the base of the Tower, to stare at the bulk and the dazzle of it, until a guard politely requested me not to linger.

So I picked up a passing buggy, and at four o'clock sharp the car arrived for me on the waterfront. As the Caliph seemed to have got grander since 1985, so had the Caliph's car. Then it was a venerable Cadillac, now it was a very new black Mercedes with tinted windows, looking to me decidedly bullet-proof. Two swarthy uniformed men sprang from the front seat. One stood shot-gun on the pavement, so to speak; the other with a practised flourish opened the back door, and out stepped the Wazir.

'What style,' said I.

'They're Assyrians.'

But the style I meant was the man himself. He was now in his late sixties, I suppose, but looked more elegant than ever. No tarboosh ('Alas no, our suppliers in Alexandria no longer fulfil our requirements'), but a beautifully cut black suit, tan gloves and shoes and Hollywood sunglasses. He was slim as a rake, and as he sat down beside me in the car I caught a snatch of musky scent. The Assyrians slipped into their seats, there was a distant purr, and the great car glided away from the waterfront.

'Yes we are so lucky', the Wazir said conversationally, 'to have these excellent fellows. These two are among the third generation in the Caliph's employ. We lost a couple during a slight fracas soon after your last visit–'

'During the Intervention, you mean?'

'Well yes, round about then. But fortunately new recruits constantly reach us, and we still feel well looked after.'

Despite all the changes along the road, much seemed the same at the Caliph's house. The gates were freshly painted, the gravel yard was well rolled, the building looked in fine condition and two Assyrians in khaki saluted us at the entrance. And who should be there to greet us at the front door but His Holiness the 125th Caliph humself!

'Aha,' he cried, 'so you two old friends meet again, *el ham dillah*! Off you go now, you wicked Wazir, and leave Ms Morris to me. We have much to talk about, I'm sure.' The Wazir bowed low, kissed my hand and disappeared. The Caliph led me indoors.

'I suppose', he said, 'that you are here on what they used to call a fact-finding mission.' Age had not withered him, since I last set eyes on him. On the contrary, it had made him a great deal fatter. If the Wazir had become more delicate, more attenuated, his master had grown visibly more consequential. He was a heavy man now, dressed in a heavy brown cassock, carrying a lumpish string of prayer-beads. 'If so, I must ask you to tread very delicately with your questions and surmises. I spoke very frankly to you last time, and my people tell me that in your book (which unfortunately I have not had a chance to read) you recorded your impressions with commendable circumspection. Thank you. My situation in Hav is, as you know, always fragile, and recent developments have made it even more necessary than before to be careful in what I say.

'However, Ms Morris, my people tell me that the Government is hoping to make use of your talents during your visit here, and I too would like to let a few ideas drop into your ear. You will know, I am sure, how best to make use of them. By the way, did old Porvic wear a tarboosh when you met him the other day? What did you think of it?'

One tarboosh looks to me much like another, but when I said so the Caliph looked disappointed in me.

'Oh no, you're quite wrong there, quite wrong. A first-class tarboosh is a work of high art, a design icon, as they say. I thought you might be able to tell me whether the standard of work of the Nakhla people in Alex really has fallen off, as my Wazir assures me. Never mind. Let us proceed.'

But he was plunged in silence then, so to cheer things up I asked what had happened to the picture of the lovely dancer which, as I remembered it, used to hang on the walls of the room.

'Naratlova? You mean Kolshok's Naratlova? Some people did not think she was suitable, for several reasons. One, she was a woman. Two, she was a Russian. Three, she was a Christian. Four, she was beautiful. Five, she was a Christian. You understand me? Two out of five?'

I took him to mean that Islamic sentiment had expelled the lady, but before I could say anything he continued: 'I'm not sure how much you know about the relationship between the Caliphate and the Cathars.'

'Not much, but Yasar Yeğen said you might perhaps be willing to tell me more.'

'Oh yes, Yeğen. I suppose he took you on his rally route? Rather an unreliable man. One day he is going to kill himself, by one means or another. He nearly did, you know, in the former times.

'Well, then, perhaps you don't know about the Holy Compact concluded between the Caliphate and the Cathar Séance, long before our separation from the Sultanate, back in the fifteenth century in fact, when the Ottomans first took this place. The Compact was maintained when the Caliphate was officially abolished, and upheld by all my predecessors until the present day. In fact it is why I am here at all – I remember telling you that my own relationship with Ankara has always been, shall we say, precarious.

'The Holy Compact was of course highly secret from the first – I am talking now in strictest confidence, you realize. The Turkish Governorate in Hav would have considered it highly seditious, and so would our late Government here, before the Intervention. It is only because of our new arrangements that I am able to say anything about it now. And I am still governed, Miss Jan – I may call you Miss Jan? Thank you – I am still restricted in what I tell you by the Holy Oath which was part of the Compact from the very beginning.'

Surely, said I, an alliance between a heretical Christian sect

and the descendants of the Prophet's own family was not terribly popular among Muslims?

'You are right. The secret leaked out long ago, and that is
one reason why my situation here has been so dangerous, and
why I need all these bodyguards – Assyrian Christians, you
must surely have noticed, every one. There are several factions
in the Arab world who would happily see me eliminated purely on religious grounds. On the other hand . . .' He interrupted
himself to cross the room and pull a tasselled cord. 'Would you
care to join me in a coffee?'

Almost at once a burly servant in a *gallabiyeh* came to take
the order.

'Tough-looking person,' said I.

'Of course,' said the Caliph. 'They perform many kinds of
services for me.'

'But you were about to tell me–'

'Yes, yes, but let's wait for our coffee. Yes, Miss Jan, I was
sorry to have to remove that painting of the lovely Naratlova,
because I have always cherished the old story that this house
was Kolchock's love-nest long ago. The place has a very
romantic air, don't you think so? I like to think of the old
reprobate here in the garden with his paramour, like people in
a Persian miniature. We Arabs are true romantics, you know,
despite the austerities of our faith and art.

> 'Ah, Love! could thou and I with Fate conspire
> To grasp this sorry Scheme of Things entire,
> Would not we shatter it to bits – and then
> Re-mould it nearer to the Heart's Desire!

'A bad translation, in my view – "shatter it to bits" is surely
poor English, is it not? And of course I cannot approve of most
of the Rubáiyát's sentiments. But still when I wander around
my garden remembering Kolchock and *his* heart's desire, I
often quote the verse to myself.'

The servant returned, soundlessly, and poured our coffee
into exquisitely chased cups of brass, out of a tall long-spouted

jug. It was thick Arabian coffee, flavoured with camomile. The Caliph watched me sipping it. 'Better, I dare say, than the stuff they give you at Lazaretto?'

'Most certainly better,' said I, 'and a thousand times better than the tea.'

'Oh the tea,' he laughed. 'Be careful what you say about the tea. They've only just invented it – like that Aqua Hav, equally appalling I am told.'

But he was about to tell me more, I reminded him, about relations with the Arab world.

'Yes, yes, something more I can say. But remember my Oath! Also I regret we must soon cut our conversation short; I have an unavoidable engagement this evening.' He looked at his watch. 'This I can tell you: that whereas I am *persona non grata* with some of the Arab factions, I am able to play a useful role in relations with others. I am a link, so to speak, outside the sphere of diplomacy, between them and this Republic. I cannot be more specific. Suffice it to say that the people at your Legation would like to know more. There are certain aspects of trade and economics which can best be facilitated by unofficial channels, certain commodities outside more normal consignments – certain people too who can entrust their whereabouts with confidence to me. Some indeed, whose names or at least cognomens, may be familiar to you, who advocate the revival of the Caliphate itself! If you follow me, Miss Jan, if you can read me between the lines, as I believe you say, please keep your conclusions to yourself.'

I was not all sure I could read him between the lines, and told him so.

'So much the better, for the moment anyway. My Oath precludes my telling you more. But I have a proposal to make to you. In my official capacity I must attend tonight, purely as an observer, naturally, the monthly Holy Séance of the Perfects. It might be of interest of you to observe it. You cannot of course enter the Séance Hall, but there are means by which you could watch its proceeedings in private. But on no account must you allow your presence to be known.'

I thought it better, on the whole, not to tell him that I had done it once before – with Yasar.

'I'm sure I can trust you not to reveal the arrangements to a living soul, and I have already instructed my Wazir to get you to the Séance Hall without revealing to you its whereabouts. I'm sure you will understand. You agree? Yes? Then you will excuse me if I leave you now. Please make yourself at home in my house, and the Wazir will come for you in half an hour or so.'

I thanked him and walked with him to the door of the room.

'Actually,' he said, turning back at the door, 'I do very much prefer the Avery and Heath-Stubbs translation to Fitzgerald's. But it's a matter of taste, I suppose.'

The Wazir slid in. He was very light on his feet, and graceful. He must apologize, he said, for what he had to say. His Holiness had intimated that he must, well, extract from me a formal promise not to memorize, or indeed consciously observe, our route to the Séance Hall.

'Of course,' I said. 'But purely as a matter of interest, is it in the same place, wherever that was, before the Intervention?'

'I think I may say that it is. The very rare visitors allowed are usually blindfolded, but His Holiness thought that would be inapposite in your case. He tells me that your word would be perfectly sufficient. In that case, shall we make our way there? It is only a short walk.'

I felt ashamed, I admit it, to be deceiving them in this way, and resolved that I really would not try to determine the way we went. We walked to the Medina, I could not help realizing that; but once within its labyrinth I easily lost my bearings. I caught a glimpse of the Grand Mosque, but conscientiously averted my eyes. The Wazir spoke not a word, but thoughtfully guided me along alleys and around corners until, producing a very small key from his waistcoat pocket, he unlocked an unobtrusive metal door in the side of an office building and ushered me down some steps into a tunnel.

Dear God, said I to myself, yet another tunnel. The tunnel could easily be Hav's emblem, alongside the maze – like the city of Bucharest, in Romania, which seems to me obsessed with the idea of the tunnel, murky with tunnel legends, burdened with tunnel memories. The Hav *séance* tunnel was not very long, and not very murky either, for its lights were bright and its walls whitewashed, but our footsteps echoed as we walked along it, the Wazir said not a word, and the absolute emptiness did give me rather eerie feelings. Was I on the verge of revelations?

We reached the end of the tunnel. The Wazir took out his key again, and unlocked another door, into a cramped space like a decompression chamber. Inside stood Mario Biancheri, with two Chinese in dark suits. 'I'm sorry to do this to you, Jan,' he said, and as he spoke he shook hands with the Wazir. 'It is my unhappy duty, though. There is a booking for you on the ten o'clock Havair flight to Istanbul. Your bags are already checked in, your passport is at Balad, at the desk they will give you an open ticket onward, and my men here will see that you are there in good time. Ciaou.'

The Wazir bowed in my direction, breathed *salaam aleykum,* and the two of them, politely giving way to each other, disappeared.

With perfect courtesy the Chinese bustled me away into a limousine and chatted amiably as we drove to the airport. A pity, they said, that my visit had ended so abruptly. Why *was* it ending so abruptly, I asked? but they did not explain. Orders is orders was the gist of their reply, and when we parted they kissed my hand in turn, murmuring 'dirleddy' as they did so.

I had never flown over Hav before. It was dark when we left, and we took off to the south before swinging around over the sea and heading for the Escarpment. The city looked utterly isolated down there. Beyond it the continent seemed deserted, around it the sea lay dark and empty. The scene was like an allegory itself – the famous Kiruski might have designed it! For at the tip of the dark peninsula, with only the odd dim light flickering in the moorlands, Hav lay there all ablaze. There was the Medina, where the money was made, industriously glowing still. There were the long runways of Balad. I could see the Castle, like a black smudge set against the city lights below, and the H1 street-lights running away towards the cluster of Yuan Wen Kuo. Lazaretto was twinkling festively. I fancied I saw watchful lights burning in the Caliph's villa . . . And above it all rose the Tower, like a pillar of fire, scintillating, incandescent, with the great 'M' at its summit shining there fainter and fainter, smaller and smaller, until we had crossed the Escarpment and left all Hav like a dream behind.

The great 'M'! 'M' for what? 'M' really for Myrmidon, or 'M' for Mammon? For Mohammed the Prophet? For Mani the Manichaean? 'M' for Macdonald's, or Monsanto, or Microsoft? 'M' for Melchik? 'M' for Minoan? 'M' for Maze?

Or, could it possibly be, I wondered as we droned on through the darkness, and I fell into an uneasy slumber, 'M' for Me?

Epilogue

When the first part of this book, *Last Letters*, originally appeared in 1985, few readers apparently recognized it as fictional. They thought it described a real place, incomprehensibly little-known. They asked me how to get there. They wanted to know if one needed a visa. Even somebody at the Map Room of the Royal Geographical Society asked me to put him straight about Hav's location. Only one single correspondent, an octogenarian lady in Iowa, saw my little book as allegory.

But hazy allegory it was meant to be, dressed up as entertainment. After forty odd years of wandering the world and writing about it, I had come to realize that I really seldom knew what I was writing about. I did not truly understand the multitudinous forces – political, economic, historical, social, moral, mythical – that worked away beneath the forces of all societies. I blundered around the planet, groping for meanings but not often absolutely understanding them, and working only with an artist's often misguided intuition.

At the same time – to be fair to myself – societies themselves were becoming ever more complex and obfuscatory. Perhaps nobody could understand them properly, entangled as they were in the welter of new ideas, technologies, doubts and loyalties that seemed to be falling upon all with ever-increasing stress and energy. There was something ominously opaque in the air of the world, I thought.

So, having failed to master so many real places, I invented one to emblemize this new confusion of the peoples, this developing uncertainty about everything. I claim no prescience, but the brooding sense of foreboding I had sensed erupted into catastrophe on September 11, 2001, and so a still more bewildering zeitgeist was born.

This is the time-spirit of my book's second part. It is allegorical again, but in a different kind. The confusions of the old Hav were rooted in history. Overlappings of ancient cultures had given the place its complexity, together with the influences and incursions of many centuries, and the responses of travellers down many generations. It was a jumble, but a jumble in which I was able to discern familiar signposts, events, notions and even personalities: and I might indeed have been able to make some sense of it all, were it not for the abrupt denouement of the Intervention.

The enigmas of Hav have remained into the years of the Myrmidons, into the second part of my book, but they are transmuted. History indeed still plays a part, but now the conflicts between contemporary truths muddy the waters more, and the striving for authenticities, and global corruptions, and resentments stemming not from the distant past, but from contemporary events. Fundamentalist religions confuse issues in Hav as everywhere else. Hints of terrorist subversion, and the threat of alien intervention, give added pungency to Hav's peculiar kind of independence.

A whole world, indeed, has come into being since I wrote *Last Letters from Hav*. New states have emerged, and new kinds of cities suddenly erupted. At the back of my mind when I first contemplated the city-state of Hav were places like Trieste, Danzig or Beirut whose characters had been formed by the long processes of history. Twenty years later sudden new civic prodigies offered analogies – startling conurbations, in desert or tropic, hitherto inconceivable and themselves all but fictional still.

So is there one essential allegory of Hav, in both its incarnations? I really don't know myself, and the second half of my book ends even more inconclusively than the first. Just as I wrote into the narrative my own meanings, bred by experience out of instinct, so I can only leave it to my readers, apologetically, to decide for themselves what it's all about.

Novels arise out of the shortcomings of history.
Novalis (1772–1801)